Sexy, flirty, sizzling!

Soaking
little

Nights

Scorching seduction as the sun sets!

Three fabulous, flirty romances—holiday flings
have never been so much fun!

£1 Columbus

Kelly Hunter   Jessica Hart
Anne Oliver

Paradise Nights

Mills & Boon, an imprint of Harlequin (UK) Limited, Eton House,
18-24 Paradise Road, Richmond, Surrey TW9 1SR

PARADISE NIGHTS © Harlequin Enterprises II B.V./S.`a.r.l. 2011

Taken by the Bad Boy © Kelly Hunter 2008
Barefoot Bride © Jessica Hart 2007
Behind Closed Doors... © Anne Oliver 2006

ISBN: 978 0 263 88763 1

024-0611

Harlequin (UK) policy is to use papers that are
natural, renewable and recyclable products and made from
wood grown in sustainable forests. The logging and
manufacturing processes conform to the legal environmental
regulations of the country of origin.

Printed and bound in Spain
by Blackprint CPI, Barcelona

TAKEN BY THE BAD BOY

Kelly Hunter

Accidentally educated in the sciences, **Kelly Hunter** has always had a weakness for fairytales, fantasy worlds, and losing herself in a good book. Husband… yes. Children…two boys. Cooking and cleaning… sigh. Sports…no, not really—in spite of the best efforts of her family. Gardening…yes. Roses, of course. Kelly was born in Australia and has travelled extensively. Although she enjoys living and working in different parts of the world, she still calls Australia home. Visit Kelly online at www.kellyhunter.net

Kelly's novel *Sleeping Partner* was a 2008 finalist for the Romance Writers of America RITA® award, in the Best Contemporary Series Romance category!

Praise for Kelly Hunter

"Hunter's emotionally rich tale will make readers laugh and cry along with the characters.
A truly fantastic read."
—*RT BOOKreviews* on
Revealed: A Prince and a Pregnancy

"This story starts out on a light, fun and flirty note and spins into an emotional and heartfelt tale about coming to terms with the past and embracing the future."
—*RT BOOKreviews* on
Playboy Boss, Live-In Mistress

CHAPTER ONE

THERE was a lot to be said for spending a day sitting beneath a striped blue and white beach umbrella on a little Greek island. Serena Comino, however, had been sitting beneath this particular beach umbrella every day for five months now—renting fifty cc motorbikes to tourists— and there wasn't a lot to be said about it any more.

The view never changed, as glorious as it was. The faces of the tourists changed with each docking ferry but their desires stayed the same. Get wet, lie on a beach, rent a Vespa, eat… Nothing *ever* changed.

Five months. Only one more month to go until she returned to Australia and the Greek-Australian arm of the family, or better yet *didn't* return home to the family bosom at all. Serena leaned back in the rickety director's chair until the front two legs left the ground, her eyes shaded by sunglasses, her head tilted towards the vivid blue sky beyond the umbrella. Maybe it had grown somewhat more interesting in the last five minutes. A passing cloud, a bird, a plane.

Superman.

Nope.

'Who suggested this?' she muttered.

'Your father,' said an amused voice from the direction of the goat track behind her. The track started at the edge of the village and meandered up the hillside, past her grandparents' rambling whitewashed cottage, and on to the road above, where Serena and the Vespas spent the better part of the day.

'Sad, but true.' She turned her head, a minimal movement, and offered up a smile for Nico, her cousin on her father's side, which meant the Greek side. The details weren't important, they were related. And it was their turn to pull carer duty for their eighty-two-year-old grandparents, not that they needed nursing care, for they were in remarkably good health. No, truth was, she and Nico were here to run the business enterprises Pappou refused to surrender. Nico's working day started at four a.m. on the fishing trawler and finished around lunchtime. Serena's started at nine, finished at five or six, and didn't involve fish. She still thought she had the better deal. 'Lunchtime already?'

'If you wore a watch you'd know.'

'I can't wear a watch any more,' she countered. 'Once upon a time when I had places to go and things to do I wore a watch. Now it's just too depressing. What's for lunch?'

'Greek salad, calamari, and Gigia's pistachio baklava.'

Okay, so there were some advantages to small Greek islands after all. She sat up, the front two legs of her chair hitting the dirt with a thud, and looked around to see why Nico hadn't taken his usual seat in the chair beside her.

He wasn't alone. A tall black-haired man stood

beside him with the body of a god and a smile guaranteed to make any woman look twice. Serena only looked once but made up for it by taking her time. Not Superman, she decided finally. Superman was square of jaw and neat as a pin. Wholesome.

This man was what happened when Superman took a walk on the wild side.

'Do you fly?' she asked him.

'Yes.'

'I knew it. Women can sense these things.'

'What's she talking about?' he said to Nico. He had a great voice. Deep. Dreamy. Amused. Australian.

'Does it matter?' she countered. 'Are we caring about that?' She sent him a smile she knew damn well could make a man tremble. He countered by removing his aviator sunglasses to reveal eyes as bright and blue as the sky above. Impressive. She stared at him over the top of her sunglasses to see if the tint was making them brighter than they actually were.

Nope.

'Rena, this is Pete Bennett. Pete, my cousin Serena. Her heart is pure. Much to the family's dismay, the rest of her is pure sin.'

'Serena.' Pete Bennett's smile was lazy, very lazy, his eyes appreciative without being bold. Superman-for-bad-girls knew women. Knew how to woo them, knew exactly how to play them. Always a bonus. 'That's quite a combination.'

Serena felt her smile widen. 'So I'm told.'

Sighing, Nico shoved the lunchbox in her line of sight and when that didn't draw her attention away from the delectable Pete Bennett he stood in front of her and blocked the view completely.

'Thank you,' she said begrudgingly as she reached for the lunchbox.

'You're welcome,' countered Nico dryly, everything about him telegraphing a warning about flirting with handsome strangers, even ones he'd just introduced.

Nico was all Greek and wholly protective of the womenfolk in the family. Serena was half Australian and born and raised in Melbourne, and his protective streak rankled even as it amused her. 'So…' Given that the flying one wasn't here for her entertainment he was probably here for business. She put the lunchbox beside the chair, got to her feet, and set about taking care of it. 'Care to rent a Vespa, Pete Bennett?' He looked like a man who appreciated a lick of speed. Not that a fifty cc two stroke was going to provide a great deal of that. 'It just so happens I can let you have the second fastest bike on the island.'

'What happened to the fastest bike?'

'That would be my ride.'

'He's not here for a bike,' said Nico.

'Then why *is* he here?'

Pete Bennett answered the question himself. 'I'm looking for a room.'

'Tomas's room,' added Nico.

Tomas was the grizzled old charter helicopter pilot who had first claim on the bedsit at the back of her grandparents' cottage whenever his customers elected to overnight on the island. 'Tomas's helicopter landed first thing this morning and hasn't left yet,' she countered. She knew this on account of her close personal relationship with the sky. 'What happens if *he* wants to stay over?'

'Tomas is in hospital with his leg broken in two places,' said Pete. 'I'm filling in for him for a time.'

'Oh.' Serena felt a slow smile begin to spread across her face again, she couldn't help it. 'You really can fly. As in forty-five minutes to Athens. Five hours to Rome. I'm *very* impressed. Why didn't you say so earlier?'

'I did,' he said, and to Nico, 'How long has she been here?'

'Too long.' Nico eyed her narrowly. 'And she doesn't always stay in the shade.'

Pete Bennett's lips twitched and Serena favoured both men with a narrow eyed glare of her own. 'The *shade* is the size of a postage stamp. This *island* is the size of an envelope. *You* sit here for five months solid and see how well you cope.'

'I offered to swap,' said Nico. 'I offered to mix it up. A day on the boat here and there, but no…' He shook his head sadly. 'The daughter of a Melbourne fishmonger with family holdings that include three trawlers, six seafood outlets, and two restaurants, and she doesn't like fish.'

'You don't eat fish?' asked Pete Bennett.

'Wash your mouth out,' she said. 'I just don't like catching and preparing fish, that's all. Gutting them, scaling them, boning them, that sort of thing. Nothing wrong with *eating* them. We do a lot of that around here.' But back to business. 'So you want the same deal as Tomas?'

'That's the plan,' he said. 'If it's all right by you, that is. Nico wanted to run it past you before he agreed.'

'Fine by me.' Serena slid her cousin a sideways glance. 'You didn't need to ask.'

'He's younger than Tomas,' said Nico with a shrug. True.

'And single,' said Nico.

Serena felt her lips tilt. The good news just kept coming.

'Might set tongues wagging, what with the grandparents away and me leaving for work so early in the mornings,' said Nico next.

There was that. But she was feeling rebellious when it came to the gossip mafia. She'd done *nothing* but behave since coming to the island and still the gossips watched her every move as if she were about to run amok at any minute. 'Let them wag.' She eyed Pete Bennett speculatively. 'Although we may need to tweak the deal somewhat to preserve my honour and accommodate your youth. I usually make Tomas's bed up for him. You can make your own.'

'Oh, that's cruel.' Pete Bennett shook his head and turned to Nico. 'I thought you said she had a good heart?'

'I lied,' muttered Nico. 'Take it as a warning. Women are cruel, as cruel as the sea and twice as unforgiving. Sirens all of them, luring innocent men to their doom.'

Definitely *not* Nico's usual take on the world. Usually Nico embraced the notion that women were there to be cared for. He had a sweet streak a mile wide, did Nico. Thoughtfully, Serena studied her cousin. He looked much the same as usual. Same kind brown eyes, strong handsome face, and sinewy body. The unhappiness lurking within those eyes, however, ran deeper than usual. 'You've been arguing with Chloe again,' she deduced finally. Chloe ran the island's largest hotel and was the bane of Nico's otherwise peaceful island existence.

'Did you hear me argue?' Nico asked Pete. 'Did I make any comment whatsoever that could be construed as an argument?'

'Nope,' said Pete with a shake of his head. 'You did not.'

'Uh-huh,' she said. 'So what exactly *weren't* you arguing about?'

Nico scowled. 'The usual.'

Which meant they'd been arguing about Chloe's nephew, Sam. No quick fixes there. 'How bad was it?'

Nico looked away, looked out to sea. 'Breeze is picking up. Figure I'll take the catamaran out this afternoon. Don't wait dinner for me.'

Bad. 'I'll save you some,' she told him. 'And make sure you eat it when you come in.'

Nico looked back at her and this time his smile did reach his eyes. 'Tomorrow I'll bring you another beach umbrella. A bigger one.'

He would too. 'And dinner with pilot Pete here? Shall I feed him or send him down to the village?' Tomas usually ate with them. Pilot Pete might have other ideas.

'I trust him.' Nico shot a warning glance in Pete's direction. 'A man of honour would not abuse my hospitality.'

'Are you a man of honour, Pete Bennett?' she asked him.

'I can be,' he said with another one of those lazy grins that made breathing a challenge.

'I'll dress platonic,' she told him. Honourable or not, she was looking forward to his company at dinner.

'Appreciated,' he murmured.

'Dinner's at seven,' she said as a pair of likely customers rounded the bend of the road and headed towards them. 'The kitchen door's the one on the other side of the courtyard, directly opposite your door. The picnic table in the middle of the courtyard's the dining room.' She slid him a parting smile and started towards the tourists, trying to gauge where they were from. Their top-of-the-line Mercedes-quality sandals and backpacks were a dead giveaway. 'I'm thinking German,' she muttered.

'Dutch,' countered Superman, *sotto voce*.

They'd soon find out. '*Yassou, Guten mittag, Goede middag,*' she said cheerfully.

'*Goede middag,*' they responded with wide white smiles, Dutch all the way to the tips of their German-made sandals.

Bugger.

Pete Bennett settled into the granny flat out back of the little white cottage on the hill with the ease of someone with wanderlust in his soul and no fixed address.

He'd been born and raised in Australia and he still called it home, no question. It was home to childhood memories, good and bad. Home to working memories too, some of them uplifting and some of them downright tragic. Not that it was the memories that had driven him away from Australian shores. No, he wouldn't say that.

He preferred to call it exploring his options.

Pete showered away the dirt of the day beneath a

lukewarm drizzle from an ancient showerhead and dressed casual in loose khaki trousers and a white T-shirt. If the goddess could dress platonic then so could he. Besides, it was the only change of clothes he had. He checked his watch, not quite seven, grabbed his damp towel from the bed, and stepped outside, heading for the single strand of washing line strung between two poles.

Movement at the edge of the grassy garden area warned him that he wasn't alone. A small boy with black hair, big eyes, and a narrow, pinched face stood at the edge of the garden. The same boy Nico had taken under his wing down at the fishing dock earlier that day until the fiery-eyed Chloe had come for him. 'Nico's not here,' he told the boy.

'Doesn't matter,' said the boy with a shrug, finding a home for his hands in the pockets of his ratty board shorts. 'Looking for you.'

Pete slung his towel over the line and reached for a peg, wondering just why the kid would be looking for *him*. The boy would get around to revealing what he wanted sooner or later. That or head back to wherever he'd come from. 'You've found me.'

'You saw what happened earlier,' said the kid after an awkward pause. 'I thought maybe you could talk to my *aunt*.' The last word was dragged from his mouth as if he resented the family connection with every fibre of his being. 'You know…' added the kid when he stayed silent. '*Chloe*. It's not as if wanting to work on a fishing boat is a bad thing. She oughta be *glad* I want to pay my own way.'

'How old are you, kid?'

The boy scowled. 'Eleven.'

Small for eleven. But the eyes were older. Pete thought of the luscious Chloe, who'd torn strips off Nico's hide earlier that afternoon when she'd caught the boy helping him unload the day's catch. Thought of the way Nico had listened in stoic silence, his silence giving the boy hope and his eyes promising *Aunt Chloe* retribution in the not too distant future. 'Why would your aunt take any notice of me?' Why for that matter was *she* riding herd on him instead of his parents? 'I'm a stranger here.'

The kid shrugged. 'She might.'

'Why not ask Nico to talk to her? He knows you. Hell, he knows you *and* your aunt.' And all the politics involved. 'I'm assuming it's Nico's boat you want to work on?'

The kid nodded. 'She won't listen to Nico. All she does is fight with him.'

He'd noticed.

'But you…you got no percentage either way.'

'Exactly.'

'She'd listen to you without getting angry about other stuff.'

Pete ran a hand around the back of his neck and looked to the sky for inspiration. The boy reminded him of his younger brother just after their mother's death. He had that same mix of defiance and vulnerability about him and it got to him, caught at him, and tugged at memories best forgotten. 'The way I figure it, you still have a few years of schooling left before you can leave. The way I figure it, going to school is non-negotiable.'

The boy's scowl deepened.

'Doesn't mean you can't try and strike some sort of deal with your aunt when it comes to your free time though. A kid like you knows how to deal, right?'

'Maybe.'

'So you tell her you'll go to school next week—no nicking off at lunchtime to meet the boats—if she'll let you work for Nico next weekend. *If* he'll have you. You tell your aunt you haven't talked to Nico about it yet, got it? Maybe you'll save him some grief.'

'Got it,' said the boy.

'On the other hand, Nico can probably fend for himself so don't sweat it if she does skip straight to thinking this was his idea. He might enjoy telling her it wasn't.' There, he'd done as much as he could for both Nico and the boy. Got way more involved than he ever intended to.

'Yeah, well…' The boy looked away. 'Thanks.'

'No problem.'

Pete watched as the boy lit off down the hillside towards the village, half sliding, half striding down the rocky track. 'Hey, kid…' The boy skidded to a halt and looked back at him wary and waiting and so damn vulnerable it made his heart ache. 'I'll be around some, these next few weeks. Let me know how it goes.'

The boy nodded, once, then he was gone.

Pete was three strides away from the bedsit door before he felt Serena's eyes on him. Two before he spotted her standing just inside the kitchen doorway, half hidden by the fly-screen door. 'You can come out now,' he said, cocking his head in her direction. 'You could have joined us before, come to think of it.'

'What? And interrupt all your good work? I don't think so.' She emerged smiling and unrepentant, a vision of sensuality from the tips of her bare feet, up and over her white gypsy skirt and sleeveless pink stretch top that revealed more creamy skin than it covered, to the glorious tumble of chocolate-coloured curls that fell to her waist. Pete Bennett knew women, lots of women. Beautiful, funny, intelligent women, but not one of them could even come close to the one standing in front of him for undiluted sex appeal and staggering impact on a man's senses. She sauntered—clearly there was no other word for it—over to a small silver coloured garden tap and started filling the bucket beneath it before sliding him a sideways glance from beneath long, dark lashes. 'His name's Sam.'

Pete filed the name away for future reference and regarded the goddess of buckets and sensuality curiously. 'Where's his father?'

'The wording on his birth certificate says "Father: unknown".'

'His mother?'

'She died in an Athens boarding house nearly a year ago of hep C. As far as anyone can gather, the only person looking after her was Sam.'

Rough. Damn rough on a kid. 'Is the Chloe who came down to the harbour to find him this afternoon his real aunt?'

'Yeah.'

'So where was *she* when her sister got sick?'

'You sound a touch judgemental.'

'Feels about right,' he said mildly. Given the picture she was painting.

'I *do* like a man who's in touch with his feelings.'

'Let's not get carried away,' he said dryly.

Serena turned off the tap, picked up the bucket and strolled towards a cluster of herbs by the kitchen door. 'Chloe was right here, running the hotel. She hadn't heard from her sister in over a year and a half.'

'Close family.'

'You're being judgemental again,' she told him.

'Uh-huh.'

'I like that about you.' A tiny smile played at the edge of her lips. 'Where was I?'

'Aunt Chloe.'

'Oh, yeah. According to Chloe, her sister lit out for Athens some twelve years ago, defiant, disowned, and three months pregnant. She was sixteen. Chloe was thirteen at the time and tried to play peacemaker. She failed. Her parents were unmoveable and her sister didn't want either Chloe's pity or the savings she sent her. The family fractured.'

'How'd the boy end up here?'

'Chloe's sister named her next of kin.' Serena shrugged. 'Chloe loves Sam, but she can't handle him. Sam's carrying a lifetime of rejection and an ocean of resentment around on his shoulders. He's fiercely independent. Chloe's fiercely overprotective. She's determined not to fail him. They clash.'

'So where does Nico fit into all of this?'

Serena chuckled, her expression lightening as she gave each clump of herbs a drink. 'Smack bang in the middle; between a boy who desperately needs to feel worthy and a woman he's crazy in love with.'

Pete shuddered. 'No wonder he's gone sailing.'

'You underestimate my cousin, flyboy. My money's on Nico claiming them both before summer's out.'

'It's a pretty picture to be sure.' So was she. 'Tell me,' he drawled. 'What would you have been wearing if this *hadn't* been a purely platonic evening meal?'

'Lipstick for starters.'

She didn't need it.

'And probably a dress.'

'Strappy?'

Definitely.

'Short?'

'No. Something demure. Just above the knees. A first-date dress.'

'What colour?'

'For you? Blue. So that when you looked at me you'd think of something you already loved. The sky.'

'Oh, you're good,' he said in admiration.

'Yes, I am.' Her accompanying grin rammed that particular point home. 'Now you. If this wasn't a strictly platonic dinner deal where would you have taken me?'

'For you?' He didn't have to think hard. 'The Trevi Fountain in Rome. I'd buy you a gelato and give you a bright new penny so you could toss it into the fountain and make a wish. And then we'd walk wherever our feet took us—a sidewalk trattoria or a bustling restaurant—and everyone in the room, myself included, would say a heartfelt prayer of thanks for beautiful sirens in sky-blue dresses.'

'Oh, you're *very* good,' she said wistfully.

'Thank you. I aim to please.'

'I'm sure you do,' she murmured as she slid the bucket back beneath the tap. 'You interest me, flyboy, I'll give you that. There's just one thing I can't quite figure out. Something that doesn't quite fit your carefree and extremely appealing image.' She smiled archly and sent a shaft of heat straight through him. 'What you said to Sam…the way you listened to him, helped him…the way you told him to get back to you.' She turned and headed for the door with a sway to her hips that was truly distracting. 'It was nice.'

CHAPTER TWO

NICE? *Nice?* Pete Bennett had been called a lot of things by the women who sauntered through his life, but *nice* had never been one of them. It didn't feel like a compliment. Okay, so he could, on occasion, be nice. Nothing wrong with that. But what if *nice* mutated into *caring*? What if caring morphed into *really* caring? Then where would he be?

Nope. Better to disabuse the bucket goddess of all nicehood fantasies immediately. Rolling his shoulders back for good measure, and with the spell she'd woven about him still clouding his mind somewhat, he headed across the courtyard after her.

The kitchen in the whitewashed cottage consisted of a fridge, a sink, a wall full of shelving laden with fresh food and a square central bench that doubled as a table. Simple, cosy, and, to Serena's way of thinking, all about the food. She'd put a chicken—liberally seasoned with garlic and oregano—in the oven earlier, along with half a dozen salt-licked potatoes. A loaf of crusty bread and the fixings of a salad sat on the bench waiting to be sliced, diced, and tossed into a bowl just before serving. Serena came from a family of cooks, chefs, restaurateurs, and foodies. Cooking might not have been her first love, or even her second, but in her family there was *no* excuse for poor cooking.

Pete had followed her into the kitchen and now stood leaning against the doorframe. Judging by the dangerous gleam in his eyes, he'd used up his daily quota of *nice* on Sam. Serena didn't mind a bit.

Nice was a bonus, certainly, but sexy, playful, and thoroughly entertaining would do just fine.

'Call me curious,' he said, 'but if renting Vespas to tourists isn't your lifelong ambition, why do it?'

'Family,' she muttered, taking a chunk of feta from the fridge and setting it on the bench alongside a wickedly sharp cutting knife. 'All the grandchildren do a six-month stint helping out here. It's my turn.'

'What happens when all the grandchildren have had a turn? Does it rotate back to the beginning?'

'Theoretically, that's when the great-grandchildren step up. Unfortunately, the oldest great-grandchild is currently six and Nico and I are the last of the grandchildren. I think everyone was hoping one of us would fall in love with the lifestyle and offer to stay on indefinitely. Nico might,' she said thoughtfully.

'But not you?'

'No. One more month and I'm gone.'

'Where?'

"Well, now, that will depend on the jobs going at the time.' And her chances of landing one of them. 'I'm a photographer by trade. When it comes to education I majored in languages, with a slice of international politics on the side.'

He didn't look as astonished as some. The ones who thought that, with a face like hers, she was far more likely to be on the other side of the camera. The ones who thought that, with a body like hers, brains were an unnecessary extra. 'Right now I'm working on a postcard series for the Greek tourism authority but as soon as I finish my stint here I'll be chasing a photojournalism slot, preferably with one of the global media groups.'

'You'll do well,' he said.

'I will?' She couldn't quite hide her astonishment. Not the usual reaction when she told someone her plans.

'Yeah. Your looks will get you noticed, your intellect will tell you when there's a story to chase, and your people skills will get you the information you need. It's a good choice for someone with your particular skill set.'

Serena sliced the bread, sliced the cheese and stuck them together before holding it out to him with a smile. 'Just for that you get an appetiser. Possibly even dessert.'

He took the sandwich with a grin. 'I hear it's a very competitive field. You'll need ambition as well. How bad do you want it, Serena?'

Bad enough to have queried every major global newspaper and some not so global ones about upcoming positions every month for the last five months. 'Trust me, I've got the ambition thing covered. Maybe in the past I've let family commitments keep me from pursuing this type of career, but not this time. This time I'm determined to get where I'm going.'

'Just as soon as you get off this island,' he said with a hint of dryness that she chose to ignore.

'Exactly.'

'So technically speaking, apart from the Vespas, the postcard photography, and keeping an eye on your grandparents, you're a free agent this coming month.'

'That's me.' Damn but he was appealing. 'And my grandparents are visiting both sides of the family on the mainland at the moment. They left this morning, so you can count them out of the equation for a couple of months. You?'

'I'll be flying these skies until Tomas recovers the use of his leg. Six…eight weeks. Maybe longer.'

'And then?'

He shrugged. 'There's an offer from an Australian mining company to run a charter-flight operation for them in Papua New Guinea. It's a good offer.'

'Yes, but is it ethical?'

'What they're doing or what I'd be doing?' he countered with a quick smile, and Serena figured she had her answer.

'So you flit,' she said dryly. 'From one flying job to another.'

'I like to think there's a big-picture plan somewhere in amongst it all,' he said mildly.

'Ever thought about settling down?'

'You mean some place permanently or with a woman?'

'Either.'

'No.'

Serena closed her eyes, muttered a prayer. As far as potential short-term romantic interludes were concerned, the man was utterly, mouth-wateringly perfect.

'Did you just whimper?' he said, eyeing her closely. 'I thought I heard someone whimper.'

'No whimpering here.' Much. 'What can I get you to drink? Water, wine?' She gestured towards the glass of white wine already on the bench. 'I'm already set.' She didn't wait for an answer, just headed for the fridge. She thought it best to keep busy, keep that whimpering to an absolute minimum. Water, wine, she grabbed both and set them in front of him. 'Help yourself.'

He did, reaching for a couple of tumblers on the shelf nearby before pouring water for them both. He snagged another glass, a wineglass this time, and filled that too, his fingers long and lean around the neck of the bottle…fingers that looked as if they could deliver anything a woman could possibly want, from a feather-light stroke to firm and knowing pressure in all the right places.

'There it goes again,' he said. 'That sound.'

'Could be the tabby cat hereabouts. She's very noisy.'

Pete looked at the curled and sleeping cat over in the corner of the kitchen, her head firmly tucked beneath one paw. 'You mean *that* cat?'

'Yes.' She said it with an utterly straight face and Pete's admiration for her rose immeasurably. 'That cat.'

They ate from the picnic table in the courtyard, with the cottage nestled into the hillside behind them and the sea spread out before them like a promise.

'So how many brothers do you have?' Pete asked between bites of truly divine roast chicken. Chicken like this could quite conceivably make a man change his mind on the issue of not wanting a woman to come home to each night.

Serena held up two fingers and he smiled. Two brothers and an overprotective cousin wasn't so bad.

'I saw that smile,' she said darkly. 'And if you figure you can handle them you're wrong. They're half Greek. And if you're talking extended family—and with my family you should—I also have two brothers-in-law, a father, three uncles, and half a dozen male cousins my age or older. Nico is the most liberal-minded of the lot.'

'Ah.' That was quite a list of protective males. Doubtless she'd driven them insane during her teenage years. 'Bet your first date went well.'

'You have no idea,' she muttered. 'I thought he'd be all right. He had a very cool car and a bad-boy reputation. A smile that promised heaven… They were waiting for him out in the front yard when he came to pick me up. My father and my uncle.' Her eyes flashed with a mixture of amusement and annoyance. 'They'd brought home a fish from the morning's catch and were gutting it when he pulled up. With ten inch boning knives.'

'Sounds reasonable,' said Pete. 'Although I can see how you might consider the knives a touch melodramatic.'

'It was a six-foot shark.'

'Oh.' He felt a smile coming on.

'And don't you dare laugh!'

'No, ma'am. But I am impressed.'

'We didn't even get to the cinema. The poor boy took me to a burger drive-through, fed me hot chips and a sundae, and had me home within half an hour. He's probably still running.'

'Just for the record, I'd have bought you a burger as well.' He topped up her wineglass, reached for another slice of bread. 'I have three brothers, a father, and one sister. Hallie's the youngest.'

'No mother?'

'Nope. She died when I was a kid. My father took it hard, pulled back. My brothers and I took over the raising of Hallie. You'd like her. You could swap stories. My youngest brother could get downright creative when it came to deterring her more persistent suitors. He works for Interpol these days. He'd have *loved* a shark as a prop.'

'Are you sure you don't have any Greek ancestry in you?'

'Not a drop.'

'What's your position on trust and honour?'

'As in Nico trusting me not to hit on you?'

She nodded.

'It's damn near killing me.'

Her smile sliced through him, wicked with challenge. 'But you *are* sticking to it.'

'Barely.' The meal had more than satisfied Pete's appetite for food, and dusk was warming up the crowd for the coming of night. The air lay heavy with the scent of jasmine and he was self-aware enough to know that if he didn't leave soon his honour wouldn't be worth a drachma. 'Close your eyes,' he told her. 'Think back to that bad boy with his own car and a smile like a promise.'

'Why?' But she did as he asked, her back to the table, her elbows resting behind her, and her head tilted back a fraction as if to catch the moonlight.

'Work with me here,' he murmured. 'You've been to the cinema and you're on your way home. The car stereo's blaring, the windows are down, the wind is in your hair, and your bad boy has forgotten all about your father's shark-carving skills. He's young and reckless, and so are you.'

Her lips curved. 'And then?'

'He pulls up outside your front yard.'

'Does he stop the engine?'

'No. He's not insane. He's planning on a quick getaway.'

Her eyes were still closed. 'Where's the shark?'

'Your father and uncle are hauling the last of it into the freezer. The timing's perfect.'

'For what?' she whispered.

'This.' He brushed his lips over hers, a fleeting touch, nothing more, and pulled away. He planned to end it then, to say goodnight and get the hell out of temptation's way, but her eyes were still closed and before he knew it his lips were on hers again, questing, cajoling, because this time, *this* time he wanted a response.

He got one.

Serena had played his game because she wanted to. Because she was curious as to what this man with his come to bed eyes and go to hell grin could bring to an evening, a moment, a kiss.

He brought plenty.

A taste so wild and delicious she shuddered. A mouth so firm and knowing she responded instinctively, following his lead with lips and with tongue in a dance as old as time. She wanted more, slid her hand to his cheek,

to the nape of his neck in search of it, taking the kiss
deeper as she sought the recklessness in him, that piece
of him that courted danger, revelled in it, and came back
for more. She found it.

And the kiss turned wild.

He murmured something, a deep-chested rumble
that sounded like a protest but felt like surrender, and
took her under.

Her mind had clouded over by the time the kiss
ended, the rapid pulsing of her blood at odds with the
languid slide of her hand from around his neck. She
leaned back, elbows on the table, and watched as he
struggled to surface, clawing his way out of the kiss in
much the same way she had, and not bothering to hide
how hard he found it.

She liked that about him. She liked it a lot.

'Damn but he's gonna break some hearts, kissing
like that,' she murmured.

'So are you.'

She made a small hum of pleasure. 'Tell him to
kiss me again.'

'No. If he does he'll be lost and he doesn't want that.
Besides, the porch light has just come on and it's way
past time to be leaving.'

'Does he come back?'

'Try keeping him away. It's your first kiss, maybe his
third, but from that moment on there's a part of him
that'll always be yours.'

She smiled, enchanted by his whimsy.

'Thank you for the meal,' he said softly. 'Serena?'

'What?'

'I'll honour Nico's trust in me tonight, but next time I see you I'll be asking you out to dinner. I'll be holding you at the end of the evening. I'll be around these next few weeks. I'll be taking up some of your free time.'

She liked his high-handedness. She liked it a lot.

'And Serena?' He stood and looked down at her, looking for all the world like a dark angel fallen straight from the sky. 'I don't give a damn how big the shark is.'

CHAPTER THREE

PETE BENNETT lived to fly. Nothing could change that. Nothing ever had. It was simple fact that he was at his happiest with one hand on the throttle and the other on the joystick of a helicopter that responded to his slightest touch. Oh, he had his favourites, everyone did, and luckily old Tomas's Jet Ranger was one of them. She was no Seahawk—equipment-wise she was a purely civilian fit—but she had a light touch and he was close to the sea, and for now that was enough.

And if at times skimming low across the water put him in mind of other far more dangerous flights and missions, well, that couldn't be helped. A man like him did his damnedest to ignore the insistent knocking of the past in favour of whatever else was in front of him.

A man like him took great pains to ensure that whatever was in front of him had a certain basic appeal.

Island-hopping with a cargo of two tourists looking to overnight on a sleepy Greek island, for example, had enough basic appeal in the shape of meeting up with Serena again to drive every unwanted memory from his body.

He touched down at Sathi, Varanissi's picturesque seaport, just on three in the afternoon, unloaded his passengers, and herded them towards the hotel, their bags slung over his shoulder with his own.

The fiery Chloe was nowhere to be seen as he saw them checked in and arranged to meet them again at nine the following morning. He wasn't as lucky when it came to the boy, Sam. The kid had appeared in the foyer as he'd arrived and had been hovering ever since. When Pete made to leave, young Sam ventured forward.

'You're not staying here?' he said.

Pete shook his head. 'I'm staying up at Nico's. In Tomas's room.'

'Oh.' Sam paused, as if weighing his options. 'I'm heading up that way too. To see Nico. I could show you a short cut if you want.'

He knew the path the boy was talking about. He'd taken it before, with Nico. And opened his mouth to say so.

But Sam had already read him. Pete watched, eyes narrowing, as bleak resignation flashed across the kid's face, just before he lifted his chin and looked away. How the hell did a kid get to be so streetwise and still be so soft? He didn't know. But it got to him. 'Fine,' he said, perversely pleased by Sam's surprise. 'I figured I'd head on up to the Vespas and say hello to Serena after that. Join me if you want. I could use the company.' This much was true. He'd be far less tempted to reach for Serena within moments of seeing her if he had Sam with him.

Given the wildness of his fantasies about her, that was probably a good thing.

* * *

Four days. Four endless summer days. That was how long Serena had been waiting for that damn helicopter to fly over and land on the island and even then she waited another hour for the pilot of the cursed machine to put in an appearance at her brand-new blue beach umbrella by the rusty Vespa shed. By that time Serena had replayed the memory of Pete Bennett's kisses at least a thousand times and every cell in her body was screaming for more. The man was a genius.

But he wasn't alone. Sam tagged alongside him, wary and silent but nonetheless there. So much for wrapping herself around Superman right then and there.

Make that evil genius.

'Hey, sailor,' she said, smiling at Sam who'd finagled a morning out on Nico's boat tomorrow. Tomorrow being Saturday, and that being the deal he'd made with Chloe if he went to school all week. 'Got a message for you. Nico said he'll swing by on his way down to the dock at around four-thirty a.m. Speaking from experience, you'd better be ready because the tide waits for no man and neither does Nico. Wear a jumper and a hat and don't worry about gloves. He's found some for you that'll fit.'

Serena watched as Sam's face lit up like the sun, a fleeting grin, gone almost as soon as it had arrived but she'd caught it nonetheless, along with a hefty dose of hero-worship for her cousin. 'Meanwhile, there's a Vespa been coughing and spluttering and I need someone to take it around the paddock a few times to see if it gives any grief.'

'What's in it for me?' said Sam.

'Experience,' she said dryly, handing him a helmet.

'It just so happens that the bike you'll be trialling could well be the second-fastest bike on the island.'

'So Aunt Chloe went for it?' asked Pete as they watched Sam fasten the helmet, start the bike and ride slowly along the fence line. '*That's* the second-fastest bike on the island?'

'Well, no. Not any more. Maybe thirty years ago.' Right now, it was the slowest ride she had. 'And Chloe caved two days ago after two more trips to the principal's office on account of our friend here's somewhat disquieting habit of disappearing from school around mid-morning and failing to return.' The bike coped with the downhill run easily enough, but coughed and groaned all the way up the hill. 'I think it needs a new spark plug.'

'That or a decent burial,' muttered Pete.

'We don't discard our old around here. It's just not done,' she told him. 'And it's about time you showed up.'

Pete Bennett smiled. 'Miss me?'

'Maybe. Did *you* miss me?'

'Of course. How many goddesses of buckets and sensuality do you think I know?'

'Pardon?'

'Never mind. I tried to get back here earlier,' he murmured. 'Unfortunately, not many people know about this place. It's a hard sell. Maybe you should hurry up with those postcards.'

'Maybe I will.' She eyed his carryall speculatively, wondering how Sam had found him so fast, wondering exactly how long he was staying this time. 'Are you staying overnight?'

He nodded. 'What time do you finish up here?'

'The last of the bikes should be back by five, give or take half an hour,' she told him. 'Why? What did you have in mind?'

'I'm thinking of taking a stroll up the hill.'

'What hill?' She followed his gaze to the mountain looming behind them. 'Oh. That hill.' She'd climbed it before. It wasn't easy. 'That's a big hill.'

'Sam says there's a path to the top.'

'Well, yes. There is. If you're a goat.'

'And that you can see the entire island when you get to the top.'

There was that.

'Bring your camera. You might catch the sunset.'

She'd been here for five months, four days, and counting. She'd photographed *everything* more times than she cared to remember, including the sunset. 'I'll need more incentive than that.'

'It's good exercise.'

'Boy, do you have a lot to learn about women and incentive.'

'C'mon, Rena. Haven't you ever wanted to touch the sky?'

He had the soul of a poet. The smile of a devil. Serena couldn't resist either. 'All right. I give in. We'll walk to the top and touch the sky.'

His smile promised more, much, *much* more, and she knew for a fact he could deliver. 'You won't regret it,' he murmured.

'I never do.'

* * *

It was half past five before the last of the bikes were locked away for the night and Serena had shooed Sam home. Closer to six by the time they'd taken her cooler and the cashbox down to the cottage. There was enough daylight left for getting up the hill. Not nearly enough daylight for getting back down. Serena picked up a small canvas bag and went in search of a torch and a couple of bottles of water before slinging it over her shoulder. 'Ready?'

With a gesture that came as automatically to him as breathing, Pete removed the bag from her shoulder and slung it over his. 'Lead on.'

She led him behind the cottage and across the bitumen road to where the goat track began. If there was one thing she'd become used to on Varanissi, it was walking up hills. Her body had grown quite fond of it; her legs no longer gave protest. She was healthy. Fit. And still she had the feeling that if necessary, Pete Bennett with his lazy stride and easy breathing could have taken the slope at a dead run. She picked up the pace, figuring that if she had to exercise she might as well make it worthwhile.

Half an hour later they reached their destination, a desolate plateau dropping away sharply on three of its four sides, but what the rocky, barren plateau lacked in visual appeal it more than made up for with its panoramic view of the village and harbour below.

The island had charm; she'd give it that. And the people on it were as good as you'd find anywhere. Maybe better.

But the world was bigger than this, and so were

Serena's dreams. Pete Bennett knew how to dream big too. She could see it in the way he looked to the sky, sense the restlessness in him, a burning need to keep moving, keep going…to run, and to fly. 'You love it, don't you? Being up here.'

'Yeah,' he said simply, looking skyward. 'It's the next best thing to being up there.'

'Why helicopters?' she asked. 'Why didn't you choose to fly planes?'

'I've flown both,' he said. 'But helicopters are more sensitive, more tactile machines than planes. Planes are all about power. Helicopters are about finesse.'

'You fly planes too?'

He flashed her a grin. 'Serena, I fly everything.'

'Have you always wanted to fly?'

'Ever since I was old enough to sit on my sainted mother's knee at Richmond RAAF base and watch the pilots practise their touch and gos.'

'I'll take that as an always. What's a touch and go?'

'You bring the plane in, touch down, and then take off again, all in the same run. What about you?' He gestured towards the camera around her neck. 'Has it always been photography for you?'

'Not always. I've done lots of things. Managed restaurants, designed their interiors, done the branding work for the family seafood outlets, written articles for magazines. But I keep coming back to my camera and the stories a picture can tell.' She took a mouthful of water. Watched as Pete did the same, slaking his thirst the same way he'd climbed the hill: effortlessly and with every appearance of enjoyment. 'So you spent a goodly portion of your childhood hanging over the fence of the local RAAF base. What then? How did you become a pilot?'

'I was all set to join the Air Force but somewhere along the way I got to stand on a deck full of Navy Seahawks and that was it for me. Nothing else would do.'

'You joined the Navy?' It didn't seem to fit with his carefree bad-boy image. 'What about the discipline? All those rules and regulations? Dedication to duty?'

'What about them?' He shot her a quizzical glance.

She figured she might as well give it to him straight. 'You don't seem the type.'

'Look harder,' he offered, his voice noticeably cooler.

Good idea. Excellent idea. She slipped the cap from her camera and studied him through the lens. 'Okay, I'm seeing it now.' But only because he was letting her see. This was a part of himself that playboy Pete Bennett preferred to keep hidden. She took the shot, and then another. 'So how long were you in the Navy?'

'Regular squadron? Seven years.'

'And then?'

'Then I transferred to air-sea search and rescue helicopters for a while.'

'For how long?' There was something about his expression that didn't invite questions.

'Eight years.'

He looked away, all shut down, but not before she'd caught with her camera a hint of pain that ran deep. She wondered at it, wondered why a man who'd spent fifteen years in service to others was currently flying tourists around these islands and contemplating hauling cargo around PNG. A man didn't walk away from the kind of work he'd been doing for no reason. Did he? 'Do you miss it?'

'Miss what?'

'The howling winds and heaving seas. The adrenalin rush that'd come with battling the elements and saving lives. It's pretty heroic stuff.'

'I'm not a hero, Serena. Far from it. Paint me as one and you'll be in for disappointment,' he said quietly.

'Thanks for the warning,' she countered dryly. 'You know, my father is a fourth-generation fisherman. My brothers are fishermen. My cousins are fishermen. I *know* who they look to for miracles when the sea turns ugly and a vessel goes down. I know what you used to do.'

'I don't do it any more.' The reckless charmer had disappeared, and in his place stood a complex warrior. The rogue had been irresistible enough. The warrior was downright breathtaking. 'Take your photos,' he said, but she already had and they wouldn't be appearing on any picture postcard.

'C'mere,' she said softly and he looked towards her, wary and wounded for reasons she couldn't fathom, his dark glare daring her to probe and prod for answers he didn't want to give only she was done with questions for now. First rule of interviewing was to read your mark and when you'd pushed them as far as they'd go, pull back and come at them later from a different direction.

He stepped up in front of her, big and brooding, his hands in his pockets and his expression guarded. 'Closer,' she said, and set her hand to his chest and lightly bussed his lips. 'That's for stepping up to protect your country—even if you were seduced into it by a bunch of Navy helicopters.' She set her lips to his again and let them linger a fraction longer, watching as his eyes darkened. 'And that's for putting your life on the line to save others, day in, day out, for eight years.' She slid her hand to his shoulder and this time her kiss was more than a whisper. She felt his response, saw with satisfaction the heat of the kiss chase the shadows from his eyes.

'What was that for?' he muttered.

'Dinner,' she said, sauntering away towards the southern edge of the plateau. 'You *are* taking me to dinner, aren't you?'

He took her to dinner. To the little restaurant high in the hills where the fish stew was reputed to taste like ambrosia and the air was thin enough to have him breathing deep whenever Serena looked at him. She wore a cream-coloured dress, low cut, square necked, with delicate shoulder straps. It had little buttons all the way down the front, buttons that drove a man to distraction whenever he looked at them, and she knew it, her smile told him so and her eyes dared him to call her on it. 'That's quite a first-date dress.' His lips brushed her hair as he saw her seated. 'But it's not blue.'

'You were expecting the blue?' she said and her eyes were laughing.

'I was looking forward to it,' he said. 'With a great deal of anticipation, I might add.'

'Sorry to disappoint.'

'You haven't. I'll continue to look forward to it.'

'I'm saving it,' she said.

'For what?'

'The Trevi Fountain.'

Good call. He knew this game of seduction well. He loved the playing of it, the hunt and the chase. Loved it when his quarry provided a challenge. And heaven help him the woman sitting opposite knew exactly how to do just that.

'Unfortunately my chances of venturing that far afield are somewhat limited at the moment,' she added with a sigh. 'And I suspect you're tied to Tomas's charter operation as well. Fortunately for you I've had another idea.' She leaned back in her chair and smiled. 'It involves no fountain and no blue dress whatsoever, but it does involve water.' He was all ears. And damned if she didn't smile and change the subject. 'Tell me about your family.'

'I've already told you about them,' he said.

'Tell me more.'

He usually didn't. But this time, in this place, he relaxed into his seat and offered up more. 'My father lives in Sydney. He's an academic—a scholar of ancient Chinese pottery. My sister is married and lives in London. She inherited our father's passion for pots. Then there's Tristan, who works for Interpol. He got married at Christmas and is back living in Sydney.' Pete shook his head at the wonder of that particular notion. 'Then there's Luke. He's older than Tris, younger than me. He's a Navy SEAL.' Pete toyed with his bread and butter knife, would have left it at that, but Serena wasn't chasing a career in photojournalism without having mastered the finer art of persistence.

'You said you had three brothers,' she prompted him with a smile. 'There's one more.'

'Jake.' Thoughts of Jake always came with a serve of guilt. That he hadn't helped him out more when their mother had died. That he hadn't shouldered more of the responsibility. 'He's a couple of years older than me and runs a handful of martial arts dojos in Singapore.'

'So your family is scattered all over the globe.'

'More or less.'

'My immediate family live in Melbourne. All of them. I can't imagine them living anywhere but in each other's pockets.'

'Is this a bad thing?' he asked curiously.

'Hard to say.' She shrugged. 'Everyone always knows what everyone else is doing. Whether that's a bad thing tends to depend on whether they approve of what you're doing. If they don't…' She shrugged again.

'And do your family approve of your plans for the future? The photojournalism career? The endless travel away from the family bosom?'

'Let's just say they don't quite understand,' she said lightly, but her eyes told a different, darker story.

'Maybe one day they will.'

She smiled and leaned back in her chair. 'You're a nice man, Pete Bennett. Idealistic, but nice.'

There was that word again. Nice. She really should stop bandying it about. It made a man uncomfortable. 'You do know that *nice* isn't really on this evening's agenda?' he told her softly. 'That would be the wrong notion to be carrying around altogether.'

Her smile held equal measures of wickedness and delight. 'I'd be very disappointed if it was.'

A weathered old man appeared beside the table, glaring at him from beneath thick grey eyebrows and over a strongly hooked nose. 'You'll order now,' he said.

Pete looked to Serena and raised an eyebrow. 'Care to order?'

'My usual, Pappou Theo. The fish stew and the salad.'

'*Pappou* Theo?' he murmured.

'Honorary grandfather,' she said. 'One of my grandfather's pinochle partners.'

That explained the scowl. 'I'll have the oysters and then the fish stew,' he said. 'Serena tells me good things about it.'

'No oysters for you!' said the old man emphatically. 'Greek salad with many onions. You'll like.' The old man turned to Serena again and surveyed her critically. 'Does Nico know you're here?'

'Yes, Pappou.'

'And when does he expect you home? At a reasonable hour, I hope.'

'Yes, Pappou. Very reasonable.'

The old man muttered to himself beneath his breath and turned back to Pete. 'Drinks?' he barked.

'Some white wine?' Pete looked to Serena.

'No!' said the old man. 'No wine.'

'Raki?'

'Pig swill,' he said.

'Beer?'

'Not for you. I'll bring the water over,' said the old man, and stalked away.

Pete stared after him. 'That went well.'

'I did warn you,' she said. 'I *told* you there'd be sharks. You told *me* you could swim.'

'I can swim.' And he was enjoying the challenge of getting past her guardians. He watched as the old man ambled towards the kitchen with their order. 'I'm just rethinking our next evening meal. I have a plan.'

'Is it a cunning plan?'

'It involves travel off the island. For you.'

'I like it,' she said. 'Simple yet effective.'

'How far away do you think we'll have to get before you run out of relatives?'

'Three or four islands over,' she said breezily. 'Five at the most. Or we could play it really safe and go to Istanbul for the evening. That'd work.'

'You don't have any relatives in Turkey?'

'None we admit to.'

'So…' He began to think of more immediate options. 'What would a man have to do to earn your family's approval to court you?'

'You want to court me? I'm thinking courtship comes under the heading of *nice* again.'

'I'm speaking theoretically.'

'Well, theoretically, it'd help if you were Greek and owned a shipping line.'

'How about Australian and co-owner of a small charter airline?'

'I'd have to check. Tell me…are you of Greek Orthodox religion?'

'Catholic,' he said with a shrug. 'Lapsed.'

'You might want to keep that to yourself,' she said.

'You should probably stick to talk of undying devotion to me, an exceptionally large income, a huge wedding, and your longing to help produce half a dozen children in very short order.'

'*How* many children?' he spluttered.

'Oh, okay, five then. But that's my absolute minimum.'

'You want *five* children? In very short order? Are we *sure* about this?' She didn't look all that sure. 'Two,' he said firmly. 'Two's a good number. Any more than two and we won't all fit in the helicopter.'

'Four,' she countered with a grin. 'And we're definitely going to need a bigger helicopter. Something roomy and safe. Family-minded. A Volvo of a helicopter.'

'Oh, that's harsh,' he murmured. 'Anyone would think you didn't *want* a man to consider a serious relationship with you.'

'They'd be right.'

'God, you're perfect,' he said. 'I swear you stand a very good chance of ruining me for all other women.'

'That's quite a compliment,' she countered. 'But I really don't want to ruin you for anyone. I just want to play a while.'

'Utterly and irrevocably perfect,' he said on a sigh. 'Hell, Serena, you might just ruin me anyway.'

Their meal arrived and they ate it. Sinfully rich stew with a smattering of easy conversation on the side. Pete knew the game of seduction very well and played it with a skill that left her breathless and more than a little intrigued as to what would come next. A rakish smile or a challenging question? A sidestep here, advance, or retreat? He kept her guessing. Kept her amused and entertained.

She was a curious woman by nature, but he did a remarkable job of making her want to know more of him. Like what it was that had put the shadows in his eyes, and what he was doing here, flying tourists around the sky, when every instinct she owned told her there was so much more to him than this.

'Coffee?' he suggested as Theo cleared their plates away. 'Dessert?' Theo opened his mouth as if to refuse them that as well. Pete eyed him coolly. 'Of course, if there's nothing available here I'd be happy to take you somewhere else.'

They got their coffee and dessert. They also got a taxi without having to order it. It was leaving within the next five minutes, Theo told them. It'd be a good idea if Serena were in it. She didn't disagree.

Pete looked amused but neither did he.

They were back at the little whitewashed cottage on the hillside by a quarter to ten. Serena waited in silence as Pete paid the taxi driver and, stepping back, looked towards her front door. 'No sharks,' he said. 'There's a surprise.'

'Nico's pretty easygoing,' she said dryly. 'I can't see him objecting too much to our having dinner up at Theo's.'

'Can't you?' There was that soul-stealing smile again. 'I can.'

Nico had left the outside light on for them, but before she could decide how to end the evening, whether to invite him in, cut and run, or try and figure out something in between, the door opened and Nico stood there glaring at them both.

'You're still awake,' she said, surprised. Nico usually bedded down far earlier than this. All that getting-up-before-dawn business.

'Have you *any* idea how many phone calls I've had about you tonight?' he demanded.

'Er…more than you wanted?'

'One was more than I wanted. I've had four. Four! Two from Theo, one from Marianne Papadopoulos, and one from your mother! And don't ask me how she knew you were out on a date, because I have no idea. Anyone would think you were making love on the tabletop.' He eyed them narrowly. 'Were you?'

'No!' Serena's hands went to her hips and her temper slid up a notch. 'We were *trying* to have a meal, and a restricted one at that. When was the last time *you* went out to dinner and Theo refused you oysters and alcohol?'

Nico's lips twitched.

Serena narrowed her eyes. 'Don't you dare laugh.'

'Not laughing,' he said, and then spoiled it by grinning hugely as he turned away and stalked back down the hall. 'This isn't Australia,' he said over his shoulder. 'It isn't even Athens. What did you expect?' He spared a lightning glance for Pete. 'You've got five minutes. I need my sleep. Anything happens to Sam on board that boat tomorrow and Chloe'll skewer me with a fish-hook. Anything happens to Serena in the next five minutes that's not entirely circumspect and I'll skewer you. That's the way it works around here. Welcome to Sathi.'

'All right,' she said with a sigh as she closed the door on Nico's retreating form and turning to study the man at her side. 'So I could have been *slightly* wrong about Nico not worrying about our dinner together—although, to be scrupulously fair, he probably wasn't the one doing the worrying. Others did it for him. How do you feel? Alarmed? Afraid? Threatened?'

'Nah.' Far from looking worried, Superman looked to be thoroughly enjoying himself. 'He gave me five minutes. He likes me.'

She liked him. And that was proving more of a problem than she'd thought it would be. 'Walk with me, Pete Bennett. I'll show you my favourite place in the garden.' She clasped her arms around her waist and walked around the side of the cottage, to the edge of the garden to stare out over the moonlit sea. She did some of her best thinking just sitting there staring out to sea.

She needed to do some very serious thinking about what she wanted from this man right about now.

She'd looked at him a few days back and seen a pleasant diversion. A charming playmate with no strings attached. She looked at him now and saw something far more dangerous. A man with a generous heart, and a guarded one. A man with the potential to captivate her as well as charm her, and she didn't want that. No, she couldn't have that.

Not when for the first time in her life she could see a time up ahead with no commitments and no family ties. *Her* time. Time for chasing long-held dreams for a career she could be proud of.

'I've enjoyed your company,' Serena said at last.

Nothing but the truth in that statement. 'I'd like to enjoy it some more. But we're going to need some rules.'

'I love rules,' he said. 'What kind of rules?'

'We keep this light-hearted,' she said firmly. 'No falling in love.'

'Check.'

'And brief. We'll both be leaving here soon enough. We should make that the end of it. Clean break. Happy memories.'

'Mature of us,' he said. 'Anything else?'

'I know we're talking a brief and in no way serious relationship here, but I'm thinking exclusivity is a must.'

'You'd better be,' he said curtly.

'There *is* one more thing.'

'You're pushing your luck, Serena.'

He looked tough, forbidding, and Serena wondered afresh whether she was insane to think she could handle this man. He walked his own path, made his own rules. But this last rule was important. 'We need to be discreet.' Otherwise it would reflect badly on her family, and she didn't want that. 'It's this place…' she said with more than a little frustration.

Pete laughed at that, and the rich dark sound of it slid along her skin like water.

'You're right,' he murmured. 'We'll be discreet.' And then his lips were on hers, hard and seeking, and all her carefully thought out rules shattered beneath the weight of her desire.

Pete's body betrayed him the moment he reached for her. He'd known it would. The searing heat. The outrageous, all-consuming need to possess that which he held and, in doing so, offer up a part of himself. She was all luscious curves, made for a man's hands, *his* hands, as he curled his fingers around her buttocks and brought their lower bodies into languid and intimate contact. He could be discreet. If that was what she wanted. He'd do it. He would.

Soon.

Just as soon as he'd finished feasting on her mouth.

She dug her hands in his hair and her lips turned ravenous, but he was ready for the staggering hunger of her kisses this time and he ate them up, spun them round, and served them straight back at her.

Serena had thought she was prepared for the passion this man brought to lovemaking, but she wasn't prepared for this. It was like a meeting of souls, locked in a kiss, and she feared it…heaven help her she feared it…even as she gloried in it. Whatever she wanted, however she wanted it, he had it in him to give. And she wanted it all.

Shuddering at the sensations threatening to overwhelm her, she dragged her lips free of his kiss and set trembling fingers to his mouth instead. A barrier, a slowdown, only her fingers had a mind of their own, exploring his upper lip, the strong shapely curve of it, before dragging the sensitive pad of her forefinger across the sculpted fullness of the rest.

Serena watched as those perfect lips curved into a smile; a smile for her attempts to regain control maybe; and then she was urging his mouth open and replacing fingertips with lips and with tongue for a kiss so staggeringly potent she clear forgot to breathe.

Whatever she wanted, she thought helplessly as his

tongue duelled delicately with hers. Just the way she wanted it, as his fingers tightened on her butt and he surged against her, and with a ragged groan spun them into the maelstrom again.

His eyes were black, as black as sin and deep enough to drown in, when finally, finally, they stood apart.

'Discreet.' He ran a hand around the back of his neck. 'We might have to work on that one,' he said raggedly. And then he was gone.

CHAPTER FOUR

NICO scowled at her when she staggered into the kitchen. Serena ignored him and headed for the sink, filling a tall glass to the brim with tap water and downing it in one long swallow. 'So…' she said, finally turning to face her cousin. 'How was your night?'

Nico's eyes narrowed. 'I *said* five minutes.'

'It *was* five minutes.'

'It was ten minutes, your mouth's all swollen, and your hands are shaking.'

Oh.

'You can't take a man like that seriously, Serena.'

'I don't intend to.'

'I mean, what do we know about him? Apart from the fact that he was able to pack up his life in an instant and come out here when Tomas called. Seriously, what does that say about a man?'

'That he's a good friend to Tomas?'

'He's a drifter. A man with no responsibilities.'

'You should ask him what he used to do for a living,' she said wryly. 'It's quite illuminating.'

'He's trouble. I thought you could handle him or I'd never have introduced you.'

'I *can* handle him,' she snapped. She'd had enough of Nico's and everyone else's well-meaning interference. 'I know damn well he's trouble. I don't need you to tell me that. I know it wouldn't work out. I don't *want* it to work out. All right?' Her voice broke but the rest of her stood tall as she glared across the table at Nico and dared him to take her to task for a passion she couldn't control. 'I know.'

Pete was fresh out of a cold shower in the little bedsit, a towel slung around his waist and his hair still dripping water, when he took it in his head to call his older brother. In Singapore.

''Lo.' Jake's voice sounded raspy, sleepy.

'Jake? What time is it there?' He did the maths, winced a little at the early morning hour. 'I, ah, didn't interrupt anything, did I?'

'Not unless you count sleep as something. Which you should.'

'Never mind. I'll call back later.'

'You in trouble?' asked Jake.

'Not really.'

Jake said nothing. Jake was really good at waiting in silence while the other person squirmed and tried to put feelings into words. Something to do with inner stillness and meditation. He'd never quite managed to get the hang of it, himself. 'All right, so I could have a *slight* problem.'

'Define "slight".'

'There's this woman.'

Dead silence at that. Fraught silence. Not a lot of inner stillness in that silence at all. And then, 'Why me?' said Jake, his voice long-suffering. 'I live a frugal life. I keep to myself. I pay my taxes… Why?'

'Is this a bad time to call?' he said. 'Because I can call back later. When you're making more sense.'

'Is she terminally ill?'

'No.'

'Are *you* terminally ill?'

'No.'

'Is she married to a Mafia Don who wants to cut off your balls?'

'She's not married at all.'

'So there's no bodily danger to you at this particular point in time?'

'No.' It was his soul he was worried about. 'My body thinks it's found heaven.'

'Colour me envious,' said Jake, 'but what the *hell* is your problem?'

'She doesn't want to be tied down.'

'So? Neither do you. The minute a woman starts getting serious, you're gone.'

'This one's kind of interesting.'

Silence.

'You've fallen for her,' said Jake finally.

'I have not!' he said indignantly. 'I did *not* say that. I was just wondering what the next step up from a strictly casual relationship might be. You know…casual yet slightly meaningful. Comes before commitment. But I can't remember what it's called.'

'Self-delusion,' said Jake dryly. 'Run.'

'That's your advice? Run?'

'Yep.'

'Any *other* advice?'

'Nope.'

'You are no help whatsoever.'

'Not in this,' said Jake with grim humour. 'Call Tris,' he said, and hung up.

No way, thought Pete as he shoved the phone back in his bag. No way was he calling *anyone* else in his family tonight. One delusional phone call an evening was enough. He towelled his hair, found a fresh pair of boxers in his carryall and looked at the bed.

He was nowhere near ready for bed.

He found a book, tossed it on the bed as incentive.

Still not ready for bed. The image of a dark-eyed goddess in an ivory-coloured sundress flashed through his mind, closely followed by an image of her lying in his bed with no ivory-coloured sundress on at all.

Now he'd *never* get to sleep.

So she wanted nothing more than a light hearted romp. Was this a bad thing? No. Light hearted romps were his speciality.

So he'd wondered, *briefly*, about a relationship that involved a little bit…more. Clearly not a good idea. He'd get over it. *Was* over it. A short-term relationship was fine. Just fine.

Fidelity he could do.

As for discretion… Pete thought back to the kisses they'd shared and chuckled as he stripped the towel from his body and ran it over his hair.

Heaven help them both.

* * *

Breakfast the following morning was a revelation. Serena had rapped on the bedsit door at seven and told him that breakfast was available in the kitchen if he wanted it. Ten minutes later he made his way over there, showered, shaved and ready for whatever lay ahead as far as light hearted, short-term, discreetly exclusive relationships were concerned.

And then he stepped through the kitchen doorway and she stopped grinding fresh coffee beans and smiled at him and every rational thought he'd had about her left his head.

She wore modest shorts and a bright pink T-shirt—Pete recognised it as her Vespa hire attire—and had pulled her hair back into a pony-tail. Nothing overtly seductive about any of it—no slinky sleepwear or artfully tousled hair, and still her innate sensuality punched into him like a fist.

'What would you like for breakfast?' she asked as she loaded up the breakfast bench with far more food than he could possibly eat.

'You don't have to do this, you know,' he said as he relieved her of the orange juice and gestured towards the bench. 'I can get my own cereal.'

'All part of the service.' She stifled a yawn and padded over to the kitchen sink, leaning over to open the window above it. 'You want anything cooked? Sausages? Bacon and eggs?'

What he *wanted* was to drag her back to bed and make love to her until the sleepiness left her eyes and satisfaction took its place. What he *wanted* was to ask her what she had planned for the day and then rearrange his own schedule to fit in around hers so he could see her again later. What he *said* was, 'No, thanks. This is fine.'

'So…' she poured herself a cup of coffee and cradled it in her hands as she leaned back against the kitchen counter and studied him '…what do you usually talk about at breakfast?'

'Usually I'm by myself.'

'When you're not,' she said dryly.

He tried to think. Couldn't. Not when she strolled over and settled into the chair opposite him and her scent wrapped around him like a promise. 'Work. We talk about work. What that person is doing with their day. That sort of thing. '

'Oh,' she said. And with another one of those lazy, loaded smiles, 'What are you doing with your day, Pete Bennett?'

'Well…' He wished his mind would return from wherever he'd dropped it. It was probably somewhere over by the door. 'First up is Corfu to drop passengers, then Cyprus to pick up some cargo, then back to mainland Greece. I'll overnight in Athens.'

'Skite,' she muttered. '*I'm* going to the Vespa shed. I'll be there until five.'

'I'll think of you.' Nothing but the truth.

'What else do you talk about?'

'Anything. Everything. Except for home improvements. A woman starts talking home improvements and I start to get nervous.'

'Really?' she said archly. 'So you don't think this kitchen needs a bigger window? I think it needs a much bigger window. I mean, look at that view! It's just begging to be taken advantage of.'

'It doesn't work when you talk about improvements to *your* home,' he told her smugly as he reached for the cereal. 'It only works when the house in question is *mine*.'

'Ah. I should have guessed.'

'You should be grateful,' he told her. 'You don't *want* a man who's looking for a woman to improve his home, remember?'

'Not yet, anyway,' she murmured.

'So…you *do* want one eventually?' This was interesting.

'Well, yes,' she said with a toss of her head. 'Eventually. But now is not convenient.'

'Why not?'

'I want to travel for a while. Concentrate on my career. Be free of family for a bit. Family commitments are messy. They confuse things.'

'So…you're streamlining.' Pete looked around at the mass of food, remembering the easy way she dealt with Nico and with Sam, with everyone who crossed her path, and stifled a grin.

Serena's eyes narrowed. 'Something amusing you?'

'If I had to hazard a guess I'd say you *liked* life a little messy and complicated.'

'Maybe in the past,' she said. 'Maybe for another few *weeks*. But in a month's time life is going to be sleek, career-focussed, and ever so slightly narcissistic.'

'Hence our rules for this relationship.'

'Exactly. I knew you'd understand. More coffee?'

Pete kept his expression deadpan as she breezed her

way through the breakfast ritual. Toast, animated discussion of a story in the newspaper, a grocery list for Nico… He ate his cereal, watched her put a load of Nico's work clothes in the washing machine, and wondered afresh at humankind's capacity for self-delusion. The fresh-brewed-coffee goddess didn't have a narcissistic bone in her body. Oh, she might have looked the part, but beneath all that blatant sensuality lay an innate regard for the welfare of others that he doubted she'd ever shake.

No matter what kind of plans she'd made for the future.

His watch told him it was time to fly. His stomach told him there was no reason to linger over breakfast any longer. Sighing, Pete stood and took his breakfast bowl and coffee-cup over to the sink.

'You're right. You do need a bigger window here,' he said as she came to stand beside him.

'I knew you'd see it my way.' Serena smiled and leaned back against the counter, her hands either side of her as he stepped in closer, effectively trapping her between himself and the counter. Her smile widened.

'Maybe instead of dinner next time, we could do something your honorary protectors don't object to quite so much. We could go sightseeing.' He brushed her lips with his. 'Swimming.' Another kiss, just as fleeting. 'Something.'

'When will you be back this way?' she murmured, leaning towards him and lifting her mouth towards his for a kiss rich with promise and in no way fleeting. His mind had fogged and he was a whisper away from taking things further when finally she drew away.

'Soon.'

Just over one week later, Serena sat at the desk in her grandparents' tiny sitting room that doubled as an office and waded through her latest batch of job applications. She'd commandeered one of Nico's fishing crew to run the Vespa hire business for the afternoon so she could get this latest lot done and on their way. Trouble was, she was doing more daydreaming than working and her pile of completed job applications didn't seem to be getting any bigger. Time was wasting. Flying.

Wrong word. Serena scowled and tried very hard not to think of other things that might be flying, a particular *person* who might be flying for example, although he certainly hadn't been flying *her* way of late.

He'd *said* he'd be back soon. One week did not qualify as *soon*.

When it came to life on the island, one week bore a startling resemblance to eternity.

'Nico said I'd find you here,' said a deep voice from the doorway and Serena caught her breath at the sudden rapid pounding of her heart. She turned slowly, her brain wrestling her wayward body for control of her next actions. Her body was all for launching itself into his arms and getting frantic fast. Her brain wanted something a little more demure and nonchalant. Something composed.

She settled for leaning back in her chair and swirling round to face him, chin high in silent defiance of the effect he had on her body. She could control this. She could. 'You're late,' she said darkly, drinking him in, those startling good looks, the smile in his eyes and the way his lips tilted at her words.

'How goes the job hunting?' he said.

'It's probably best if you don't ask about the job hunting right now.'

'That bad, huh?'

'Let's just say there's not a lot here that makes my heart go pitter patter.' Apart from the obvious.

'So can I persuade you to take some time out to go for a Vespa ride or a swim?'

With a smile like that he could doubtless persuade her to do *anything*. Not that he needed to know that.

'I can probably spare a few hours. Distractions aren't all that common around here. When they arrive we tend to make time for them. It's just the island way.' There. Nonchalant had been well and truly nailed. Who said she had no control around this man? She looked at the carryall at his feet. 'Are you staying overnight?'

'Two hours.'

'That's *it*?' Her nonchalance headed south, never mind the nails.

'I have a pick-up in Santorini later this afternoon. Business is booming.'

Bummer. She stacked her papers into a pile and shut down her laptop. Two hours was still two hours. No point wasting it. 'I hope you have a towel in your bag. And swimmers.'

'Happens I do,' he said.

Hers were in her room. 'I'll meet you in the courtyard in three minutes. Help yourself to some food from the kitchen on the way.'

Three minutes later she stood by the fastest Vespa on the island—which wasn't saying much—with Superman beside her munching an apple as she contemplated their next step. 'What would you rather do first? Swim or sightsee? There's a good swimming cove nearby. Some pretty little churches up in the hills. Do you like churches?'

'They have their uses. But I'd rather swim first and repent later,' he said with a decidedly unangelic smile.

'I like your thinking.' Such a good catholic. She looked at the Vespa, looked back at Pete. 'Who's driving?'

His lips twitched as his gaze met hers. 'Now there's a question.'

'I'm the one who knows where we're going,' she said reasonably.

'True,' he said with a sigh, shoving his hands in his pockets and staring dejectedly at the bike for good measure. 'There's no arguing with that.'

Serena rolled her eyes at the pitiful image of male self sacrifice before her. 'Or we could go past the shed and get another Vespa. Then we could both be in the driver's seat.'

'A marginally better idea,' he said. 'If you discount the wasted fuel.'

They stared at the bike some more.

'You could always give me directions,' he said.

'Can you *take* directions?' she asked sceptically.

'Why wouldn't I?'

'There doesn't need to be a *reason*.' Clearly he'd never been in the car with her parents.

'Not only can I take directions, I also have an equal

opportunity plan of attack for this particular dilemma,' he said. 'Me being a thoroughly modern man and all.'

Serena snorted. 'Let's hear it, then.' He wasn't quite as traditional in his thinking as her father and brothers when it came to womenfolk and their place in the world. But he wasn't that far off it.

'I'll drive us to the beach, you can drive us to the church,' he said with a grin. 'We'll start tossing coins after that.'

'My hero.' Wonders would never cease.

He handed her his carry bag and straddled the bike. She slung the bag over her shoulder, next to her own, and slipped onto the bike, her hands at his waist and her sundress riding high on her thighs so that when she settled into place behind him her bare thighs nudged the lightweight cotton material of his trousers and the tightly muscled buttocks beneath. Maybe there was something to be said for not being in the driver's seat after all. This was very nice. Very…liberating. Perfect, in fact.

But wait. She'd wrinkled his shirt and she couldn't have that. So she let her hands roam all over that wide muscled back; a wrinkle smoothed here, a wrinkle made there. Really, there was just no getting rid of them.

'Serena—' His voice was husky, more than a little strained.

'Hmm?'

'What *are* you doing?'

'Ironing.'

'Well, can you do it later?' he muttered. 'I'm trying to concentrate here.'

'Oh.' She slid her hands beneath his shirt and set them to his waist, set her feet to the footpegs, her knees tucking in behind his and bringing her thighs into even closer contact with the back of his. 'Sorry. Ready when you are.'

'Serena—' He sounded long suffering, his voice a deep delicious rumble that started in his chest and carried all the way to the tips of her fingers as well as her ears. There was just no *end* to the sensory delights to be found on the back of this bike. 'The directions—'

'Oh. Right.' Serena grinned as he started the bike. 'Turn left and drive. The road follows the coastline. I'll tell you when we're there.'

'That's it?' he said. 'Those are the directions?'

'They're good, aren't they?' she said and settled back to enjoy the ride.

Serena took him to a secluded cove with white sand, clear blue water and a swimming cave she knew damn well he'd want to explore. Sure enough his eyes lit up when he saw it and he wasted no time stripping down to his board shorts. He wore clothes well, no denying it. But he wore next to no clothes better. He was all lean and sculpted muscle, not an ounce of fat on him. Sheer perfection, but for a thin, wicked-looking scar that started high on his back and headed up and over his left shoulder.

She stepped closer and traced its path with gentle fingers. 'What's this?'

'A reminder,' he said gruffly. 'And you're underdressed.'

She took care of that, stripping down to her bikini before rummaging through her shoulder bag for some sunscreen. She smoothed it over her shoulders and down her arms, noting with some satisfaction that she'd managed to divert his attention from the cave. She slid her hand behind her hair and lifted it forward, over her shoulder, and handed him the sunscreen before presenting her all but bare back to him. 'Do you mind?' she murmured. She wanted his hands on her. She wanted her hands on him. She'd been dreaming of it.

Pete stood back and surveyed the vision splendid in front of him with the appreciative eye of a true connoisseur. So many curves, all of them lethal. And they were his for the coating. Pete tried to remember when life had last been this good…

Nope. Nothing.

Life had *never* been this good.

'Nice day for a swim,' said a voice beside him, and he turned his head to find an elderly Greek woman standing beside him wearing a scary black one-piece swim suit. Sturdy body. Thighs. And a white bathing cap covered in plastic yellow flowers. 'Marianne Papadopoulos,' she said briskly. 'I run the local bakery. We haven't met.'

Serena tilted her head, one hand still holding the bulk of her hair. 'Hello Mrs Papadopoulos.' Serena sounded amused. Resigned. 'This is Pete Bennett. He's filling in for Tomas. But you probably already know that.'

'Of course,' said Marianne, deftly removing the sunscreen from Pete's grasp and squirting a generous amount into her palm before sending the bottle of sunscreen over Serena's shoulder and tapping her none too gently with it.

'Thanks.' Serena's voice was dry, very dry, as she reached up to take it back.

'You can't be too careful about sun damage these days,' said Marianne, rubbing her hands together before slapping them down onto Serena's back and moving them about with vigour. White streaks began to form; a criss-cross of streaks on a canvas of glorious golden skin. Picasso would have been impressed. Pete wasn't so much impressed as resigned. They really did need to get off this island and onto another one.

Tahiti sounded nice.

'Will you be staying overnight?' asked Marianne.

'No, ma'am,' he told her politely. 'I'm only here for a couple of hours.'

'Just enough time for a swim and maybe a trip up into the hills before we head back to Sathi,' said Serena, turning round and squaring up to Marianne Papadopoulos with admirable aplomb.

But Marianne was undeterred. 'I noticed you only brought one bike,' she said.

'Pete's very fuel-conscious,' countered Serena. 'For a pilot.'

'You should take two bikes next time. Your grandfather would not mind.' She looked meaningfully towards him and Pete stifled the urge to reach for his clothes and start pulling them on. 'Your grandfather would prefer it.'

'I might just…swim,' he said, seeking escape, finding a likely avenue in the crystal-clear water of the cove.

'Good idea,' said Marianne. 'Swim. Cool off. I'll come too. It's not good to swim alone.' And she headed majestically towards the water.

'Another one of your grandfather's pinochle partners?' he muttered.

'Uh-huh.'

'Frightening.'

'You have no idea.'

'Maybe I'll just swim on over to the cave and *you* can swim with Marianne.' Sharks he could handle. White bathing caps with plastic yellow flowers were *way* beyond his sphere of experience.

'Leave me alone with her and you're a dead man,' she muttered.

Pete contemplated his options. There was really nothing for it but to take Serena with him. He grabbed her hand and raced towards the water, Serena giggling helplessly as they sped past their latest chaperon, kicking up spray as feet met water, before finally getting far enough into the water to plunge beneath it.

He surfaced a fair way out, with Serena right beside him, and turned back towards Marianne, who clearly preferred a more leisurely entry into the water. 'We're just heading over to the cave. We'll be right back.'

Marianne's hands went to her hips. Pete grinned and set off for the cave at a fast crawl with Serena matching him all the way, agile as a seal and just as sleek.

'I'm ruined,' she said with a reckless smile.

'But you haven't done anything,' he argued. Nor had he. Yet.

'You're right.' She gave Marianne a wave. 'Maybe I'm only partially ruined. If we stay within her sight and you stay, oh…' she gestured about a body length's distance with her hands '…about this far away from me, we might even manage discreet.'

Oh, yeah. Discreet. Vaguely platonic. He'd forgotten about that. 'Do we *need* to manage discreet?' he queried. 'Is it really essential?'

'This is Sathi,' she said. 'It's a necessity.'

So he played by the rules and they dived for shells in the shallows and stayed within sight of Marianne and finally swum back to her and floated about and made small talk about the various sights to be seen on the island. By the time they left the water and had dried off an hour had passed and there was no time left for sight-seeing anyway.

'I'd better be heading back.' He slung his towel in his carryall, watched with a sigh as Serena slung a dress over all those glorious curves and twisted her hair back into a pony-tail.

'You can drive,' she said, picking up her carry bag and heading across the sand towards the bike.

'Are you sure?' he said, deftly catching her bag and slinging it over his own shoulder. He didn't much like riding shotgun but he'd said he'd do it. Fair was fair.

'Very sure. Go ahead.' A tiny smile played about her lips. 'I insist.'

Three days later, Serena sat on the little beach at the water's edge, paintbrush in hand as she touched up the name on her grandfather's prize fishing boat. Not changed it, mind. The name of a fishing boat *never* changed once it had been bestowed, but touch-ups were allowed, and the free flowing black scrawl was sorely in need of it. The boat was called *Plenty*, and Serena was trying very hard to convince herself that that was exactly what she had.

Nico had decided that she needed another break from the Vespas and had organised one of his fishing crew to cover for her for the day, so one thing she had was plenty of time. He'd convinced her to come down to the beach beside the fishing-boat docks and repaint the name on the boat while he rolled out the nets and set to repairing holes. Sam had found them not long after they'd beached the boat, Chloe had found them not long after that, but instead of ordering Sam home she'd sat down and started repairing the holes in the net too, with a deftness that spoke of previous experience. Technically, thought Serena, she had plenty of company.

In just under two weeks her stint on the island would be up and she'd be free to do whatever she wanted.

Plenty to think about there.

It was a crying shame that the only thing she *had* been thinking about lately was a laughing, complicated man with the smile of a rogue, the soul of an eagle, and a heart that seemed to beat in time with her own.

'Fool,' she muttered.

'There she goes again,' said Sam, looking up from his inspection of the net and shooting Nico one of those man-to-man looks. 'Talking to herself.'

'Let it be a lesson to you, Sam,' murmured Nico. 'Wear a hat.'

'How do you know I'm not talking to you?' she said to Nico, reloading her brush with paint before spearing him with a dark glare. 'It's possible. Extremely possible.'

Nico rolled his eyes at Sam. Sam grinned back. 'I saw that,' she said darkly.

'She's been twitchy for days,' continued Nico with a sigh. 'Moody. Some might even say pining. One might even hazard a guess as to what she's been pining *for*.'

'Oh, good. A man with a death wish,' she said with a toss of her head. 'And I am *not* pining for anything. I'm just…contemplating the universe.'

And then a helicopter appeared on the horizon where sea met sky, heading towards them low and fast.

'Look! It's Pete,' said Sam, and Nico sniggered.

The chopper drew closer. Close enough for Serena to see Pete and two passengers. Sam leapt to his feet and waved. Chloe waved too. Even Nico looked up and grinned.

Serena gritted her teeth and turned her attention back to the Greek word for *Plenty*.

'Can I go see if he's staying over?' asked Sam as the chopper headed for the landing pad behind the hotel. 'He might want to come and mend nets too.'

'*If* he's staying,' she muttered. 'Sometimes he doesn't.' Sometimes he just dropped by to torture her.

'If he is staying he'll probably be after a room at the hotel,' Nico told Chloe.

'You banished him?' said Chloe.

'You *banished* him?' demanded Serena.

'Had to,' he said. 'By order of Marianne and Theo. They fear for your virtue.'

'Quite right,' said Chloe. 'A girl can't be too careful. Not on this island. You have no idea how people gossip.'

'We went *swimming*,' said Serena. 'That's *all* we did.'

'That's not what I heard,' said Chloe dryly. 'Marianne had to save you from total ravishment at the cove. She got there just in time. One second later and he'd have had his hands all over you. That's her story and she's sticking to it.'

'It's a good story,' said Serena with a wistful sigh. 'I even vaguely recognise some parts of it.' She turned to Nico and eyed him narrowly. 'Exactly *when* did you banish him?'

'The day you went swimming,' he said amiably. 'I phoned him and explained the situation and he offered to bunk down at the hotel straight away. Said he had his reputation to think about. And yours. Mentioned the word discreet a few times. Mentioned something about a whale shark and a yellow-flowered bathing cap.' Nico shuddered. 'I didn't want to know.'

Serena sniggered.

'So he's staying at the hotel?' Sam asked Nico, his eyes bright.

Nico nodded. 'Most probably.'

Sam took off across the beach with an unguarded enthusiasm Serena envied, only to halt abruptly some ten metres away. Serena watched as he turned back, not towards her or Nico this time, but towards Chloe. It was the first time he'd paid her the slightest attention all morning. 'What room can we give him?' he asked her. 'The big one? Number seventeen?'

'Provided no one's in it,' she said, looking up at him from her spot on the sand, her hands full of fishing net as she considered his question. 'Otherwise he can have number two. That's another one we sometimes use for upgrades. Tell Reception to put it through at the discount rate.'

Sam left at a run and Chloe watched him go, her face alight with happiness. 'Did you hear that?' she said in wonder. 'Sam said *we*. As in him and me. He didn't even think about it. He just said it.'

'You give the pilot your best room?' demanded Nico. 'At a discount rate? For what?'

'I like him,' she said, pleasure easing to puzzlement.

Nico glared at her.

Serena glared at her too.

'Well, I do,' she said defensively. 'He's nice to Sam. He talks up the hotel to his passengers…'

'Yeah, but what else do you know about him?' muttered Nico.

Chloe's eyes took on a decidedly teasing gleam. 'He's handsome, polite—?

'Almost penniless, not Greek, a lapsed Catholic…' added Serena, although the penniless bit was probably a stretch. Not if he co-owned an air-charter business. 'And, oh, yeah, he's running from something. Don't forget to factor that in.'

'How romantic.' Chloe slid her a sideways glance. 'What do you think he's running from? A tragedy? A world full of injustice? A woman?'

'A life of crime?' muttered Nico. 'Come on, Chloe.

He's not a saint. He flies tourists around the sky, for heaven's sake.'

'And before that, he used to fly air-sea rescue helicopters,' said Serena.

Nico stared at her in silence. So did Chloe.

'All right,' her cousin said finally. 'So he hasn't always been a penniless drifter. That's quite a job. Some women might even think it sounds romantic—although they'd be *wrong*.' He glared at Chloe. 'But can he fish?'

CHAPTER FIVE

PETE was five steps from the front door of Chloe's hotel, his duffel slung over his shoulder and his mind on a dark-eyed goddess he'd promised to court discreetly, when Sam hightailed it past him to hold the door open for him before making a beeline for the reception desk. The passengers Pete had flown to the island were staying with family, he had no need to help anyone else check in, no one else's belongings but his own to carry, no one to answer to until mid-morning the following day. Nothing to do but suit himself.

As far as Pete was concerned, suiting himself involved checking in, grabbing something to eat at some stage, and finding Serena.

Furious whispering ensued as he headed towards the desk. Maybe they were booked out? Maybe that was what all the fuss was about? Because, without question, they were fussing about something. Sam beamed. The receptionist blushed.

'Checking in, sir?' she said. 'Do you have a booking?'

'Not yet. I'm after a room for the night. If you have one.'

'Certainly, sir. One person?'

Pete nodded.

'You'll be in room seventeen.'

He handed over his credit card and she processed his payment and handed him a key. 'Enjoy your stay.'

'You want me to carry your bag?' asked Sam.

'Why? You working here now too?'

'Nope.' Sam paused as if to consider the notion, his eyes brightening. 'Not yet. But I could. Do you think she'd pay me?'

'Who? Your Aunt Chloe? Maybe.' He studied the boy. 'You need money?'

'Doesn't everyone?'

'What for?'

'Stuff.'

'What kind of stuff?'

The boy shrugged. 'Just stuff.'

Pete opened the door to room seventeen and looked around. 'Nice room,' he said.

Sam's smile broadened.

Pete dumped his duffel on the end of the bed and deliberately turned to survey the minibar. 'Do you drink, Sam?'

Sam's mouth set into a thin stubborn line. 'No.'

'Smoke?'

'No.'

'Shoot?'

'I *said* no!'

'Good for you,' he said mildly. 'Then why are you so determined to start work and earn money?'

Sam didn't answer him, just stood silently in the doorway with a stubborn set to his jaw that Pete was more than familiar with having grown up in a household full of siblings who were anything but malleable. He held Sam's gaze and waited, not stern, not demanding, just waiting. Borrowing the technique from Jake—hell, it always seemed to work for *him*.

'What if I need to buy food, or shoes?' said Sam abruptly. 'What if I need to buy medicine for—' The boy stopped, looking as stricken as Pete suddenly felt. 'What if I get sick?' he said in a small, thin voice.

'Your family will take care of that kind of stuff for you, Sam,' he said gruffly.

'And if they don't?'

'They will. Your aunt Chloe will.'

There was a world of mistrust in Sam's eyes. 'You don't know that.'

'You're right, I don't.' He'd lost his mother, just like Sam. But he'd never been alone. He'd always had his brothers to rely on. Even when their father had fallen apart, he'd always had his siblings. Sam had had no one and Pete couldn't begin to imagine what the boy had gone through—was still going through if his dogged determination to work and to earn his own way was any indication. 'But I'll bet you fifty euros that if you get sick your aunt will get you the medicine, or the doctors, or the hospital care you need.' He fished his wallet from his pocket, withdrew a fifty euro-note and tossed it down on the bed. He withdrew another note. 'I'll bet you another fifty she'll never let you go hungry.'

Sam stared at him with those dark, haunted eyes. Wanting to believe, thought Pete. Desperately wanting it to be so, when experience had only ever taught him otherwise. 'I don't have a hundred euros to bet with,' Sam said at last.

'You don't need it. If your aunt lets you down the money's yours. If she doesn't, you give it back. That's the deal,' he said, but still the boy hesitated. 'Take it or leave it.' Pete turned away, started to unpack his duffel. When he turned back Sam was standing by the bed and the money was gone.

'Deal,' said Sam awkwardly.

Pete nodded. Maybe with some money in his pocket the kid would feel slightly more secure. He hoped so.

'Everyone's down at the beach fixing nets,' Sam said next. 'You could come down too.'

'I have a few things to do here first.' He was trying to be discreet. Trying very hard not to go looking for Serena the minute he set foot on the island. Although… Maybe seeing her now was *better* than seeing her later. Maybe being seen with her openly, in the company of others, was the epitome of discreet in Sathi. Who knew?

Sam studied him curiously. 'Serena's down there.'

'So I saw.'

'She keeps talking to herself. Nico reckons she's pining for something.'

'Does he now?'

'Yeah. Serena reckons Nico's got a death wish.'

'Maybe I will come down,' he said, stifling a grin. After all, Sam *had* come looking for him. Nico and Serena and Chloe had to be thinking it was okay for him to join them otherwise they wouldn't have let Sam come looking for him in the first place. Right?

Besides, denial wasn't exactly one of his strong suites.

What Pete Bennett wanted, he usually got.

Fast.

Serena had decided to be cool, calm, and in control if the flying one decided to join them down on the beach. Cool was a shoe in given that she was wearing short white shorts, a pink and lime bikini top, and currently stood knee deep in water. Calm and in control were proving a little more problematic given that her heart was hammering and her brain had chosen to replay the beach kiss scene in *From Here To Eternity* and suggest it as a viable greeting option.

'*Not!*' she muttered vehemently and glared at Nico when he laughed.

Maybe if she'd had a little more forewarning she might have been able to manage calm and in control. Honestly, couldn't he have called ahead to let her know he'd be flying in?

Didn't the man know how to use a *phone*?

On the other hand, maybe he wasn't even stopping, just dropping passengers and flying on. That was possible too.

Not that she cared if he stayed or if he left. No. He was a distraction, nothing more, and distractions could always be replaced by other distractions.

Trying to paint signage while scanning the waterfront walkway every few seconds, for example, was very distracting.

She botched the curve of the middle letter about the same time she spotted Pete and Sam heading towards the beach from the direction of the village. Not the most direct route from the hotel by any stretch of the imagination, but the reason for their detour could probably be explained by the newspaper Pete carried in one hand, and the woven blue and white shopping bag he carried in the other. The reason for her botched paint job probably had something to do with the way he filled out a white crew-necked T-shirt and an old pair of cargo trousers cut off at the knee.

'There they are,' said Chloe.

'Mmm.' She was trying for an indifferent-sounding 'mmm,' but figured from Chloe's smirk that it had emerged as a whimper. Hopefully Chloe would think she was staring at the shopping bag.

Pete took his own sweet time making his way down to the boat. He stopped to kick off his shoes when he reached the sand. Stopped again to share a few words with a couple of elderly tourists.

When he stopped with Sam to poke at a mound of seaweed and watch a tiny soldier crab scuttle back into its hole in the sand she could have screamed.

He knew *exactly* what he was doing to her. Making her wait. And want. And want some more.

Damn but he was good at this game.

'Serena,' said Pete with a nod, when he and Sam finally reached her. He leaned into the boat and set the shopping bag and the papers inside it before sending her a lazy, non-committal smile, but it wasn't enough. She wanted more. Exactly how much more currently being a subject of much internal debate between her body and her brain.

'Hey, flyboy.' She was *not* changing her plans for him.

'Apple and honey cake?' he said affably.

She was going to become a successful international photojournalist! She didn't *want* to be a suburban house-wife. 'No,' she snapped, before reconsidering the question actually on the table. 'Yes.' She jammed the paintbrush back into its pot. 'Thank you.'

'You're welcome.' He eyed her warily. 'Something wrong?'

'It's this island,' she muttered.

'She needs to get off it,' said Nico, zeroing in on that woven shopping bag like a seagull after a crust. Chloe wasn't far behind him. Not that she blamed them. Marianne Papadopoulos might have been the biggest gossip on the island, but her pastries could make grizzled Greek fisherman get down on their knees and beg. The woven shopping bag Pete had carried down to the boat was one of the ones she saved for special treats and Nico knew it. 'What's in the bag?'

'Apple and honey cake,' she said. 'And it's for *me*.'

'Actually, I bought it for all of us,' said Pete. 'I *would* have bought something just for you but I'm being discreet.'

'Makes sense to me,' said Nico, delving into the bag. 'Look, she even sliced it for us. Who's the big bit for?'

'Sam,' said Pete. 'As directed by Mrs Papadopoulos herself.'

'She likes you, Sam,' said Chloe, eyeing the slice. 'That's a *big* bit of cake.'

Sam looked at the cake, looked at Chloe. 'You can have it if you like,' he offered awkwardly. 'I'm not that hungry.'

Chloe stared at him in startled silence, Nico smiled, and Pete turned away but not before Serena caught the hefty dose of concern in his eyes. Serena didn't know what was going on. But it felt big.

'Thank you, Sam, but I couldn't. I'd never hear the end of it,' said Chloe, trying to make light of his unexpected gesture and not quite managing it. Her eyes were too bright. Her voice wobbled too much. 'It's yours.' She reached into the box and selected a smaller piece. 'Save it for later if you don't feel like eating it now.'

Later, by Sam's reckoning, turned out to be approximately two seconds later. He took the cake and, head down, went back to examining the nets for holes. Loading themselves up in similar fashion, Nico and Pete did the same.

'I should have taken it, shouldn't I?' whispered Chloe anxiously, her gaze still on Sam. 'He offered, and I turned it down. I did it all wrong.'

'No.' Serena laid a hand on the other woman's arm. 'It's okay, you did fine. It was sweet of Sam to offer, and right of you to turn it down.' Her thoughts turned to Nico and to what she as a good and helpful cousin might do to support his cause. 'Of course, if you wanted to capitalise on the whole food sharing business you'd go over there and very casually offer to help Sam cook up the sea bass he caught this morning, and even more casually suggest that Nico come over later and help you eat it.'

Chloe blushed furiously, her eyes wide and panicked as she turned back to Serena. 'But, Serena, I couldn't! That would put Nico in a terrible position. It'd be almost like a *date* or something.'

'What if it was? Would that be so bad?' Serena shook

her head. 'Get to know my cousin, Chloe. You might be surprised.'

'I don't *want* to be surprised! Nico will leave here soon. They always leave.' She shrugged and looked back towards the village. 'Whereas me…I couldn't leave here even if I wanted to. My parents are old. Someone has to run the hotel. That someone is me. I have to make good, especially now I have Sam.'

'You know from my point of view Nico's leaving here is somewhat negotiable,' said Serena, after a moment. 'He could make this place his home, given the right incentive. Look at him showing Sam how to roll the nets. He *likes* fishing. He likes being a part of this community. He likes *you.*'

Chloe stayed silent, but her gaze skittered back to Nico and Sam. She was scared of opening herself up to hurt, Serena got that. But surely she could see that in this case the prize was well worth the risk? 'So if you like *him*, maybe you need to think about giving the man a reason to stay.'

Serena ate apple and honey cake while Chloe headed up the beach towards the nets and Pete headed back down the beach towards her. They stopped midway to chat, while Serena brushed the crumbs from her hands and wet sand from her legs and tried to remember how she was supposed to be acting around this man. Cool, calm and collected, that was it.

Definitely a stretch.

But he made it easy for her as he made small talk about the island and his charter customers, settling back against the boat and leafing through the newspapers he'd brought with him. *The Times* was one of them; *The Australian* was the other one.

'I saw a job in here for you earlier,' he said as he reached into the cake box for another slice of cake. Serena eyed it wistfully. If she had any more of that cake she'd be up for some serious exercise afterwards. Tempting…but no. 'They're looking for a political foreign correspondent. It's based in Jerusalem though.'

'I could do Jerusalem.'

'Can you do Hebrew?'

'Do I need to?'

'Beats me.' He pulled out the jobs section and passed it to her. 'Keep it.'

She waded the few feet to the shore and set her paint pot down, pushing it into the wet sand to stop it from spilling before settling down beside it and opening up the paper. Nothing like a world of possibilities to distract her from a vision sublime of man and cake, both of which she wanted far more than common sense allowed.

'There's one in here for you too,' she said after a few minutes of silent browsing. 'Feel like flying climate-control scientists around Greenland?'

'No.'

'Why not?'

'Because I'd freeze. Here's another one.' He'd been leafing through *The Australian*. 'They're looking for a Wilderness Society photographer. This one's based in Tasmania.'

'You think I have environmentalist tendencies?'

'Serena, you're trying to send me to *Greenland*.'

Good point. 'Tasmania might be a little too close to home,' she told him. 'I'm thinking further afield.' Pete glanced at her and shook his head. Serena lifted her chin. She knew that look. Usually it preceded a lecture about setting goals that were realistic, not to mention closer to home. 'What? You think I'm wrong to want my freedom?'

'I think you should be choosing your future career based on the work you'll be doing and whether it'll satisfy you, not on how far away it is from your family.'

Another good point.

'You'll miss them, you know.' He wasn't looking at her. He was looking at Sam, thinking of Sam, unless she missed her guess. 'You don't know how lucky you are to have a family who cares for you. People you can rely on because they love you.'

'He's talked to you, hasn't he?'

Pete looked at her but said nothing.

'Sam. He's talked to you. About his mother.'

'No.'

'About Chloe, then? And not fitting in here.'

'No.' And at her look of disbelief, 'What?'

Honestly, men! They had no idea how to communicate. 'Well, what *did* you talk about?'

'Money, and stuff.'

Serena sighed heavily and shook her head. '*Talk* to him next time. See if you can get him to open up to you about his feelings.'

Pete snorted. 'Not gonna happen, Serena.'

'Why not?'

'Because it won't.' He glanced back at Sam. 'He's doing okay.'

Serena followed his gaze to where Sam and Nico sat mending the net. She narrowed her eyes, automatically framing the shot as she waded out into the water and reached for the camera she'd tucked inside the boat. The pattern of the nets contrasted with the ripples in the sand beneath and presented an interesting juxtaposition, but it was the focus both Nico and Sam brought to their task that interested her. The wordless connection between them as boy looked to man for guidance. Nico's nod of approval; the pleasure and quiet pride Sam took in it… She captured every heart wrenching nuance, and knew instinctively that somewhere amongst the photos she'd just taken she'd find the final image for her postcard series and that it could well be the best photo she'd ever taken.

'Here, grab a brush and let's get this done,' she said to Pete, picking up the paint pot and handing it to him. 'We're getting out of here.'

'We are?' He took the paint pot with the brush sticking out of it and wandered around to the bow of the boat to survey her work. 'I only just got here.'

'How do you feel about spending the afternoon working on postcard photos?'

'Do I have a choice?'

'No. You'll like it. Trust me.'

'Does it involve a darkroom?' He smiled a pirate's smile. 'I love darkrooms.'

'Excellent,' she said. 'Start painting.'

'I thought you said you had a darkroom,' Pete muttered half an hour later. They were up at her grandparents' little whitewashed cottage, in a neat little sitting room that looked as if it doubled as an office. A widescreen laptop computer sat on a table in the corner beside a printer. Half a dozen folders stood beside that. There was nothing wrong with it, as far as rooms went. But it wasn't quite what he'd had in mind. 'You know, dark, private, *discreet.*'

'I said no such thing,' Serena said cheerfully and pulled down the window shades, switched on the computer, and sat down in front of it. 'You just *assumed* we'd need a darkroom. Welcome to the age of digital photography. The days of broom-cupboard darkrooms and messy, smelly chemicals are long gone.'

Pity. He'd had a fantasy or two about broom cupboards, beautiful women, and the mingling thereof. Guess it'd have to stay a fantasy. 'These photos had better be good,' he said with a sigh as he pulled up a chair and settled down beside her to watch her work.

The photos were better than good. They were outstanding. From a wide-angle shot of Mrs Papadopoulos watering the geraniums out the front of her shop to the latest shot of Nico and Sam, they showed the power of the human spirit, with all its strengths and frailties.

'Forget the words, Serena,' he told her bluntly. 'Your pictures don't need them.'

'There's another one you might like to see,' she said after a moment. 'It's not for the postcard series, though.'

'What's it for, then?'

'You.' She trawled through her files until she found it. Pete sat back in his chair, aiming for distance, and wished to hell she hadn't. It was one of the photos she'd taken of him when they were up on the plateau. She'd captured his solitude, he thought, trying to be objective. And she'd captured a pain he'd thought he'd buried deep.

'If I were a curious woman,' she said with a tiny half-smile, 'I'd ask you what you were thinking about.'

'If I were the sharing kind I'd tell you.' He glanced away; he didn't want to look at his picture any longer. One day he'd stop running. He'd turn and face his past and all that went with it. Maybe one day he'd even make his peace with it. But not today.

'No great tragedy?'

'No,' he muttered as she stood and pushed the laptop aside before leaning her backside on the table, curling her hands around the edge of the table, and regarding him solemnly. 'You're very persistent, aren't you?'

'So I'm told.'

Not that it seemed to bother her.

'*Something* put that look in your eyes,' she said at last.

'Experience.' He spanned her waist with his hands and slid her towards him in one effortless movement. She was still perched on the edge of the table. He still sat in the chair. Their bodies weren't quite touching, not yet, but if…when…he pulled her into his lap she'd be straddling him. 'Nothing more, nothing less.' His hands were rough, her stomach was silky smooth and just begging to be kissed. He slid her closer and set to tracing lazy circles across her stomach with his fingertips, before leaning back in the chair and glancing up at her face to gauge her reaction.

If the flush of colour riding high on her cheeks and the lip she'd caught between her teeth were any indication, she liked his hands on her just fine. So did he. 'I went into air-sea rescue battle-trained and ready for anything,' he said wryly. 'Or so I thought.'

'Cocky,' she murmured as her hands settled on his shoulders. 'Invincible.'

'Yeah. And when you save a soul that would have been lost that's exactly how you feel.' He didn't know why he was telling her this. He should stop now, leave it be, but her eyes didn't judge him and the hands on his shoulders were warm and somehow soothing, and he offered up more. 'It's the best feeling in the world. The best *job* in the world. But when you don't…' He paused and drew in a long breath before continuing. 'They take a little piece of you with them.'

Somewhere along the way he'd stopped tracing circles on her skin. He started up again, slower this time, lower, until they scraped the waistband of her shorts. 'Got that way there wasn't much of me left. Got that way that the person I needed to save most was me. I couldn't do it any more, Serena. So I left.' He leaned back in the chair, concentrating on the present, on those little white shorts, and the woman in his arms. *Hell* of a way to woo her, he thought with a twist of his lips. *Hell* of a way to make her think well of him.

'You think you've failed them, don't you? The people who trained you? The people you couldn't save?'

'I did fail them.'

'Don't be so hard on yourself,' she said quietly. 'No one gets to save them all. Not even Superman.'

'You believe in Superman?' He tried for a smile and

almost managed it. Enough soul-baring. Enough. He couldn't do this.

'I believe in you.'

'Oh, hell, Serena.' He drew her closer, wrapping his arms around her waist and resting his forehead on her stomach. 'Don't.'

'Too late.' She wound her hands in his hair and drew his head back before sliding from the table and into his lap as if she belonged there, as if she'd always belonged there. His body responded instantly, even if his brain was still playing catch-up. He felt himself harden beneath her slight weight, inhaled the essence of her and the scent of the sea, and shuddered.

'You know what you need?' she said lightly. 'Right this very moment?'

'A change of subject,' he said curtly. No question.

'Comfort.' She shifted, and those little white shorts she wore shifted right along with her, all softness and warmth against his growing hardness. 'Lucky for you I give good comfort.'

But it wasn't comfort that he wanted from her. 'What about distraction?' Because she was way off on the comfort angle. Way off. 'Do you provide that too?'

'Mmm hmm.' She set her lips to his earlobe and her hands slid from his shoulders to his waist and then lower, stopping only to create havoc beneath the hem of his T-shirt. 'I think you'll find me an excellent distraction.'

And then her lips were on his, teasing, giving, and the world and his struggle to find a place in it disappeared beneath the weight of his desire for her. His passion built and so did his urge to bury himself deep inside her; to take and take still more, until the only name he remembered was hers.

He tried to damp it down. He called on every last bit of skill he possessed to keep things simple and easy between them, just as she wanted. Just as he'd always been able to do with a woman before. With words and with every drop of control he'd ever been taught, he tried to delay the inevitable. 'I'm still waiting on that blue dress,' he told her raggedly as he twined a strand of her hair, that midnight-dark hair, around his finger, around his fist.

'Maybe if you'd told me you were *coming*,' she countered as she slid his T-shirt heavenward.

He helped her take it off, dropping it on the floor beside him before reaching for her again, finding the curve of her throat with his lips as he surged against her, heat to heat, centre to hard, unyielding centre. 'Trust me, Serena. I guarantee you'll know when I'm coming.'

He watched her face as he traced a path from the hollow of her throat, down over the curve of her breasts with his fingers, smiling his satisfaction when her eyes grew slumberous and her nipples peaked for him beneath the slippery material of her bikini top. 'Distract me some more,' he murmured, leaning back in the chair, still trying for lightness between them, and her smile turned impish.

'You're a beautiful man, Pete Bennett,' she said as she leaned back and lifted her hand to the bikini tie at the back of her neck, sliding it forward so that it lay on the curve of her breast. 'Sculpted enough to make a woman sigh her gratitude. Hard enough to make her tremble in anticipation.' She toyed with the end of that string, back and forth, back and forth, until his fingers twined with hers and he took over that particular duty.

He tugged on it gently, not enough to loosen it altogether, not yet, and she shuddered and bit back a whimper, playing the game he'd asked of her, playing it to perfection. He *could* have tugged that string loose completely and covered the tightly peaked nubs of her nipples with his mouth but he wasn't quite ready to give up his sanity just yet.

He smoothed his hands over those golden shoulders, played his hands along her arms until his hands found hers and he set them palm to palm, smiling a little at the contrast. She had beautiful hands, smooth, feminine. A direct contrast to his much larger, rougher hands, and one that pleased him. She studied their joined hands with a tilt to her lips that told her the contrast amused her too, and then she threaded her fingers through his and made his hands prisoners.

'You'd rather I didn't touch you?' he queried as her lips traced a path from his jaw to the edge of his mouth. 'That's a pity.'

'I *do* want you to touch me,' she assured him. 'Soon. Very soon. But it's *very* distracting and that's not good, because right now *I'm* the one who's doing the distracting.'

'You're right. You're absolutely right,' he murmured, closing his fingers over hers. 'But you'll let me know when you're done with that?'

'Of course.' Her lips met his for a kiss so deeply drugging that he groaned beneath the onslaught.

'Are you done yet?' he demanded raggedly.

'No.' Another kiss followed, more potent than the first. 'How about now?'

'Patience, flyboy.' But she punctuated her remark by loosening her grasp on his hands as she arched back, her body undulating ever so gently against his—like the lapping of the tide—and any patience he might have laid claim to disappeared beneath a wave of exquisite pleasure.

His hands left hers to slide over her skin, over her belly button, over the thin cotton material of those little white shorts, as he played his knuckles across the area just above where his body met hers. Back and forth, back and forth, while his body demanded more.

'I think I'm done distracting you,' she whispered.

'You're sure?'

She looked down to where his hand played over those little white shorts and shuddered hard against him, all feminine strength and outrageous heat. 'Positive.'

'Because I'd hate to rush you.'

Her eyes met his, dark and needy, as her fingers found her bikini string and tugged it loose. 'You're not.'

Her breasts were full and round, dusky tipped and perfect, and fitted his hands as if they belonged there. She gasped, her hands coming up to cover his as she pushed against him. She *knew* this game, revelled in it, and, heaven help them both, so did he.

With a ragged groan he wrapped his arms around her waist and her behind, carried her to the day-bed in the corner of the room, and tumbled her onto it.

Her clothes went, his did, and his need turned fierce.

He feasted on her lips, her skin, her breasts, and every-where he touched she responded with a sigh, a shudder, a whimper. Tight, so tightly responsive, her eyes as black as her hair, hot colour riding high on her cheeks as he eased inside her, back and forth, each time filling her that little bit more.

She reared up beneath him, her hands clutching at his arms and her lips finding his for a kiss that seared clear through to his soul. He'd had lovers before, bedmates he'd enjoyed, but no one had *ever* played him like this. Not like this.

'More,' she whispered as he rolled onto his back, bringing her with him, still buried inside her.

'You'll get it.' He found her centre with his thumb, and she found a rhythm guaranteed to send him soaring, arching back, her breath coming in short sharp gasps. And then he was flying apart, touching the sky, taking her with him as he emptied himself into her and gave her what she asked for.

She laughed in the aftermath. Deliciously satisfied laughter that slid through Pete's body as he lay on his back, his hands still holding her in place while his muscles twitched and rippled in response to the demands he'd placed on them. So much for finesse. For taking his *time*. Taking the edge off his hunger for her.

The only thing he'd well and truly taken, he thought ruefully, was Serena. 'You okay?' he asked huskily. Not a question he normally had to ask. Usually, he made sure of it somewhere along the way. Usually, he didn't lose his *mind*.

'I swear I just went to heaven,' she said, and laughed some more. 'Am I dead?'

'You have a pulse.' He could feel it, intimately. 'You're not dead.' Judging by his returning hardness, neither was he. Yet.

'What's that?' she asked as he stirred inside her.

'A minor miracle.' Possibly an opportunity to show her he could be a civilised lover when he put his mind to it. Of course, first he had to *find* his mind. 'You did say you wanted more.'

Her lips curved as she trailed lazy fingers up his arms towards his shoulders. 'So I did.'

'I aim to please,' he told her, rolling her over onto her back before setting his lips to the corner of her mouth, the underside of her jaw, the curve of her neck, and then lower still, to a part of her he'd rushed over earlier.

'Oh, you do.' He closed his lips over her nipple and bit down gently, and she gasped and arched beneath him as her hands threaded though his hair, urgent and demanding. 'You really do.'

CHAPTER SIX

PETE BENNETT was both passionate and extremely thorough when he put his mind to it, decided Serena some half an hour later as she stood beneath a lukewarm shower. Pete had showered with her briefly, kissing her senseless beneath the spray, and, cursing her roundly as his body responded to hers again, had made himself scarce.

She watched him through the gap between the shower curtain and the cubicle as he dried off and pulled on his shorts and then his shirt. Such a tough, hard body. Such pleasure to be found from exploring it. He had another scar, in addition to the one on his shoulder. This one was nasty—a couple of centimetres wide running across his lower back. She couldn't be sure but it looked like a burn of some kind, maybe a rope burn, and she wondered what the hell had been on the other end of that rope to carve a gash that deep. He was a warrior, this man, never mind the façade. Beneath his reckless, charming ways lay the heart of a fighter.

Right this minute her warrior was a very sated man, she'd stake her life on it. His body had been to heaven and back. She knew this because he'd taken her with him. His brain, on the other hand, didn't seem to have made the trip at all.

She stepped out of the shower and met his gaze in the mirror, hers questioning, his bleak.

'Light-hearted,' he said grimly.

'Yes.'

'And brief.'

'Yes.'

'Civilised.' His eyes were anything but.

'You forgot exclusive,' she told him.

'I didn't forget.' He turned around to scowl down at her, a thoroughly disgruntled dark angel, all the way from the spikes of his midnight black hair right down to his toes. 'This is a disaster,' he said as he pulled her closer. 'You're a disaster.' And with a kiss so unguardedly needy she trembled beneath the force of it, he turned on his heel and left the bathroom.

Pete sagged against the bathroom door the minute he closed it, willing himself not to go back in there, willing his feet to take him down the corridor and out of the cottage and to keep on walking, straight down the hill to the village. He needed to think. To regain the balance he'd lost in the arms of a siren.

One step. He dragged his extremely happy body away from the door and took it. And stopped abruptly as he looked up, straight at Nico—at Nico and Sam— who stood beside him.

'We're gonna cook the sea bass I caught this morning,' said Sam. 'Me and Nico. And we're inviting

Chloe and Serena and you to come and help us eat it for dinner.'

'Oh.' He struggled for words, for some sense of normality, a modicum of discretion, while Sam looked up at him hopefully and Nico eyed the bathroom door. 'How big is this fish?'

'Big,' said Sam with a grin. 'Where's Serena?'

Not a question he wanted to answer. 'She's been downloading the photos she took of you and Nico this morning onto her computer. I think she wants to use one of them for her postcard series. Go take a look. In the sitting room.'

Sam didn't need any more urging. Nico, on the other hand, stayed right where he was.

The bathroom door swung open the tiniest bit, an inch or so, nothing more, and Pete stepped in front of it, blocking Nico's view as he reached for the handle and pulled the door firmly closed.

Nico stared at him, studying his wet hair with a narrowed gaze. Pete stared back with not a lot to say. He tried putting himself in Nico's place. Tried to pretend he'd just caught some poor schmuck coming out of his sister's bathroom, with every indication of his sister still being in there. What would *he* do?

Castration seemed like a reasonable option.

Hopefully Nico was of a more civilised bent.

'You want to explain why that bathroom door suddenly seems to want to swing open by itself?' asked Nico silkily.

'Not really.' But for the sake of discretion he gave it a shot. 'Could be the wind.'

'Wind?' said Nico flatly.

'Uplift. Downdraft. Air. Wind.'

Nico didn't look convinced.

'O-or it could be that the door's set on a slant and swings open by itself.'

'It doesn't.'

'Pity.' He was running out of plausible excuses. 'Maybe it's possessed.'

Nico's lips twitched. 'Nice try.' But he wasn't buying it. 'Serena's a grown woman,' he said after a lengthy pause. 'She makes her own choices. I try and respect that.'

Castration didn't seem to have entered Nico's mind. This was a good thing.

And then Nico's gaze swung from Pete to the bathroom door and his face hardened. 'Hurt her and I'll hunt you down.'

Or maybe it had. 'No one's going to get hurt,' he said curtly. 'Serena knows what she's doing, and so do I.'

'Do you?' Nico rapped on the door with enough force to make it vibrate. 'Dinner's at seven. Chloe and Sam are eating with us,' he said loudly and stalked off.

No sooner had Nico disappeared than Serena stalked out, as fully dressed as a person could get in skimpy white shorts and a pink and lime bikini top. She glared at him, thoroughly miffed about something, possibly his parting shot about her being a disaster, but it was too late to take it back now. Besides, he didn't want to. 'What?' he said. What *now*?

'You call that discreet?'

'Well…yeah. It could have been worse.'

'How?' she demanded. 'Nico *knows* I was in there;

that you were in there with me. How on earth could it get any worse?'

'Hell, Serena,' he said, darkly amused by her indignation. 'Five minutes earlier and he'd have found us naked on the day-bed.'

Chloe arrived shortly after that and added her voice to the dinner invitation. 'It started with me offering to cook for you all at my place,' she told them ruefully as she set a big basket on the kitchen bench and turned to look back out the kitchen door to where Sam and Nico were cleaning the barbecue. 'I'm still not sure how the invitation got turned around to having it here. I hope you don't mind. I brought the fixings for a salad with me and some bread and wine. Nico says he's cooking the fish.'

'I love it when he says that,' said Serena.

'So you don't mind?' Chloe turned towards her and Pete, her expression faintly apologetic. 'You weren't planning to go out to dinner? Just the two of you?'

'Well…we could?' said Pete. 'I hadn't thought much about dinner at all. Yet.' He caught her gaze, a question in his, and that small act of courtesy and uncertainty after all that had gone before was Serena's undoing.

'If we stay here I can guarantee us a glass of wine or beer with dinner,' she said lightly, opening the fridge and raiding it for both items and setting them on the counter. She had no idea how much their disastrously wonderful lovemaking had changed things. Absolutely no idea what he wanted from her. All she knew was that he was welcome at her table and that she didn't want him to leave. 'Matter of fact I can guarantee them now.'

'There is that,' he said, with the whisper of a smile.

'So you'll stay for dinner?' said Chloe hopefully. 'The more the merrier, I say.' She didn't want to dine alone with Sam and Nico was what she *meant*. 'There'll be plenty of food.'

There was that word again, thought Serena wryly. Plenty. She looked at Pete and that was exactly what she saw. 'Here.' She passed him the beer, got another bottle from the fridge and a lemonade for Sam and handed those to him as well. 'Go help Nico and Sam man the barbecue while Chloe and I get busy in the kitchen.'

'Does this feel light-hearted to you?' he muttered, shooting her an enigmatic glance as she held the kitchen screen door open to let him through. 'It doesn't feel light hearted to me. Feels kind of family-oriented.'

'I know.' She smiled wryly. 'But stay anyway.'

Having Pete stay on for dinner was a bigger mistake than she'd thought it would be, decided Serena an hour later as she sat at the garden table and watched him bond with Sam and Nico over slow-barbecued potatoes and soon-to-be-barbecued sea bass. She didn't want to notice the way Sam looked up to him, or how much Nico seemed to enjoy his company, never mind Nico's earlier words of warning outside the bathroom door. Pete Bennett charmed without thinking, without understanding what it would do to a woman fresh from his lovemaking to watch him interact so easily with the people she loved.

'If I were a betting woman—which I'm not,' said Chloe, coming up beside her and handing her one of the two glasses of champagne she held in her hands, and sipping delicately on the other, 'I'd say the universe you've been contemplating of late was standing right there by the barbecue. And what a universe it is,' she murmured with a wicked smile, and Serena felt her own lips curve in reluctant agreement.

'It's only a temporary universe,' she told Chloe. 'He'll be leaving soon. *I'll* be leaving soon.'

'Haven't we just had this conversation?' said Chloe dryly.

'No, that was a different conversation. You and Nico have a shot at something beautiful. Pete and I…well…he's going in one direction and I'm going in another. I don't *want* to change direction to accommodate him.'

'Perhaps he'll change direction to accommodate you.'

The thought slid through her, bright and beckoning, demanding closer examination.

'He's very good with Sam,' said Chloe. 'He cares for people.'

She'd noticed. And all of a sudden she was standing there wondering just what kind of father he would make, what kind of husband. And what it would take to capture his heart.

No.

Some other woman could glory in his passionate lovemaking and delight in the compassion beneath his strength. Not her.

Some other woman could heal a heart too heavy and too wounded to carry any more loss. *Not* her. She had dreams of her own to chase. Dreams that didn't involve him.

Serena tore her gaze away from Pete to stare out at the ocean with a growing sense of panic.

If only she could remember what they were.

It was almost ten p.m. when Chloe deemed it time for her and Sam to head back to the village. Dinner had been served and savoured and Sam was fading fast in the wake of his early morning. Pete stood as well, offering to walk back to the hotel with them, and the happy family picture the three of them made set Serena's eyes to narrowing. Never mind that it wasn't real, Serena didn't like it. Neither did Nico.

'Aren't you going to walk down with them?' she muttered to her cousin.

'Aren't you?' he countered darkly.

'No.'

Nico scowled. 'I'll join you,' he said to them abruptly.

Pete nodded, as if he'd expected no less, and started clearing plates and empty glasses from the table, carrying them into the kitchen while Nico helped Chloe and Sam gather their belongings ready for departure. Better, much better.

'What time are you heading out in the morning?' she asked him lightly as he set the dishes on the sink. No pressure. No clinging. Much.

'Around ten. My clients want to go to Santorini.'

Santorini. Plenty of night-life in Santorini. 'Staying overnight there, are you?'

'Yeah.' He leaned forward and kissed her cheek.

'What was that?'

'Discreet.'

Oh. She thought of him not being around tomorrow, or the day after that. Thought of the pleasure to be found in his kisses and decided to scrap discretion and go with need instead. She ached for his touch, for what it could bring, and she dumped her own armful of dishes into the sink, stepped in close and touched her lips to his, teasing at first, and then ravenously hungry as she dragged them deeper and deeper into uncharted waters.

'I'll call you,' he said raggedly when at last the kiss ended. 'I'll be back. Soon. As soon as I can.'

'I'll be here,' she said and felt her heart tremble. 'For the next couple of weeks.'

Pete called her mid-afternoon the following day.

'Where are you?' she wanted to know.

'Sitting in a café in Santorini, reading the paper.'

Lucky him. She was sitting beneath the beach umbrella beside the Vespa shed.

'How do you feel about working for a fashion photography house in New York?' he asked her.

'Unenthusiastic.' She leaned back in her chair. 'Although it does satisfy the requirement of being some distance from my family.'

'Just checking,' he said. 'Wedding photographer in Vegas?'

'Only if I'd be working for Elvis.'

'It's possible.' She could feel the smile in his voice, closed her eyes and let it warm her through. 'Okay, here's something you might be more interested in. It's a photography competition and it's global. They want you to capture and celebrate the essence of humanity.'

'I'm listening.'

'I'm glad. I'll bring you the details.'

'When?'

'Soon.'

Serena sighed. She knew what soon meant. It meant he had no idea when he'd be back. 'Enjoy Santorini. It's a pretty place.'

'You're prettier,' he said, and disconnected.

He phoned her again the following day. This time she was ready for him.

'What are you doing?' Pete asked her.

'The crossword in *The Sydney Morning Herald*.' She was sitting in her usual place beneath the beach umbrella by the old Vespa shed, but time was passing more quickly this morning. 'A British rock god needs a helicopter pilot to keep on retainer.'

'Just shoot me now,' he said.

'Just checking. There's also a need for a medivac helicopter pilot along the Northern Australian seaboard.'

Silence.

'I'm sensing some reluctant interest in that one,' she said with a grin. 'I'll keep the paper for you. Meanwhile I have a job interview in Athens tomorrow with a big daily newspaper. They're after a photojournalist who can cover politics one day and human-interest stories the next. It sounds promising.'

'How are you getting there?' he asked her.

'I thought I'd take the ferry.'

'I can get you there faster than a ferry,' he muttered. He could get her there faster than anybody on the planet, and she was pretty sure he knew it. 'Are you free tomorrow? I could hire your charter services.'

'You can have them for free. When's your interview?'

'Four in the afternoon.'

'I'll come for you at midday. We can go out for a meal afterwards. Spend the night in Athens. If you've a mind to.'

'I'd love to.' She already had a teenager from the village organised to take charge of the Vespas for a day. Why not for two days? She had good reason, and heaven help her she had a fierce need to spend some time alone with Pete without having to be discreet about it. 'I've missed you, flyboy.'

'I want you in my arms again,' he told her, with a rasp to his voice that set her skin to tingling. 'Preferably sitting on my lap.'

He wasn't the only one. 'Am I naked?'

'Very.'

'Are *you* naked?'

'I'm at the airport in Athens. If I was I'd be arrested.'

'So…I'll see you tomorrow, then?'

'I'll come for you,' he said.

She was counting on it.

CHAPTER SEVEN

THERE was a world of difference between life on a sleepy Greek island and the vibrant energy that came with being in the middle of a major city. People moved faster, talked louder, dressed smarter and for the most part looked a whole lot tenser. Six months ago Serena would have thrived on the bustle and the crowds. Now she found it slightly unnerving.

Or maybe it was just the thought of the up-coming job interview that unnerved her.

She and Pete were standing outside the newsgroup building. It was almost time to head inside. She'd gathered her hair up into an elegant chignon and had donned a charcoal-grey business suit for the occasion. She looked good. If her portfolio of work was any sharper it'd grow fangs and bite someone. The only thing missing was her enthusiasm for walking through those double glass doors.

'Time to go, Rena,' he said as she looked at the doors for the tenth time in half as many minutes.

'How do I look?' she asked him.

'Smart. Sophisticated. Like you belong here.'

'Really?' He was wearing cargo trousers, a collared shirt and a smile that scattered her wits. No charcoal-coloured business suit for him and he still managed to look more at home on these streets than she did. How did he do that? She fiddled nervously with the collar on her shirt, scrunching it up; Pete smoothed it out.

'Where's your confidence?' he said, tilting her chin up with his forefinger so that her gaze met his.

'Gone.'

'Happens that way sometimes.' He pressed his lips to her cheek, a man who knew not to mess with lipstick at a time like this. 'Time to remember who you are. What you are. And what you want.'

Oh, boy. It'd help if she *knew*. 'I could use a reminder.'

'You're talented, educated, smart, savvy, and determined.'

'You're right,' she said straightening. 'I am.'

'You want this job?'

'I do.'

He put his hands to her shoulders and turned her in the direction of the door. 'Go get it.'

Pete watched the traffic go by while he waited for Serena's interview to finish, wondering at her last-minute hesitation. He knew her best when she wore gypsy skirts and sleeveless cotton shirts, but it came as no surprise to him that she could look perfectly at home in a business suit. If she wanted this kind of life all she had to do was reach out and take it. He was that certain of her talent and her ability to succeed.

She didn't belong on the island; anyone with eyes could see that. Whether she belonged *here* was up to her.

It was a quarter to five before she reappeared. He figured it for a good sign. 'How'd it go?' he asked her when she stood in front of him.

'It was a panel interview,' she told him, chewing on her lower lip. 'There were five of them. It was hard to tell what they thought—either collectively or individually.' She lifted her chin a fraction. 'They said I'd hear from them in a few days. *I* thought it went well.'

'Hold that thought.' He slung his arm around her shoulders, she wrapped her arm around his waist and together they started walking. 'Where to now?' he asked her. 'Dinner? A drink? A show?'

'Yes,' she said with a vigorous nod for good measure. 'All of them.'

'Any particular order?'

'Surprise me.'

He did surprise her. He took her to the art gallery Medusa where a modern photographic exhibition was showing, and fed her creativity. After that he took her to dinner at a restaurant that boasted candlelit corners, Spanish cuisine, and a Lebanese entertainer with a repertoire ranging from 'Zorba the Greek' to 'Dancing Queen'. The meal fed her stomach, the entertainment fed her sense of humour. The place was a mish-mashing clash of cultures with a boisterous crowd, a little bit of whimsy, and plenty of romance thrown in for free and it matched her mood perfectly. *He* matched her mood perfectly, played to it, and at the end of the evening when the music slowed he took her into his arms and the night turned to magic.

'What next?' he murmured when the music drew to a close.

'You and me,' she said without hesitation. 'Alone.' Always it came back to this.

The colours from the streetlights played over his face, such a beautiful face, as he hailed them a taxi. He didn't touch her on the way back to the hotel, not until they reached the lift and then it was only to put his palm to the small of her back as they stepped inside. His hand dropped away after that. He looked like a man with a lot on his mind, not all of it welcome.

'Penny for them,' she said.

His smile belonged to a rogue but his eyes were somewhat more sombre. 'I was wondering what you'd do if you landed this job. Where you'd live… Who'd take charge of the Vespas…'

'I'd probably stay with my aunt and uncle—Nico's parents—for a while until I found a place of my own.'

'And the Vespas?'

'Currently have my second cousin Marina's name on them. It's her turn to come and contemplate the universe for a while.'

'You didn't mind it that much,' he said dryly.

'You're right,' she admitted. 'I didn't. I got to take some beautiful pictures and live in a beautiful part of the world. But I wouldn't want to do it on a permanent basis. It wouldn't satisfy me. It's not enough.'

'And the job you went for today will be enough?' he asked her as they reached the hotel room.

'Maybe,' she muttered as he ushered her inside. She didn't know. 'If I get it I guess I'll find out. But it's a step in the right direction, that's the main thing. I've already spent too much time doing things I never really wanted to do, mainly to keep my family happy.' She shrugged out of her jacket and slipped off her shoes with a sigh of relief. 'I got my photography and language qualifications by fitting them in around the work I've done in the family businesses. Had I wanted to be a restaurateur like my brother, or had a vision for growing and marketing the seafood arm of the business like my sister, everything would have worked out just fine, but unfortunately I don't want to do either of those things. I want to tell stories. Take photos that tell stories. *Use* those qualifications it took me so long to get.' Pete said nothing, just watched and listened. 'You probably think I'm selfish,' she said, turning away from him so she wouldn't see the confirmation in his eyes. She'd heard that particular opinion voiced often enough times over the years that she'd learned to anticipate it, brace for it. 'That I should appreciate all the opportunities my family have given me and take one of them.'

'If you're waiting for me to tell you to sacrifice your own needs for those of your family you'll be waiting a long time, Serena,' he said, punctuating his words with a tiny tilt of his lips. 'I lit out of home as soon as the Navy would have me, chasing the sky and a childhood dream. I left behind a grieving father, an older brother, two younger brothers, and a sister—all of whom needed me—because I had to go my own way. I know what it is to sacrifice family for freedom. I've done it.' His lips twisted. 'The worst part is when they tell you to go and that they'll be there when you need them and that they're proud of you for going after what you want.'

'I'd have been proud of you too,' she said quietly. 'If you'd been mine.' His words had comforted her, settled her conscience. He knew what it was to chase a dream. He understood.

'Tell your family what you've just told me,' he said. 'Hell, just show them your photos. If that doesn't convince them you're wasted on the fishing business, nothing will.'

'They've seen them. To them photography is just a hobby, something to do on the side. Photojournalism is marginally more acceptable.'

His eyes narrowed. 'So which one would *you* prefer to spend your time doing? Straight photography or photojournalism?'

Now there was a question. One she'd spent a great deal of time trying to answer. 'For the sheer joy of it? Probably the photography.'

'In that case why the *hell* did you just go for a photojournalist job?'

His voice was curt, his expression formidable. Maybe he didn't understand quite as much as she thought. 'It gets me good subject material for my camera. It's a time-honoured road for photographers to take. The job might not be perfect, but moments of it will be, and those are the ones I'll savour. 'She sent him a wry smile. 'Surely you of all people can understand that.'

He laughed abruptly; it seemed he could.

'But enough about work,' she said lightly. Here they were in a room with a blissfully large bed in it and an entire night at their disposal. Her thoughts turned wicked as she started pulling pins from her hair, the ones that had kept her businesslike chignon in place. 'I'd like a shower,' she said, shaking her hair free and dropping the pins on the bedside table before padding towards the minibar, her stockinged feet sinking into the deliciously plush carpet. 'A glass of wine…' She opened the fridge, selected a bottle and tossed it on the bed. 'Some chocolate…' She perused the selection on top of the counter, chose the Swiss variety, and tossed that on the bed too. 'I know it sounds trite but I'd like to slip into something a little more comfortable.' She had a white silk cami and matching panties in her luggage. She found them, threw them onto the bed as well. 'And then I'd like you.' She looked meaningfully at the pile on the bed and then back at Pete. Pete's lips twitched. 'Feel free to arrange yourself any way you like.'

'I'd like to oblige,' he said. 'Really. And I'm sure we can come to some sort of mutually agreeable arrangement at some point in time.' He was peeling off his shirt as he spoke, heading towards her, grabbing her by the hand. 'But *my* fantasy started the minute you mentioned the shower.'

He made her laugh as he turned on the shower taps and pulled them both under the spray, and her still fully dressed. Made her gasp as he peeled her out of her clothes and set about devouring her body.

Later, much later, he wrapped her in a towel, carried her to the bed and fed her wine and chocolate as she relived the high points of her interview for him, and the low. And then the wine and chocolate went on the counter and the towel went on the floor and he reached for her again.

This time, the sheer perfection and intensity of his lovemaking nearly made her cry.

Pete flew her home the following morning, his body utterly exhausted and his mind fogged with the pleasure only Serena's touch could bring. He'd had lovers before. Generous, accomplished lovers, but not one of them had ever brought to lovemaking what Serena gave to him.

A sensuality that held him breathless. A generosity that left him reeling.

And a hunger for more that he didn't know how to deal with.

She had to get back to Sathi. He had to get her there and then go take care of Tomas's business. That was his agenda for today. He couldn't think any further than that. He didn't want to think further than that. Because then he'd start thinking about what he'd begun to want from this woman and it had for ever written all over it.

And he sure as hell didn't want to think about *that*.

So he took her home and he played the game she'd asked of him and grinned at the scene that greeted him when they touched down in Sathi.

There was no shark, no ten-inch boning knives, no father and uncle with narrow-eyed glares and faces carved from rock. But Theo was sitting on the bench across from the helipad sharpening a box full of frighteningly large fish hooks and the majestically built Marianne Papadopoulos was there as well, pounding octopus on a flat weathered rock with a glint to her eye and a strength to her wrist that put him in mind of a cat o nine tails and some poor unsuspecting sod's back.

It was a warning, beautifully executed, almost effective. Serena slid him a long-suffering glance. Pete grinned at her.

'This is the part where you *leave*,' she told him dryly.

'I knew that,' he said.

'And never come back.'

'Now that's unlikely.' He gave Theo a nod, Marianne Papadopoulos a smile he reserved for the hardest of hearts and laughed when she narrowed her eyes and stopped pounding in favour of grinding that octopus hard against the rock with a swift, twisting motion. 'I'll be back,' he said and lightly bussed her lips. 'Count on it.'

CHAPTER EIGHT

WHEN it came to women and the wooing of them, Pete Bennett could justify just about any hare-brained scheme. Everything from a daily bombardment of flowers to remote location helicopter joyrides with a picnic basket and blanket packed for good measure. From tandem parachute jumps to Symphony Orchestra concerts by way of a spot of deep-sea marlin fishing in between. But he'd never, ever, done anything as stupid as jumping in a helicopter when he should have been working and setting off for a sleepy little Greek island that no one else seemed to want to go to on the off chance that once he got there the ache around his heart might ease.

He *should* have been checking into an Athens hotel, grabbing a bite to eat, and bedding down early in readiness for the five a.m. start his clients had requested the following day. He had a schedule to stick to, passengers to collect. He should have *phoned* Serena when he'd got the urge to talk to her. That was what a sane man would have done.

Instead he was flying the little Jet Ranger fast and low

en route to Sathi, his mind firmly fixed on getting to his destination before the sun disappeared over the horizon.

After that…well…after that he didn't much care what he did so long as Serena was a part of it.

Pete touched down just on dusk, secured the rotors, and locked the little helicopter down for the night before finally heading for Chloe's hotel. Discretion. He knew the need for it, tried to think of a way to act with it and still make contact with Serena. He pulled his phone out of his pocket and dialled. 'Where are you?' he said when she answered the phone.

'Halfway down the goat track,' she said somewhat breathlessly. 'And if that wasn't you in that damned helicopter I'm going to strangle you.'

Always nice to feel appreciated. Pete grinned. 'Have dinner with me.'

'Where?'

'Anywhere. I'm heading for Chloe's.'

'I'm two steps in front of you. Is it too late to be coy about dinner and tell you I'll check my calendar and get back to you?'

'How fast are you coming down that hill?'

'Fast.'

'It's too late. Besides, coy doesn't suit you. Neither does discreet. Feel free to jump me in the foyer.'

'Keep dreaming,' she said. 'I can be *very* discreet when I need to be. Get a room. Order something from room service. And wait.'

'If there's a God this fantasy will include you, a short black skirt, a frilly white apron, and not a lot else.'

'God is not a minimalist,' she told him blithely. 'God is bountiful.'

'Amen,' he muttered, and finished the call before he fell over his feet in his haste.

'No,' Chloe told Serena sternly. 'You can *not* be a room-service maid. Nico would kill you. Then he'd kill me for letting you.'

'Who's going to tell him?' countered Serena, not begging, not yet. 'Not me.'

'This is Sathi, Serena. Everyone will tell him because five minutes after I put you behind the room-service trolley everyone will know. Wait. Meet the man in public, where everyone can see what you're doing. And what you're not.'

'But I *told* him to call for room service.'

'And I'll tell him he can't have any. Anticipation is good for a man.'

'That's all well and good, Chloe, but it's killing *me*.'

'You need a distraction.'

'He *is* the distraction,' she said earnestly.

'Then you need another distraction. Here, read the paper. I circled a job in there for you.'

'What is it with people thrusting newspapers with job applications in them at me?' she grumbled, reluctantly taking the paper Chloe held out to her.

'Gee,' said Chloe. 'Could it have something to do with your burning ambition to leave this place and make your mark on the world?'

There was that.

'You can read it in my office,' said Chloe.

'Why can't I read it here at the reception desk?' While waiting for Superman to show up.

'Office,' said Chloe. 'I mean it. Think of your reputation. Everyone else will be. And if that doesn't stop you think of your family.'

'I'm going,' she muttered darkly. 'But I want you to know you ruined a perfectly good fantasy. My body hates you.'

'There's baklava in the office. Marianne Papadopoulos brings it in as payment for letting her use one of the tables in the taverna for her bridge game.'

'My body forgives you.'

'Your body is fickle.'

'No, it's just a sucker for perfection in all its many and varied forms.'

'Office,' said Chloe. 'And stay there 'til Pilot Pete has gone to his room.'

'I'd like a room,' Pete said to Chloe, his duffel at his feet and his anticipation running rampant.

'And it's nice to see you again too,' she said dryly, leaning against the counter and all but ignoring the credit card he held out to her. Finally, she took it and proceeded to open the bookings ledger with not nearly enough haste for his liking. 'Looking for someone?' she added as he scanned the foyer for a wanton goddess wielding a room-service cart.

'If I were being indiscreet I'd say Serena, but I'm not so I can't. And it's nice to see you too, Chloe. How's Sam?'

'Waiting impatiently for the weekend, so he can go out fishing with Nico again. What kind of room?'

'Any room.' He paused to reconsider. 'Something out of the way. Possibly soundproof, with a domed-glass roof and a view of the hinder stars.'

'Uh-huh.'

A slight sound came from the direction of Chloe's office, just behind the reception desk. The door was almost shut. Almost but not quite. 'Did you just whimper?'

'Excuse me?'

'Never mind.'

'You can have room seventeen, the same room you were in last time,' she said. 'Or I can offer you a smaller room, discreetly placed at the back of the hotel.'

'You *have* seen Serena.'

'Uh-huh.'

'So how do I order room service?'

'You don't. Nico heard you fly in, along with half the island's population. Theo's here, Marianne Papadopoulos is here. The room service you require is not available right now. Have a drink or a meal in the taverna instead. Nico might join you there. Then perhaps Serena and I later on.'

'So…no room service?' he said.

'None whatsoever.'

'No glass ceiling and view of the stars?'

'Lie on your side and look out the window.'

'Chloe, Chloe, Chloe,' he chided with a grin. 'Where's the romance in your soul?'

'Buried beneath the weight of my responsibilities, which for some reason have grown to include both you and Serena. You don't know this place or the people here. Even if you care nothing for your own reputation you need to think of Serena's and that of her family. Trust me on this.'

'I do trust you, Chloe. Which is why I'll take your advice,' he said with a sigh as he kissed his French-maid fantasies goodbye. 'Any more advice?'

'Yeah, it's Theo and Marianne's bridge night in there at table two and they're a player short. Resist. And Peter…'

He waited.

'I realise seduction comes as naturally to you as breathing, but try and travel a little slower than the speed of light this evening. Seduction's frowned upon around these parts. Try something else.'

'Like what?'

'You could always try courtship.'

Courtship. Right. 'As in bring a goat along for Serena's grandfather?'

'She's Greek, Peter, not a Bedouin.'

'So…no goat?'

'Just respect her.'

'You think I don't?'

'I think women come easily to you and always have. I think you don't know the difference between courtship and seduction.' She handed him the key. Not room seventeen. 'And I think it's time you learned.'

Pete made it to the out-of-the-way room at the back of the hotel, set his bag by the bed, took a fast shower and changed into fresh trousers and a collared white shirt. He could use a haircut, he decided after checking his appearance in the mirror. His hair was getting more and more like Tris's mop, less and less like Luke's regulation crew cut, but then, he didn't need a crew cut these days anyway. He wasn't Navy any more.

He didn't know what he was.

Hungry, he was that, and Chloe had suggested he head for the hotel taverna. Hopefully he'd find Nico there already. There were worse chaperons. Then again, Nico might not be there at all. He might end up sitting there alone, which wouldn't bode well for him when it came to resisting bridge invitations. He needed something to do while he waited, figured it might as well be the mail and paperwork he was supposed to have waded through a week ago.

Make that two weeks ago, he decided, eyeing the bulging black folder in his carryall with trepidation. He could run the flying component of Tomas's business with his eyes closed. The paperwork and scheduling side, however, was a nightmare.

Tomas was out of hospital and starting to get up and around. Maybe if Pete got the paperwork up to date Tomas could take the running of that part of the business *back*. Pete picked up the folder and headed for the door, no further incentive required. He'd do it while he waited.

Except that Nico was already at the taverna when he got there, looking tired and not altogether sociable. Still, he nodded when he saw him and Pete figured it for an invitation of sorts.

'So how'd they get you down here midway through a working week?' he said by way of greeting.

'Chloe rang and said she needed me,' said Nico

offering up a wry grin. 'A statement guaranteed to get me down here any time of night, or day, for that matter. Then she mentioned you, Serena, room service, Theo, and Marianne Papadopoulos in her next breath and that was the end of *that* fantasy.'

'I know the feeling,' said Pete with heartfelt sincerity. 'What do you know about courtship?'

'Do you see Chloe standing here, breathless to be in my company?'

'No.'

'Exactly,' said Nico darkly. 'I've been here almost six months and I still can't get her to notice me. I know *nothing* about courtship.'

'But I do see her and Sam over in the doorway waving at you.'

Nico turned sharply, his face splitting into a grin, and then he was heading towards them. Maybe he knew more about courting than he thought. The middle-aged barman behind the counter removed Nico's empty beer glass. 'I'll have one of those,' Pete told the barman.

'No beer for you,' said the barman. 'You can have coffee.'

'In that case, I'll have it at a table.' He took himself and his paperwork towards a corner table, only to be stopped by the majestically built Mrs Papadopoulos greeting him and wanting to know how Tomas was. 'He's out of hospital and up walking around,' said Pete. 'The cast comes off in another few weeks.'

'So you will leave us, once he mends, eh?' she countered.

'That's the plan.'

'Plans change,' said the lady. 'Isn't that right, Theo?'

Theo scowled.

'Tell me, Peter,' she continued, thoroughly undaunted by Theo's surly demeanour. 'Do you play bridge?'

'Never did get the hang of it, Mrs Papadopoulos. Besides, I have some paperwork to see to.'

'And friends to greet,' she said, eyeing the doorway behind him. 'The taverna's a busy place, this evening.'

He turned, following her gaze, and there stood Serena, looking exceedingly demure in an ankle length yellow sundress that, if he had to hazard a guess, he'd say belonged to Chloe. And then she smiled and he wouldn't have been able to describe what she was wearing. 'Excuse me.'

He made it to the door without falling over his feet, made it through small talk with Chloe and saying hello to Sam, who had homework and then bed to look forward to rather than socialising in the taverna, according to Chloe.

'I could stay here for a while,' said Sam. 'With Nico and Pete and Serena. I'm not tired.'

'Not on a school night,' said Chloe and Sam's frown turned mutinous.

'I'll do my homework in the morning.'

'You've had all afternoon to do it. You'll do it tonight.'

'Homework being part of the renegotiated deal involving Sam fishing with Nico on Saturday *and* Sunday mornings,' murmured Serena.

'Ah.'

'Do what your aunt says,' said Nico. 'She gives you

more freedom than I ever had as a boy, and receives more than her share of criticism because of it. Cut her a break, Sam, and honour your bargain.'

Sam's face grew even more thunderous, but he turned on his heel and stalked through the hotel without another word. Nico watched him go with a frown. 'A boy needs limits,' he said finally.

'When I want your help, Nicholas Comino,' said Chloe icily, 'I'll ask for it!' And then she too was gone and silence reigned supreme.

'I'm pretty sure she'll be back,' said Pete finally.

Serena nodded. 'Me too.'

Nico glared at them both. 'And if she doesn't come back?'

'Beer?' said Pete.

'Bridge?' said Serena, looking towards Theo and Mrs Papadopoulos.

'I like his suggestion better,' said Nico. '*You* play bridge.'

Serena shook her head emphatically. 'I like his suggestion better too. I was just giving you options.'

'The man doesn't need options, Serena. He needs hope,' said Pete. He thought of seduction and of court-ship and wondered where a compliment might fit in the grand scheme of things. 'And may I say you're looking divine this evening, as usual. Care to join me and my melancholy friend here for a drink?'

'You can have ten minutes,' she told him with a toss of her head. 'Then I'm off to check on Chloe. She's a little sensitive right now to the influence Nico has over Sam.'

'And you couldn't have mentioned this earlier?' demanded Nico, shooting her a dark glare.

Serena shot him a halfway apologetic glance. 'I thought you knew.'

'I'm curious,' said Pete, steering them both towards a table. 'Does Nico supporting Chloe's authority over Sam count as courtship or seduction?'

'Pardon?' said Serena.

'I'm saved,' he told Nico. 'She doesn't know either.'

'Huh?' said Nico.

'Never mind. Coffee?' he asked Serena. 'Have you eaten?'

'No, and no. But I'd rather have wine with my meal than coffee.'

'Good luck with that,' he murmured, and turned to browse the blackboard menu. 'What's good here?'

'The fish,' said Nico dryly. 'I caught it this morning. And *I'll* order the wine.'

They got their wine but held off on ordering meals in favour of waiting to see if Chloe returned.

'Bring any passengers in?' asked Nico.

'They're still in Athens. I'll go back for them in the morning. They're booked to go to Kos.' Pete relaxed back into his chair, more content than he'd been at any point during the last two days. 'Was my coming here tonight on the off chance of meeting up with Serena an act of courtship or seduction, do you think?'

Nico shook his head. 'Hell, I've got it pegged as an act of desperation.'

'I think it was sweet,' said Serena, favouring him with a smile. 'What's in the folder?'

'Mail and scheduling paperwork in case I ended up sitting here by myself. Chloe warned me about the bridge party. I figured I might need a prop.'

'Good move.' Serena flicked open the folder and began to browse. 'Aerial cattle mustering in the Northern Territory? Really?'

He'd forgotten about the job ads he'd shoved in there. 'It could be fun,' he said.

'Yeah, for about five minutes.'

'It's seasonal, Serena. Read on. Five minutes is as long as it takes.'

'I was thinking of it as a more permanent position.'

'No.'

'Oh.' She flicked over to the next page. Pete sighed. This one involved transporting men and supplies to and from oilrigs off the Western Australian coastline and this one *was* permanent. Doubtless he'd hear her opinion on it too.

'It's not exactly family-oriented, is it?' she said after a read through.

'It doesn't need to be,' he countered. 'Does it?'

'I'm just saying that it's something you might want to think about if you're looking at a long term position, that's all.'

'Interesting advice,' he said mildly. 'Coming from you.'

Nico snorted, Serena ignored them both, turning that paper over to stare down at the next one. A fax this time, marked urgent, and not strictly a job advertisement. 'What's this?'

'Private.'

She looked up, her startled gaze clashing with his.

'Sorry.' She shut the folder and pushed it back towards him. Yours, her actions said, but there was a question in her eyes and on her lips. Knowing Serena, it wouldn't be long before she voiced it.

'They want you back, don't they? They've asked you to go back and fly rescue helicopters for them again.'

He didn't reply. Didn't think he needed to. It was Nico who broke the silence. 'Your ten minutes is up, Serena. It's time to go find Chloe. Please,' he added.

'For you,' she told her cousin as she scraped back her chair and stood to leave. 'Because I love you and I know she'll come round. You'll see. And as for you…' Pete found himself on the receiving end of an apologetic smile. 'I'm sorry I pried. Even sorrier about the lack of room service. But I *am* glad you're here.'

Serena found Sam and Chloe in Chloe's tiny two-bedroom apartment nestled at the back of the hotel grounds. Sam looked up from his seat at the kitchen table but there was no smile for her as she greeted him. Instead he nodded curtly and turned his attention back to the schoolbooks surrounding him. Chloe stood at the kitchen bench chopping salad ingredients into a bowl. A steaming dish of moussaka sat cooling on the stove. Sam still looked mutinous. Chloe still looked upset. The silence pervading the room could have been heard over a full scale military tattoo it was that loud. 'So… you're eating over here?' she said lightly.

'Yes.'

'How about joining us for coffee a little later, then?'

'I can't, Serena.'

'You're angry with Nico.'

'I'm angry with everyone, including myself,' said Chloe tightly.

Wholesale anger. Not good. 'You need company. Anger loves company.'

'You mean misery.'

'Exactly. So we'll all come and eat over here with you and Sam, then, shall we?'

Chloe picked up a knife and began dicing carrots, dumping them into an already overflowing salad bowl. Clearly Chloe hadn't been paying a whole lot of attention to the amount of salad she actually needed when she'd been cutting it up. Serena looked from the salad to the oversized casserole dish full of fragrant moussaka. 'How many people were you planning on feeding tonight?'

Sam looked up briefly and caught her eye, a smile tugging at his lips before he ducked his head and went back to his homework.

'C'mon, Chloe,' she said quietly. 'Nico's beside himself. He thinks he's hurt you. Both of you.'

Chloe remained silent, so did Sam.

'He was only trying to help.'

More silence.

'You think walking a line between what you want and what Sam wants is easy? It damn near rips my cousin in two sometimes, Chloe. He doesn't deserve your anger.' Sam slid her another furtive glance from his spot at the table. 'And he certainly doesn't deserve yours,' she told him bluntly. 'Finished your homework yet?'

Sam nodded warily. 'Just now.'

'Perfect,' she said, turning back to Chloe. 'Sam's ready to eat. We're all ready to eat. And here you are with enough food to feed a dozen people. Invite us over. It'll make everyone feel better.'

'What do you think, Sam?' said Chloe faintly. 'Shall we invite them over here for dinner?'

Sam shrugged. 'It's your house. Your food.'

'Yours too,' said Chloe.

Sam looked away, all shut down.

Chloe looked down at the bench, but not before Serena caught the sheen of tears in her eyes. She reached up and tucked a strand of Chloe's straight dark hair back behind her ear with gentle fingers. Chloe looked up and shot her a miserable smile. 'Sorry,' she whispered.

'Don't be. Just send Sam to go get Nico and Pete. I'll stay here and help you set the table. Trust me. It'll be fun. It'll work.' She reached over to the little radio by the kitchen sink and switched it on. 'We'll make it work.'

Pete wasn't averse to having dinner at Chloe's place rather than the taverna. Judging by the swiftness with which Nico pushed back his chair and stood to leave, neither was he. 'What about the gossip?' Pete asked Nico, surreptitiously eyeing the formidably gossipy Marianne Papadopoulos and co. Gossip being the reason they'd all been meeting at the taverna in full view of everyone in the first place. 'Will having us to dinner be a problem for Chloe?'

'Do I look like I *care*?' said Nico.

Good point.

They had to pass the bridge party table on the way out. Pete nodded to them. Nico went one better. Nico stopped.

'I need some flowers,' he said to Marianne Papadopoulos.

She pursed her lips, her old eyes shrewd. 'Happens I have a garden full of them. I'm open to trading suggestions.'

'Two kilos of fish from tomorrow's catch,' said Nico, ignoring the amused glances of the other card players at the table. 'For a fistful of whatever I like from your garden.'

A glimmer of a smile played about those thin wrinkled lips. 'My scented pink roses are in flower,' she said with the air of someone bestowing something special. 'They're not just any old flower. You want some of those, you'll need to trade up.'

Nico eyed her narrowly. 'The *best* of tomorrow's catch for the best in your garden.'

Marianne's smile bloomed. 'Agreed.'

'I need them now,' he said.

'You can have them now. Mind you use the secateurs hanging on the tool shed door to cut them. I'll have no ragged stems in my garden.'

'Anyone care to concentrate on the *cards*?' asked Theo, his voice long-suffering.

'Ho! Listen to you!' said Marianne Papadopoulos. 'Was a time you asked for flowers from my garden in just the same way, old goat!'

'I gave them back to you, didn't I?'

Nico snorted. Theo glared. Pete edged away from the table, Sam was right behind him. The boy had a good eye for a fast brewing storm. Best not to get caught in the eye of it.

'I'll meet you up at Chloe's,' said Nico when they reached the hotel grounds. 'You two go on ahead.' He strode off down the laneway in the direction of the village. Sam looked after him, his expression wistful.

The boy had delivered Chloe's invitation with a wariness Pete had found painful to watch, and he wasn't nearly as invested in the kid as Nico. Nico had probably found it excruciating.

'Reckon I can find my own way to Chloe's apartment if you'd rather go with Nico,' he told the boy, offhand.

'He wouldn't want me around,' mumbled Sam.

Pete shrugged. 'I say he would. Matter of fact I think it'd mean a lot to him if you helped him pick those flowers for Chloe.'

Sam slanted him a gaze. 'You don't know that.'

'You're right, I don't. But that's what I think.'

Sam stared at him, his face a study of indecision as hope warred with fear. And then the boy was racing after Nico, falling into step beside him and shoving his hands in his pockets for good measure. Not a word passed between them but Nico slowed to accommodate the boy and the shadow of a smile flitted across the kid's face.

'Guess I was right,' he murmured, and, leaving them to the choosing of flowers and the careful cutting of stems, he turned on his heel and headed for Chloe's.

'Sam and Nico will be along soon,' he told Chloe when she opened the door to him. 'Thanks for the dinner invite.'

'What are they doing?' Chloe wanted to know.

'Just some business they had to take care of.'

'What *kind* of business?'

'Their business,' he said with a grin. 'Have a little faith, Chloe. Alternatively, have a glass of wine. You look like you could use one.' He handed her the half-full bottle the waiter had recorked for them at the taverna. 'From Nico. I'd have bought some too only no one lets me buy alcohol around here.'

Chloe smirked. 'So I've heard. The general consensus is that you're quite forward enough without it. Come through.' Stepping aside, she gestured for him to enter.

Serena was setting the table when he entered the kitchen and Pete felt something shift and fall gently into place at the sight of her performing that simple task. Mealtimes and the setting of the dinner table had been important to his family too, once upon a time. Before his mother had died. Before his father had fallen apart, leaving Jake, and him as next eldest, to step in and make sure that clothes got washed and people got fed. He'd been sixteen at the time, Jake had been eighteen, and they'd managed well enough. Managed just fine, considering…

But food had generally made it to a person's stomach directly from the fridge or by way of the kitchen counter. Food had rarely stopped by the dinner table *en route*. Not his choice. No one's choice really. That was just the way things had shaken down.

He'd grown used to eating meals on the run. To loading up a food tray in a Navy mess hall, or stopping for take-away the way home from work. Food was fuel, no need to celebrate the eating of it.

Maybe that was why the simple act of Serena laying knives and forks on the table cut at him so deeply, reminding him of his mother and of family the way it should be.

Maybe that was why he crossed over to the domestic goddess, set his palms to her face and touched his lips to hers for a kiss that spoke of tenderness, and thanks, and a moment in time he wanted to cherish.

Serena's eyes fluttered closed and the cutlery she'd been holding clattered to the table as Pete's lips met hers. There was passion in his kiss; there always was. A lick of heat and a dash of recklessness that called to her and made her tremble. But this time his passion was tempered with sweetness and a longing she'd never felt from him before. This wasn't a hello kiss. It wasn't seduction.

This kiss was all about coming home.

'What was that for?' she said shakily when he finally released her.

'Would you believe for setting the dinner table?'

'Are you serious?'

He sent her his charming, reckless smile. 'Maybe.'

She narrowed her eyes, mulled over his words and cursed him for being so much more than she wanted him to be. 'You love the idea of coming home to this every night, don't you? Coming home to family. You're not a carefree playboy at all. You're a fraud!'

'Only lately. Sorry I interrupted.' He picked up the cutlery and dumped it back in her hand. 'Feel free to continue. You looked like you were enjoying it and Lord knows I'll enjoy watching you.'

'Don't get any ideas,' she snapped. 'I'm a career woman.'

His smile deepened. 'I know that.'

'Guess you're not the only fraud around here,' Chloe murmured to him as she handed him a glass of wine. Serena opened her mouth to protest, Chloe raised a delicate eyebrow and shoved a glass of wine in her free hand too. 'Watch her deny it,' she said to Pete.

'Just because I don't mind setting a dinner table doesn't mean I want a life of domestic servitude,' she muttered loftily, taking a sip of her wine before putting it down and carrying on with the task of laying out the cutlery.

'Just because I like watching you set a dinner table doesn't mean you couldn't chase your chosen career.' He leaned forward, battle ready, a blue-eyed black-haired thief of hearts who could have charmed the moon down from the sky if he put his mind to it. 'I'm quite capable of setting a table myself. Or not at all if it comes to that.'

'You were right,' Chloe told her from the counter, her movements deft and practised as she swiftly uncorked another bottle of wine. 'Standing here listening to you two argue about a simple everyday task that takes about two minutes is *so* much better than standing here brooding.'

Sam and Nico arrived not long after that, the latter with pink roses, white daisies and green ferny things in hand. 'Pretty,' said Serena as Nico handed them over to a suddenly tongue-tied Chloe. 'A man who can find flowers like that at this time of night is both romantic and re-sourceful.'

'Although not entirely discreet,' murmured Pete.

'He doesn't need to be discreet,' countered Serena. 'His intentions are pure.'

'Not that pure,' said Nico.

'What about honourable?' said Pete.

'They're mostly honourable,' said Nico.

Chloe glared at them both. 'Do you *mind*? There's a *child* present.'

Sam rolled his eyes, Pete grinned his sympathy. 'I just figured Sam should probably know the difference between courtship and seduction too. You know…for future reference. At first I thought it had something to do with speed, seduction being the faster of the two methods of wooing a woman. Then I got to thinking it might have something to do with a man's intentions, but, no, man's intentions are a grey area. Who in their right mind would base it on that?'

'A woman might,' said Nico. 'They get some strange notions in their heads at times.'

'You're right,' said Pete.

'Aren't they sweet?' said Serena. 'All that brawn, so little brain… Puts me in mind of Winnie the Pooh. He was a bear of little brain too.'

'But cuddly,' said Pete. 'Generally happy with his lot.'

'Well, that rules you out, flyboy,' she murmured, handing him a plate of food. 'You can't even *find* your lot.'

She was right. But it still stung. 'I'll know it when I see it,' he said defensively.

'It's in your folder,' she said dryly. 'Three pages in.'

Pete unwound over the course of the dinner, everyone did, with the help of Chloe's excellent cooking and hospitality skills and Serena's knack for turning conversation into entertainment. Caring bubbled beneath the surface; bonds of friendship and of blood; ties of affection and of love.

The ache around his heart was gone.

They didn't make it a late evening, what with early starts for him and Nico the following morning and Sam looking increasingly sleepy.

'Walk me to the door,' he murmured to Serena as Nico made his farewells to Chloe and Sam.

'I'm sorry the evening didn't quite go to plan,' Serena said to him when they reached Chloe's front step. 'It probably wasn't what you had in mind. It certainly wasn't what I had in mind.'

'I'm not unhappy with the way it turned out,' he told her.

'The lack of mind-blowing sex doesn't bother you?'

'Is this a trick question?' Because he didn't have the faintest idea how to answer it.

'No, it's just a regular question.'

He still didn't know how to answer it. 'Hell, Serena.' He opted for the simple unvarnished truth. 'I just wanted to see you again.'

'Are you courting me, Pete Bennett?'

'Damned if I know.' He thought he might be. He thought he might just keep that bit of information to himself.

'When are you leaving in the morning?' she asked.

'Early.'

'When will you be back?'

'Soon. Alternatively, you could come up with another reason to get off this island. You could come with me in the morning.'

'You *do* miss the mind-blowing sex!'

Pete reached out to run a wayward strand of her hair through his fingers, noting with interest the way her eyes seemed to darken at his nearness and his touch. 'Maybe a little.' Maybe he wasn't the only one.

'The need is there, don't get me wrong,' she told him. 'But practically speaking it's just not possible to get away right now. I have Nico and Chloe to throw together…Vespa hire to arrange so I don't let my grandparents down. How about we aim to meet up in Athens in a few days' time?'

'We can do that,' he said. And with more bravado than sense, 'It doesn't bother you that I had to come and see you tonight?'

'Should it?' she whispered, her eyes dark and fey.

'I don't know,' he muttered. 'But it sure as hell bothers me.'

'Where's Nico?' Serena asked Chloe when she came back into the kitchen. 'And Sam?'

'Nico's gone to talk to Theo about fish-hooks for tomorrow,' said Chloe. 'I dare say he'll also find a way to casually mention that dinner's over, Pete's back in his hotel room, and that you and he are about to head back to the cottage. He'll be back in a few minutes. Sam's putting the rubbish out.'

Serena started stacking plates in the dishwasher while Chloe found containers for the remaining food.

'I was watching you with Pete Bennett tonight,' said Chloe, uncharacteristically hesitant. 'He's more than passing fond of you, Serena.'

Serena shook her head. 'He's playing a game, that's all. And he's very, very good at it.'

'Maybe he is,' murmured Chloe. 'Maybe that's exactly what he's doing. But for what it's worth I think you should start thinking about what you're going to do if he ever decides to stop.' Sam swung in through the back door and Chloe turned towards him. 'Thank you, Sam.'

Sam shrugged awkwardly.

'Had enough to eat?' Chloe said next.

He nodded.

'Then it's bedtime.' Chloe paused awkwardly. 'Would you like me to come up with you?'

'I'm not *six*,' he said scathingly, shooting her a dark glare before scooping up his schoolbooks and heading from the room.

'I thought things were improving,' said Serena into the silence Sam left in his wake.

'They are. This is one of our better days,' said Chloe with a strangled laugh. 'I don't know how to help him, Rena. He wants nothing from me. He's so defensive. So fiercely independent.'

'Maybe he's had to be,' she said gently. 'It can't have been easy looking after his mother.' Watching her die.

'I know.' Tears welled in Chloe's eyes. 'I hate the thought of it. There was no *need* for it. One phone call from my sister, one single phone call, and I'd have been there. She *knew* that, but no. She was too proud for that; too damn selfish. Even if she wanted nothing for herself why didn't she ask it for Sam, Serena? Why? What kind of mother makes an eleven-year-old bear the brunt of her illness alone?'

There was a slight shuffling noise in the doorway and Serena turned just in time to see Sam's retreating form. Her stomach clenched. The kitchen and dining area was a large one. The doorway stood a fair distance away. He probably hadn't heard them. And yet…

'He heard us.'

'No,' Serena muttered, desperately trying to believe it. 'He was too far away. And even if he did hear us, we didn't say anything wrong.'

'I criticised my sister.' Chloe's eyes were like bruises. 'I shouldn't have done that, even if I believed it. Not in front of Sam.'

'He didn't hear you.' Serena held Chloe's panicked gaze with her own. 'He couldn't have,' she said firmly. And prayed that it was so.

CHAPTER NINE

THERE was something to be said for sitting beneath a stripy blue beach umbrella next to a little tin shed half full of Vespas and dreaming about a man. It helped pass the time, decided Serena. It kept a brain agile and a body…aware. The breeze playing with her hair put her in mind of Pete's hands in it, the sun on her skin reminded her of the warmth of his body. She wanted to be back in his arms. Soon. That was a given. The trick lay in figuring out how to get there without disgracing her family in the process.

Nico delivered her lunch a little later than usual. He looked tired, subdued. As if he carried the weight of the world on his shoulders and then some. But he handed her the day's mail and her lunchbox, same as usual, and hunkered down in the chair beside her.

'Chloe was waiting down at the docks when the boats came in this morning,' he said finally.

That sounded promising. 'Moon kissed roses will do that to a girl.'

'Sam's not at school.'

That didn't sound promising at all.

'She thought he might have been waiting for the boats to come in. Waiting for me. He wasn't.'

'Oh.'

'Chloe told me what she'd said about his mother. She thinks Sam overheard her.' He ran a hand through his already untidy hair. 'Some of his clothes are gone. His wallet…Chloe thinks *he's* gone.'

'Gone where?'

Nico shrugged helplessly. 'I checked the ferry terminal, the ticket office. He didn't buy a ticket off the island, no one saw him getting onto a ferry. Chances are he's somewhere on the island. I thought I'd take a Vespa out and look around. He's probably just gone for a swim, or a walk. He does that sometimes. Skips out for a while. That's probably all that's happened.'

Serena nodded. 'Yeah. He'll be around.' She looked up at the hill, looked out over the sea. 'Where could he go?'

By mid-afternoon all the Vespas bar the one Nico had taken out were back in the shed. None of Serena's customers had seen Sam; *no one* had seen Sam, according to Chloe, and Serena had decided to shut up shop for the rest of the day.

Chloe was helping her.

When Nico rode up and told them his sea catamaran was missing, Chloe's face crumpled. Nico watched in silence, his own face a study in indecision before finally he reached out and drew Chloe into his arms.

'Not quite the way I imagined it,' he murmured softly to Chloe. 'Not quite the reason why.'

Chloe laughed through her tears, a choked, strangled sound, and her arms tightened around him.

'You think Sam's taken it out?' Serena asked him quietly.

'It's too big for him, Serena. If he tips it he'll never get the sail back up.' Nico looked out to sea. 'The wind's blowing North East. I'll take Theo's speedboat out. If Sam *has* taken the cat he won't have got far.' He rattled off Theo's radio frequency, Serena wrote it on her hand. She wrote it on Chloe's hand too, the one still wrapped around her cousin.

'I'm coming with you,' Chloe told Nico shakily.

'No.' He set her away and smoothed the hair from her face with gentle hands. 'You keep looking for him here. Keep asking around. Get Marianne Papadopoulos onto it.'

'I've already called her,' mumbled Chloe. 'I've called everyone on the island. There's no one left to call.'

Maybe not on *this* island. Serena pulled out her cell phone and started scrolling through her directory for a newly familiar number. Nico's gaze sought hers as she put the phone to her ear and he gave her the tiniest of nods. He already knew where her thoughts were headed. She was calling Pete.

'Where are you?' she said when he answered the phone.

'Kos,' he said cheerfully. 'Tell me you're about to walk through this restaurant door in a sky-blue sundress and make my day.'

'Sam's missing,' she said baldly.

Silence from Pete's end, silence from hers while she waited for him to comprehend the situation and change direction. He did it in a heartbeat, moving smoothly from lover to warrior and earning her undying admiration in the process. 'Have you reported it to the authorities?'

'Chloe's doing it now. He hasn't been gone all that long, only a few hours, but Chloe's worried about him. We all are.' She gave him the worst of it. 'Nico's super-cat is missing too.'

'Where's Nico?'

'On his way to the harbour. He's taking Theo's speedboat out to look around.'

'What's his radio frequency?'

She gave it to him, along with Nico's mobile number.

'Give him mine,' said Chloe anxiously, and she gave him that too.

'Pete—'

'Keep in contact with Nico,' he said. 'Try and contact some of the other boats you know are in the area. Ferries, fishing boats, charter boats. Concentrate on finding that cat.'

'How soon can you get here?' She wanted him here. *Needed* him here. They all did.

'Soon.'

Serena had never felt more at a loss for direction in her life. She and Chloe had taken a Vespa and scoured the nearby beaches for Sam but they'd seen no sign of him and after an hour of fruitless searching they'd decided to head for the village and for Marianne Papadopoulos's shop. The older woman had the best gossip network on the island, they reasoned. If anyone could get people mobilised and out looking for Sam, she could.

She did. With efficiency more suited to a general than a baker Marianne Papadopoulos assembled her ranks, appointed her colonels and set them loose. Theo would contact all the vessels in the area. Other key people would organise land search parties if Sam didn't show up soon. It was still early, she told Chloe gently. If Sam was on the island they'd find him. If he'd taken to the sea then Nico would find him. She didn't say what they were all thinking. That for a city boy like Sam, the sea was a dangerous place and that if something happened to him out there they might never find him.

It was a big sea.

Chloe was too tense to eat; Chloe existed on coffee. Serena bypassed the coffee in favour of cake. Each to their own.

It was Marianne Papadopoulos who first heard the helicopter coming in.

'You called Tomas's pilot?' she asked Serena bluntly. 'The one you've been stringing along these past few weeks?'

'Not stringing along,' she said defensively. 'Getting to know, and, yes, I called him.'

'Good girl,' said Marianne. 'Here he comes now.'

'Time to go,' Serena told Chloe, wresting the half full cup of coffee from Chloe's fingers and setting it on the counter. 'Pete's here.' And to the older woman, 'You have our numbers? You have Nico's?'

'You just get me your young man's radio contact details and I'll have them all,' said Marianne and handed her a cake box. 'For when you get hungry,' she said. 'For when you need hope.'

* * *

'Have you found him?' were Pete's first words as he stepped out of the helicopter.

Serena shook her head.

'I need to refuel,' were his second. 'We'll be in the air in five minutes. Get in.' He was all business, but he had a kiss for Chloe's forehead as he saw her seated in the rear of the cockpit and a smile for Serena as he pointed her to the seat beside him in the front. 'I'm glad you called,' he said.

'I'm glad you came.'

'Who's your ground-crew co-ordinator?'

'Marianne Papadopoulos. She wants your contact details.'

'She'll get them. I've already spoken to Nico. He's concentrating his search in the North Eastern corridor. We'll broaden ours.'

He radioed Mrs P, gave Serena a map and told her to grid it up. He got them airborne, explained the search pattern they'd use and told them how best to scour the sea below them without courting excess eyestrain and fatigue. He kept positive, kept Chloe calm, kept them looking. With cool deliberation Pete Bennett, air-sea rescue helicopter pilot, took charge.

Serena had never seen anything more beautiful in her entire life.

They searched for what felt like for ever, until the little helicopter needed to refuel. He sent them to the bathroom when they landed, made them drink and eat cake while he arranged with Theo to find spotlights, search-lights he could attach to the helicopter when they refuelled next. If they didn't find Sam soon, they'd be searching in the dark.

With just over two hours of daylight left he took them up again.

Serena shaded in more little boxes on the map on her knees and scoured the water below them for some sign of Nico's catamaran, some sign of Sam. But they didn't find either.

The wind blew stronger as the day wore on. Tiny whitecaps formed on top of the waves and the light started to fade, making searching for things like small boys alone in the water harder. Serena's eyes felt dry and gritty but she didn't stop looking. No one did.

It felt like hours later when Chloe spoke up. 'There,' she said, her voice thready with fatigue. 'There's something over there.' There being over to the west, straight into the sun. The *something* that Chloe was referring to being a white speck that Serena had to strain to see.

'I see it,' said Pete, and something in his voice made Serena sit up straighter and catch her breath as they changed course, dipping lower as they sped towards that speck of white. He was on the radio to Nico, relaying coordinates, almost before Serena could make out the shape of a sail in the water and a small figure clinging to an overturned catamaran hull.

'It's him. We found him!'

Pete smiled grimly. 'Yeah, but we still can't *get* to him.'

'He's not moving,' said Chloe, panic lacing her voice as she fumbled with her seat harness. 'He's hurt. His head's all bloody!'

Pete brought the chopper in for a closer look, balancing their need to know more with Sam's need to stay clinging to that hull. The noise should have roused the boy; the spray kicked up by the hovering helicopter should have done it... Not too close, not too close...

'His hand moved,' muttered Serena.

Not moved, thought Pete grimly. Slipped.

'He's letting go,' said Chloe, wrenching a life-jacket from beneath her seat and opening the door.

'What are you doing?' Pete swivelled round in his seat to glare at her.

'Chloe—' began Serena, unbuckling her own seat belt.

Chloe ignored them both, tugging the inflator tag on the lifejacket and hurling it out and down. Pete watched the life-jacket settle on the water a good fifty metres away from the target.

Chloe swore. Serena sought to calm her. 'Sam doesn't need it. He's got the hull. Nico'll get him.'

'Tell him to hurry,' said Chloe and disappeared out the door after the life jacket.

Pete felt the weight of the helicopter shift, adjusted for it, swinging high and wide and swearing long and loud as Chloe hit the water. 'Fifteen feet!' he raged. 'A swimmer jumps from fifteen feet, dammit!' Thirty feet and a body could break a leg. Fifty feet and people started dying. 'Where is she? Where the *hell* is she?' Had she gone in feet first? The clearance between the door and the rotor blades on this thing was tiny. Had she crossed her arms as she'd gone out the door or flung them above her head? Hell! Did she have any arms *left*?

'It's okay.'

He wrestled with the helicopter, got it back where he

wanted it, off to one side of where Chloe had gone in and far enough away from Sam so as not to disturb his hold on the hull. He looked back to find Serena hanging out the door, looking for Chloe, and his heart did stop. 'Get back in the cockpit,' he roared. 'So help me, Serena, if you follow her I'll kill you myself!' His words were drowned by the thumping of the rotor blades but she heard him, looked back at him, her hair flying about her face as she grinned at him.

'I'm not!' she roared back. 'She's okay. She's got the lifejacket!'

'She'd have had it to start with if she'd put it *on* before she *jumped*!' He longed for a Seahawk, and a crew. Sean running the winch and Merry in the water. A safety line and a basket, *some* damn way of getting Sam—and now Chloe—into the helicopter and headed for land, but a man made do with what he had and got on the radio and told Nico that there were two in the water now and to get a move on.

Nico's savage curses echoed his feelings perfectly. The other man didn't need to ask who else was in the water and Pete had no mind to tell him. The two most important people in the world to Nico were down there—he'd get there as fast as he could.

'It's all right,' muttered Serena, putting her hand to his shoulder as she climbed back through to the front and settled into the seat beside him. 'Chloe's a good swimmer. A good sailor. She'll right that cat and sail it if she has to. Where's Nico? How far away?'

'He'll be here,' he told her and edged the helicopter higher and wider so as not to impede Chloe's passage to the catamaran. She was almost there, was there, and he watched in grim satisfaction as she hauled herself up on the hull, straddled it and put the lifejacket on before edging towards Sam. Finally some sea craft and some sense.

'Look,' said Serena in a choked voice and he watched as Chloe inched towards the boy, talking to him, all the time talking to him, as tears coursed down her face. Sam's eyes fluttered open, and his hand moved towards her, just a fraction. And then Chloe was hauling him onto the hull, gathering him up in her arms and he was clinging to her as if he'd never let go. 'It's going to be all right. Chloe's got him. Look. She won't let go.'

Pete nodded curtly, not wanting to tell her that it was far from okay. They didn't know how bad Sam's head wound was—whether it was just a bump or if he'd done some real damage. He didn't want to remember the times when not letting go simply hadn't been enough to see a soul through. Not this time, he prayed to whatever God cared to listen. Please, not this time.

He manoeuvred the helicopter higher. There was nothing they could do but give Chloe and Sam smoother seas and less noise. Nothing to do but lift that bird higher so that Nico could see them; so that they could see him coming. He radioed Marianne and the authorities, arranged for the doctor to be waiting when Nico brought them in. There was nothing left to do.

He waited until Nico appeared on the horizon, skimming across the water in Theo's speedboat like a low-flying bullet. He kept the Jet Ranger hovering until Nico reached them. Watched as Sam's arms suddenly found strength and he clung to Chloe until finally, finally Nico persuaded him to let her go.

When Nico had settled Chloe in the speedboat with Sam back in her arms and blankets around them both, Pete turned to Serena and smiled his relief.

Mindless of the throttle and the controls she covered his face, his cheek, his hair with kisses and promptly burst into tears.

When her tears and her kisses had diminished somewhat he ordered her back in her seat and finally headed for land.

The locals who had joined in the land search for Sam had already gathered in Chloe's taverna by the time Pete and Serena stepped into the hotel a good half an hour after landing. He accepted the beer Theo and Marianne Papadopoulos set in front of him with a grin, accepted the congratulations they offered, but he wasn't quite ready to celebrate, not yet.

Yes, they'd found Sam, but until a doctor or a medic had checked the boy over and cleared him of serious injury Pete's celebrations would remain subdued.

Serena sat beside him at the bar, her eyes weary but her smile impish. They'd bought her a beer too. 'We found him,' she said as she touched her glass to his. 'Cheer up, flyboy. Smile a little.'

He smiled a little. 'It's a start.'

'It's a good start,' she corrected him.

More locals filtered into the room, drawn by shared concern and hope of good news. This was a tight-knit community and for tonight at any rate they were willing to let him be part of it. They knew who he was. They congratulated him on his efforts and on finding Sam.

'It's my job,' he started to say more than once, only that was a lie and he refused to be caught in it. He wasn't an air-sea rescue pilot any more. He didn't know what he was.

He wanted to know how serious the boy's injuries were. He wanted the relief that would come with knowing that Sam was going to be fine. *Then* he could celebrate.

Serena's phone rang and she covered her free ear from the din as she took the call, leaning forward, resting her elbows on the bar.

'Shh,' said Marianne, her eyes as sharp as ever and her senses honed for gossip. 'Shh!'

The crowd quietened a little, not a lot, and Pete placed his hand on the small of Serena's back, seeking her warmth, offering his. The eyes of the crowd were upon them this night but he didn't care what gossip might come of his actions. Serena mattered to him; her happiness and her future mattered to him. So did Sam's.

He was through with being discreet.

He leaned forward, his brow almost touching hers as she tucked a thick fall of hair behind her ear with shaking fingers before seeking his free hand with hers, twining her fingers through his and holding on tight. 'They're back,' she whispered. 'Sam's with the doctor now. Nico says he's talking, that his eyes are clear and that the cut on his head doesn't look that big now that they've cleared most of the blood away.' Her eyes sought his, filling with tears. 'Nico says the doctor says he's fine!'

She stood up abruptly, repeated her words in Greek

and the crowd erupted. People started kissing him, his face, his hair, and somehow he was standing and Serena was kissing him too.

The mood really turned celebratory after that and by the time Nico and Chloe walked in, Nico carrying a drowsy boy with a big sunburn and a mercifully little bandage on his head, it was standing room only. The three of them stayed a few minutes, just long enough for Sam to receive the kissing treatment and Chloe to thank everyone for their help and declare drinks on the house. And then, stating firmly that Sam needed to rest, all three of them made their escape.

Pete stayed long enough to collect more congratulations, stayed long enough to see Serena drawn into the laughing crowd, part of it in a way he would never be, before he too took his leave.

Serena knew it the minute he left. She thought he'd be back. That maybe he'd gone to check in. He was hero of the hour and he'd been enjoying it, she could have sworn he had, but as twenty minutes slipped by and then another twenty and he still hadn't returned, Serena began to doubt that he would. Would he leave without telling her?

She didn't know.

He'd seemed subdued. Even after seeing Sam, talking to him, and telling Chloe to never *ever* jump out of his helicopter like that again, he'd been subdued. Adrenalin was a funny beast. Hours later her body still thrummed with it. The air tasted sharper, the lights shone brighter. She was hyper alert, almost bursting

out of her skin with energy. Did he feel that way too?
The bulk of the decision-making regarding the search
had rested with him these past few hours. Did he feel
more?

How the hell did a person handle more adrenalin
than *this*?

She checked with Reception only to find that he'd
booked a room but wasn't in it. She checked with Chloe
and Nico but he wasn't there either. She walked outside,
her eyes drawn to the track that led up to her grandparents' cottage and beyond.

She looked to the sky and thought she knew where
she might find him.

Serena stopped off at the cottage on her way. She needed
a jacket against the coolness of the night air, never mind
that her walk up the hill would conceivably keep her
warm. She grabbed the lightweight blanket at the foot
of her bed at the last minute, and, trusting to moonlight
rather than a torch she set off up the goat track.

She found him on the plateau, with the lights of the
village spread out below him and the stars shining
above. She dumped the blanket at his feet and waited
for him to speak.

He looked at the blanket, looked at her, and the
faintest of smiles crossed his lips.

'Is that a hint?' he said.

'You left early.'

He shrugged. 'I'd had enough.'

'You don't like it when people honour you?'

'I like it well enough.'

'So why leave?' Why leave without *me*? was what she meant.

He looked at her, his eyes dark and unfathomable. 'I'm tired, Serena. I couldn't think back there. And I needed to.'

He was thinking about other rescues, other times when his best just hadn't been enough. She could see it in his eyes.

'You were wonderful today. You know that, don't you?'

He shrugged. 'It's a situation I'm familiar with. It's just training.'

'Then I'm glad you chose to undertake it.' She took a deep breath. 'I watched you today. Watched you come alive in a way I've never seen before. Watched you be what I've always known you could be. It was a beautiful thing. Made me realise something I think you already know in your heart.' She moved forward to cup his cheek, drawing his gaze to hers. 'You don't belong here, Pete Bennett. Flying tourists around these islands or mustering cattle or hauling cargo or whatever else it is you think you might do next. People need those skills you've learned. The air-sea rescue service needs them. Go home.'

'That's your advice?'

'Well, yeah. I realise it's a little short on ways to manage those feelings that made you run in the first place, but I'm working on that.'

'You are?' He smiled a crooked smile. 'Let me know how it goes.'

She planned to. 'I know it gets personal when you don't save a soul. It cuts deep. Because you care. Because failure isn't an option for you when it comes to saving lives.'

'It's an option, Serena. It's a reality.'

'I know. But when you're up there searching for someone it's not *your* reality. Not until death rams it down your throat.'

He didn't disagree with her. Couldn't, she thought with an ache in her heart. 'Ask me why I called you when Sam went missing.'

'Because you needed a helicopter?' He brushed her cheek with the back of his knuckles, gentle, so very gentle for a man with such strength.

'Because we needed *you*. Because you care. Because failure just isn't an option for you when it comes to saving lives. It's quite a conundrum you've got there, flyboy. Because if you didn't feel the loss of the people you couldn't save quite so keenly you wouldn't be nearly as good at saving the ones you do.'

'That's not advice, Serena. It's a summary.'

She had to laugh at the stubborn jut of his chin, had to step in closer and set her lips to it. 'All I'm saying is that if you accept the bad as a necessary part of the work you do, it might not weigh so heavy on your soul.' Now *that* was advice. Whether or not he would take it was anyone's guess.

'I'll think about it later.' His eyes darkened as his gaze came to rest on her lips. 'I'm thinking about something else right now.'

'Oh?' Her hands settled on his shoulders. So much strength in this man, so much heat. 'What might that be?'

'You.'

'Excellent. Because I'm hoping you'll give *me* some advice. Happens I find myself standing here with an overabundance of energy I can't seem to get rid of.'

'Leftover adrenalin.' His lips brushed hers, lingering, promising, dragging gently and setting her nerves on fire. 'You need to give it direction.'

'I'm so glad you agree.' She set her lips to his for a hot, open-mouthed kiss and directed it, all of it, straight at him.

He wasn't prepared for it. He hadn't realised just how fast she could ignite his passion and rouse his hunger. Too much. More than he could handle and still be careful of her. And still he let his need for her come and when it did he feared it and gloried in it in turn as her mouth played his; hot, soft, knowing.

'Slow down,' he murmured as sensation crashed over him like a wave, dragging at his control, trying to wrest it from him. 'Please, Serena. Slow down.'

'Can't,' she muttered. 'There's only you, only this. Help me.'

But her words had pushed him beyond helping anyone.

He fisted his hand in her hair and tugged, exposing her neck to his lips, grazing her collar bone with his teeth not nearly as lightly as he would have wished. He found the throbbing pulse at the base of her neck, tasted salt on his tongue as she threaded her hands in his hair, tilted her head back and offered up more.

He wanted to savour her, to take his time, but his hands rushed down her back, over her curves, and his grip turned hard and biting as he dragged her lower body against his. 'I'm sorry,' he muttered as he surged against her, but she didn't seem to mind at all.

'The blanket,' she muttered as she writhed against him, her fingers dealing swiftly with the buttons of his shirt.

He backed off, letting her go long enough to find it and spread it out before reaching for her again and dragging her to the ground. He wanted her on her back, naked and open. That was the start of it. Heaven only knew where his hunger would take them after that. He fumbled with the buttons at the front of her dress. No, not a button, it was a snap. He tugged. One snap. Two. A flurry of snaps as she shrugged out of the dress altogether and she was lying down, her eyes not leaving his face as she crossed her wrists above her head and offered her body to him and the night, to the sky, like some pagan goddess.

'I don't want to hurt you.' It was a plea, a warning, and came straight from his soul. His hands were at her hips, on her thighs, too rushed, too needy. Just like his mouth as it followed his hands, teasing, biting, ravenous.

'You won't,' she whispered, and with a ragged oath he pushed her thighs wide open and set his mouth to her.

Serena bucked beneath the lash of his tongue and the wild desire that speared her body. Her hands fisted and she cried out, a high keening sound that spoke of a pleasure so intense it bordered on pain, but she did not make him stop. And that hungry, knowing mouth drove her higher and higher with ruthless precision. Too fast, but she couldn't slow down, too much and still she ached for more. She was out of control, out of her depth with this man, but she didn't care. She needed him. And then climax ripped through her and Serena closed her eyes as need vanished beneath the onslaught of outrageous, all-consuming pleasure.

He was looming over her when finally she surfaced, his hair mussed, and his eyes sharp with desire. She murmured her approval as he shed his shirt but it wasn't enough. 'I want more,' she muttered, her hands moving down the taut planes of his stomach towards the huge, hard bulge in his trousers.

'How much more?'

'All.' She undid his trouser buttons and then his fly. Pushed them down his legs until he was as naked as she was. 'Everything.'

His curse was succinct. Appropriate. He sheathed himself inside her with one smooth stroke and she cried out at the urgency and the wildness in him. He rolled onto his back, dragging her with him and she rode him, blind with need, her body demanding its due as she took him deep inside her, until there was nothing between them, not even moonlight.

'No,' he whispered as he started to move, ragged strokes to match his breathing, every magnificent line of him radiating tension. 'Not all. Not everything. I can't.'

But he did.

With every fierce caress, he gave it. With every shudder of his body he showed it.

'You and me, Pete Bennett. Whatever you want. Whatever you need from me. Take it.' She was spiralling out of control, tightening around him, moments away from orgasm. 'Because heaven help me I'm going to take what I need from you.'

'All right,' he muttered and it was both a curse and a prayer. 'All right, then.' His lips crushed down on hers, drinking her in, driving her insane. 'Together.'

* * *

He honoured his word. In the lovemaking that followed they reached the stars together. He honoured his word in the way he roused her from sleep at dawn and pulled her against him; back to front, like spoons in a drawer as they watched the sun rise from the ocean.

Serena watched, breathless, until the sun gained its freedom from the water and then she rolled over onto her back and looked her fill at another view just as breathtaking. The sunrise had held a soft and gentle beauty. The man leaning on his elbows staring down at her possessed a different kind of beauty, his face all angles and planes, his mouth straight and unsmiling. She looked to his eyes, unprepared for the utter bleakness she saw in their depths. And then he smiled and his eyes warmed.

'I want my camera,' she murmured.

'For the sunrise?'

'For you.' She breathed deep to catch his scent. 'You're magnificent. When you smile you fill my heart. When you're solemn you damn near break it.' She couldn't get enough of this man. Every time she touched him, kissed him, made love to him, she wanted more.

He ran a hand through his hair and sat upright, taking most of the blanket with him.

'Places to go, flyboy?'

'Exactly. Not to mention someone else's business to run.'

'Does that mean that if it were *your* business you'd be inclined to linger?'

'Probably. You do strange things to my perception of what's important. Now get up.'

Pleasure warred with indignation. Pleasure won as

she trailed a finger down his back. 'Five more minutes,' she said.

'No.'

She trailed a finger up his back, pleased when he shuddered beneath her touch. 'Four and a half.'

He turned swiftly, pinning her to the ground, his eyes stormy but his touch gentle. 'Three,' he said gruffly.

But he gave her ten.

'What's your current position on discretion?' Pete asked her as they staggered down the hill towards the cottage. He needed coffee, food, and a scalding shower, all of which could be found at the hotel if his knees would carry him that far. Right now he was aiming for the cottage.

'I'm thinking it's a lost cause.' She stumbled over a rock, cursed as she got her feet beneath her and kept moving. 'Nico's at work. Or should be. There's food at the cottage. Coffee,' the word was almost a whimper. 'Fresh clothes.'

'I'll take the food and the coffee,' he muttered. 'Keep the clothes. Put them on. *Keep* them on.'

'Good idea.'

They all but fell into the kitchen and Serena headed straight for the fridge and a tin of fresh coffee beans that she dumped, double strength, into the coffee-maker before shoving a mug beneath the spout and turning it on. Civilisation poured into the cup, hissing and steaming, bringing with it rational thought and a groan of pure appreciation.

Breakfast began to happen in front of his eyes; a skillet full of sausages and tomatoes, bread in the toaster, another pan of eggs. 'Is that enough?' she wanted to know. 'It doesn't look like enough.'

'It's enough.' Never half measures with Serena, not in anything. He loved that about her. Despaired of it.

'Where will you be today?' she asked, keeping it casual, keeping it light, but he was fresh out of casual. He'd tried to play it her way this morning, tried to play the game, but his heart wasn't in it and therein lay the crux of the problem. His heart lay elsewhere.

'Kos.'

'You're going back to collect your passengers from yesterday?

'Yes.'

She shot him a wary glance before taking a quick sip of her coffee. He had that grim look about him again. The one that said don't push me, don't poke, but she wasn't. Was she?

She'd been doing her utmost to pretend that the events of yesterday and last night hadn't shaken her to the core. Seeing firsthand his compassion and his strength. Demanding it for Sam, watching him deliver, and even after the job was done she hadn't had the courtesy to leave well enough alone. Rearranging his life for him, telling him where she thought he belonged, never mind his own thoughts on the matter. She didn't even know what his thoughts on the matter were.

'About what I said last night…' she muttered awkwardly.

He regarded her coolly. 'You said a lot of things last night, Serena.'

'About your work.'

'What about it?'

'I mean, it's up to you. Why should I have a say in what you do?'

His lips twisted. 'Why indeed?'

He set his coffee down on the bench, took the tongs from her unresisting hand and set about turning the sausages she'd forgotten. 'It's all right, Serena,' he said quietly. 'You didn't say anything I wasn't already thinking.'

'So… You're going home?'

'Yes.'

Sausage fat spat in the pan as her conviction that he was doing the right thing warred with a piercing sense of loss. She summoned a smile. 'I'm glad for you. I think. When will you go?'

'As soon as I find a replacement pilot. It shouldn't be too hard to persuade someone to come fly around paradise for a few weeks.'

'No. No, it shouldn't.' The pain grew sharper and she tried to absorb it. She admired his decision to return to the world of air-sea rescue. Knew in her heart he belonged there. It was the thought of him leaving that hurt. She didn't think she'd be able to look at a blue summer sky without thinking of him, and that was bad because there were a lot of blue summer skies in a lifetime.

At least, there should be.

'I guess now's the time to start being all civilised and mature about you going one way and me going another,' she said, striving for lightness and failing miserably.

'No.'

'No?'

'I can't do it.' He doused the flame beneath the skillet and turned to face her, his expression grave. 'You asked for everything last night, Serena,' he said quietly. 'I gave it.'

He'd never done this before. He'd never been the one to ask for more than a casual relationship. But he was asking it now. 'I'm going home, Serena. I want you to come with me. Be with me.' There was no easy way to say it. 'Marry me.'

He'd shocked her. He could see it in her eyes, in the way she stood so utterly still. It was too soon in their relationship, he knew it, knew damn well he was rushing her. But he'd run out of time. There was no other way. 'I know the timing's bad. And the last thing I want to do is stand in the way of your dreams or your job opportunities. We can talk about it. Work something out.' His heart faltered at her continued silence. 'Serena, say something.'

'I—' She reached out towards him with her hand as if pleading for something, only he didn't know what. She already had all of him. He had nothing left to give.

He jammed his hands in his trouser pockets and took a deep breath as he turned to stare out the kitchen window at the sea beyond. 'Think about it,' he said gruffly. 'I have a home on the Hawkesbury, just north of Sydney. It's set in the hills overlooking the water. There's a jetty there. A boat. It's peaceful. Beautiful. A little bit like this place. With Sydney on the doorstep.' Why wasn't she saying anything? 'You could work if you wanted to. You could freelance from home. Commute to Sydney.

Whatever you'd prefer. We could get a bigger helicopter.' She hadn't moved since he'd started talking. She just stood there in silence. An ocean full of silence. So this was what it felt like to drown. '*Dammit*, Serena, say something!'

'Like what?' He turned his head to look at her and she stared back at him, her eyes blazing and her face pale. She looked tragically, heartbreakingly magnificent in her anger—if it was anger, she still hadn't said enough for him to be sure. Maybe it only looked like anger. But it sure as hell didn't look like joy. 'That you're tearing me in two? Well, you are!'

She put her hands to her head and stalked towards the table, turned and stalked back until she was level with him. 'I thought we agreed,' she said hotly. 'I thought we were playing. That we were *both* playing. You *know* this game, Pete Bennett. Don't you dare tell me you don't!'

'I know it,' he said quietly, while his heart shattered into pieces at her feet. 'I just can't play it any more. Not with you. I've never been able to play it right with you.'

'But you have to!' she said, her eyes filling with tears. 'You have to, don't you see? I got the Athens job. The one you helped me get.' And with a choking laugh, 'Damn you, Pete Bennett, I got the job!'

He watched her race across the kitchen and slam out the door, out of his sight.

So much for asking her to be his wife.

Guess that was a no.

CHAPTER TEN

BLEAK didn't begin to describe Serena's feelings. She couldn't understand how a day that had begun with such happiness and such promise had degenerated so swiftly into a day full of hurt and despair. Her fault, she knew it. She'd asked for too much, demanded all Pete had to give, craving it all, taking it all, and never realising that there would be a reckoning; that he would make her pay.

Bastard.

Anger took the edge off her misery, never mind that it was misdirected. It was there, inside her. No point wasting it. So she stewed and she brooded and by the time Nico found her at lunchtime, in her usual place beside the Vespa shed, she'd acquired a head full of steam and an ocean of resentment towards the traitorous, thieving marauder of hearts, Peter, *Superman, flyboy,* Bennett.

Nico looked tired but happy as he handed over her lunchbox and settled into the chair beside her. Nico— if the unlived-in state of the cottage this morning was any indication—had not made it home last night. Good for him. 'How's Sam?'

'He'll mend,' said Nico, opening her cooler and pinching one of her cans of cola.

'And Chloe?'

'She'll mend too once she stops blaming herself for what happened. She's fussing over Sam something awful.' The hint of a smile touched Nico's lips as he set the cola to his lips and drank deeply. 'He's letting her.'

'Good.' Good for all of them.

'Chloe said she saw Pete this morning before he left,' he continued with a studied casualness she didn't believe one little bit. 'She said if he looked any more miserable she'd have bundled him up next to Sam for the day and mollycoddled them both.'

Serena said nothing.

'She asked him when he'd be back,' said Nico. 'She wanted to thank him properly for what he did for Sam. Take him out for a meal or a drink. *Something.*' Nico slid her a sideways glance. 'He said he didn't know.'

Serena felt the tears start to well and blinked them away, grateful for the sunglasses that hid her eyes until Nico set his drink on the ground and gently removed her sunglasses from her face and left her defenceless.

'He hurt you.'

'No.' *Yes.* 'It's nothing.'

'Then why are you crying?'

'I'm not crying,' she muttered, dashing the tears from her cheeks. 'You just took the sunglasses away too soon, that's all.' She took a deep shuddering breath. 'Pete's heading back to Australia. To his old job with air-sea rescue.'

Nico studied her intently. 'So you're crying because he's leaving?'

'No.' *Yes.* 'He asked me to go with him. To marry him.'

'Oh.' Nico leaned forward, scratched his head, and developed a sudden fascination with the ground beneath his feet. 'I would speak with your father on Pete's behalf if you wanted me to. If you thought he might not approve.'

'That's not it.'

'Didn't think so,' he said, turning his face towards her, his eyes sharp and searching. 'You refused him.'

'Not exactly.' She hadn't meant to ask for everything. She really hadn't. She stared at Nico helplessly, not knowing how to explain. Not knowing where to start. 'I just—' She waved her hand in the air.

Nico sighed. 'Did you say yes?'

'No.'

'Trust me. You refused him.'

Serena felt the tears start to come again. 'I got the job in Athens.'

'Well…' he said, and followed up with a lengthy pause. 'Congratulations. But that doesn't necessarily mean you have to take it.'

'If I don't take it…if I don't step out on my own *now* I'll never know if I could have succeeded.'

'Women,' he muttered.

'You don't understand,' she said hotly. 'This was supposed to be my time. *Mine.* You don't know how long I've waited for it!'

'I do know,' he said gently. 'And it still *is* your time, Serena. There's just another offer on the table now, that's all.' He sent her a wry smile. 'All you have to do is decide which one you want to take.'

Pete stayed away from sleepy Greek islands and soul-stealing sirens for well over a week but he couldn't stay away from the island for ever. Not when passengers wanted to go there. Not when passengers wanted to be picked up from there and flown to Athens.

His one saving grace was that he knew who his passengers were and Serena wasn't one of them. It was Chloe and Sam.

Chloe greeted him like a long lost brother when he touched down, which was sweet of her. Sam greeted him with something akin to awe.

'Where do you want to sit?' he asked the boy as they headed towards the Jet Ranger. 'Front or back?' His gaze slid to Chloe, his eyes narrowed. 'Actually, you take the back. Last time your aunt was in the back of my helicopter she jumped *out* of it. And don't think I've forgiven you either,' he muttered to Chloe. 'The memory of it will haunt me to the day I die.'

Chloe sent him an angelic smile. 'I knew what I was doing.'

'You did not!'

'Did she really jump out of your helicopter?' said Sam.

'Yes.' He didn't want to think about it.

'Chloe says you found me.'

'It was a group effort. Chloe spotted you, Nico came and got you, Mrs Papadopoulos had people out looking for you.' He gauged Sam's readiness to hear what he had to say next. Thought the boy ready for it. 'Pretty stupid move, Sam.'

'I know.' Sam's thin frame stiffened but he held Pete's gaze. 'I'm sorry.'

'I'm glad.' Pete gestured for him to get in the helicopter, showed him how to buckle up, and where the life-jackets were. 'Where were you headed, anyway?

'Athens.'

'Flying's faster.'

'Yeah, but I can't fly a helicopter.'

'You can't sail either, but did that stop you trying? No.'

Chloe giggled first. Sam grinned. 'I'm gonna learn to sail first. Then I'm gonna learn how to fly.'

'Why not?' said Pete. 'So why the trip to Athens today? Something special on?'

Sam's smile faltered. Chloe answered for him. 'It's an anniversary—of a kind. Sam's mother died a year ago. We have a visit to make.'

'My mother died when I was not much older than you,' Pete told the boy gently. 'I do the same. Every year. It helps you remember.'

They touched down in Athens without incident, Sam helping him secure the rotor blades as Chloe gathered up all their stuff. The boy looked edgy. Tense. But it was a big day for him. He had a right to be tense and Pete left him well enough alone.

Sam's hands went to his pockets, nothing untoward about that except that when he withdrew his hand he clutched two fifty euro notes in it. He held them out to Pete, his expression guarded. 'They're yours,' he said.

'Are you sure?'

Sam nodded jerkily. 'Nico and Chloe are getting married. Nico says he's going to adopt me so that we'll all belong to each other. Like a family.' The wonder in Sam's eyes pierced Pete to the core.

'Take care of them, Sam,' he said gruffly.

'I will.' The words were a promise. Sam held out the money. 'Here. It's yours. I don't need them any more.'

Chloe had more words for him as they walked across the tarmac to the arrivals building.

'Serena left the island last week,' she told him.

Pete said nothing.

'She's staying with Nico's family while she tries out this new job. She has a two-week trial period.'

Pete shrugged. 'She won't need it. Her work is brilliant.'

'I hear she's conflicted,' said Chloe. 'She had another offer on the table that was tempting.'

Pete smiled bitterly. 'Congratulations on your engagement.'

'You're changing the subject,' she said.

'Yeah.'

'We're meeting her for coffee later. Care to join us?'

'No.'

'No message for her?'

'Yeah.' Pete's gut clenched. He'd never known how hard it was to be the one letting go. 'Tell her I'm proud of her.'

'You've seen Pete?' said Serena as Chloe gave Sam the okay to go and check out the pastries in the cabinet.

They were sitting in a café in Athens before Chloe and Sam headed back to Sathi. The question revealed more than it should but Serena asked it anyway.

'Of course I've seen him,' said Chloe. 'He flew us here. He's flying us back.'

'What did he look like? How did he seem?'

'He looked the way he always looks. Heartbreakingly handsome. He seemed fine.'

'Bastard,' she muttered.

'You, on the other hand, look miserable.'

'I'm not miserable. I'm fine.'

'How's the job going? Is it as fulfilling as you expected?'

'I've only been there a week,' she said dryly. 'Fulfilment takes time.'

'If you ask me, without the right man at your side, fulfilment's going to take for ever,' muttered Chloe. 'Not that you asked.'

'Since when did you become the expert?'

'Since your cousin asked me to marry him,' said Chloe shyly, and lifted her hand to display the sweetest diamond ring.

'Really?' A smile began to bloom deep in Serena's heart. Finally, something that was going right. 'I knew it,' she said as she leaned over and hugged Chloe tight. 'I knew it!' She sat back and beamed. 'He'll bring you laughter and happiness.'

'And fish,' said Chloe with a grin.

'And children,' said Serena, slanting a glance at Sam who was still glued to the sweets counter, seemingly unable to make a decision about which one to have.

'More children. You'll have a good life together, Chloe. I can feel it.'

'You could have had a good life too,' said Chloe quietly. 'With Pete.'

'I know.' Serena looked away.

'Call him,' said Chloe.

'And say what? Don't go back to Australia? Stay in Athens and cart tourists around for a living? It won't satisfy him, Chloe. I can't ask it of him.'

'Maybe he could get air-sea rescue work here. Have you asked him that? No. Have you discussed the possibility of you getting the kind of work you want back in Australia? No. You took the first job offered, and sold yourself short.'

'I had to start somewhere,' she said defensively.

'Don't get me started,' said Chloe curtly. 'Your photographs are wasted on a daily newspaper. Your pictures don't need words. You're an artist. That your family didn't encourage you in that direction long ago is shameful, but enough about my feelings on that.' She cut off her words with an abrupt wave of her hand. 'If you want to be a photojournalist, fine. Be one. But why on earth do you have to be one *here*?'

'It's not just that,' she said doggedly. 'I know it sounds selfish but I wanted to concentrate on me for a while. My wants. My wishes. My career. If I'd met him a few years from now it might have been different… *Would* have been different,' she admitted. 'I'd have been ready for what he offered me, Chloe, but right now I just don't know. Sometimes I want him with me so bad I ache. But I want my freedom too.'

'Marriage isn't a cage,' said Chloe, and held up her hands when Serena would have protested. 'Okay, I know it brings with it responsibilities and duty to other people. It brings complications when it comes to working out whose wants and needs should take priority. It can bring sacrifice and heartache, children to love, relatives to worry about, and more ties than you know what to do with and they just keep coming until they're wrapped around you like a cloak. But it's a cloak of gold, Serena—rich with dreams and with wishes, full of strength and of joy. It'll keep you warm in the winter and it'll be there for you to come home to after a hard day's work taking pictures that break your heart. It'll keep you strong for when you come home to a man who's been up in the sky all day scouring raging seas for non-existent survivors. Talk all you want about freedom, Serena, but what you found with Pete Bennett? It's worth something.'

'I know,' she said quietly.

'He said to tell you he's proud of you,' said Chloe.

Serena swallowed hard. Nodded. She couldn't speak.

'Do you love him?'

Serena nodded again.

'I can't tell you what to do, Serena, but if you love him the way he loves you?' Chloe smiled gently. 'It's worth everything.'

Serena stewed over her options another week before finally gathering the nerve to call Pete. Her two weeks trial working period was up. She'd found the work satisfying, occasionally exhilarating, and the deadlines tight. They were happy with her work. *She* was happy with it. Time to start looking for an apartment and carving out a life for herself in Athens if that was what she wanted.

But it wasn't.

She wanted something else more.

She needed to find out if it was still on offer. With shaking hands she reached for her phone. A recorded message told her his phone was out of range. She called the helicopter charter service. Tomas answered.

'How's the new job?' he wanted to know.

'It's a good job. Tomas, is Pete around?'

'Didn't he tell you?' said Tomas. 'His old air-sea rescue unit were desperately short a helicopter pilot. He's back in Australia. He went home.'

CHAPTER ELEVEN

THE plane from Athens, by way of Paris and Singapore, touched down in Sydney early Saturday morning, not quite one week after Serena's conversation with Tomas. The newspaper job had been a good one but in the end she'd respectfully declined it. She would find something closer to home, closer to where her heart was. Serena looked to the sky, such a bright and vivid blue sky, as she made her way from the arrivals terminal to a waiting taxi and told the driver to take her to a cityside hotel.

She needed to make plans before she tracked Pete Bennett down. She needed to figure out what to say and what to ask for. And what she would do if he turned her away.

She needed to try and ensure that didn't happen.

It was time to accessorise.

Pete Bennett was happy to be home. He'd slipped back into his old job as if he'd never left it: the training and the camaraderie, the Seahawks and the purpose behind it all. He was back, he was ready, and he had a newfound philosophy about dealing with the missions that didn't turn out the way he wanted them to. Whether that particular philosophy would work without Serena there to remind him of it was open to speculation.

He'd wondered about calling her before he left Greece. He could have asked her how the job was going, told her he was heading home. But in the end he hadn't called. He'd said everything he wanted to, offered everything he had, and she'd chosen not to take it.

There was nothing left to say.

So here he was, back in Sydney, back within reach of his family and all the stronger for it. His brothers were in town, all of them. Jake, who'd flown in from Singapore for reasons of his own that Pete had yet to fathom. Luke, who was home on shore leave. And Tristan, who lived here in Sydney these days. It wasn't often they were all together in the one place, it was something of an event and one that needed celebration.

Jake and Tristan had argued the where of it, but in the end they'd decided to take a trip down memory lane and spend the better part of this lazy Sunday afternoon at the local hotel down by the beach. Just like old times as Luke and Tristan started arguing the relative merits of different law enforcement agencies and Jake wheedled a set of darts from the barman and commandeered the dartboard. Home turf. There was no place quite like it for healing a wounded heart. No better company to do it in.

He'd get over her. He would.

Give it fifty, sixty, years he'd be just fine.

They paired up to play darts, him and Jake against Tristan and Luke. He liked darts. He could have whipped them all but for their incessant questions about Greece and beautiful women.

'So what does she do?' Luke asked him as he lined up his shot.

'Who?'

'The woman you left behind. The one who broke your heart.'

'Whatever she damn well wants,' he muttered, missing his mark by a good three centimetres.

'A wayward woman,' said Tristan. 'I like her already. Why didn't you bring her back with you?'

'Did you ask her?' said Luke curiously.

Pete glared at the pair of them. 'What is this? An inquisition?'

'Just curious,' said Luke. 'What are you going to do about her?'

'Nothing. She had another offer on the table. She took it. End of story.'

'What kind of offer?' asked Luke. 'An offer from another man? And you couldn't see it coming?'

'A job offer,' he said curtly. 'And I did see it coming.'

'A wayward *career* woman,' said Tristan. 'Now I'm really intrigued. What did *you* offer?'

'Everything,' he muttered.

'Ouch,' said Luke. 'You finished with those darts yet?'

Pete threw his last dart and headed across to the board to retrieve all three of them and mark down his score on the nearby chalkboard. 'You ready to try and hit the dartboard yet, junior, or shall I just save time and mark you down as a no score?' he countered with an edge to his voice that warned Luke that if he wanted a rumble tonight he was going the right way about getting it. But Luke had fallen strangely silent. The room itself felt as if it had drawn a giant breath.

He looked round for the reason for all that silence, and all but swallowed his tongue.

She wore a sky-blue dress that could have been demure but for the perfection of the body beneath it. She was all heavenly curves and sensual grace and as her gaze swept the room several bellies were ruthlessly sucked in, but to no avail.

Her gaze rested on him, her brown eyes thoughtful, and then she smiled; a reckless, challenging smile that promised the kind of trouble a man might just well beg for one more taste of. Someone beside him whimpered. He thought it might have been Luke.

She sauntered towards them, there was no other word for it, and Pete straightened. They all straightened.

'You think that's her?' muttered Tristan.

'He just stabbed himself with the darts,' said Jake. 'It's her.'

The bar was decidedly down-market—a little on the rough side, a little too dark. Serena didn't know what had possessed her to think that walking into a bar like this, *dressed* like this, was a good idea but she tossed her head back and kept right on walking, her eyes firmly fixed on her mark. She'd trawled through the Bennetts in the phone book and finally got lucky in the form of Jake, the brother who usually lived in Singapore but could currently be found manning the family home in Sydney.

He'd given her Pete's phone number, and, just in case she gathered enough courage for it, she'd asked where she might look if she wanted to find Pete in person.

Jake had told her where. And when. But he'd neglected to mention just how many other people might be around. Or how they would stare.

She'd dressed carefully for the occasion. A blue silk sundress, as blue as a summer sky. A first-date dress that flared gently over her hips and ended just above the knee. The strappy bodice favoured skin over fabric, the three little buttons in the middle were a masterful touch and guaranteed to make a man's fingers itch. Her hair fell in waves to her waist and her mouth glowed a shade darker than natural courtesy of some very expensive lipstick. She'd been aiming for elegant sophistication but, judging by the reaction of the crowd, she'd also nailed sexy. Never mind. Faint heart would never hold this man.

Fortunately, she didn't have one.

'Hey, flyboy,' she said when she reached him.

'Serena,' he said gruffly.

She glanced around at the men ranging on either side of him, three of them in total, all of them dangerous-looking enough to make grown women preen and the rest of the patrons in the bar eyeball them carefully. 'Aren't you going to introduce me to your friends?'

'No.'

'Then I'm guessing a drink is out of the question?' she said with the raise of an eyebrow.

'Get her a drink,' said the man to Pete's right, one of Pete's brothers if his dark good looks were any indication.

'Get her a chair,' said another one.

'Get her number,' said the third and winced when Pete dumped the darts into his hand points down.

'What are you doing here?' said the only man whose words she wanted to hear.

'You left without saying goodbye,' she said quietly.

'He usually has better manners,' said one of them.

'Maybe he lost his *mind*,' said another. 'I'm Tristan. This is Jake,' he said, gesturing towards the one she'd pegged earlier as a brother. 'The one with the holes in his hand is Luke.'

Great. *All* of them brothers. Nothing quite like meeting the family *en masse*. 'Gentlemen.' Serena sent them a smile. If she didn't miss her guess, they were giving their man time to regroup. That or deliberately trying to rile him. She didn't mind him riled. She much preferred snarling to cool indifference.

'They were just leaving,' said Pete. 'Now.'

'And miss all this?' said Tristan, sharing a glance with his brothers that had more than a whisper of rogue about it. 'You have *got* to be kidding. I *love* reunions.'

'Then *we're* leaving.' Pete grabbed her by the hand and started dragging her towards the door before she could so much as summon a protest. Not that she felt inclined to protest. Chances were she was about to humiliate herself completely. For that she only needed an audience of one.

Once they were clear of the hotel, he headed for the beach across the road, his stride ground eating and his silence oppressive. He stopped to let her slip off her sandals when they reached the sand and then he was off again, heading towards the water's edge. When he reached it he dropped her hand and shoved both of his in his pockets before turning to face her.

'Why are you here?' he said.

'You asked me a question back on the island. One that took me by surprise. I wasn't expecting it. Didn't know how to answer it.'

His lips twisted. 'You left for Athens two days later, Serena. I thought you answered it fairly comprehensively, all things considered.'

'Then let me ask you a question,' she said. 'If I'd asked you to come with me to Athens…to be with me, build a life with me…would you have?'

He looked at her for what seemed like an eternity, the tension in him a living thing. 'Yes,' he said curtly. 'But you never did ask.'

'Because I knew damn well you needed to be *here*, not there!' she countered, stung by the chill in his eyes.

'I *needed* you. Maybe I didn't make that clear enough for you, Serena. I love you. I'd have done whatever it took to be with you. The only reason I let you go was because I thought you didn't want *me*. That you'd rather be free.' He turned away from her and stared out to sea. 'When my mother died my father took down every picture we had of her and packed them away in a box in the attic. I could never understand why he did it, but I understand now. Lord, it hurts to look at you.'

Three observers stood on the deck of the nearby hotel and watched with varying degrees of concern.

'He's blowing it,' said Luke.

'Have a little faith,' said Tristan.

Jake said nothing.

It wasn't meant to play out like this, thought Serena with increasing desperation. He wasn't supposed to tell her he loved her with one breath and refuse to even look at her the next.

'What happened with the job?' he said abruptly.

'It was a good job, don't get me wrong,' she said. 'For a long time I'd dreamed of landing one just like it, but dreams change.' Serena hesitated, not at all sure of her next move in the face of his continued silence. 'These days I dream of you.'

Desperate times called for desperate measures. She waded out into the water so that she stood in front of him, facing him, her hands on her hips and her chin held high. A wave caught the edges of her dress, lifting it higher, plastering it to her thighs, but she didn't care. A wave could drench her completely and she wouldn't care.

'Your father put those pictures away because he couldn't bear to see what he'd lost,' she told him bluntly. 'You look at me, Pete Bennett. You look your fill because I'm not dead and I'm sure as hell not lost to you. I came here because I wanted to be with you. I want to live with you in your little cottage on the hillside. I can work from home. I can work in Sydney if I've a mind to. I can compromise. Because the most important thing in my life isn't my work…it's you.'

The ghost of a smile touched his lips, reached his eyes, and Serena let out the breath she'd been holding with a shudder. Until the smile in his eyes turned into an all too familiar gleam.

'You love me?' he said.

'I love you,' she told him. 'I'm absolutely stark raving bonkers about you, in case you hadn't noticed.'

'Prove it,' he said. 'Discreetly.'

'We don't do discreet, remember? But for you I'll try.' She knew how to play this game. Damn sure she did. She smiled sweetly as her fingers went to the buttons on her dress, loosing them swiftly before lowering crossed arms to the hem of her dress and peeling it skywards.

Back on the deck Jake choked on the beer he'd just set to his lips.

'Sweet Mary Mother of God,' said Tristan.

'Amen,' muttered Luke.

'Don't panic,' said Jake. 'No need to panic! She *is* wearing swimmers. People do that at the beach. Maybe she just wants to go for a swim to cool off...or something. No one's going to arrest them.' Jake watched with fatalistic resignation as his brother caught her by the waist and tumbled her to the sand, dragging her more or less beneath him, pinning her to the ground. 'Yet.'

'Maybe he'll grow a brain and remember where they are,' said Luke.

'Would you?' countered Tristan.

Luke sighed. 'Maybe *she'll* remember.'

Three men watched in silence as the couple on the beach rolled until Pete lay on his back with Serena plastered all over *him*, in a manner reminiscent of a very old movie.

'She did remember,' said Jake dryly, rolling his eyes. 'That's *so* much better. No way anyone's going to arrest them *now*.'

'I want four children,' said Pete as he wrestled with his libido and the knowledge that if they weren't careful they'd end up making love right there and then.

'You'll get them.' She wound her arms around his neck.

'A garage full of Vespas.'

'That can be arranged.'

'A helicopter on a hillside.'

'Beats driving.'

'Award-winning photographs on the walls.'

'I'll do my best.' His lips scraped over the curve of her jaw, warm and easy. She wanted more. Much *much* more.

'And you.'

A wave rushed up the sand, splashing between them, around them. 'Trust me Pete Bennett,' she murmured, just before his lips found hers, still lazy and teasing but with an edge of hunger in them that made her tremble. 'You'll get that too.'

BAREFOOT BRIDE

Jessica Hart

Jessica Hart was born in West Africa, and has suffered from itchy feet ever since, travelling and working around the world in a wide variety of interesting but very lowly jobs, all of which have provided inspiration on which to draw when it comes to the settings and plots of her stories. Now she lives a rather more settled existence in York, where she has been able to pursue her interest in history, although she still yearns sometimes for wider horizons.

If you'd like to know more about Jessica, visit her website www.jessicahart.co.uk

Praise for Jessica Hart

"Sweet and witty, with great characters and sizzling sexual tension, this one's a fun read."
—*www.RTbookreviews.com* on
Honeymoon with the Boss

"Strong conflict and sizzling sexual tension drive this well-written story. The characters are smart and sharp-witted, and match up perfectly."
—*www.RTbookreviews.com* on
Cinderella's Wedding Wish

CHAPTER ONE

'GUESS who I bumped into in town?'

Beth bounced down the steps into the garden and plonked herself onto the lounger next to Alice.

Alice had spent a blissful morning by the pool, feeling the tension slowly unwinding as the tropical heat seeped into her bones, and guiltily enjoying some time on her own. There was a puppyish enthusiasm about Roger's wife that could be quite exhausting at times, and, ever since she had arrived two days ago, Alice had been conscious of how hard Beth was trying to distract her from the fact that Tony was getting married tomorrow.

No one could be kinder or sunnier-natured than Beth, though, and Alice would have been very fond of her even if she wasn't married to Roger. And this was, after all, Beth's pool that she had been lying beside all morning. A good guest would be opening her eyes and sitting up to take an interest in her hostess's morning.

On the other hand, Beth *had* told her to relax before she'd gone out. Alice had done as she was told, and was now so relaxed she honestly couldn't summon the energy to open her eyes, let alone care which of Beth's many acquaintances she had met in town.

'Umm... Elvis?' she suggested lazily, enjoying the faint stir of warm breeze that ruffled the parasol above her.

'No!' Beth tsk-tsked at Alice's failure to take her exciting news more seriously, but she was much too nice to take offence. 'Someone we know... At least, I think you know him,' she added, suddenly dubious. 'I'm pretty sure that you do, anyway.'

That meant it could be anybody. Beth was unfailingly sociable, and gathered lame ducks under her wing wherever she went. When Roger and Beth had lived in London, Alice had often been summoned to parties where Beth fondly imagined her disparate friends would all bond and find each other as interesting as she did.

Sadly, Alice was by nature as critical and prickly as Beth was sweet and kind. She settled herself more comfortably on her lounger, resting an arm over her eyes and resigning herself to one of her friend's breathless accounts of someone Alice had met for five minutes several years ago, and who she had most likely hoped never to see again.

'I give up,' she said.

At least she wouldn't have to pay much attention for the next few minutes. Beth's stories tended to be long, and were often so muddled that she would get lost in the middle of them. All Alice would be required to do was to interject an occasional 'Really?' or the odd 'Oh?' between encouraging murmurs. 'Who did you meet?' she asked dutifully.

It was the cue Beth had been waiting for.

'Will Paxman,' she said.

Alice's eyes snapped open. 'What?' she demanded, jerking upright. *'Who?'*

'Will Paxman,' Beth repeated obligingly. 'He was a friend of Roger's from university...Well, you must have known him, too, Alice,' she went on with an enquiring look.

'Yes,' said Alice in a hollow voice. 'Yes, I did.'

How strange. She had convinced herself that she'd forgotten Will, or at least succeeded in consigning him firmly to the past, but all it had taken was the sound of his name to conjure up his image in heart-twisting detail.

Will. Will with the quiet, serious face and the stern mouth, and the disconcertingly humorous grey eyes. Will, who had made her heart jump every time he'd smiled his unexpected smile. He had asked her to marry him three times, and three times she had said no.

Alice had spent years telling herself that she had done the right thing.

She felt very odd. The last four years had been consumed by Tony, and she'd been braced for memories of him, not Will. Ever since Tony had left, she had done her best to armour herself against the pain of if onlys and what might have beens, to convince herself that she had moved on, only to be ambushed now by the past from quite a different direction.

Alice was totally unprepared to think about Will. She had thought that relationship was long over, and that she was safe from those memories at least, but now all Beth had to do was say his name and Alice was swamped by the old turbulence, uncertainty and bitter-sweetness of that time.

Beth was chatting on, oblivious to Alice's discomposure. 'I didn't recognize him straight away, but there was something really familiar about him. I've only met him a couple of times, and the last time was at our wedding, so that's…how long?'

'Eight years,' said Alice, carefully expressionless.

Eight years since Will had kissed her one last, fierce time. Eight years since he had asked her to marry him. Eight years since he had turned and walked away out of her life.

'It's hard to believe Roger has put up with me for that long!' Beth smiled, but Alice had seen the faint shadow cross her eyes and knew that her friend was thinking of the years she had spent trying to conceive. She and Roger had been open about their plans to start a family as soon as they were married, but it hadn't worked out that way. And, although they were unfailingly cheerful in company, Alice knew the sadness they both felt at their inability to have the children they wanted so much.

'Where did you meet Will?' she asked, wanting to distract Beth.

'In the supermarket, of all places!' Alice was pleased to see Beth's expression lighten as she swung her legs up onto the lounger and settled herself into a more comfortable position to recount her story. 'Isn't that an *amazing* coincidence? I mean, bumping into someone in a supermarket isn't that unusual, I know, but a supermarket in *St Bonaventure*? What are the odds of us all ending up on a tiny island in the Indian Ocean at the same time?'

'Will *is* a marine ecologist,' Alice felt obliged to point out. 'I guess the Indian Ocean isn't that odd a place to find him. It's more of a coincidence that Roger's been posted here. Not many bankers get to work on tropical islands.'

'No, we're so lucky,' Beth agreed happily. 'It's like being sent to Paradise for two years! And, now you're here, and Will's here, it's not even as if we've had to leave all our friends behind.'

She beamed at Alice, who immediately wondered if Beth was hatching a plan for a cosy foursome. It was the kind of thing Beth would do. It was Beth who had suggested that Alice come out for an extended visit while Tony was getting married.

'There are lots of single men out here,' she had told Alice. 'They won't be able to believe their luck when you turn up! A few weeks of uncritical adoration, and you won't care about Tony any more!'

Alice had no fault to find with this programme in principle, but not with Will. He knew her too well to adore her, and the last thing she wanted was Beth taking him aside and telling him how 'poor Alice's' world had fallen apart. He might be persuaded to take pity on her, and pretend he didn't remember how she had boasted of the great life she was going to have without him.

She would have to squash any matchmaking ideas Beth might have right now.

'I'm only here for six weeks,' she reminded Beth. 'And Will's probably just on holiday too. I don't suppose either of us will want to waste our precious holiday on politely catching-up on old times,' she added rather crushingly.

'Oh, Will's not on holiday,' said Beth. 'He's working here on some long-term environmental project. Something to do with the reef, I think.'

'But you'd have met him already if he'd been working here,' Alice objected. 'St Bonaventure is such a tiny place, you must know everybody!'

'We do, but Will's only been here a week, he said. I got the impression that he knows the island quite well, and that he's been here on various short trips, probably before Roger and I came out. But this is the first time he's brought his family with him, so I imagine they're going to settle here for a while.'

Alice's stomach performed an elaborate somersault and landed with a resounding splat, leaving her with a sick feeling that horrified her. 'Will's got a *family*?' she asked in involuntary dismay. She sat up and swung her feet to the warm tiles so that she could stare at Beth. 'Are you sure?'

Beth nodded, obviously surprised at Alice's reaction. 'He had his little girl with him. She was very cute.'

Will had a daughter. Alice struggled to assimilate the idea of him as a father, as a husband.

Why was she so surprised? Surely—*surely*, Alice—you

didn't expect him to stay loyal to your memory, did you? she asked herself.

Why on earth would he? She had refused him. End of story. Of *course* he would have moved on and made a life of his own, just as she had done. It wasn't as if she had been missing *him* all these years. She hadn't given him a thought when she'd been with Tony. Well, not very often, anyway. Only now and then, when she was feeling a bit low. If things had worked out, she would have been married by now herself.

Would that have made the news less of a shock? Alice wondered with characteristic honesty.

She could see that Beth was watching her curiously, and she struggled to assume an expression of unconcern. So much for her fears about Beth's matchmaking plans!

'I didn't know that he had married,' Alice said, hoping that she sounded mildly surprised rather than devastated, which was what she inexplicably felt. 'What was his wife like?'

'I didn't meet her,' Beth admitted. 'But I asked them to your welcome party tomorrow, and he said they'd like to come, so I guess we'll see her then.'

'Oh.' The sick feeling got abruptly worse. Somehow it seemed hard enough to adjust to the mere idea of Will being married, without having to actually face him and smile at the sight of him playing happy families, Alice thought bitterly, and then chided herself for being so mean-spirited.

She ought to be glad that Will had found happiness. She *was*, Alice told herself.

She was just a bit sorry for herself, too. None of the great plans she had made for herself had worked out. How confidently she had told Will that her life would be a success, that she wanted more than he could offer her. Alice cringed now at the memory. She wouldn't have much success to show off tomorrow. No marriage, no child, not even a job, let alone a good one.

Will, on the other hand, apparently had it all. He probably hadn't even been thinking about her all those years when the thought of how much he had loved her had been somehow comforting. It was all very...dispiriting.

'It's not a problem, is it?' asked Beth, who had been watching Alice's face rather more closely than Alice would have liked. Beth might be sweet and kind, but that didn't mean that she was stupid.

'No, no...of course not,' said Alice quickly. 'Of *course* not,' she added, although she wasn't entirely sure whether she was trying to convince herself or Beth.

How could it be a problem, after all? She and Will had split up by mutual agreement ten years ago, and she hadn't seen him for eight. There was no bitterness, no betrayal to mar their memories of the time they had spent together. There was absolutely no reason why they shouldn't meet now as friends.

Except—*be honest, Alice*—that he was married and she wasn't.

'Honestly,' she told Beth. 'I'm fine about it. In fact, it will be good to catch up with him again. It was just funny hearing about him suddenly after so long.'

She even managed a little laugh, but Beth was still looking sceptical, and Alice decided that she had better come clean. Roger was bound to tell his wife the truth anyway, and, if she didn't mention how close she and Will had been, Beth would wonder why she hadn't told her herself, and that would give the impression that she *did* have a problem with seeing Will again.

Which she didn't. Not really.

Slipping her feet into the gaudily decorated flip-flops she had bought at the airport at great expense, Alice bent to adjust one of the straps and let her straight brown hair swing forward to cover her face.

'You know, Will and I went out for a while,' she said as casually as she could.

'No!' Beth's jaw dropped. 'You and Will?' she said, suitably astounded. 'Roger never told me that!' she added accusingly.

'We'd split up long before he met you.' Alice gave a would-be careless shrug. 'It was old news by then. Roger probably never gave it a thought.'

'But you were both at our wedding,' Beth remembered. 'I do think Roger might have mentioned it in case I put you on the same table or something. I had no idea!' She leant forward. 'Wasn't it awkward?'

Unable to spend any more time fiddling with her shoe, Alice groped around beneath her lounger for the hair clip she had put there earlier.

'It was fine,' she said, making a big thing of shaking back her hair and twisting it carelessly up to secure it with the clip, all of which gave her the perfect excuse to avoid Beth's eye.

Because it hadn't been fine at all. There would have been no way she'd have missed Roger's wedding, and she had known that Will would be there. It had been two years since they had split up, and Alice had hoped that the two of them would be able to meet as friends.

It had been a short-lived hope. Alice had been aware of him from the moment she'd walked into the church and saw the back of his head. Her heart had jerked uncomfortably at the sight of him, and she had felt ridiculously glad that he was wedged into a pew between friends so that she wouldn't have to sit next to him straight away.

She had been going out with someone from work then. Clive, his name had been. And, yes, maybe he *had* been a bit of a stuffed shirt, but there had been no call for Will to talk about him that way. They had met, inevitably, at the reception after the service, and Alice had done her best to keep up a flow of increasingly desperate chit-chat as Will had eyed Clive and made absolutely no attempt to hide his contempt.

'You've sold out, Alice,' he told her later. 'Clive is boring, pretentious and self-obsessed, and that's putting it kindly! He's not the man for you.'

They argued, Alice remembered, in the hotel grounds, away from the lights and the music, as the reception wore on into the night. Clive had too much to drink, and to Alice's embarrassment was holding forth about his car and his clients and his bonuses. Depressed at her lack of judgement when it came to men, she slipped away, but, if she had known that she would encounter Will out in the dark gardens, she would have stuck with Clive showing off.

Will was the last person she wanted to witness Clive at his worst. She had been hoping to convince him that her life had been one long, upward curve since they had agreed to go their separate ways and that she was happily settled with a satisfying career, a stable home and a fulfilling relationship. No chance of him thinking that, when he had endured Clive's boasting all evening.

Mortified by Clive's behaviour, and tense from a day trying not to let Will realise just how aware she was of him still, Alice was in no mood for him to put her own thoughts into such brutal words.

'What do you know about it?' she fired back, glad of the dim light that hid her flush.

'I know you, and I know there's no way on earth a man like Clive could ever make you happy,' said Will, so infuriatingly calm that Alice's temper flared.

'You didn't make me happy, either!' she snapped, but Will just shook his head, unfazed by her lie.

'I did once,' he said. 'We made each other happy.'

Alice didn't want to remember those times. She turned her head away. 'That was then and this is now,' she said.

'We haven't changed.'

'*I* have,' Alice insisted. 'It's been nearly two years, Will. I'm not the same person I was before. I've got a new life, the life I always wanted.' She lifted her chin. 'Maybe Clive gives me what I need now.'

'Does he?' Will took a step towards her, and instinctively Alice backed away until she found herself up against a tree.

'Does he?' Will asked again softly, taking her by the wrists and lifting her arms until she was pinned against the tree trunk. 'Does he make you laugh, Alice? Do you lie in bed with him and talk and talk?' he went on, in the same low voice that reverberated up and down Alice's spine. 'The way you did with me?'

Her heart was thumping and she could feel the rough bark digging into her back through the flimsy material of her dress. She tried to pull her wrists away, but Will held her in place with insulting ease. He wasn't a particularly big man, but his spareness was deceptive, and his hands were much stronger than they looked.

And Alice, too, was conscious that she wasn't fighting as hard as she could have done. She could feel her treacherous body responding to Will's nearness. It had always been like that. Alice had used to lie awake sometimes, watching him while he slept, and wondering what it was about him that created such a powerful attraction.

It wasn't as if he were especially good-looking. In many ways, he was quite ordinary, but there was something about him, something uniquely Will in the line of his jaw, in the set of his mouth and the feel of his hands, in all the lean, lovely planes and angles of him that made her senses tingle still.

Will's voice dropped even further as he pressed her back against the tree. 'Do you shiver when he kisses you here?' he asked, dropping a light kiss on Alice's bare shoulder where it curved into her throat, and in spite of herself Alice felt that familiar shudder of excitement spiral slowly down to the very centre of her, where it throbbed and ached with memories of all the times they had made love.

Closing her eyes, she sucked in her breath as Will pressed warm, slow kisses up the side of her throat. 'That's none of your business,' she managed unsteadily.

'Does he love you?' Will whispered against her skin, and the brush of his lips made her shiver again.

She swallowed hard, her eyes still squeezed shut. 'Yes,' she said, but she knew it was a feeble effort. 'Yes, he does,' she tried again, although it sounded as if she was trying to convince herself.

Alice wanted to believe that Clive loved her, otherwise what was she doing with him?

'No, he doesn't,' said Will, and, although she couldn't see him, she knew that he was shaking his head. 'Clive doesn't love anybody but himself.'

There was a long pause, then Alice opened her eyes and found herself staring up into Will's face, the face that had once made her heart clench with the knowledge that she could touch it and kiss it and feel it whenever she wanted.

'Do you love Clive, Alice?' Will asked quietly.

Alice couldn't answer. Her throat was so tight it was hard enough to breathe, and all she could do was stand there, her arms pinioned above her head, and look back at him while the world stopped turning, and there was only Will and the feel of his hands over her wrists.

To her horror, her eyes filled with tears, and Will bent with a muffled curse to kiss her, a fierce, hard kiss that seared Alice to the soul. Nearly two years since they had said goodbye, but her mouth remembered his instantly, and she found herself kissing him back, angrily, hungrily, until Will released her wrists at last and yanked her into him to kiss her again.

Instinctively Alice's arms reached round him and she spread her hands over his back. It had been so long since she had held him, so long since she had felt the solidity and the hardness of the body she had once known as well as her own. She had forgotten how much she missed the feel of him and the wonderfully warm, clean, masculine scent of his skin.

'I've missed you,' Will echoed her thoughts in a ragged voice. 'I don't want to miss you again.'

'Will…' Alice was reeling, shocked by the emotion surging between them and the power of her own response.

'I'm going to Belize next week to work on the reef,' he went on, taking her face between his hands. 'Come with me,' he said with an urgency she had never heard from him before. 'Come with me and marry me, Alice. We need each other, you know we do. Clive has got his big, fat bonuses to keep him warm. He won't even notice you're gone. Say you'll come with me, and we can spend the rest of our lives making each other happy.'

And the truth was, Alice remembered by Beth's pool in St Bonaventure, that for a moment there she hesitated. Every fibre of her body was clamouring to throw herself back into his arms and agree.

And every cell in her brain was clanging a great, big warning.

She had the security she had yearned for at last. She had a good job, and in a year or two she would be in a position to get a mortgage and buy her own flat. Wasn't that what she had always wanted? A place of her own, where she could hang up her clothes in a wardrobe and never have to pack them up again? She was safe and settled. Did she really want to give that up to chase off to the Caribbean with Will, no matter how good it felt to kiss him again?

'Say yes,' Will urged her, encouraged by her hesitation.

Very slowly, Alice shook her head. 'No,' she said.

She would never forget the expression on his face then. Alice felt as if she had struck him.

'Why not?' he asked numbly.

'It wouldn't work, Will.' Alice pulled herself together with an effort. 'We went through all this two years ago. We agreed that we're different and we want different things. Our lives were going in different directions then, and they still are now. What's the point of pretending that they're not?'

'What's the point of pretending that what we have doesn't exist?' he countered, and she swallowed.

'It's just sexual chemistry,' she told him shakily. 'It's not enough.'

'And Clive and his bonuses are, I suppose?' Will made no attempt to hide the bitterness in his voice.

Alice didn't—couldn't—answer. It wasn't Clive, she wanted to tell him. It was the way her life seemed finally under control. She was settled, and had the kind of reassuring routine that she had craved when she was growing up.

And, yes, maybe Clive and the other boyfriends she had had weren't kindred spirits the way Will had been, but at least she knew where she was with them. They didn't make her entrails churn with excitement the way he had done, it was true, but they didn't make her feel superficial and materialistic for wanting to root herself with tangible assets either. Will was like her parents. He wanted things like freedom, adventure and independence, but Alice had learnt that you couldn't count on those. You couldn't put them in the bank and save them for when you needed them. Freedom, adventure and independence might be great things to have, but they didn't make you feel safe.

So all she did was look helplessly back at Will until he

dropped his hands, his expression closed. 'That's three times I've asked you to marry me,' he said bleakly as Alice lowered her trembling arms and rubbed them unsteadily. 'And three times you've said no. I've got the message now, though,' he told her. 'I won't ask you again.'

He had stepped away from her then, only turning back almost against his will for one last, hard kiss. 'Goodbye, Alice,' he said, and then he turned and walked out of her life.

Until now.

Alice sighed. For a while there, the past had seemed more vivid than the present, and her heart was like a cold fist in her chest, just as it had been then.

'Are you sure?' asked Beth, whose blue eyes could be uncomfortably shrewd at times.

'Of course.' Alice summoned a bright smile. 'It was fine,' she repeated, knowing that Beth was afraid that tension between her and Will would mar the party she had planned so carefully. 'And it will be fine this time, too. Don't worry, Beth. I promise you I don't have a problem meeting Will or his wife,' she went on bravely, if inaccurately, as she got to her feet. 'Will probably won't even remember me. Now, why don't I give you a hand unpacking all that shopping?'

Will watched anxiously as Lily took Beth's hand after a moment's hesitation and allowed herself to be led off to the pool, which was already full of children squealing excitedly. His daughter had looked apprehensive at the thought of making new friends, but she hadn't clung to him or even looked to him for reassurance. He was almost as much a stranger to her as Beth was, he reflected bitterly.

'She'll be fine.' Roger misread Will's tension. 'Beth loves kids, and she'll look after Lily. By the time the party's over, she won't want to go home!'

That was precisely what Will was afraid of, but he didn't want to burden Roger with his problems the moment that they met up again after so long. He'd always liked Roger, and Beth's delight at bumping into him the day before had been touching, but the truth was that he wasn't in the mood for a party.

He hadn't been able to think of a tactful way to refuse Beth's invitation at the time, and this morning he had convinced himself that a party would be a good thing for Lily, no matter how little he might feel like it himself. Beth had assured him that it would be a casual barbecue, and that several families would be there, so Lily would have plenty of other children to play with.

Will hadn't seen his daughter play once since they had arrived in St Bonaventure, and he knew he needed to make an effort to get her to interact with other children. But, watching Lily trail reluctantly along in Beth's wake, Will was seized by a fresh sense of inadequacy. Should he have reassured her, or gone with her? He was bitterly aware that he was thrown by the kind of everyday situations any normal father would take in his stride.

'Come and have a beer,' said Roger, before Will could decide whether to follow Lily and Beth or not, so he let Roger hand him a bottle so cold that the condensation steamed. There wasn't much he could do about Lily right now, and in the meantime he had better exert himself to be sociable.

The two men spent a few minutes catching up and, by the time Roger offered to introduce him to the other guests, Will was beginning to relax. He didn't know whether it was the beer, or Roger's friendly ordinariness, but he was definitely feeling better.

'Most people are outside,' said Roger, leading the way through a bright, modern living-area to where sliding-glass doors separated the air-conditioned coolness from the tropical heat outside.

Will was happy to follow him. He had never minded the heat, and, if he was outside, he'd be able to keep an eye on Lily at the pool. Roger glanced out as he pulled open the door for Will, then hesitated at the last moment.

'Beth did tell you who's staying with us, didn't she?' he asked, suddenly doubtful.

'No, who's that?' asked Will without much interest as he stepped out onto the decking, shaded by a pergola covered in scrambling pink bougainvillaea.

He never heard Roger's answer.

He saw her in his first casual glance out at the garden, and his heart slammed to a halt in his chest.

Alice.

She was standing in the middle of the manicured lawn, talking to a portly man in a florid shirt. Eight years, and he recognized her instantly.

Even from a distance, Will could see that her companion was sweating profusely in the heat, but Alice looked cool and elegant in a loose, pale green dress that wafted slightly in the hot breeze. She was wearing high-heeled sandals with delicate straps, and her hair was clipped up in a way that would look messy on most other women, but which she carried off with that flair she had always had.

Alice. There was no one else like her.

He had thought he would never see her again. Will's heart stuttered into life after that first, jarring moment of sheer disbelief, but he was still having trouble breathing. Buffeted by a turbulent mixture of shock, joy, anger and something perilously close to panic, Will wasn't sure what he felt, other than totally unprepared for the sight of her.

Dimly, Will was aware that Roger was saying something,

but he couldn't hear it. He could just stare at Alice across the garden until, as if sensing his stunned gaze, she turned her head, and her smile froze at the sight of him.

There was a long, long pause when it seemed to Will as if the squawking birds and the shrieking children and the buzz of conversation all faded into a silence broken only by the erratic thump of his heart. He couldn't have moved if he had tried.

Then he saw Alice make an excuse to the man in the ghastly shirt and turn to walk across the garden towards him, apparently quite at ease in those ridiculous shoes, the dress floating around her legs.

She had always moved with a straight-backed, unconscious grace that had fascinated Will, and as he watched her he had the vertiginous feeling that time had ground to a halt and was rewinding faster and faster through the blur of the last ten years. So strong was the sensation that he was half-convinced that, by the time she reached him those long years would have vanished and they would both be back as they had been then, when they'd loved each other.

Will's mouth was dry as Alice hesitated for a fraction of a second at the bottom of the steps that led up to the decking, and then she was standing before him.

'Hello, Will,' she said.

CHAPTER TWO

'ALICE.' Will's throat was so constricted that her name was all he could manage.

Roger looked from one to the other, and took the easy way out. 'I'd better make sure everyone has a drink,' he said, although neither of them gave any sign that they had even heard him. 'I'll leave you two to catch up.'

Will stared at Alice, hardly able to believe that she was actually standing in front of him. His first stunned thought was that she hadn't changed at all. There were the same high cheekbones, the same golden eyes and slanting brows, the same wide mouth. The silky brown hair was even pulled carelessly away from her face just the way she had used to wear it as a student. She was the same!

But when he looked more closely, the illusion faded. She must be thirty-two now, ten years older than the way he remembered her, and it showed in the faint lines and the drawn look around her eyes. Her hairstyle might not have changed, but the quirky collection of dangly, ethnic earrings had been replaced by discreet pearl studs, and the comfortable boots by high heels and glamour.

Alice had never been beautiful. Her hair was too straight, her features too irregular, but she had possessed an innate stylishness and charm that had clearly matured into elegance and sophistication. She had become a poised, attractive woman.

But she wasn't the Alice he had loved. That Alice had been a vivid, astringent presence, prickly and insecure at times—but who wasn't, when they were young? When she'd talked, her whole body had become animated, and she would lean forward and gesticulate, her small hands swooping and darting in the air to emphasise her point, making the bangles she wore chink and jingle, or shaking her head so that her earrings swung wildly and caught the light.

Will had loved just to watch the way the expressions had chased themselves across her transparent face. It had always been easy to tell what Alice had been feeling. No one could look crosser than Alice when she was angry; no one else's face lit like hers when she was happy. And when she was amused, she would throw back her head and laugh that uninhibited, unexpectedly dirty laugh, the mere memory of which was enough to make his groin tighten.

Ironically, the very things that Will had treasured about her had been the things Alice was desperate to change. She hadn't wanted to be unconventional. She hadn't wanted to be different. She'd wanted to be like everyone else.

And now it looked as if she had got her wish. All that fire, all that quirkiness, all that personality…all gone. Firmly suppressed and locked away until she was as bland as the rest of the world.

It made Will very sad to realise that the Alice who had haunted him all these years didn't exist any more. In her place was just a smart, rather tense woman with unusual-coloured eyes and inappropriate shoes.

'How are you, Alice?' he managed after a moment.

Alice's feet were killing her, and her heart was thumping and thudding so painfully in her chest that it was making her feel quite sick, but she produced a brilliant smile.

'I'm fine,' she told him. 'Great, in fact. And you?'

'I'm OK,' said Will, who was, in fact, feeling very strange. He had been pitched from shock to joy to bitter disappointment in the space of little more than a minute, and he was finding it hard to keep up with the rapid change of emotions.

'Quite a surprise bumping into you here,' Alice persevered in the same brittle style, and he eyed her with dismay. When had the fiery, intent Alice learnt to do meaningless chit-chat? She was treating him as if he were some slight acquaintance, not a man she had lived with and laughed with and loved with.

'Yes,' he agreed slowly, thinking that 'surprise' wasn't quite the word for it. 'Beth didn't tell me that you were here.'

'I don't think she made any connection between us,' said Alice carelessly. 'It wouldn't have occurred to Beth to mention me to you. She didn't know that we'd been…'

'Lovers?' suggested Will with a sardonic look when she trailed off.

A slight flush rose in Alice's cheeks. 'I didn't put it quite like that,' she said repressively. 'I just said that we had been close when we were students together.'

'It's not like you to be coy, Alice.'

She looked at him sharply. 'What do you mean?'

'You and Roger were *close*,' said Will. 'You and I were in love.'

Alice's eyes slid away from his. She didn't want to be reminded of how much she had loved him. She certainly didn't want a discussion of how in love they had been. No way could she cope with that right now.

'Whatever,' she said as carelessly as she could. 'Beth got the point, anyway.'

He had changed, she thought, unaccountably disconsolate. Of course, she had known in her head that he wasn't going to be the same. Ten years, marriage and children were bound to have had an effect on him.

But in her heart she had imagined him still the Will she had known. The Will she had loved.

This Will seemed taller than she remembered, taller and tougher. His neck had thickened slightly and his chest had filled out, and the air of calm competence she had always associated with him had solidified. He still had those big, capable hands, but there was none of the amusement she remembered in his face, no familiar ironic gleam in the grey eyes. Instead, there were lines around his eyes and deeper grooves carved on either side of his mouth, which was set in a new, hard line.

It was strange, talking to someone at once so familiar and so much a stranger. Meeting Will like that was even worse than Alice had expected. She had planned to be friendly to him, charming to his wife and engaging to his child, so that they would all go away convinced that she had no regrets and without the slightest idea that her life wasn't quite the glittering success she had so confidently expected it to be.

She might as well have spared herself the effort, Alice thought ruefully. In spite of all her careful preparations, her confidence had evaporated the moment she'd laid eyes on him, and she was as shaken and jittery as if Will had turned up without a moment's warning. She knew that she was coming over as brittle, but she couldn't seem to do anything about it.

'Beth said that you were working out here,' she said, opting to stick with her social manner, no matter how uncomfortable it felt. It was easier than looking into his eyes and asking him if he had missed her at all, if he had wondered, as she had done, whether life would have been different if she had said yes instead of no that day.

Will nodded, apparently willing to follow her lead and stick to polite superficialities. 'I'm coordinating a major project on sustainable tourism,' he said, and Alice raised her brows.

'You're not a marine ecologist any more?' she asked, surprised. Will had always been so passionate about the ocean, she couldn't imagine him giving up diving in favour of paperwork.

'I am, of course,' he corrected her. 'But I don't do straight research anymore. A lot of our work is assessing the environmental impact of major development projects on the sea.'

Alice frowned. 'What's that got to do with tourism?'

'Tourism has a huge effect on the environment,' said Will. 'The economy here desperately needs the income tourists can bring, but tourists won't come unless there's an international airport, roads, hotels, restaurants and leisure facilities…all of which use up precious natural resources and add to the weight of pollution, which in turn affects the delicate balance of the environment.'

Will gestured around him. 'St Bonaventure is a paradise in lots of ways. It's everyone's idea of a tropical island, and it's still unspoilt. Its reef is one of the great undiscovered diving spots in the world. That makes it the kind of place tourists want to visit, but they won't come all this way if the development ends up destroying the very things that makes this place so special.

'The government here needs to balance their need to get the money to improve the living standards of the people here with the risk to the reef,' he went on. 'If the reef is damaged, it will not only destroy the potential revenue from tourism, it'll also leave the island itself at risk. The reef is the most effective protection St Bonaventure has against the power of the ocean.'

Will stopped, hearing himself in lecture mode. The old Alice might have been interested, but this one certainly wasn't. Instead of leaning forward intently and asking awkward questions, the way she would have done before, she wore an expression of interest that was little more than polite.

'Anyway, the project I'm coordinating is about balancing the needs of the reef with the needs of the economy before tourism is developed to any great extent,' he finished lamely.

'Sounds important,' Alice commented.

He glanced at her, as if suspecting mockery. 'It is,' he said.

Alice had deliberately kept her voice light to disguise the pang inside. For a moment there he had been the Will she remembered, his face alight with enthusiasm, his eyes warm with commitment.

What would it be like to work on something you believed in, something that really mattered, not just to you but to other people as well? Alice wondered. When it boiled down to it, her own career in market research was just about making money. It hadn't changed any lives other than her own.

That had never bothered her before, but she had had to question a lot of things about her life in the last year. What did her much-vaunted career amount to now, after all? Nothing, thought Alice bleakly.

Will had built his career on his expertise and his passion. He had done what he wanted the way he'd wanted to do it. He had found someone to share his life and had fathered a child. His life since Roger's wedding had been successful by any measure, while hers... Well, better not go there, Alice decided with an inward sigh.

'What about you?' Will asked, breaking into her thoughts and making her start.

'Me?'

'What are you doing on St Bonaventure?'

Alice wished she could say that she was here for some interesting or meaningful reason. 'I'm on holiday,' she confessed, immediately feeling guilty about it.

'So you'll just be here a couple of weeks?'

She was sure she detected relief in his voice. He was

probably delighted at the idea that she wouldn't be around for long so that he could get on with his happy, successful, *married* life without her.

The thought stiffened Alice's resolve not to let Will so much as guess that all her careful plans had come to nothing. It wasn't that she begrudged him his happiness, but a girl had her pride. She needed to convince him that she had never had a moment's regret. She wouldn't lie—that would be pathetic, obviously—but there was no reason why she shouldn't put a positive slant on things, was there?

'Actually,' she said, 'I'm here for six weeks.'

He lifted one brow in a way that Alice had often longed to be able to do. 'Long holiday,' he commented.

'I'm lucky, aren't I?' she agreed with a cool smile. 'Roger and Beth have been telling me I should come and visit ever since they were posted here last year, but I just haven't had the opportunity until now.'

Redundancy could be seen as an opportunity, couldn't it?

'You must have done well for yourself,' said Will. 'Not many people get the opportunity for a six-week holiday.'

'It's not strictly a holiday,' Alice conceded. 'As it happens, I'm between jobs at the moment,' she explained, tilting her chin slightly.

That wasn't a lie, either. She might not have another job lined up just yet, but when she went home she was determined that she was not only going to get her career back on track, but that she would be moving onto to bigger and better things. With her experience, there was no reason why she shouldn't aim for a more prestigious company, a promotion *and* a pay raise.

'I see,' said Will, his expression so non-committal that Alice was afraid that he saw only too well. He had no doubt interpreted being 'between jobs' as unemployed, which of course was another way of looking at it, but not one Alice was prepared to dwell on.

'I was in a very pressurised work environment,' she told him loftily. 'And I thought it was time to take a break and reassess where my career was going.'

Strictly speaking, of course, it had been the company who had taken over PLMR who had decided that Alice could have all the time she wanted to think about things, but Will didn't need to know that. It wasn't as if it had been her fault. Almost all her colleagues had been made redundant at the same time, she reminded herself. It could happen to anyone these days.

'Market research—it *is* market research, isn't it?—obviously pays well if you can afford six weeks somewhere like this when you're between jobs,' said Will, with just a hint of snideness. 'But then, you always wanted to make money, didn't you?'

'I wanted to be secure,' said Alice, hating the faintly defensive note in her voice. 'And I am.' What was wrong with wanting security? 'I wanted to be successful, and I am,' she added for good measure.

Well, she had been until last year, but, when your company was the subject of a hostile takeover, there wasn't much you could do about it, no matter how good you were at your job.

It hadn't been a good year. Her only lucky break had been winning nearly two thousand pounds in the lottery, and that had been a fluke. Normally, Alice wouldn't even have thought about buying a ticket, but she had been in a mood when she was prepared to try anything to change the dreary trend of her life.

It wasn't as if she had won millions. Two thousand pounds wasn't enough to change her life, but it was just enough for a ticket to an out-of-the-way place like St Bonaventure, and Alice had taken it as a sign. At any other time, she would have been sensible. She would have bought herself a pair of shoes and put the rest of the money towards some much-needed repairs on her flat—the unexpected windfall would have covered the cost of a new boiler, for instance—but that hadn't been any other time. That had been the day she heard that Tony and Sandi were getting married.

Alice had gone straight out and bought a plane ticket. *And* some shoes.

Still, there was no harm in letting Will think that she had earned so much money that she didn't know what to do with it all. Not that it would impress him. He was more likely to disapprove of what he thought of as her materialistic lifestyle, but Alice was desperate for him to believe that she had made it.

'We all make choices,' she reminded him. 'I made mine, and I don't have any regrets,'

'I'm glad you got what you wanted, then,' said Will flatly.

'You too,' said Alice, and for a jarring moment their eyes met. It was as if the polite mask they both wore dropped for an instant, and they saw each other properly for the first time. The sense of recognition was like a blow to Alice's stomach, pushing the air from her lungs and leaving her breathless and giddy and almost nauseous.

But then Will jerked his head away, the guarded expression clanging back into place with such finality that Alice wondered if she had imagined that look.

'You didn't marry Clive, then?' he asked abruptly.

'Clive?' Alice was thrown by the sudden change of subject.

'The Clive you were so in love with at Roger and Beth's wedding,' Will reminded her with an edge of savagery. 'Don't tell me you've forgotten him!'

'I didn't—' Alice opened her mouth to strenuously deny ever loving Clive and then shut it again. If she hadn't loved Clive, why had she let Will believe that she did? Why hadn't she been able to tell him the truth that day?

'No, I didn't marry Clive,' she said quietly. 'We split up soon after…after Roger's wedding,' she finished after a tiny moment of hesitation.

She had so nearly said 'after you kissed me', and she might as well have done. The memory of that dark night in the hotel gardens jangled in the air between them. Those desperate kisses, the spiralling excitement, the sense of utter rightness at being back in each other's arms.

The tightness around her heart as she'd watched him walk away.

Alice could feel them all as vividly as if they had kissed the night before.

Will had to be remembering those kisses too. She wanted to be able to talk about it, laugh about it even, pretend that it didn't matter and it was all in the past, but she couldn't. Not yet.

So she drew a steadying breath and summoned another of her bright smiles. 'Then I met Tony, and we were together for four years. We talked about getting married, but…well, we decided it wouldn't have worked.'

Tony had decided that, anyway.

'We stopped ourselves making a terrible mistake just in time,' Alice finished.

OK, it might not be the whole story, but why should she tell Will all her sad secrets? Anyway, it might not be the *whole* truth, but it *was* the truth. It *would* have been a mistake if she and Tony had gone ahead with the wedding. Nothing but unhappiness would have come from their marriage when Tony was in love with someone else. Alice's world might have fallen apart the day Tony had sat her down to tell her about Sandi, but she'd accepted even then that he had done the right thing.

Today was Tony and Sandi's wedding day, Alice was startled to remember. She had spent so long dreading this day, imagining how hard it would be for her to think about another woman taking what should have been her place, and, now that it was here, she hadn't even thought about it.

Perhaps she ought to be grateful to Will for distracting her?

Will drained the last of his beer and turned aside to put the empty bottle on the decking rail. 'Still avoiding commitment, I see,' he commented with a sardonic glance over his shoulder at Alice, who flushed at the injustice of it.

She wasn't the one who had called off the wedding. If it had been down to her, she would be happily married to Tony right now, but she bit back the words. She had just convinced him that ending her engagement to Tony had been a mutual decision, so she could hardly tell him the truth now.

Which was worse? That he thought she was afraid of commitment, or that he felt sorry for her?

No question.

'Still determined not to get married until I'm absolutely sure it's perfect,' she corrected Will. 'So…I'm fancy free, and on the lookout for Mr Right. I'm not going to get married until I've found him, and, until then I'm just having fun!'

Will was unimpressed by her bravado. 'You seem very tense for someone who's having fun,' he said.

Alice gritted her teeth. 'I am *not* tense,' she snapped. Tensely, in fact. 'I'm a bit jet-lagged, that's all. I only got here a couple of days ago.'

'Ah,' said Will, not bothering to hide the fact that he was totally unconvinced by her explanation. Which just made Alice even crosser, but she sucked in her breath and resisted the temptation to retort in kind. She didn't want Will to think that he was getting to her, or that she cared in the slightest what he thought of her.

Friendly but unobtainable, wasn't that how she wanted him to think of her? Pleasant but cool. His long-lost love who had turned into a mysterious stranger. Anything but sad and tense and a failure.

She fixed a smile to her face. 'I gather you weren't as hesitant about taking the plunge,' she said.

'The plunge?'

'Marriage,' she reminded him sweetly, and a strange expression flitted over his face.

'Ah. Yes. I did get married,' he agreed. 'Why? Did you think I would never get over you?'

'Of course not,' said Alice with dignity. 'If I thought about you at all—which I can't say was that often—' she added crushingly, 'it was only to hope that you were happy.'

Will raised his brows in disbelief. 'Really?'

'Yes, really.' Alice had been nursing a glass of Roger's lethal tropical punch, but it didn't seem to be having a very good effect on her. She set it on the rail next to Will's empty bottle.

'*Have* you been happy?' she asked him, the words out of her mouth before she had thought about them properly.

Will didn't answer immediately. He thought about Lily, about how it had felt when he had held his daughter in his arms for the first time. About drifting along the reef, fish flitting past him in flashes of iridescent colour and looking up to see the sunlight filtering down through the water to the deep blue silence. About sitting on a boat and watching dolphins curving and cresting in the foamy wake, while the water glittered and the sea breeze lifted his hair.

He had been happy then. It hadn't been the same feeling as the happiness he had felt lying next to Alice after they had made love, holding her into the curve of his body, smoothing his hand over her soft skin, breathing in her fragrance, marvelling that this quirky, contrary, vibrant woman was really his, but, still, he *had* been happy since.

In a different way, but, yes, he'd been happy.

'I've had times of great happiness,' he said eventually, very conscious of Alice's great golden eyes on his face. 'But not in my marriage,' he found himself admitting. 'We weren't as sensible as you. We didn't realise what a mistake we were making until it was too late.'

It had been his fault, really. He had vowed to move on after Roger's wedding, had been determined to put Alice from his mind once and for all. The trouble was that every woman he'd met had seemed dull and somehow colourless after Alice. They might have been prettier and nicer, and certainly sweeter, but, when he'd closed his eyes, it had always been Alice's blazing golden eyes that he saw, always Alice's voice that he heard, always Alice's skin that he tasted.

Nikki had been the first woman with the strength of personality to match Alice's, and Will had persuaded himself that she was capable of banishing Alice's ghost once and for all. They had married after a whirlwind holiday romance in the Red Sea where he had been researching at the time.

It had been madness to take such a step when they'd barely known each other. Will should have known that it would end in disaster. Because Nikki hadn't been Alice. She had been forceful rather than colourful, efficient rather than intense. The only thing the two women had shared, as far as Will could see, was a determination to make a success of themselves.

Nikki, it had turned out too late, had had no intention of wasting her life in the kind of countries where Will felt most at home. 'My career's at home,' she had told him. 'There's nothing for me to do here, nothing works, and, if you think I'm having the baby in that hospital, you've got another think coming!'

Lily was the result of a failed attempt to make the marriage work. She'd been born in London, just as Nikki had planned, but by then Nikki had already sued for divorce. 'It's never going to work, Will,' she'd told him when he came to see his new daughter. 'Let's just accept it now rather than waste any more time.'

'We were married less than two years,' he told Alice.

'So you're divorced?' she said, horrified at the instinctive lightening of her heart, and ashamed of herself for feeling even a smidgeon of relief that his life hadn't turned out quite as perfectly as it had seemed at first.

And that she wouldn't have to face his wife after all. Although she wished now that she hadn't said that about 'looking for Mr Right'. She didn't want Will thinking that she would try and pick up where they had left off the moment she realised that he was single.

'I'm sorry,' she said, when he nodded curtly. 'I didn't realise. Beth said that you had your family with you, so we just assumed that you were married.'

'No, it's just me and Lily,' he said. 'My daughter,' he added in explanation. 'She's six.'

'Is she spending the holiday with you?' Alice didn't have much to do with children, and was a bit vague about school terms, but she supposed mid-March might conceivably mean the Easter holidays. It seemed a bit early, though. Perhaps it didn't matter so much for six-year-olds?

'No, she lives with me,' said Will, almost reluctantly.

'Oh? That's unusual, isn't it?' Alice looked surprised. 'Doesn't the mother usually have custody?'

'Nikki did,' he said. 'She died recently, so now Lily only has me.'

'God, how awful!' Alice was shocked out of her cool pose, and Will was absurdly pleased to see the genuine compassion in her eyes. He had been wondering if there was anything left of the old Alice at all. 'What happened? Or maybe you don't want to talk about it?' she added contritely.

'No, it's OK. People are going to have to know, and obviously it's difficult to explain in front of Lily.' Will sighed. 'That's why I couldn't tell Beth when we met her in the supermarket. Lily is finding it hard enough to adjust without hearing the whole story talked over with perfect strangers.'

'I can imagine.'

'Lily used to go to the after-school club, and Nikki would pick her up after work. But that day there had apparently been some meeting that had run on, so she was going to be very late at the school. They'd warned her before about being late, so she was rushing to get there, and I suppose she wasn't driving as carefully as she should …'

'A car accident?' said Alice when he trailed off with a sigh.

'She was killed instantly, they said.' Will nodded, and Alice wondered just how much his ex-wife still meant to him. You could say that the marriage had been a mistake, but they had had a child together. He must have had some feelings still for Lily's mother.

'Meanwhile, Lily is still waiting for her mother to come and pick her up?' she said gently.

Will shot her a curious look, as if surprised by her understanding. 'I think she must be. She hasn't talked about it, and she's such a quiet little girl anyway, it's hard to know how much she understands.'

He looked so tired suddenly that Alice felt guilty for being so brittle and defensive earlier. 'It must have been a shock for you, too,' she said after a moment.

Will shrugged his own feelings aside. 'I was in Honduras when I heard. It took them some time to track me down, so I missed the immediate aftermath. I wasn't there for Lily,' he added, and, from the undercurrent of bitterness in his voice, Alice guessed he flayed himself with that knowledge.

'You weren't to know,' she said in a deliberately practical voice. 'What happened to Lily?'

'Nikki's parents live nearby so the school called them when she didn't turn up, and they looked after Lily until I got there. My work's kept me overseas for the last few years, though, and I haven't had the chance to see her very often, so I'm virtually a stranger to her.' Will ran his fingers through his hair in a gesture of defeat. 'To be honest, it's all been a bit…difficult.'

Difficult? Alice thought about his small daughter. Lily was six, he had said. What would it be like to have the centre of your world disappear without warning, and to be handed over instead to a father you hardly knew? Alice's heart was wrung. Her own parents had been dippy and unreliable in lots of ways, but at least they had always been there.

'When did all this happen?' she asked.

'Seven weeks ago.'

'Seven *weeks*? Is that all?' Alice looked at Will incredulously, her sympathy evaporating. 'What are you doing out here?'

Will narrowed his eyes at her tone. 'My job,' he said in a hard voice. 'I've already delayed the project by over a month.'

'You shouldn't be thinking about your *job*,' said Alice with a withering look. 'You should be thinking about your daughter!'

'I am thinking about her.' Will set his teeth and told himself he wasn't going to let Alice rile him. 'I'm hoping that the change of scene will help her.'

He couldn't have said anything more calculated to catch Alice on the raw. His casual assumption that a change of scene could only be good for a child reminded her all too painfully of the way her own parents had blithely uprooted her just when she had settled down in a new country and started to feel at home.

'We're off to Guyana,' they had announced gaily. 'You'll love it!'

After Guyana, they had spent a year on a croft in the Hebrides. 'It'll be good for you,' her father had decided. Then it had been Sri Lanka— 'Won't it be exciting?'—followed by Morocco, Indonesia, Exmoor (a disaster) and Goa, although Alice had lost track of the order they had come in.

'You're so lucky,' everyone had told her when she had been growing up. 'You've seen so much of the world and had such wonderful experiences.'

But Alice hadn't felt lucky. She hadn't wanted any more new experiences. She had longed to settle down and feel at home, instead of being continually overwhelmed by strange new sights and sounds, smells and people.

And she hadn't had the loss of a mother to deal with at the same time. Alice's heart went out to Will's daughter.

Poor Lily. Poor little girl.

CHAPTER THREE

'YOU don't think it would have helped her more to stay in familiar surroundings?' Alice asked Will sharply, too irritated by his apparent disregard for his daughter to think about the fact that it was probably none of her business.

A muscle was twitching in Will's jaw. 'Her grandparents offered to look after her,' he admitted. 'But they're getting on. Besides, we all thought that it would be easier for Lily to start a new life without continual painful reminders of her mother. She's going to have to get used to living with me some time, so it's better that she does that sooner rather than later.'

His careful arguments were just making Alice crosser. 'Why couldn't *you* get used to doing a job that meant you could stay where Lily would feel at home?' she demanded.

'There's not a lot of work for marine ecologists in London!'

'You could change your job.'

'And do what?' asked Will, stung by her tone, and annoyed with letting himself be drawn into an argument with Alice, who was typically holding forth on a subject she knew little about.

Her brittleness had vanished, and she was vivid once more, her cheeks flushed and her tawny eyes flashing as she waved her arms around to prove her point. Suddenly, she was the

Alice he remembered, and Will was simultaneously delighted and exasperated.

It was an uncannily familiar feeling, he thought, not knowing whether he wanted to shake her or catch her into his arms. The rush of joy he felt at realising that the real Alice was still there was tempered by resentment of her unerring ability to home in on the very issue he felt most guilty about. He wouldn't have minded if they'd been arguing about something unimportant, but this was his daughter they were discussing. Will was desperate to be a good father, and he didn't need Alice pointing out exactly where he was going wrong five minutes after meeting him again.

'Marine ecology is all I know,' he tried to explain. 'I have to support my child financially as well as emotionally, and the best way I can do that is by sticking with the career that I know rather than launching wildly into some new one where I'd have to start at the beginning. Besides,' he went on as Alice looked profoundly unconvinced. 'Lily isn't my only responsibility. This project has taken five years to set up, and a lot of futures depend on it being successful. Of course Lily is important, but I've got responsibilities to other people as well. That's just the way things are, and Lily's going to have to get used to it.'

'That's an incredibly selfish attitude,' said Alice, twirling her hand dramatically so that she could poke her finger towards Will's chest. 'It's all about what suits *you*, isn't it? All about what *you* need. What about what *Lily* needs?'

'I'm her father,' said Will tersely. 'Lily needs to be with me.'

'I'd agree with you, if being with you meant staying in a home she knew, with her grandparents and her friends and her routines.'

Alice knew that it wasn't really her business, but Will's complacency infuriated her. 'Losing a mother would be hard enough for her to deal with even if she had those things to hang on to, but you've dragged her across the world to a strange country, a place where she doesn't know anyone or anything, and by your own admission she doesn't even know you very well!'

She drew an impatient breath. 'Did you ever think of asking Lily what *she* wanted to do?'

'Lily's six.' Will bit out the words, too angry by now to care whether Alice knew how effectively she was winding him up. 'She's not old enough to make an informed decision about anything, let alone where she wants to live. She's just a little girl. How can she possibly judge what's best for her?'

'She's old enough to know where she feels comfortable and who she feels safe with,' Alice retorted.

Will gritted his teeth. Her comments were like a dentist drilling on a raw nerve. Did she really think he didn't feel guilty enough already about Lily? He hated the fact that he was practically a stranger to his own daughter. He *hated* the fact that Lily was lost and unhappy and he seemed powerless to help her. He was doing the best that he could, and, yes, maybe it wasn't good enough, but he didn't need Alice to point that out.

That brief surge of joy he had felt at her transformation from a brittle nonentity into the vibrant, fiery creature he remembered was submerged beneath a wave of resentment, and he eyed her with dislike.

'I thought you'd changed, Alice,' he said. 'But you haven't, have you?'

She tilted her chin at him in a characteristically combative gesture. 'What do you mean?'

'You still hold forth about subjects you know absolutely nothing about,' he said cuttingly. 'You know nothing about my daughter, nothing about the situation and nothing about me, now, but that doesn't stop you, does it?'

He gave a harsh laugh. 'You know, I used to think it was quite amusing the way you used to base your opinions on nothing more than instinct and emotion. For someone so obsessed with fitting things into neat categories, it always seemed odd that you refused to look at the evidence before you made up your mind. But I don't think it's very funny anymore,' he went on. 'It's pointless and narrow-minded. Perhaps, just once, you should try finding out the facts before you open your mouth and start spouting your personal prejudice!'

There was a stricken look in Alice's golden eyes but Will swept on, too angry to let himself notice and feel bad about it.

He was fed up. It had been a hellish seven weeks. He was worried sick about his daughter, and he had a daunting task ahead to get a complex but incredibly important project off the ground. The last thing he needed was the inevitable turmoil of dealing with Alice.

This was typical of her. Time and again over the last eight years, Will had told himself that he was over her. That he was getting on with his life. That he wouldn't want her even if he *did* meet her again. And then he would catch a glimpse of a straight back through a crowd, or hear a dirty laugh at a party, and his heart would jerk, and he would feel sick with disappointment to realise that it wasn't Alice after all.

And now—*now* when he had so much else to deal with— here she was, with characteristically perverse timing, threatening to turn his world upside down just when he least needed it!

Well, this time it wasn't going to turn upside down, Will determined. He had wasted the last ten years of his life getting over Alice, and he wasn't going to waste another ten minutes. It was just as well that they had come face to face, he decided. It had reminded him of all the things about her that had used to irritate him, and that made it so much easier to walk away this time.

'You know, I could stand here and pontificate to you if I could be bothered,' he told Alice, his words like a lash. 'I could tell you that you've thrown away everything that was warm and special about you, and turned yourself into someone brittle and superficial with dull earrings and silly shoes, but I won't because, unlike you, I don't believe in passing judgement on people I've only met for five minutes!'

Alice only just prevented herself from flinching at his tone. She had no intention of showing Will how hard his words had struck home. She managed an artificial laugh instead, knowing that she sounded just as brittle as he had accused her of being.

'You've got a short memory, if you think we've only known each other for five minutes!'

'You're not the Alice I knew,' said Will in the same, hard voice. 'I liked her. I don't like you. But that doesn't give me the right to tell you how to live your life, so don't tell me how to live mine. Now, if you'll excuse me, I'll go and find the daughter you seem to think I care so little about before you accuse me of neglect.'

And, with that, he turned and headed down the steps towards the pool, leaving Alice alone on the decking, white with fury mixed with a sickening sense of guilt. She shouldn't have said all that about his daughter. Will was right, she *didn't* know the situation, and she had probably been unfair. She had let the bottled-up resentment about her own childhood get the better of her. She should apologise.

But not yet.

I don't like you. Will's bitter words jangled in the air as if he had shouted them out loud. Alice felt ridiculously conspicuous, sure that everyone had heard and everyone was looking at her. They were probably all thinking that they didn't like her either, she thought miserably

Her throat was tight with tears that she refused to shed. She hadn't let anyone see her cry about Tony, so she certainly wasn't about to start blubbing over Will. She didn't care if he didn't like her. She didn't care what he thought. She didn't care about anything.

'You haven't got a drink, Alice.' Roger materialised beside her. 'Is everything OK?'

Roger. Alice nearly did cry then. Dear Roger, her dearest friend. The only one she could rely on through thick and thin.

She blinked fiercely. 'You like me, don't you, Roger?'

'Oh, you're all right, I suppose,' said Roger with mock nonchalance, but he put his arms round her and hugged her close. 'What's the matter?' he asked in a different tone.

'Nothing,' said Alice, muffled against his chest.

'Come on, it's just me. Was it seeing Will again?'

Alice drew a shuddering breath. 'He's changed,' she muttered.

'We've all changed,' said Roger gently.

'You haven't.' She lifted her head and looked up into his dear, familiar face. She had met Roger on her first day at university, and they had been best friends ever since. For Alice, he was the brother she had never had, and not Beth, not even Will, had come between them. 'That's why I love you,' she said with a wobbly smile.

Roger pretended to look alarmed. 'An open declaration of affection! This isn't like you, Alice. You *are* upset!'

'Only because Will was rude about my shoes,' said Alice, tilting her chin. 'They're not silly, are they, Roger?'

Straight-faced, Roger studied the delicate sandals, decorated with sequins and blue butterflies. 'They're fabulous,' he told her. 'Just like you. Now, come and have another drink before we both get maudlin and I tell you I love you too!'

'All right.' Alice took a deep breath and steadied her smile. 'But only if you introduce me to all these single men Beth promised me,' she said, determined to put Will Paxman right out of her mind. 'And not that guy in the awful shirt with the per-spiration problem,' she added, following Roger into the kitchen.

'Colin,' said Roger, nodding knowledgeably as he handed her another glass of punch. 'No, we'll see if we can do better for you than that!'

He was as good as his word, and Alice soon found herself the centre of a circle of admiring men, all much more attractive and entertaining than the hapless Colin. Alice was under no illusions about her own looks, but she appreciated that, living in a small expatriate community with a limited social life, these men would be interested in any single, available female, and she did her best to sparkle and live up to the reputation Beth had evidently created for her. But it was hard when all the time she was aware of Will's dark, glowering presence over by the pool.

Alice turned her back pointedly, but it didn't make much difference. She could practically feel his cold grey eyes boring into her spine, and the thought made her shiver slightly and take a gulp of her punch.

Why was he bothering to watch her, anyway? There were no shortage of women simpering up at him by the pool, all of them wearing shoes and lipstick and apparently indulging in small talk. Alice was prepared to concede that she might be wrong, but none of them gave the impression of being intellectual giants. How come Will didn't find *them* prickly and false?

Defiantly, Alice emptied her glass and let someone whose name she had already forgotten rush off to get her a refill. If Will thought her brittle and superficial, superficial and brittle she would be!

Flirting was not something that came naturally to her but it was amazing what she could do when glacial grey eyes were watching her with open disapproval. What right had Will Paxman to disapprove of her, anyway? She was just being sociable, which was more than he was doing, and she was damned if she was going to skulk away to the kitchen just because he didn't like her.

So she smiled and laughed and made great play with her eyelashes while she shifted her weight surreptitiously from foot to foot to try and relieve the pressure from her shoes, which might look fabulous but which were, in truth, becoming increasingly uncomfortable. Not that Alice would ever have admitted as much to Will.

The tropical sun combined with Roger's punch was giving her a thumping headache, and Alice's bright smile grew more and more fixed as she concentrated on being fun and ignoring Will. Still, she was doing all right until someone mentioned honeymoons and suddenly she remembered that today was Tony's wedding day.

All at once Alice's bottled-up misery burst through its dam and hit her with such force that she only just managed to stop herself doubling over as if from a blow. The pain and anger and humiliation she had felt when Tony had left her for Sandi was mixed up now with a nauseating concoction of shock, regret, guilt and hurt at Will's reaction to meeting her again after all this time.

Not to mention an excess of Roger's punch.

Unable to keep up the façade any longer, Alice murmured an excuse about finding a hat and headed blindly for the house. At least there it would be cool.

And full of people. She hesitated at the bottom of the steps leading up to the decking. The large, airy living area would be packed with people enjoying the air conditioning and someone would be bound to see her sneak off to her room. The next thing Beth would be there, knocking on the door, wanting to know what was wrong.

Changing her mind, Alice glanced over her shoulder to

make sure that Will wasn't watching her, and realised that she couldn't see him. All that time she had spent simultaneously ignoring him and trying to convince him that she was having the best time of her life, and he hadn't even been there!

Humiliation closed around her throat like a fist. She had been so sure that he was watching her—he *had* been at first!—and now the idea that he had got bored and gone off while she'd been still desperately performing for his benefit made her feel an idiot. No, worse than an idiot. *Pathetic*.

Close to tears, Alice slipped unnoticed along the side of the house and ducked beneath an arch laden with a magnificent display of bougainvillaea that divided the perfectly mani-cured front garden from a shady and scrubby patch of ground at the back behind the kitchen and servants' quarters.

Beth had a maid to help with the housework, a smiling woman called Chantelle, and this was her domain. There were wooden steps leading down from the kitchen verandah where she would sit sometimes, her fingers busy with some mindless task while she sang quietly to herself. Alice wouldn't normally have intruded, but Chantelle, she knew, was busy clearing up after the barbecue lunch, and Alice didn't think she would mind if she sat there for a little while on her own.

The garden here was blissfully shady and overgrown, so dark that Alice was almost at the steps before she realised that she was not the only person needing some time alone. A little girl was sitting on the bottom step, half-hidden in the shadow of a banana tree. Her knees were drawn up to her chin, and she hugged them to her, keeping very still as she watched a butterfly with improbably large iridescent blue wings come to rest on her shoe.

Alice stopped as soon as she saw them, but the butterfly had already taken off and was flapping languidly in and out of the patches of sunlight. The child spotted her at the same time, and she seemed to freeze. Alice was reminded of a small, wary animal trying to make up its mind whether to bolt for cover or not.

She was sorry that she had interrupted, but it seemed rude to turn on her heel and walk off without saying anything. Besides, there was something very familiar about the scene. Alice couldn't work out what it was at first, but then she realised that the little girl reminded her of herself as a lonely, uncertain child.

'I'm sorry, I didn't mean to disturb you, or the butterfly. I was just looking for somewhere quiet to sit for a while.' She paused, but the little girl just looked guardedly at her, still poised for flight.

She wasn't a particularly pretty child. She had straight, shapeless hair and a pinched little face dominated by a pair of huge, solemn dark eyes. Her expression was distrustful, but Alice was conscious of a pang of fellow feeling.

How many times had she slipped off to find a place to hide while she'd waited for her parents to take her back to wherever they were calling home at the time? This child's parents were probably having a great time by the pool, totally oblivious to the fact that their daughter had slipped away, intimidated by the other children who were noisy and boisterous and seemed to be able to make friends without even trying.

'I wanted to escape from the party for a bit,' Alice explained. 'It's too noisy and I didn't know anyone to talk to properly. Is that what you did?' she asked as the girl glanced sharply at her.

The child nodded.

'The thing is, I don't want to go back yet,' said Alice. 'And I can't think of anywhere else to hide. Do you mind if I sit next to you, just for a little while? I won't talk if you don't want to. I hate it when people talk to me when I'm trying to be quiet.'

There was a flash of recognition in the girl's watchful eyes, and, while she didn't exactly agree, she didn't say no either, and as Alice went over she shifted along the step to make room for her. Encouraged, Alice settled next to her, drawing her knees up to mirror the child's posture.

A strangely companionable silence settled round them. In the distance, Alice could hear the buzz of party conversation, punctuated by the occasional burst of laughter, and the squeals and shrieks and splashes from the pool, but they seemed to be coming from a long way away, far from the dark, drowsy green world of the kitchen garden where there was only the squawk of a passing raucous bird and the low-level hum of insects to break the hot quiet.

She was glad of the chance to settle her nerves. Meeting Will again had left her jangled and distressed, and it was hard to disentangle her feelings about him from all the hurt and confusion she had felt since Tony had left. Between them, they had left her feeling utterly wretched.

If only she could rewind time and do things differently, this afternoon at least, Alice thought miserably. Seeing Will hadn't been at all the way she had imagined. *He* wasn't the man she had imagined him to be. If she had become brittle and superficial, he had grown hard and bitter. The young man with the humorous eyes and the reassuring steadiness had gone for good. Now that she knew what he had become, she couldn't even dream of him the way he had been.

The realisation that the Will she had loved was lost for ever felt like a bereavement. Alice's throat worked, and she pressed her lips hard together to stop herself crying.

There was no point in this, she told herself. She was upset because it was Tony's wedding day, but that was no excuse. She had behaved badly. She had been defensive and unsympathetic and rude. No wonder Will hadn't liked her. Now he had obviously left the party without saying goodbye, and she might not have another chance to say that she was sorry.

It was no use trying to tell herself that she didn't care. Here in the quiet garden with her restful companion she could acknowledge that she did.

'There's the butterfly again.' The little girl broke the silence in hushed tones, and they both sat very still as the butterfly alighted on an upturned bucket. It was so big that it seemed almost clumsy, its wings so heavy that it blundered from perch to perch, flapping slowly through the hot air as if barely able to keep itself aloft.

The child's eyes were huge as she watched it. 'I've never seen such a big butterfly before!'

She obviously hadn't been on the island that long, Alice reflected, although she could probably have told that anyway from her pale skin.

'When I was a little girl I lived in Guyana,' Alice said. 'That's in South America, and it was hot and humid, like this. Our house was on the edge of the jungle, and the garden was full of butterflies—blue ones and green ones and yellow ones, and butterflies with stripes and spots and weird patterns. Some of them were enormous.'

'Bigger than that one?'

'Much bigger.' Alice spread out her fingers to demonstrate the wing span. 'Like this.'

The girl's eyes widened further as she looked from the butterfly to Alice's hand and back again, clearly trying to imagine a garden full of such creatures.

'It must have been pretty,' she commented.

'They were beautiful,' Alice remembered almost in surprise. Funny, she hadn't thought about the garden in Guyana for years. 'I used to sit on the verandah steps, just like we're doing now, and watch them for hours.'

The little girl looked solemn. 'Didn't you have any friends?'

'Not then,' said Alice. 'It was very isolated where we lived, and I didn't know many other children. I used to pretend that the butterflies were my friends.'

How odd to remember that now, after all these years! She smiled, not unkindly, at her younger self.

'I imagined that they were fairies in disguise,' she confided to her small companion. It was strange how she felt more comfortable sitting here with the child than she had in the thick of a party thrown especially for her. Alice had never been a particularly maternal type, but she felt a strong sense of affinity with this quiet, plain little girl with her dark, wary eyes.

'Fairies?' the child breathed, riveted.

'At night I thought their beautiful wings would turn into silk robes and gorgeously coloured dresses.' Somehow it didn't sound silly in this dark, tropical garden. 'You know the sound the insects make when it's dark here?'

The girl nodded but her mouth turned down slightly. 'I don't like it. It's loud.'

'It was loud in Guyana, too,' said Alice. 'I used to think it was frightening, and then my father told me one night that it was just the sound of all the insects having a great party!'

Her father had been good at nonsense like that. He'd told the young Alice extravagant stories, embellishing them until they were more and more absurd, and she had struggled to know how much to believe. She ought to remember the good times more often, Alice thought with a sudden pang. It wasn't often that she thought of her childhood with affection, but it hadn't been all bad.

'So after that, whenever I couldn't sleep because it was too hot, I'd lie there listening to the noise and imagine the butter-flies talking and laughing and dancing all night.'

She laughed softly, but the little girl looked struck. 'I was a bit frightened by the noise too,' she confessed. 'But now I'll think about them having a party like you said, and it won't seem so strange.'

'You'll soon get used to it,' Alice reassured her, and then nudged her, pointing silently as the butterfly came lumbering through the air towards them again. They both held their breath as it came closer and closer, fluttering indecisively for what seemed like ages before it settled at last on Alice's foot.

The child's eyes widened in delight as she noticed for the first time that Alice's shoes were decorated with tiny fabric butterflies, their beads and sequins catching the light, and she put a hand to her mouth to smother a giggle.

'He likes your shoes,' she whispered. 'Do you think he knows those butterflies aren't real?'

Alice considered. 'I'm not sure. Probably not. He doesn't look like a very clever butterfly, does he?'

A laugh escaped through the rather grubby little fingers, rousing the butterfly to flight once more, but Alice didn't mind. It was such a pleasure to see the small, serious face lighten with a real smile. She guessed it didn't happen very often and her heart constricted with a kind of pity. A little girl like this should be laughing and smiling all the time.

'I like your shoes,' she said to Alice, who stretched out her legs so that they could both admire them.

'*I* like them too,' she agreed. 'But somebody told me today that they were silly.' Her face darkened as she remembered Will's comment.

'I don't think they're stupid. I think they're really nice.'

'Well, thank you.' Alice was ridiculously heartened by her approval. She peered down at the small feet next to her. 'What are yours like?'

'They're just shoes,' the child said without enthusiasm.

Alice could see what she meant. She was wearing sturdy

leather sandals which were perfectly practical but lacked any sense of fun or fashion.

'When I was little I wanted a pair of pink shoes,' she said sympathetically. 'I asked my parents for years, but I never got them.'

'I'd like pink shoes too, but my dad says these are more sensible.' The little girl sighed.

'Dads don't understand about shoes,' Alice told her. 'Very few men do. But, when you grow up, you'll be able to buy any shoes you want. I bought a pair of lovely pink shoes as soon as I was earning my own money. Now I've got lots of shoes in different colours. Some of them are lots of fun. I've got shoes with polka dots and zebra stripes,' she said, illustrating the patterns by drawing in the air. 'Some of them have got sequins, or bows, or fancy jewels or—'

'*Jewels?*' she interrupted, starry-eyed. 'Real ones?'

'Well, no, not *exactly*,' Alice had to admit. 'But they look fabulous!'

The child heaved an envious sigh. 'I wish I could see them.'

Alice opened her mouth to offer a view of the collection she had brought with her, but before she could ask the little girl her name a voice behind them made them both jump.

'Lily?'

Will stepped out of the kitchen onto the wooden verandah, letting the screen door bang into place behind him. He had been looking for his daughter everywhere.

Unable to bear the sight of Alice flirting any longer, he had been avoiding the front lawn, and had endured instead a tedious half-hour making small talk in the air-conditioned coolness of the living room. Only when he'd thought that he could reasonably make an excuse and leave had he realised that Lily was not among the children around the pool where he had left her.

Since then he had been searching with rising panic, flaying

himself for ever taking his eyes off her in the first place, and now acute relief at finding her safe sharpened his voice.

'What do you think you're—'

He stopped abruptly as he reached the edge of the verandah and saw who was sitting at the bottom of the steps next to his daughter, both of them staring up at him with identically startled expressions.

'Alice!'

Will glared accusingly at her. If Alice hadn't annoyed him so much, he wouldn't have left the poolside, and he would have kept a closer eye on Lily. This was all her fault.

'What are *you* doing here?' he asked rudely. It was bad enough when he had imagined her out front, making a spectacle of herself with all those fawning men, but it was somehow worse to find her here with Lily, a witness to his inadequacies as a father.

Why did it have to be *her*? He wouldn't have minded finding anyone else with Lily, would even have been glad that his daughter had found a friend, but not Alice. She had been free enough with her opinion of him as a father earlier. There would be no stopping her now that she had met Lily. Alice would have taken one look at his quiet, withdrawn daughter and decided just how he was failing her, Will thought bleakly.

CHAPTER FOUR

ALICE took her time getting to her feet. Slowly brushing down the back of her dress, she wondered how best to deal with him. She didn't want to argue in front of Lily—how stupid of her not to have guessed who she was, but she didn't look anything like Will—but it was obvious that Will was still angry with her.

Obvious too that he hadn't liked finding her with his daughter. She just hoped he wouldn't think that she had done it deliberately.

'We were just talking about shoes,' she said carefully at last. 'We hadn't got round to introducing ourselves, had we?' she said to Lily, who had turned away from her father and was sitting hunched up, her fine hair swinging down to hide her face.

Lily shook her head mutely. With the appearance of her father, she had lost all her animation.

'I'm Alice,' said Alice, persevering. 'And you're…Lily? Is that right?'

Lily managed a nod, but she peeped a glance under her hair at Alice, who smiled encouragingly.

'Nice to meet you, Lily. Shall we shake hands? That's what people do when they meet each other for the first time.'

It felt like a huge victory when Lily held out her hand, and Alice shook it with determined cheerfulness. She wished she could tell Will to stop looming over his daughter. He looked so forbidding, no wonder Lily was subdued.

'What are you doing out here, Lily?' Will asked stiffly. 'Don't you want to play with the other children in the pool?'

Lily's face was closed. 'I like talking to Alice,' she said, without turning to look at him.

There was an uncomfortable silence. Alice looked from Will to his daughter and back again. He had told her that he was practically a stranger to his own child, but she hadn't appreciated until now just what that meant for the two of them. Will was awkward and uncertain, and Lily a solitary child still trying to come to terms with the loss of her mother. Neither knew how to make the connection they both needed so badly.

It wasn't her business. Will wanted her to leave him alone with his daughter, that much was clear. She should just walk away and let them sort it out themselves.

But when Alice looked at Lily's hunched shoulders, and remembered how she had laughed at the butterfly, she couldn't do it. Will didn't have to accept her help, but his little girl needed a friend.

'I liked talking to you, too,' she said to Lily. 'Maybe we can meet again?' She glanced at Will, trusting that he wouldn't jump on the offer before Lily had a chance to say what she wanted. 'Do you think your dad would let you come round to tea one day?'

'Can I see your shoes?' asked Lily, glancing up from under her hair.

'You can see some of them,' said Alice. 'I'm only here on holiday, so I didn't bring them all with me, but I've got some fun ones. The others are at home in London.'

Lily thought for a moment and then looked over her shoulder at her father. 'Can I?'

Most other little girls would have been jumping up and

down, swinging on their daddy's hand and cajoling him with smiles and dimples, supremely confident of their power to wrap their fathers round their perfect little fingers, but not Lily. She would ask his permission, but she wouldn't give him smiles and affection. Not yet, anyway.

A muscle worked in Will's jaw. He wished that he knew how to reach her. He knew how sad she was, how lost and lonely she must feel. If only he could find some way to break down the barrier she had erected around herself.

Torn, he watched her stiff back helplessly. He wanted to give Lily whatever she wanted, but Alice and her shoes and her talk about London would only remind her of her mother and her life in England, and she would be unsettled all over again. Surely that was the last thing she needed right now?

He was still hesitating when Beth burst through the screen door with her customary exuberance. 'Will?' she called. 'Are you out here? Did you—' She stopped as she caught sight of the three of them. 'Oh, good, you've found her—and Alice too!'

Belatedly sensing a certain tension in the air, she looked from one to the other. 'I'm not interrupting anything, am I?'

'Of course not.' Alice forced a smile. 'I was just inviting Lily round for tea one day.'

'What a lovely idea!' Beth clapped her hands together and beamed at Will. 'Come tomorrow!'

Will could feel himself being swept along by the force of her enthusiasm and tried to dig in his heels before it all got out of hand. 'I'm sure you'll have had enough visitors by then,' he temporised while he thought up a better excuse.

'Nonsense,' said Beth briskly. 'I've hardly had a chance to talk to anyone today. You know what it's like at a party. You're always saying hello or goodbye or making sure everyone's got a drink. It would be lovely to see you and Lily tomorrow. Otherwise it'll all feel like an awful anticlimax, and we'll get scratchy with each other. At least, if you come, Roger and Alice will have to behave.' She laughed merrily. 'It's not as if you'll be working on a Sunday, is it?'

'No,' Will had to admit.

'And Lily needs to make friends for when you're not there,' Beth reminded him.

'I've brought a nanny out from England,' said Will, irritated by the implication that he hadn't given any thought to child-care arrangements. What did they think? That he was planning to go off to work and leave Lily alone in the house every day?

'Oh, you should have brought her along today.' Beth was blithely unaware of his exasperation, but Alice was keeping a carefully neutral expression, Will noticed. She would know exactly how he was feeling.

'It's her day off,' he said, forcing a more pleasant note into his voice. It wasn't Beth's fault that Alice was able to unsettle him just by standing there and saying nothing. 'She wanted to go snorkelling.'

'Well, bring her tomorrow,' Beth instructed. 'Then she'll know where we are, and she and Lily can come again when you're at work.'

Will glanced back at Lily. She had lifted her head and was watching the adults talking. Her face was brighter than he had seen it, he thought, and his heart twisted.

I like talking to Alice, she had said. He couldn't refuse her just because he remembered talking to Alice himself. And what would be the harm, after all? He didn't have to have anything to do with Alice. He could just have tea and then let Dee take over the social side of things.

'All right,' he succumbed, and was rewarded by a flash of something close to gratitude in Lily's eyes. 'Thank you, we'd like to come.'

* * *

Alice disliked Dee, Lily's nanny, on sight. What had Will been thinking of, hiring someone quite so young and silly to look after his daughter? Or had he been thinking more about what a pretty girl she was? How long her legs were, how sparkling her blue eyes, how soft the blonde hair she tossed back from her face as she giggled?

Lily was subdued, and Will positively morose, but Dee made up for both of them with her inane chatter—and he had called *her* superficial! Alice listened in disbelief as Dee rambled on about her family and her friends, and what a good time she had had learning how to snorkel the day before.

As far as Alice could tell, she had absolutely nothing in common with Will or Lily. It was hard to imagine anyone less suited to dealing with a quiet, withdrawn child, she thought disapprovingly. Still, if Dee's particular brand of silliness was what Will wanted to come home to in the evening, that was his business. She was only thinking about Lily.

Unable to bear Dee's inanities any longer, Alice leant over to Lily. 'Would you like to come and see my shoes?' she whispered as Dee talked on, and Lily nodded. She took the hand Alice held out quite willingly and trotted beside her to the bedroom, where a selection of Alice's favourite shoes had been spread out on the bed.

'Which ones do you like best?' Alice asked, after Lily had examined them all seriously.

After much thought, Lily selected pair of black high heels with peep toes and floppy bows covered in polka dots.

'Good choice,' said Alice approvingly. 'They're my favourites too. Why don't you try them on?' she added, and watched as Lily slipped her small feet into the shoes and turned to look at herself in the mirror.

'Wait!' Alice rummaged in a drawer and pulled out a diaphanous sarong. Tying it round the little girl, she draped some pearls over her and added her favourite straw hat with its wide brim. 'There!'

She stood back to admire the effect, delighted by the look on Lily's face as she studied her reflection. The sullen expression was gone and, animated, the piquant face looked positively pretty beneath the hat.

Will would like to see her like this, Alice thought. 'Let's show the others,' she suggested casually.

Biting her lip as she concentrated on her balance, Lily teetered down the corridor. 'May I introduce Miss Lily Paxman?' Alice announced grandly as she flung open the door.

There was a chorus of oohs and aahs, and a broad smile spread across Lily's face. Alice happened to glance at Will just then, and the expression in his eyes as he watched his daughter smile brought a lump to her throat. She would never be able to accuse Will of not caring about Lily now.

Feeling as if she had intruded on a very private moment, she looked away and caught Roger's eye.

'OK?' he mouthed.

Alice nodded and went over to stand next to him, leaving Beth and Dee exclaiming over Lily. Dee, in particular, was going completely over the top with her compliments. Probably trying to impress Will, Alice thought sourly. Too bad Dee didn't know that Will didn't go in for gushing sentimentality.

At least, he never used to. He had changed so much that for all Alice knew sweet, fluffy women were just his type nowadays. He certainly didn't have much time for sharp, astringent ones, that was for sure.

Without quite being aware of it, Alice sighed.

'What's the matter?' asked Roger.

'Oh…nothing.'

Not wanting to look at Will, Alice watched Beth instead.

'She's fantastic with kids, isn't she?' she said, and Roger's smile twisted as his eyes rested on his wife.

'She loves children.'

Roger and Beth had never talked much about their inability to conceive, but Alice knew how much having a baby would mean to both of them. She tucked her hand through Roger's arm and leant against him, offering wordless comfort. 'It must be hard for her at times like this,' she said quietly. 'For you, too.'

'It's just that you can't help imagining what it would be like if it was your own child dressing up …' Roger trailed off, and Alice hugged his arm closer in silent sympathy. He and Beth were both so easy-going and good-humoured that it was easy to forget that they had their own problems to deal with.

On the other side of the room, Will watched Alice standing close to Roger and frowned. Only a moment ago he had been feeling grateful to her. Lily's smile might not have been meant just for him, but still it had warmed his heart, and it was down to Alice, he knew. She had been able to connect with his daughter in a way that eluded him.

But, when he looked at her to try and indicate his gratitude somehow, he saw that she wasn't even aware of Lily any more. Instead she was leaning against Roger, her arm tucked through his and her head on his shoulder. It was a very intimate pose.

Too intimate for a man whose wife was only a few feet away.

Will glanced at Beth, who was smiling at Lily as she adjusted her hat. She seemed unaware of Roger and Alice over by the window, but Will had noticed a fleeting expression of sadness in her face more than once now, and he wondered how much Beth knew, or guessed, about her husband's feelings for Alice.

It was a long time since he and Roger had shared that drunken evening, but Will had never forgotten the look in Roger's eyes as he confessed the truth. He couldn't remember where Alice had been, but Roger had just split up with yet another girlfriend, and Will had been deputed to help him drown his sorrows and provide a shoulder to cry on.

'I don't want him to be alone,' Alice had said. She'd always been very protective of Roger, which was ironic in its own way, Will reflected.

It had been very late and very dark when Will had helped a reeling Roger home at last. He had never known if Roger had meant to tell him that all the other girls were just an attempt to disguise how he felt about Alice, or if the next day he had even remembered the truth he had blurted out. Neither of them had ever mentioned it again, but Will couldn't shake the memory of the bleakness in Roger's face.

'I'm just her friend,' he had said, slurring his words. 'I'll only ever be her friend.'

Had Roger decided to settle for second best with Beth? Will hoped not. He liked Roger's wife. She deserved better than that.

What was Alice doing, snuggled up to Roger like that? Will scowled. Did she know how Roger felt about her? Had she guessed?

'I'm looking for Mr Right,' she had told him with that bright, brittle smile he hated. Easy to see how Roger might fill that role for her. He was kind, loyal, funny, the rock Alice had fallen back on more than once. It wouldn't be hard to imagine the scales falling from her eyes as friendship turned to love...

But Alice wouldn't do that to Beth, would she? Will's frown deepened. The old Alice would never do anything to hurt her friends, but what did he know of her now? The old Alice wouldn't have stood that close to Roger, either.

She would have been standing close to *him*, leaning against him, touching him.

Will pushed the thought aside and got abruptly to his feet. 'It think it's time we went,' he said.

'What did you think of Dee?' Beth asked Alice when Will had chivvied a disappointed Lily and Dee out to the car.

'Not much,' said Alice, unimpressed. She felt oddly disgruntled. It wasn't that she had wanted to see Will, but he could have stayed a bit longer instead of rushing them off like that. It wasn't very fair on Lily. 'She tries too hard. You can tell she's desperate to impress Will.'

Beth looked at her strangely. 'You can?'

'Well, it's a classic, isn't it?' Alice sniffed. 'Child, nanny, single father...alone together on a tropical island... Of *course* she's going to fall for him!'

'It's interesting you should say that,' said Beth. 'I wouldn't have said that she was the slightest bit interested in Will. He's too old for her.'

'Old?' repeated Alice, outraged. 'He's not *old*! He's only thirty-five!'

'I expect that seems old to Dee,' said Beth, choosing not to comment on how well Alice remembered Will's age. 'She can't be much more than twenty. I'd say she was much more impressed by that hunk who taught her how to snorkel yesterday. Didn't you hear her going on about him?'

'No.' Alice frowned. She wasn't as openly friendly as Beth, and had frankly tuned out most of Dee's prattling. She wasn't quite ready to believe that Dee had no interest in Will, either. He might be a bit older, but Dee could hardly have failed to notice that he was an attractive man—any more than Will would have missed the fact that she was young and very pretty. One could accuse Will of being lots of things, but unobservant wasn't one of them.

'I don't know how Will could possibly have thought she would make a suitable nanny,' she said crossly.

Beth laughed. 'Nannies aren't buxom old ladies in mob caps any more, you know! Dee is young and friendly and enthusiastic. I expect Will thought she would be fun for Lily to have around.'

'Or fun for *him* to have around?' suggested Alice, her voice laced with vinegar. 'You're not going to tell me he didn't clock those long legs and that body when he interviewed her?'

'She's certainly a very pretty girl,' Beth agreed equably. 'But it wasn't Dee he was watching today, and it wasn't Dee he couldn't take his eyes off yesterday.'

Alice, who had prowling restlessly around the room, stopped and stared at Beth, who smiled blandly back.

'I don't think you need to worry about Dee,' she said.

'I'm not worried about Dee,' snapped Alice, severely ruffled. 'Will can do what he likes. *I* don't care. We don't even like each other any more.'

'Ah.' Beth nodded understandingly. 'Right. That'll be why you both spent the entire time watching each other when you thought the other one wasn't looking.' She paused. 'I think there's still a real connection between you.'

Alice flushed. 'There's no connection,' she insisted. 'Not any more.'

And there wasn't, she reminded herself repeatedly over the next few days. Will had hardly spoken to her at the tea, and she certainly hadn't been aware of him watching her. Whenever she'd happened to glance at him—and it wasn't that often, no matter what Beth had said—he'd seemed intent on talking to Roger or Beth, or watching Lily and Dee. If he'd even noticed that *she* was in the room, he'd hidden it extremely well, she thought grouchily.

There certainly hadn't been any opportunity for her to tell him that she was sorry for her tactless comments at the party.

Not that Will would care whether she apologised or not. He had made it very clear how he felt about her now. Beth's idea of a connection between them was ludicrous, Alice thought more than once over the next week, refusing each time to consider why the realisation should make her feel so bleak. Any sense of connectedness that had once existed between her and Will had been broken long ago, and there was no hope of repairing it now.

And she wouldn't want to, even if it had been possible, Alice reminded herself firmly. She hadn't been lying when she had told Will that this time in St Bonaventure was her chance to think about what she really wanted out of life. Redundancy and Tony's rejection had brought her to a crossroads, and, if the last miserable few months had taught her anything, it was that she needed to look forward, not back.

There was no point in hankering after the past or what had been. Of all the options that lay open to her now, the one route she wouldn't take was the one she had already travelled. She had to make her own future, and that certainly didn't include resurrecting old relationships that had been doomed in the first place.

No, she was going to have a good time while she was here, Alice decided, and then she was going to go home and rebuild her life so that it was bigger and better than before. She would get herself a really good job. She might even sell her flat, and make a fresh start somewhere new where memories weren't lurking behind every door, waiting to ambush her when her resistance was low.

And she would do it all by herself. She wasn't going to rely on anyone else to make her happy this time. The only way to be sure was to do it alone.

In spite of all her resolutions, Alice found her mind wandering to Will uncomfortably often over the next few days. Having been catapulted back into her life without warning, Will had disappeared again so completely, it left Alice feeling mildly disorientated.

Had that really been Will standing there, after all these

years? Sometimes she wondered if she had dreamt the entire episode, but she knew that she hadn't made up Lily. That guarded little face with the clouded dark eyes were all too vivid in her memory. Alice hoped that she was adjusting to her new life and learning to trust Will. She kept thinking about the look in his eyes when he had seen his daughter smiling, and every time it brought a lump to her throat.

She would have liked to be able to help them understand each other, but then she would remind herself that they didn't need her help. They had Dee, and no doubt they were already well on the way to being a happy little family.

Alice imagined Will going home every night to Dee, who would already know how he liked his tea—strong and black. By now she would know that he hated eggs, and his gestures would be becoming familiar to her. She would recognize how he rubbed his hand over his face when he was tired, how amusement would light the grey eyes and lift the corner of his mouth.

Oh, yes, Lily and Will would be fine without Alice. They didn't need her when they had Dee.

Which left her free to enjoy her holiday.

She should have been delighted at the prospect, but instead Alice felt scratchy and increasingly restless as the days passed. She had longed and longed for a few weeks doing absolutely nothing in the sunshine, but the truth was that she was getting a bit bored of sitting by the pool all day.

Beth had a full social agenda, and Alice was included in all the invitations, but there were only so many coffee mornings and lunches at the club that she could take. All that gossip and moaning about maids, school fees, how hard it was to get bacon or a decent gin and tonic! Beth was so open and friendly that she was welcome anywhere, but Alice knew that her own brand of acerbity went down rather less well.

In spite of having grown up overseas, she had never come

across the expat lifestyle like this before. Her parents would never have dreamed of joining a club with other expatriates. They didn't care about air-conditioning or supermarkets, and chose to live in remote tribal villages where they could be 'close to the people', a phrase that still made Alice nearly as uncomfortable as a lunch with some of Beth's fellow wives.

Why was it she never seemed to fit in anywhere? Alice wondered glumly. All she had ever wanted was to belong somewhere, but the only place she felt really at home was work. At least this break had taught her one thing, and that was how important her career was to her. Will might think her superficial, but at least she was prepared to go out and do a proper job, not sit around smiling all day like Dee.

'Are you sure you don't want to come?' Roger asked her the following Sunday. He and Beth were off to yet another barbecue, where they would meet all the people who had come to their barbecue the previous weekend, and Alice had opted out. 'Will might be there. They're bound to have invited everybody.'

If Will had wanted to see her, he knew where she lived. Alice had spent far too much of the week wondering if he would think about dropping round some time, and she was thoroughly disgusted with herself for being disappointed when he hadn't. She certainly wasn't about to go chasing after him at some party now!

'I don't think so, thanks,' she said, ultra-casual. She could hardly change her mind just because Roger had mentioned Will. What a giveaway *that* would be! 'I'll just stay here and finish my book.'

But, when Roger and Beth had gone, Alice sat with her book unopened on her lap and wished perversely that she had let herself be persuaded. After all, Will could hardly suspect her of chasing him if she just happened to bump into

him at party, could he? She would have been able to see
how he—how *Lily*, Alice corrected herself quickly—was
getting on.

Then, of course, Dee might be at the party too. What could
be more natural for Will to take her along since they were all
living together? Did she *really* want to see that they were all
getting along absolutely fine?

No, Alice acknowledged to herself, she couldn't honestly say
that she did. Much better not to know. She was better off here.

Determinedly, she opened her book, but it was impossible
to concentrate when all the time she was wondering if Roger
and Beth had bumped into Will at the party, and, if they had,
whether he would notice that she wasn't there. Would he ask
where she was? Would he miss her?

'Oh, for heaven's sake!' Alice slammed her book shut,
furious with herself. Will didn't even like her now. *Remember
that little fact, Alice?* Why on earth would he miss her?

And why was she wasting her time even *thinking* about him?

When the doorbell went, she was so glad of the interruption that she leapt to her feet. It was Chantelle's day off, and
she hurried to the door, not caring who it was as long as they
distracted her from her muddled thoughts for a while.

Flinging open the door, she smiled a welcome, only to
find the smile wiped from her face in shock as she saw who
was standing there.

It was Will, with Lily a small silent figure beside him. The
last people she had expected to see. The sight of them
punched the breath from Alice's lungs, and, winded, she hung
onto the door.

'Oh,' she said weakly. 'It's you.' She struggled to get some
oxygen into her lungs but her voice still sounded thin and
reedy. 'Hi…hello, Lily.'

''Lo,' Lily muttered in response.

Will cleared his throat. He looked as startled to see Alice as she was to see him, which was a bit odd given that he knew perfectly well that she was living there. 'Is Beth around?'

'No, she and Roger have gone to a party.' Alice had herself under better control now. It had just been the surprise. 'At the Normans, I think.'

'Damn, I'd forgotten about that …'

Will raked a hand through his hair and tried to concentrate on the matter in hand and not on how Alice had looked, opening the door, her face alight with a smile. Her hair swept back into its usual messy but stylish clip, and she was wearing loose trousers and a cool, sleeveless top. Her feet were thrust into spangled flip flops, and she looked much more relaxed than she had done at the party.

Much more herself.

'Is there a problem?' she asked.

He hesitated only for a moment. 'Yes,' he said baldly. Alice might be the last person he wanted to ask for help, especially under these circumstances, but he didn't have a lot of choice here. Too bad if she gave him a hard time about neglecting Lily. He had survived worse.

'There's been an accident on the project,' he said, his voice swift and decisive now that his mind was made up. 'I don't have many details yet, and I don't know how bad it is, but I need to go and see what's happened and if anyone's hurt. I can't take Lily with me until I know it's safe.'

'Where's Dee?' asked Alice, going straight to the heart of the problem as was her wont.

'She left yesterday.'

'Left?'

'She met some guy at the diving school last weekend.' Will wondered if he looked as frazzled as he felt. Probably, judging by Alice's expression. 'She's known him less than a week, but when he told her he was going back to Australia she decided to go with him.' He tried to keep his voice neutral, because he was afraid that if he let his anger and frustration show he wouldn't be able to control it.

Alice opened her mouth to ask how on earth that had happened, and then closed it again abruptly. Will was worried about Lily, worried about the accident. He didn't need her exclaiming and asking questions.

'Perhaps Lily could stay with me,' she said instead. 'You wouldn't mind keeping me company this afternoon, would you, Lily?'

Lily shook her head and, when Alice held out her hand, she took it after only a momentary hesitation.

'You go on,' Alice said to Will. 'I'll look after her until you get back.'

Astonished and relieved at her lack of fuss, Will could only thank her. He turned to go, but as he did he saw Alice nod imperceptibly down at his daughter. God, he'd almost forgotten to say goodbye! What kind of father did that make him?

'Goodbye, Lily,' he said awkwardly. If only he could be sure that if he crouched down and hugged her she would hug him back. 'Be good.' She was always good, though. That was the problem. 'I'll be back as soon as I can.'

Alice had to be one of the few people who knew less about parenting than he did, he thought bitterly as he reversed the car out of the drive and headed towards the project headquarters as fast as he could, but she was still able to make him realise how badly he was getting it wrong.

Alice, still able to wrong-foot him after all these years. Will shook his head. He had been waiting for her to take him to task for putting the project before his own child. He couldn't have blamed her if she'd pointed out that it was his fault for employing a silly girl like Dee who would run off and leave him in the lurch after barely more than a week as a nanny. She could have criticised him for not even thinking to say goodbye to Lily.

But she had done none of those things. She had recognized the problem and done exactly what he needed her to do. He would have to try and tell her later how much he appreciated it.

CHAPTER FIVE

'LILY's asleep,' said Alice, opening the door to him nearly four hours later and motioning Will inside.

'Asleep?' He was instantly anxious. 'Is she OK?'

'Of course. She's just tired, and she dropped off a few minutes ago. It seems a shame to wake her just yet. Why don't you sit down and have a drink?' Her polite façade vanished as she watched Will drop into a chair. 'You look tired,' she added impulsively.

Will rubbed a hand over his face in a gesture so familiar that Alice felt a sharp pang of remembrance. 'I'm OK,' he said gruffly, but he was glad to sit down, he had to admit. The room was cool and quiet after the chaos at the hospital. 'Thanks,' he said as Alice came back with one of Roger's beers, and he drank thirstily.

'Was it a bad accident?' Alice asked. She sat on the end of the sofa, far enough away to be in no danger of touching him by accident, but not so far that it looked as if she was nervous about being alone with him.

'Bad enough.' Will lowered the bottle with a sigh. 'A couple of our younger members of staff had taken one of the project jeeps to the beach. It's their day off, and they had a few beers…you know what it's like. They're not supposed to take any of the vehicles unless they're on project business, but they're just lads.'

He grimaced, remembering the calls he had had to make to the boys' parents after he'd contacted the insurance company. 'Perhaps it's just as well they took one of our jeeps: It had our logo on the side, so when someone saw it had gone off the road they raised the alarm with the office, and the phone there gets switched through to me at weekends.'

'Are the boys OK?'

'They'll survive. They've both recovered consciousness, and the doctors say they're stable. The insurance company is making arrangements to fly them back to the UK, and the sooner that happens the better. The hospital here isn't equipped to deal with serious accidents.' He shook his head. Hospitals were grim enough places at the best of times.

'I'm glad I didn't have to take Lily there,' he said abruptly. 'I don't know how to thank you for looking after her, Alice.'

Alice avoided his eyes. 'It was no trouble,' she said with a careless shrug. 'Lily's good company.'

'Is she?' Will took another pull of his beer, unable to keep the bitterness from his voice. 'I can't get her to talk to me.'

'You need to give her time, Will. Everything's very new to her at the moment, and she's just lost her mother. You can't expect her to bounce back immediately.'

'I know, it's just…I don't know how to help her,' he admitted, the words wrenched out of him.

'You can help her best by being yourself. You're her father, and she knows that. Don't try too hard,' Alice told him. 'Let her get to know you.'

'Who made you such an expert on child care?' Will demanded roughly.

There was a tiny pause, and then, hearing the harshness of

his voice still echoing, he put down the beer and leant forward, resting his elbows on his knees and raking both hands through his hair. 'I'm sorry,' he said after a moment. 'That was uncalled for. Sorry.'

'You've got a lot on your mind at the moment,' said Alice after a moment.

'Still.' He straightened, and the grey eyes fixed on hers seemed to reach deep inside her and elicit a disturbing thrum. 'It's no excuse for rudeness.'

With an effort, Alice pulled her gaze away and reached for her lime juice with a hand that was not nearly as steady as she would have liked it to be.

'You're right, I don't know much about children,' she said. 'But Lily reminds me a lot of myself when I was younger. I was shy, the way she is, and I know what it's like—oh, not to lose my mother—but that feeling of not really knowing where you are or what you're doing there …' The golden eyes clouded briefly. 'Yes, I remember all that.'

'Is that why you were so angry with me at the party?'

Alice flushed. 'Partly. I shouldn't have said what I did, Will. I'm sorry, I was out of order. It wasn't any of my business.'

'No, you were right. I overreacted, mainly because you'd put your finger on all the things I felt most guilty and unsure about.' He smiled briefly. 'So it looks as if neither of us behaved quite as well as we might have done.'

He paused, his eyes on Alice, who had tucked her feet up beneath her and was curled into the corner of the sofa.

'What was the other reason?' he asked.

'Reason?' she said blankly.

'You said that was "partly" the reason you were angry,' he reminded her.

'Oh…' The colour deepened in Alice's cheeks, and she fiddled with the piping on the arm of the sofa. 'It's stupid, but

I suppose it was meeting you again after all this time. I was nervous,' she confessed.

'Me too,' said Will, and her eyes flew to his in disbelief.

'Really?'

He lifted his shoulders in acknowledgement. 'You were the last person I expected to see,' he told her with a rueful smile. 'I was completely thrown.'

'Oh,' said Alice with an embarrassed little laugh. 'Well… I'm glad it wasn't just me.'

'No.'

An awkward silence fell, and stretched at last into something that threatened to become even more difficult. Will drank his beer. Alice traced an invisible pattern on the arm of the sofa and kept her eyes lowered, but beneath her lashes her eyes kept sliding towards the fingers curled casually around that brown bottle.

Those fingers had once curved around her breast. They had drifted over her skin, stroking and smoothing and seeking. They had explored every inch of her, and late at night, when they had been intertwined with her own, she had felt safe in a way she never had before or since.

Alice's throat was dry, and that little thrum inside her was growing stronger and warmer, spreading treacherously along her veins and trembling at the base of her spine.

She reached forward for her glass with something like desperation. She shouldn't be remembering Will touching her, kissing her, loving her. They weren't the same people they had been then. Will was a father, and had more on his mind right now than remembering how the mere touch of his hands had been enough to melt her bones and reduce her to gasping, arching delight.

Sipping her lime juice, she sought frantically for something to say, but in the end it was Will who broke the silence.

'Roger and Beth still out?'

The question sounded too hearty to be natural, but Alice fell on it like a lifeline.

'Yes,' she said breathlessly. 'You know what party animals they are.'

'Why didn't you go?' Will asked her.

'I didn't feel like it.'

She didn't quite meet his eyes as she adjusted her hair clip. Telling him how she had dithered over the possibility of meeting him again wouldn't help. The atmosphere was taut enough as it was, even though they were both labouring to keep the conversation innocuous.

'I've spent all week going to coffee mornings and lunches, and we've been out to supper twice, and every time you meet the same people,' she said. 'To be honest, I had a much better time with Lily this afternoon.'

Will had finished his beer, and he looked around for a mat to put the bottle down on. 'What did you do with her?'

'Oh, you know…we just pottered around.'

'No, I really want to know,' he said. 'I'm going to have to spend more time with Lily, and it would help if I knew what she liked doing.'

'Well, she's very observant,' said Alice, glad to have moved the conversation into less fraught channels. 'And she's interested in things. We spent some time wandering around the garden, and she was full of questions, most of which I couldn't answer, like why the butterflies here are so colourful and why don't bananas grow in England… I think you'll make a scientist of her yet!'

Will's expression relaxed slightly. 'It's reassuring to know that she'll ask questions like that. She's always so quiet when she's with me.'

'She's not a chatterbox,' Alice agreed. 'But she'll talk if

she's got something to say. She got quite animated going through my wardrobe. She loves dressing up.'

'She gets that from her mother.' Will sounded faintly disapproving. 'Nikki was a great one for clothes. Her appearance was always very important to her.'

'Appearance is important to a lot of us,' said Alice, sensing the unspoken criticism in his comment. 'It doesn't always mean that you're superficial,' she added with a slight barb, remembering how his jibe at the party had stung.

'No, I suppose not,' said Will, although he didn't sound convinced, and Alice noticed darkly that he didn't take the opportunity of apologising for calling her superficial.

'It's perfectly normal for Lily to like dressing up,' she said with some tartness. 'Most little girls do. It doesn't mean she's condemned to life as an empty-headed bimbo! Some of us manage to dress well *and* hold down a demanding job.'

'You sound like Nikki,' he said, and from the bleak expression that washed across his face Alice gathered that it wasn't a compliment.

She longed to ask what Nikki had been like and what had gone wrong with their marriage, but it seemed inappropriate just then. Besides, she wasn't sure she wanted to know just how much she resembled Lily's mother.

'At least I stick at my jobs,' she pointed out with a slight edge. 'Unlike Dee.'

'Quite.' Will acknowledged the hit with a sigh. 'I should never have employed her, but she seemed so bright and lively that I thought she would be more fun for Lily to have around than some of the more experienced nannies. We obviously weren't fun enough for her, though,' he said, his mouth turning down at the memory of that dire week with Dee. 'She couldn't wait to go out as soon as I got home in the evening. I should have guessed she'd take the first chance to leave. I just didn't realise it would come quite so soon.'

'You couldn't have anticipated she'd throw up a good job to follow a guy she'd only known for a week,' said Alice, even as she wondered why she was trying to make him feel better.

Perhaps that was what superficial people did.

'If I'd been more experienced, I might have read the signs,' said Will. 'She was the only nanny the agency had on their books who could leave at such short notice, and now I know why!'

'What are you going to do now?'

Will put his arms above his head and tried to stretch out the tension in his shoulders. 'Get another nanny, I guess.' He leant back in his chair with a tired sigh. 'I'll have to get onto the agency tomorrow. I just haven't had a chance today.'

'It might take them some time to find someone suitable,' Alice pointed out. 'What happens in the meantime?'

'I'll just have to manage,' said Will, rubbing his face again. 'Lily's due to start school in a few weeks' time. I might be able to find someone locally who could help out until then, or maybe she could come to the project headquarters some days. It's not a very suitable place for a child, but I can hardly leave her on her own.'

'I'll look after her.'

The words were out of Alice's mouth before she had thought about them, and she was almost as startled by them as Will was. He sat bolt upright and stared at her.

'You?'

'Why not?' Some other person seemed to be controlling her speech. Was she really doing this? Arguing to look after Will's daughter for him? She must be mad! 'I managed this afternoon.'

'But …' Will looked totally thrown by her offer. Almost as thrown as Alice felt herself. 'You're on holiday,' he pointed out.

'I'm not suggesting I take on the job permanently. I'm just offering to help out until you can find a qualified nanny.'

'It's extraordinarily kind of you, Alice,' said Will slowly. 'But I couldn't possibly ask you to give up your holiday to look after Lily. You told me yourself that you were here for a complete break.'

'A break from routine is all I need.' Alice got to her feet and walked over to the sliding doors, trying to work out why it felt so important to persuade him.

'I thought I wanted to spend six weeks doing absolutely nothing,' she told him. 'When Beth told me about her life here, about the mornings by the pool, about the parties and the warmth and the sunshine, I was envious, jealous even.'

She remembered sitting at her desk, staring out at the rain and remembering Beth's bubbling enthusiasm. Tony hadn't been long gone, then, and she had still been at the stage of dreading going home to an empty flat.

'It was a bad time for me,' she told Will. She wasn't ready to tell him about Tony yet. 'The idea of just turning my face up to the sun and not thinking about anything for a while seemed wonderful, and when I got the chance to come I took it…'

'But?' Will prompted when she paused.

Alice turned back from the window to face him. 'But I'm bored,' she said honestly. 'It's different for Beth. She makes friends wherever she goes. She likes everybody, even if they're really dull, and she always sees the good side of people, but I'm …'

'… not like that?' he suggested, a hint of amusement in his eyes, and he looked suddenly so much like the Will she remembered that Alice's heart bumped into her ribs and she forgot to breathe for a moment.

'No,' she agreed, hugging her arms together and drawing

a distinctly unsteady breath. 'You know what I'm like. I'm intolerant, and I get impatient and restless if I'm bored.'

'They don't sound like ideal characteristics for a nanny,' Will pointed out in a dry voice, and she made herself meet his eyes squarely and not notice that disconcertingly familiar glint.

'Lily doesn't bore me,' she said. 'I like her. She reminds me of me, and I'm never bored when I'm on my own. Besides, I'm not planning on being a nanny. If this week has taught me anything, it's how important my career is. I need to work, and if I can't work, I need to do *something*.

'I enjoyed spending this afternoon with Lily,' she told Will. 'I'd much rather spend the next few weeks with her than twitter away at endless coffee mornings.'

'If that's how you feel, why don't you just cut short your trip?'

'Because I can't change my ticket. It was one of those special deals which means you can't get any refund if you change your flight. And Roger and Beth would be hurt if I said I was bored and wanted to go home. They've gone to so much trouble to make me welcome,' Alice added guiltily.

'They might be hurt if you choose to spend the rest of your time with Lily,' Will commented.

'I don't think so. Not if we present it as me helping you out.' Alice hoped she wasn't sounding *too* desperate, but, the more she thought about it, the more she liked the idea.

'I love Roger and Beth,' she said carefully. 'Of course I do. No one could be kinder or more hospitable, but I'm used to being independent and having my own space, making my own decisions.

'When you're a guest, you just fit in with everyone else,' she tried to explain. 'And I'm finding that harder than I thought. It's as if I'm completely passive. I don't decide what we're going to do, or what we're going to eat, or where we're going to go. I just tag along. At least if I was looking after Lily I'd have some say in how we spent the day.'

'I certainly wouldn't try and dictate what you did,' said Will. 'You know what would keep Lily happy better than I do. I do have a cook but I expect she'd be happy to make whatever you felt like.'

By the window, Alice brightened. 'You mean you're going to accept my offer?'

Will studied her eager face, puzzled by her enthusiasm and disconcerted by the way her mask of careful composure kept slipping to reveal the old, vivid Alice beneath.

'I don't know …' he said slowly. 'It doesn't seem right somehow.'

'Is it because it's me?' she demanded. 'You wouldn't be hesitating if the agency had sent me out on a temporary assignment, would you?'

'Of course not. That would be a professional arrangement and I'd be paying you for your time.'

Alice shrugged. 'You can pay me if it makes you feel better, but it's not necessary. It's not as if I'm doing it for you, you know. I'd be doing it for me—and for Lily,' she added after a moment's thought.

Still, Will hesitated. Getting to his feet, he took a turn around the room, hands thrust into his pockets and shoulders hunched in thought. Finally he stopped in front of Alice.

'You don't think it would be a bit…difficult?' he asked. 'Living together again after all these years?'

'I'm not suggesting we sleep together,' said Alice, a distinct edge to her voice. 'Presumably Dee had her own room?'

'Of course.'

'Well, then.' She glanced at him and then away. 'It's different now, Will. What we had before is in the past. We agreed at the time that we would go our separate ways, and we have. There's no going back now.'

She was presenting it as something they had both decided together, but it hadn't been quite like that, not the way Will remembered it, anyway. It had been Alice who had wanted to end their relationship. 'Our lives are going in different directions,' she had said. 'Let's call it a day while we're still friends.'

'I think we both know that there's no point in trying to recreate what we had,' she was saying. 'I don't want that and neither do you, do you?'

'No,' said Will, after a moment. Well, what was he supposed to say—yes, I do? I do want that? I've never stopped wanting that?

That would have been a very foolish thing to say. He had tried to say it at Roger's wedding, and he wasn't putting himself through that again. He had enough problems at the moment without getting involved with Alice again. She was right; it was over.

'So what's the problem?' she asked him. 'It makes much more sense for you to have me living with you than some other woman who might fall in love with you and make things *really* awkward.'

It was her turn to pause while she tried to find the right words. 'We've both changed,' she said eventually. 'We're different people and we don't feel the same way about each other as we did then. We're never going to be lovers any more, but there's no reason why we couldn't learn to be friends, is there?'

Except that it was hard to be friends with someone whose taste you could remember exactly, thought Will. Someone whose body you had once known as well as your own, someone who'd been the very beat of your heart for so long.

With someone who'd made you happier than you had ever

been before. Someone who'd left your life empty and desolate when she had gone.

'It would only be for a few weeks,' Alice went on. 'And then I'd be gone. That wouldn't be too difficult, would it?'

'No,' said Will. 'We could do that for Lily.'

He had a feeling that it was going to be a lot harder than Alice made out, but it would be worth it for Lily. She liked Alice, that was clear, and Alice's presence would help her to settle down much more effectively than introducing yet another stranger into her life. He would just have to find his own way of dealing with living with Alice again.

And living without her once more when she had gone.

'All right,' he said, abruptly making up his mind. 'If you're sure, I expect Lily would love you to look after her until I can find a new nanny.'

He was glad that he had agreed when he saw Lily's face as the news was broken to her that Alice was going to stay with them for a while. She was never a demonstrative child, but there was no mistaking the way her dark eyes lit up with surprise and delight.

'You're going to live with us?'

'Just for a little while,' cautioned Alice. 'Until your dad can find you a new nanny.'

'Why can't you stay always?'

Will waited to see how Alice would handle that. It was a question he had wanted to ask her himself in the past. He had never understood why she had been so determined to end their relationship when they had been so good together. It was as if she had been convinced that everything would go wrong, but she hadn't been prepared to give it a chance to go right.

'Because I have to go home, Lily,' Alice told her. 'My life

is in London, not here. But until I do go back we'll have a lovely time together, shall we?'

Lily seemed to accept that. 'OK,' she said.

Alice was more nervous than she wanted to admit about how Beth would react to the news that she was moving out that night to live with Will and Lily. The last thing she wanted to do was to hurt Beth's feelings. But, once the situation about the missing nanny had been explained, Beth was very understanding, and even surprisingly enthusiastic about the idea.

'It sounds like the perfect solution,' she said, smiling, her gaze flickering with interest between Will and Alice. 'I'm sure you're doing the right thing.'

'I'm doing it for *Lily*,' said Alice pointedly. She didn't want Beth getting the wrong idea.

Beth opened her eyes wide. 'Of course,' she said. 'Why else?'

Roger was less convinced that it was a good idea. 'Are you sure about this, Alice?' he asked under his breath as they came to say goodbye.

'I'm sure,' she said. 'Don't worry about me.'

Roger glanced at Will. 'Maybe it's not you I'm worrying about.'

'We've talked about it,' said Alice firmly. 'It's going to be fine.'

'Well, you're a big girl now, so I guess you know what you're doing.' Roger swept her up into a hug. 'Look after yourself, though.'

'I'm only going up the road!'

'I'll still miss you. I've got used to coming home to find you drinking my gin.'

'I'll miss you, too. I always do.' Alice hugged her dearest friend, holding tightly onto his big bear strength, and her eyes were watery when he finally let her go.

'Oh, good God, she's going to cry!' exclaimed Roger in mock horror. 'Take her away, man!'

Will, who had observed that tight hug, thought it would not be a bad idea to get Alice away from Roger for a while. He was worried about Beth. At first glance, she seemed as bright and cheerful as ever, but on closer inspection Will thought there was a rather drawn look about her. It might be best all round if Alice came with him.

'Come on, then,' he said to Alice and Lily. 'Let's go home.'

They had decided that Alice might as well start her new role straight away, so she had already packed a bag by the time Beth and Roger got home. Now Will slung it in the back of his four-wheel drive and hoped to God he was doing the right thing.

Will's house had no pool, no air-conditioning, and was some way away from the exclusive part of St Bonaventure up on the hill where Roger and Beth lived in manicured splendour, but Alice felt instantly much more at home there. An unassuming wooden house set up on stilts, it had a wide verandah shaded by a corrugated-iron roof, and ceiling fans that slapped at the air in a desultory fashion.

It was set on a dusty, pot-holed road and an area of coarse tropical grass at the rear led down to a line of leaning coconut palms. 'The sea's just there,' said Will, pointing into the darkness. 'Go through the coconuts, cross a track and you're on the beach.'

He carried Alice's cases inside and put them in what had been Dee's bedroom. 'I need to make some calls, I'm afraid,' he said. 'I want to ring the hospital and see how the boys are, and then I'll have to talk to our head office in London. Lily, perhaps you could show Alice the house?' he suggested.

'That was a good idea, getting Lily to show me round,' Alice said to him later when they had eaten the light supper left by his cook and Lily had gone to bed. They were sitting out on the back verandah, listening to the raucous whirr of the insects in the dark and, in the distance, the faint, ceaseless suck of the sea upon the sand. Alice could just make out the gleam of water through the trunks of the palms. 'Knowing more about the house and where everything was made her realise that she was more at home than she thought. It was good for her to be able to explain everything to me,' Alice told Will. 'She might not have been talking much, but she's certainly been taking it all in.'

'I'm glad about that.' Will handed her a mug of coffee that he had made, unthinkingly adding exactly the right amount of milk. He hadn't forgotten how she took hers any more than she had forgotten how he liked his tea, Alice thought with an odd pang. She took the mug gingerly, taking care that her fingers didn't brush against his.

'This is going to be her home for a couple of years at least,' he went on, picking up his own mug and sipping at it reflectively. 'So she needs to feel that it's where she belongs.'

He paused to look sideways at Alice, who was curled up in a wicker chair, cradling her coffee between her hands. The light on the verandah was deliberately dim so as not to attract too many insects, but he could make out the high cheekbones that gave her face that faintly exotic look and the achingly familiar curve of her mouth. It was too hard to read her expression, though, and he wondered what she was thinking.

'I want to thank you, Alice,' he said abruptly. 'I know I didn't seem keen when you first suggested it, but I think it will be a very good thing for Lily to have you here.'

'I hope so,' she said.

'What about you? Do you think you'll be comfortable at least?' He glanced around him as if registering his conditions for the first time. 'I know it's not as luxurious as Roger's house.'

'No, but I like it better,' she said. Tipping back her head, she breathed in the heady fragrance of the frangipani that blossomed by the verandah steps. The wooden boards were littered with its creamy yellow flowers. 'This reminds me of the kind of places I lived in as a child.'

Will grimaced into his coffee. 'I'm not sure that's a good thing. You hated your childhood.'

'I hated the way my parents kept moving,' she corrected him. 'It wasn't the places or the houses—although we never lived anywhere as nice as this. It was the fact that I never had a chance to feel at home anywhere. My parents never stuck at anything. They had wild enthusiasms, but then they'd get bored, or things would go wrong, and they'd be off with another idea.'

She sighed. She loved her parents, but sometimes they exasperated her.

'I was shy to begin with. It was hard enough for me to make friends without knowing that in a year or so I'd be dragged somewhere new, where I'd have to learn a new language and make completely new friends. After a while, it didn't seem worth the effort of making them in the first place. It was easier if I was just on my own.'

It was her unconventional upbringing that had made Alice stand out from the other students. Will had noticed her straight away. It wasn't that she'd been eccentric or trying to be different. She'd dressed the same as everyone else, and she'd done what everyone else did, but there had been just something about the way she'd carried herself that drew the eye, something about those extraordinary golden eyes that had seen places that most of the other students barely knew existed.

Alice might complain about being endlessly uprooted by her parents, but continually having to adapt to new conditions had given her a self-sufficiency that could at times be quite intimidating.

It was a kind of glamour, Will had always thought, although Alice had hooted with laughter when he'd suggested it. 'There's nothing glamorous about living in a hut in the middle of the Amazon, I can tell you!' she had said.

'That's why I identify with Lily, I think,' she said now, sipping reflectively at her coffee. 'She's a solitary child too.'

'I know,' said Will, anxious as always when he thought about his daughter. 'But I hope she'll have a chance to settle down now. I should be here for two or three years.'

'And then?'

'Who knows?' he asked, a faint undercurrent of irritation in his voice. He wasn't her parents, moving his child around the world on a whim. 'It depends on my job. I'm not like you. I don't plan my life down to the last minute.'

'I've learnt not to do that either, now,' said Alice, thinking about Tony and the plans they had made together. 'There are some things you just can't plan for.'

Will arched a sceptical brow. 'I can't imagine you not planning,' he said. 'You were always so certain about what you wanted.'

'Oh, I still know what I want,' she said, an undercurrent of bitterness in her voice. 'The only thing that's changed is that now I'm not sure that I'll get it.'

CHAPTER SIX

'I GUESS that's something we all learn as we get older,' said Will. 'You can't always have what you want.'

His voice was quite neutral, but Alice found her head turning to look at him, and as their eyes met in the dim light she was suddenly very sure that he was thinking about Roger's wedding when he had told her what he wanted and she had said no.

She kept her own voice as light as possible. 'That's true, but perhaps we get what we need instead.'

'Do you think you've got what *you* need?'

Alice looked out into the darkness to where the Indian Ocean boomed beyond the reef.

'I've got a career,' she said, ignoring the little voice that said it wasn't much of one at the moment. 'I've got a flat and the means to pay my mortgage and earn my own living. I've got security. Yes, I'd say I've got everything I need.'

'Everything?' She didn't need to be looking at Will to know that his brows had lifted sardonically.

'What else would I need?'

'Let's say love, just for the sake of argument,' he said dryly. 'Someone you love and who loves you. Someone to hold you and help you and make you laugh when you're down.

Someone who can light up your world, and close it out when
you're too tired to cope.'

Someone like he had been, Alice thought involuntarily,
and swallowed the sudden lump in her throat.

'Why, Will, you've turned into a poet!' she said, deliberately flippant. 'Have they started doing an agony column in
Nature and *Science Now*?'

'I read books too,' he said, unmoved by her facetiousness.
'So, do you?'

'Need love?' Alice leant down to put her coffee mug on the
table between them. 'No, I don't. I used to think I did, but I've
discovered I can manage quite well without it.'

'That's sad,' said Will quietly.

'Love would be great if you could rely on it, but you can't,'
she said, wrapping her arms around herself as if she were cold.
'You can't control it. You think it's going to be wonderful and
you trust it, and then you end up hurt and humiliated.' Her jaw
set, remembering. 'If you want to be safe, you need to look after
yourself, not put your whole happiness in someone else's hands.'

She glanced at Will. 'You asked me what I need. Well, I need
to feel safe, and that's why I'm not looking for love any more.'

'You've been hurt,' he said, and she gave a short, bitter laugh.

'You can tell you've got a Ph.D., the speed you worked
that one out!'

Will ignored her sarcasm. 'What happened?'

He thought at first that she wasn't going to answer, but
suddenly Alice needed to tell him. It was too late to pretend
that her life was perfect now. Will's clearly wasn't, so he
might as well know the truth.

'I met Tony four years ago,' she began slowly. 'I'd had a
few boyfriends, but there hadn't been anyone serious.'

There hadn't been anyone like Will. Alice pushed that
thought aside and carried on. 'I hadn't exactly given up on

meeting someone special, but I'd decided it probably wasn't going to happen. And then Tony came to work in my office.'

She paused, remembering that day. 'He was everything I'd ever wanted,' she said, oblivious to the wry look that passed over Will's face. 'We clicked immediately. We had so much in common. We liked doing the same things, and we wanted the same things out of life. I really thought he was The One,' she said, with an effort at self-mockery.

'Tony's careful,' she went on, even though she knew Will wouldn't understand. 'I felt safe with him. He's committed to his career, and he makes sure he invests his money sensibly. He thinks before he acts. He doesn't take stupid risks. That's why...'

She stopped, hearing her voice beginning to crack like a baby. Swallowing hard, she forced herself to continue. 'That's why I found it hard to believe that he would do something so out of character.'

'What did he do?' asked Will, part of him still grappling with disbelief at the idea that his lovely, vibrant Alice had decided after all to settle for safe, sensible and boring. He wouldn't have minded so much if she had fallen in love with someone wild, passionate and unsuitable, but how could she choose a man whose main attribute seemed to be a sensible approach to financial investments?

Alice drew a breath. 'He went out one day and fell in love at first sight.'

For a moment, Will was nonplussed. 'It happens,' he said, remembering that dizzy, dropping feeling he'd had the first time he'd laid eyes on Alice.

'Not to someone like Tony,' she said almost fiercely. 'We were together three and a half years, and I thought I knew him through and through. He was never impetuous. He never did anything without thinking it through.'

God, Tony sounded dull, thought Will. He wasn't a particularly reckless man himself, but he got the feeling that he would seem a positive daredevil next to Tony. What on earth had been his appeal for Alice?

'I couldn't believe it when he told me,' she was saying. 'He was very honest with me. He said that he'd thought that he did love me, but he realised when he met Sandi that he hadn't known what love was. It had taken us three years to decide that we would get married,' she added bitterly. 'It took him three minutes to know that he wanted to marry Sandi.'

'I'm sorry,' said Will, not knowing what else to say.

'Sandi's sweet and good and kind and pretty,' Alice went on. 'She really is,' she insisted, seeing Will's sceptical look. 'It's really hard to dislike her, and, believe me, I've tried. No one who meets her is at all surprised that Tony fell for her. The only surprising thing is that he thought he loved *me* for so long. Sandi's about as different from me as she could be.'

'She doesn't sound very interesting,' Will said, but Alice wasn't to be consoled.

'Tony doesn't want interesting. Interesting is too much like hard work,' she said. 'I thought I was making an effort for him, but it turned out I was "challenging" him,' she remembered, bitterness creeping back into her voice. 'I don't know how. I didn't think I had particularly high expectations, but there you go. Apparently I'm very demanding.'

'You're not easy,' Will agreed. 'But you're worth the effort. If Tony couldn't be bothered to make that effort, you're better off without him.'

'It didn't feel that way,' said Alice bleakly. 'We have lots of friends in common, so I see Tony with Sandi quite often. I don't think he's regretted his decision for a minute. In fact, I think he wakes up in a cold sweat sometimes, realising what a narrow escape he had!'

She tried to sound as if she didn't mind, but Will could hear the thread of hurt in her voice.

'They're still together, then?'

'They got married last week,' said Alice, her eyes on the dull gleam of the sea through the darkness. 'The day I met you at Roger and Beth's party.'

Will remembered how tense she had been that day. Alice had always been too proud to show how much she hurt inside. He should have guessed that something more than the passage of time was wrong, but he had been too shaken by his own reaction to give any thought to hers.

'I'm sorry,' he said again. 'It must have been difficult for you.'

Alice lifted her chin. She had always hated any suspicion of pity. 'I survived,' she said curtly. 'But that's why I'm doing without love at the moment.'

'You know, we all get hurt sometimes,' said Will mildly. 'Some of us more than once.'

'Once is enough for me,' said Alice.

Silence fell. They sat together in the hot, still night, each wrapped in their own thoughts, while the insects shrilled frantically in the darkness and the lagoon whispered onto the sand.

Alice was very aware of Will beside her. It was strange, being with him again, feeling that she knew him intimately, and yet hardly at all. He wasn't the same man he had been, she reminded herself for the umpteenth time. He was harder, more contained than he had been, and he had grown out of his lankiness to a lean, solid strength.

Her eyes slid sideways under her lashes to rest on the austere profile. She couldn't see them in the darkness but she knew there were new lines creasing his eyes, a tougher set to his jaw, a sterner line to his mouth.

That capacity for stillness was the same, though. She had often watched him sitting like that, his body relaxed but alert, and envied his ability to withdraw from the chaos and just be calm. She had loved his competence, his intelligence, the ironic gleam in the humorous grey eyes. Even as a young man, he had had an assurance that was understated, like everything else about Will, but quite unmistakeable.

There was something insensibly reassuring about his quiet presence. Whatever happened, you felt that Will could deal with it and everything would be all right. Even now, after everything that had happened, he made her feel safe.

If only that was all he had made her feel! The initial attraction she had felt for the ordinary-looking student had deepened into a dangerous passion that made Alice uneasy. She didn't like feeling out of control, and the strength of her emotions scared her.

Will had started out a good friend, a good companion, and he had become a good lover, but soon it went beyond even that. Alice was out of her depth. She didn't like the feeling of needing him, of not feeling quite complete without him. All her experience had taught her to rely on herself, and she had forced herself to resist the lure of binding herself to him for ever.

Because she had been so in love she hadn't seen that they wanted very different things out of life. The future Will enthused about hadn't been the one Alice had dreamed of. She had yearned all her life for security, and that had been the one thing Will couldn't offer. He'd wanted to continue his research, to work wherever he could find a coral reef, to do what he could to protect them. She'd wanted a wardrobe, somewhere she could hang up her clothes and never have to unpack them. She'd wanted a place she could call her own. She'd been sick of scrimping and saving to put herself through university. She'd been sick of window shopping. If she saw a pair of wonderful shoes in a window, she wanted to be able to go in and buy them.

There were no shoe shops on coral reefs. If she'd married Will, as he had asked her to, she'd have had to give up all her dreams to live his. Alice had decided that she couldn't, wouldn't, do that.

She had made the right decision, she told herself, but there was no denying that the physical attraction was still there. It was very hard to explain. There was nothing special about the way Will looked. He had a lean, intelligent face that could under no circumstances be called handsome, but the contrast between the severe mouth and the humorous grey eyes made him seem more attractive than he actually was.

The first time Alice had seen Will, she hadn't been conscious of any instant physical attraction. Later, that seemed strange. She'd thought he was nice, but it was only as she'd got to know him that she'd begun to notice those things that made him uniquely Will: the firmness of his chin, the texture of his skin, the angle of his jaw. The way the edges of his eyes creased when he smiled.

Once she had start noticing, of course, it had been impossible to stop. It hadn't been long before Alice had found her body utterly in thrall to his, and she'd only had to look at his mouth for her breath to shorten and for her entrails to be flooded with a warmth that spread through her until it lodged, tingling and quivering with excitement, just beneath her skin.

The way it was doing now.

Alice tucked her feet beneath her once more and drew herself in, willing the jangling awareness to fade. 'It's not enough,' she had told Will at Roger's wedding, and she knew that she had been right. If she let herself be sucked back into those dark, swirling depths of sexual attraction, she would lose control of her life and her self completely, and the last ten years would have been for nothing.

She swallowed, hard. 'So, what about you?' she asked to break the lengthening silence. 'Do you know what you want?'

For years Will would have been able to say instantly that he wanted her. And then he would have said that he wanted to forget her. Now ...

'Not really,' he said slowly. 'I've learnt not to want anything too specific. I don't want a Porsche or a knighthood or to win a million pounds. But I want other things, I suppose,' he went on, thinking about it.

'I want to keep Lily safe. I want her to grow up with a sense of joy and wonder at the world around her. I don't want her to be afraid of it.' He turned his head to look at Alice. 'I don't want her to end up frightened of love or too proud to admit that she needs other people.'

'Oh, so you don't want her to end up like me?' Alice asked flippantly, but there was no answering smile on Will's face as he met her gaze steadily.

'No,' he agreed. 'I want her to be happy.'

Was that really how he saw her—unhappy and afraid? Alice lay in bed that night, scowling into the darkness, hating the memory of the pity she had seen in Will's face. She didn't need him to be sorry for her. She was fine. She could look after herself. She didn't need anybody.

She had thought that she needed Tony, and look where that had got her. She had placed him at the centre of her life and told herself that she was safe at last. Tony hadn't made her head whirl with excitement, it was true, but it wasn't passion that Alice was looking for. She had had that with Will, and the power of those unmanageable emotions had left her uneasy and out of control. With Tony, she had felt settled and as if her future was safe at last. It had been a wonderful feeling.

Until Sandi had come along, and her carefully constructed world had fallen apart.

All those years she had dreamed of feeling secure, and with one meeting it had been shattered. Was it the loss of that dream that hurt more than losing Tony himself? Alice wondered for the first time. And did that mean that she had never really loved Tony at all?

For some reason, it was that thought that made Alice cry in a way she hadn't been able to cry since Tony had left. Trapped in a straitjacket of hurt and humiliation, she had taken refuge in a stony pride, but all at once she could feel the careful barriers she had erected around herself crumbling, and she lay under the mosquito net and wept and wept until at last she fell asleep.

Her eyes were still puffy when she woke the next morning, but she felt curiously released at the same time. Having spent her childhood trying not to let her parents guess how unhappy she was, Alice felt uncomfortable with crying. Until now, it had just seemed another way of admitting that everything was out of control, and she'd been afraid that, once she started, she might never be able to stop.

But this morning it felt as if a heavy hand had been lifted from her heart.

Perhaps she should try tears more often, Alice thought wryly.

Will had gone by the time she got up. She found Lily in the kitchen with the cook, a severe-looking woman called Sara. Alice was quite intimidated by her, but Lily seemed to accept her and was already picking up some words of the local language, a form of French Creole.

Alice was relieved not to have to face Will just yet. She might feel better for a good cry, but she had told him more than she wanted about herself last night, and now she felt exposed. At least she hadn't cried in front of him—that was something—but he had still been sorry for her, and that wasn't a feeling Alice liked at all.

She spent the morning exploring the garden with Lily, and together they crossed the track to the beach. In the daylight, the lagoon was a translucent, minty green, its surface ruffled occasionally by a cat's paw of breeze from the deep blue ocean that swelled and broke against the protecting reef. The leaning coconut palms splashed the white sand with shade, but it was still very hot and Alice was glad to keep on the shoes she had put on to pick her way through the coarse husks and roots that littered the ground beneath the trees.

She had bought the sandals on impulse at a market the previous summer, and Lily was frankly envious. They were cheap but fun, their garish plastic flowers achingly bright in the dazzling sunshine.

'I wish I could have some shoes like that,' said Lily wistfully.

'Let's see if we can find you some in town,' Alice said without thinking, and Lily's face lit up.

'*Could* we?' She sounded dazzled by the prospect.

'We'll go this afternoon,' said Alice.

'Look what I've got,' Lily said to Will when he got home that evening, and she lifted one foot so that he could admire her new shoes.

There hadn't been a great deal of choice in town—St Bonaventure would have to give some thought to modernising its shops if it wanted to attract large numbers of tourists and relieve them of their money, Alice thought—but they had found a pair of transparent pink sandals in Lily's size, and she could hardly have been more delighted if they were Manolo Blahniks.

Will shot a glance at Alice before studying the shoe Lily was showing him so proudly. 'They're very…pink,' he said after a moment.

'I know,' said Lily, deeply pleased.

'Lily and I thought we'd do a spot of shopping,' said Alice, who could tell that Will was considerably less delighted with the shoes but was trying hard not to show it.

'So I see.'

Lily looked earnestly up at her father. 'Alice is good at shopping,' she said, and Will's jaw tightened.

'There are more important things to be good at in life than shopping,' he said.

'Did you have to be quite so crushing?' Alice demanded crossly much later, when Lily was in bed. 'She was so thrilled with her shoes. It wouldn't have killed you to have shown some interest.'

'How can you be *interested* in a pair of shoes?' snarled Will, who was in a thoroughly bad mood, exacerbated by guilt at so comprehensively pricking his daughter's balloon earlier.

It had been the first time Lily had volunteered any information when he'd come home. Part of him had been ridiculously moved that she had come to show him her new shoes without prompting. She had been chattier than usual, too, but he had had to go and spoil things by his thoughtless comment.

Will sighed. He was very tired. It had been a long day, dealing with the fall-out from yesterday's accident, and it hadn't helped that he had slept badly the night before. His mind had been churning with what Alice had told him about her broken engagement. In the small hours, Will had had to acknowledge that he didn't like the fact that Tony had obviously been so important to her.

It was Tony who had given her what she wanted, Tony she was missing now. Alice could say all she wanted about not needing anybody; it was clear that she had loved Tony, and that he was the one she was always going to regret. Will knew exactly what that felt like.

He was sorry, of course, that she had been hurt so badly. But his pity was mixed with resentment at the years *he* had spent believing that he would never find anyone who could make him feel the way she did, the years spent hoping that somehow, somewhere, she was missing him too, and was sorry that she had ended things when she had.

And all the time she had been in love with Tony, dull, safe, sensible Tony who had broken her heart! Will was furious with her for making it so clear how ridiculous his fantasy had been all along, and more furious with himself for caring.

As if that wasn't enough of a slap in the face, now she was the one who was getting through to Lily. It was Alice who was making the bond with his daughter that should really be his, and he resented that too. Will knew that he was being unreasonable and unfair, and he was ashamed of himself, but there it was, something else to add to the mix of his already confused feelings about her.

The next few weeks were going to be even harder than he had feared. Lily went to bed early, which meant that there would just be the two of them alone together every evening like this. Alice still stirred him like no other woman he had ever met. She made him feel angry, and resentful and regretful and grateful and irritated and amused and sympathetic and muddled and disappointed and exhilarated and aroused, often all at the same time. And all it took was for her to turn her head and he was pierced by such joy at her presence that it drove the breath from his lungs.

'Look,' he said, 'I'm sorry I wasn't more enthusiastic about the shoes. I know she likes them. I just don't think it's a good idea for you to encourage her to think that happiness lies in shopping.'

Alice was exasperated. 'I bought her a pair of cheap shoes,' she said tightly, and was aware, deeply buried, of relief that

Will was being so objectionable. It was much easier to be cross than to be aware of him and his mouth, his hands and the way he made her *feel* again. 'It wasn't a philosophical statement, and it won't turn her into a raging materialist. It was just a present, and not a particularly expensive one at that.'

'It's not about the money,' said Will irritably. 'It's about giving her false expectations of the kind of life she's going to have now. Nikki used to buy her things the whole time—toys, clothes, the latest brands, whatever made her feel better for being away at work so much—but that's not going to happen now. I'm not going to try and buy Lily's love, even if I had the time to do it. Little shopping trips like today's will just remind Lily of a life that's gone, and I'm afraid it will just make it harder for her to settle down here.'

'There's a difference between buying affection and giving your child some security,' snapped Alice. 'Lily's been wrenched out of the only life she's ever known. Where *are* all these toys and clothes that her mother bought for her? Did it not occur to you that she might like a few familiar things around her? Or would that have been making things too easy for her? I suppose you thought what she really needed was a clean break and the equivalent of an emotional boot camp to help her settle!'

'Of course not,' said Will stiffly. 'It's true I only brought what I could carry this time, but all her other things are being shipped out. They should arrive in a couple of weeks.'

'Oh,' said Alice, wrong-footed. She had been ready to whip herself into a fury at his stupidity and intransigence. 'Well… good,' she finished lamely.

'Is there anything else she needs—apart from pink shoes, that is—until the shipment arrives?'

'She could do with more to keep her occupied during the day.' Alice was glad that Will had given her the opening. She had intended to raise it, but was afraid she might have pushed him a bit too far to suggest it herself. 'If I didn't think you'd throw a fit at the idea of going to the shops again, I'd suggest getting her some books and maybe some paper and crayons.'

'If I give you some money, will you take her and let her choose whatever she wants?'

'What?' She clapped a hand to her chest and opened her eyes wide. 'You mean we're going to be allowed to go *shopping*?'

Will clamped down on his temper, not without some difficulty. 'For things Lily really needs,' he said repressively. 'I don't want it spent on rubbish.'

'Heavens, no! We don't want to risk Lily having something silly that would give her pleasure, do we?' Alice got up in a swish of skirt. 'That would be spoiling her, and we can't have *that*!'

He had handled that all wrong, thought Will glumly as she swept off saying that she was going to read in her room. He had to stop letting her get to him like this. He needed to forget that she was Alice and treat her the way he would any other nanny. Dee hadn't wound him up this way, and she hadn't done nearly as good a job as Alice. Somehow he would have to find a way to start again.

Alice was decidedly frosty the next morning, and Will's nerve failed at the thought of a tricky discussion before breakfast, but he was determined to make amends when he came home. He left work as early as he could, and found Alice and Lily on the back verandah playing cards.

Hesitating behind the screen door, he looked at the two heads bent close together over the little table, and his chest tightened so sharply that he had to take a deep breath before he pushed open the door.

At the sound of the door banging to behind him, Lily looked up with a shy smile. She didn't cry 'Daddy!' or throw herself into his arms, but it was such a big step for her that

Will felt enormously heartened. Alice was looking aloof, but that didn't bother him. He knew he would have to work harder to win her round, but in the meantime he was content to go over and ruffle Lily's dark hair.

'Hello,' he said with a smile. 'What are you playing?'

'Memory.'

'Who's winning?'

'Alice is,' Lily admitted reluctantly.

That was typical of Alice. She would never patronise a six-year-old by letting her win. When Lily *did* win, her victory would be the sweeter.

'It won't be easy to beat her,' Will warned Lily. 'She's got a good memory.'

Too good a memory, Alice thought, trying not to notice how the smile softened his face. She didn't want to be able to remember too well at the moment. It would be much easier if she could forget the times she and Will had played cards together. Neither of them had had any money as students, and they hadn't been able to go out very often, but Alice had been perfectly happy to stay at home with him, to sit on the floor and play cards, while outside the rain beat against the windows.

Once, when she'd got a distinction for an essay, Will had taken her out to dinner to celebrate. He had only been able to afford an old-fashioned brasserie on the outskirts of town with plastic tablecloths and a dubious taste in décor, but it had still been one of the best meals Alice had ever had. She wanted to forget that, the way she wanted to forget the long walks along winter beaches, the lazy Sunday mornings in bed, all those times when they had laughed until it hurt. She wanted to forget the feel of those hands curving over her body, to forget the taste of his mouth, of his skin. The last thing she wanted was to be able to remember the sweet, shivery, swirling and oh-so-seductive pleasure they had found in each other night after night.

She wanted to remember why it had been such a good idea to end it all.

Will was still talking to Lily. 'That was a good idea to buy cards.'

'We went shopping again.' Lily eyed her father with a certain wariness after his unenthusiastic response to her shoes the day before, but he kept his smile firmly in place.

'Did you buy anything else?'

'Some books.'

'Show me what you bought.'

Lily ran off quite willingly to find the books, and Will glanced at Alice, who immediately turned away, mortified to have been caught watching him.

'Don't lift your chin at me like that,' he said. 'I know I deserve it, but I really am sorry. I was in a bad mood yesterday, and I shouldn't have taken it out on you and Lily, but I did.'

Alice's chin lowered a fraction.

'I'm truly grateful to you, Alice, for what you've done. You've made a huge difference to Lily already, and I know I'm going to have to try harder to make things work if we're going to spend the next month together. Say you'll forgive me,' he coaxed. 'It'll make it much easier for us all if you do!'

The chin went down a bit further.

'Would you like me to go down on my knees and apologise?'

'That won't be necessary,' said Alice with as much dignity as she could muster. She wished he would go back to being grumpy and disagreeable, but she could hardly sulk for a month. 'Apology accepted.'

'I really am sorry, Alice,' Will said quietly, and, in spite of herself, Alice's head turned until she met his steady gaze.

That was something else she remembered—how those grey eyes could tip her off balance so that she felt as if she was toppling forward and tumbling down into their depths, falling out of time and into a place where there was nothing but Will and the slow, steady beat of her heart and the boom of her pulse in her ears.

And when she had managed to wrench her eyes away it had almost been a shock to find, like now, that the world had kept turning without her. Alice had once been sitting on a train, waiting for it to depart and watching the train beside them turn into a blur of carriages as they pulled out of the station. She had never forgotten the jarring shock of realising that it was another train that had left, and hers hadn't moved at all. As the last carriage had disappeared and she'd seen the platform once more, it had felt as if her train had jerked to a sudden, sickening halt. It was the same feeling she had now.

'Let's both try harder,' she muttered.

'All right,' said Will. 'Let's do that.'

CHAPTER SEVEN

'Do you want to see my books?'

It was a tiny comfort that Will seemed as startled as Alice was by Lily's reappearance. She was clutching a pile of books to her chest and watching them with a doubtful expression, as if sensing something strange in the atmosphere.

'Of course I do.' Will forced a smile. 'Let's have a look.'

Lily's face was very serious as she stood by his chair and handed him the books one by one. Will examined them all carefully. 'This looks like a good one,' he said, pulling out a book of fairy stories. He glanced at his daughter. 'Would you like me to read you a story?'

Lily hesitated and then nodded, and, feeling as if she were somehow intruding on a private moment, Alice got to her feet. She suspected that this was the closest Will had ever been to Lily, and the first time he read her a story should be something special for both of them.

'That sounds like a good idea,' she said, firmly quashing the childish part of her that felt just a tiny bit excluded. 'You two read a story together, and I'll go and heat up the supper Sara left for us. She left very strict instructions, and I'm frightened of what she'll say if I get it wrong!'

Alice lingered in the kitchen, giving them time alone

together. It wasn't a bad thing for her to have some time to herself too, she reflected. She had spent all day feeling furious with Will, and there had been something almost comforting in that, but all he had had to do was say sorry and look into her eyes and her anger had crumbled. Like a town without a wall, she was left without defences, and it made her feel oddly vulnerable and uneasy. Will shouldn't still be able to do that to her.

Oh, this was silly! Alice laid the table with unnecessary vehemence, banging down the knives and forks, cross with herself for making such a fuss about nothing. She should be glad that Will had apologised and was obviously prepared to be reasonable. She *was* glad for Lily's sake, if not her own. They couldn't have spent the next month arguing with each other. That would have been no example to set a six-year-old.

It would be so much easier if she could just think of Will as Lily's father, if she could wipe out the memories of another time and another place. It was all very well to tell him that she wanted to be friends, but that was harder than she'd thought it would be.

Alice sighed. Her feelings about Will weren't simple. They never had been and they never would be, and she might as well accept that. Nothing had changed, after all. She had meant what she had said. When her holiday was over, she was going home and she was starting life afresh on her own. No more looking back, no more wanting something from love that it just couldn't give.

When Alice went back out onto the verandah, Will and Lily were sitting close together on the wicker two-seater. Will's arm rested loosely around his daughter and she was leaning into him, listening intently to the story.

Reluctant to disturb them, Alice sat down quietly and listened too. The sun was setting over the ocean, blazing through the trunks of the palm trees, and suffusing the sky with an unearthly orange glow in the eerie hush of the brief tropical dusk. Lily's face was rapt. Will's deep voice resonated in the still air and, watching them, Alice felt a curious sense of peace settle over her. Time itself was suspended between day and night, and suddenly there was no future, no past, just now on the dusty wooden verandah.

'... and they lived happily ever after.' Will closed the book, and his smile as he looked down at his daughter was rather twisted. It was sad that Lily already knew that things didn't always end as happily as they did in stories.

'Did you like that?' he asked, and Lily nodded. 'We could read another one tomorrow, if you like,' he said casually, not wanting her to know how much it had meant to him to have her small, warm body leaning against him. It was like trying to coax a wild animal out of its hiding place, he thought. He wanted desperately for her to trust him, but he sensed that, if he was too demonstrative, she would retreat once more.

'OK,' she said. It wasn't much, but Will felt as if he had conquered Everest.

It was all getting too emotional. Alice had an absurd lump in her throat. Definitely time to bring things down to earth. 'Let's have supper,' she said.

'You're starting to make a real bond with her,' she said to Will.

Lily was in bed, the supper had been cleared away, and by tacit agreement she and Will had found themselves back on the verandah. She had thought about excusing herself and spending the evening reading in her room, but it was too hot, and anyway that would look as if she was trying to avoid him, which would be nonsense. They had cleared the air, and there was no reason for them to be awkward together.

Besides, she liked it out here. It reminded her of being a child, when she would lie in bed and listen to the whirr and click and scrape of the insect orchestra overlaid by the comforting sound of her parents' voices as they sat and talked in the dark outside her room.

She had been thinking of her father a lot this evening. He used to read to her the way Will had read to Lily earlier. He would put on extraordinary voices and embellish the stories wildly as he went along, changing the ending every time, so that Alice had never been quite sure how it was going to turn out. No wonder she had grown up craving security, Alice thought with a rueful smile. She hadn't even been able to count on books to stay the same until she could read them for herself!

Funny how she kept thinking of her childhood here. Normally, she kept those memories firmly buried, but she was conscious that she was remembering it not with her usual bitterness and frustration, and not with nostalgia either, but, yes, with a certain affection. Perhaps she should have remembered more of the good times as well as the bad.

'Lily's learning to trust you,' she went on, and Will leant back in his chair and stretched with a sigh that was part relief, part weariness.

'I hope so,' he said. 'Just doing something simple like reading a story makes me realise how much time I've missed with her. I've got a lot of catching up to do.'

Alice hesitated. 'How come you're such a stranger to her?' she asked curiously, hoping that she wasn't opening too raw a wound. 'Didn't you want a child?'

Will glanced at her and then away. 'Do you want the truth?' he said. 'When Nikki first told me that she was pregnant, I was appalled. Lily was the result of a doomed attempt to save a failing marriage. That's not a good reason to bring a child into the world. Nikki had already made arrangements to leave when she found out she was pregnant. So, no, I didn't want a child then.'

'But Nikki decided to keep the baby?'

'Yes. I don't know why, to be honest,' said Will. 'She couldn't wait to get back to her career, and as far as I could make out Lily spent more time with her grandparents than she did with her mother. Nikki made it very clear that it was her decision whether or not to keep the baby, and I had to respect that. I accepted my responsibility to support the child, but I couldn't really imagine what it would be like to be a father,' he admitted. 'I hadn't been involved in the pregnancy the way most fathers are. I didn't get to see the first scan, or go to antenatal classes. I was just someone who would be handing over a certain sum of money every month.'

'Would you rather Nikki had chosen not to have the baby?' Alice asked curiously.

'There was a time when I thought that would have been the best solution,' said Will. 'But then a funny thing happened. Nikki didn't want me there at the birth, but she did let me see Lily a couple of days later.'

'You cared enough to see her, anyway.'

He looked out at the night. 'I can't honestly say I cared, not then,' he said slowly. 'I felt responsible, that's all. Nikki was in London by then, and I was working in the Red Sea, but my child was being born. I couldn't just pretend it wasn't happening, could I?'

Some men might have done, reflected Alice, but not Will.

'So I went to visit,' he went on, unaware of her mental interruption. 'I guess Nikki thought that if she wanted me to pay maintenance she would have to let me see my own child, but she wasn't exactly welcoming. Fortunately, there was a nice nurse there. I'm not sure whether she knew the situation, or just thought I was a typically nervous first-time father, but before I could say anything she picked Lily up and put her in my arms and—'

He stopped, and in the dim light Alice could just see that his mouth was pressed into a straight line that was somehow more expressive of the feelings he was suppressing than a dramatic show of tears and emotion would have been.

'...And I felt...' he began again when he had himself under control, only to falter to a halt again. 'I can't really describe how I felt,' he admitted after a moment. 'I looked down at this tiny, perfect little thing and just stared and stared. She was so new and so strange, and yet I knew instantly—deep in my gut—that she was part of me.

'I've never felt anything like it before,' he said. 'It was such a strong feeling, it was like a tight band around my chest, and I could hardly breathe with it. It was too painful to be happiness, and there was terror in there too, but it was a wonderful feeling too... I don't know what it was.'

Surprised at how moved she was, Alice managed a smile. 'It sounds like love,' she said, lightly enough, and Will turned his head to look at her for a long, intense moment.

'Yes,' he said after a moment. 'I suppose that's what it was. But not love the way—'

He had so nearly said *the way I loved you*. Will caught himself up just in time.

'It's not the same as the love between a man and a woman,' he finished smoothly.

'Of course not,' said Alice. 'But it's still love. I've never had a child, but I recognized the feeling you described straight away.'

She remembered lying in bed next to Will and feeling just that mixture of terror and wonder, a feeling so intense that it was almost pain. Its power had seemed dangerous, overwhelming, uncontrollable, and in the end she had run away from it. She had been a coward, Alice knew, but at the time it had seemed the sensible thing to do.

And now... Well, there was no point in looking back. No

point in wondering what it would have been like if she had given in to that feeling instead of fighting it, if she had chosen love rather than security. She and Will might have had a child together. She would have discovered for herself how it felt to hold a child in her arms.

She wouldn't have been able to run away from *that* feeling.

Aware that she was drifting perilously close to regret, Alice gave herself a mental shake. She had made her own choices, and she would have to live with the consequences.

'I don't think Lily knows that you love her that much,' she said, breaking the silence.

'How could she?' said Will. 'I've hardly seen her since she was a baby. Nikki had already started the divorce process before Lily was born.'

'You'd think the baby would have brought you together,' Alice commented.

'I would have been prepared to give it another go for Lily's sake, but I suspect Nikki was right when she said that we both knew it wasn't going to work, so we'd better accept reality sooner rather than later.'

Will shifted shoulders restlessly, as if trying to dislodge the memory pressing onto them. Of course, that was what Alice had said too. *It'll never work. Let's call it a day while we're still friends. It's not worth even trying.* At least Nikki had taken the risk of marrying him. Alice hadn't even had the guts to give it a go.

'So you didn't contest the divorce?'

'No.' He shook his head. 'Our marriage was a mistake. Nikki was right about that. We should never have got married in the first place.'

'Why did you, then?' asked Alice, who had no patience with people who didn't think through the consequences of their actions. Of course, sometimes you could think about things too much, and you ended up missing opportunities, but Will was an intelligent man, and marriage was a serious business. It wasn't the kind of thing you fell into *by mistake*.

The sharpness in her voice made Will glance at her, but he didn't answer immediately. How could he tell Alice how hard he had tried to find someone else after she had given him that final 'no' at Roger's wedding? How every woman he'd met had seemed either twee or colourless in comparison to her? Nikki had been the first woman he'd met with a strength of personality to match hers. Seduced by the notion of wiping Alice from his memory once and for all, Will had convinced himself that he was falling in love with Nikki's forcefulness and vivacity, and he had been too eager to find out what she was really like until it was too late.

'I think I fell in love with the idea of Nikki, rather than with the person she really was,' he said at last. 'And I think she did the same.'

Alice opened her mouth to tell him it had been madness to even think about marrying an idea, but then closed it abruptly. Hadn't she done the same with Tony, after all? Tony had represented something that she had always yearned for, but she hadn't really known him. If she had, she might not have been so unprepared when he'd met Sandi.

'It was a holiday romance that got out of hand,' Will went on. 'She came out to the Red Sea to learn how to dive, and when we met she was incredibly enthusiastic about diving and the reef. I saw that she was fun, pretty, vivacious…and I think she saw me as someone very different from her friends and business associates in London.'

Alice could imagine it all very clearly. To Nikki, bored with men in suits and ties, escaping from a cold, grey London, Will must have seemed hard to resist with his wind-tanned skin and the glitter of sunlit sea in his eyes. He would have been a step up, too, from the surfers and beach bums. Will's shorts and T-shirts might have been as faded from the sun as theirs, but he had an air of competence and assurance that gave him the kind of authority other men had to put on suits to acquire.

'So you were both carried away by the sea and the stars?' she suggested, with just a squeeze of acid in her voice.

'You could say that,' Will agreed dryly. 'And of course, once reality set in, the sea and the stars weren't enough. Nikki was full of how she wanted to start a new life with me, but it didn't take long before she was bored, and then she started to resent me for "making" her give up her career in London.'

His mouth twisted. 'It wasn't a good time. We tried to patch things up—hence Lily—but in the end it was obvious it wasn't going to work. Nikki wanted to pick up her career where she'd left off, and the truth was that by then I wanted out of the marriage too. I just didn't count on how Lily's birth would change things.'

'It must have made everything more complicated,' said Alice, and he gave a mirthless laugh.

'You could say that. Nikki insisted on having full custody of Lily, and I was prepared to accept that. What I wasn't prepared to accept was not having any access to my daughter at all.'

'No access? But that's completely unreasonable!' Alice protested, shocked. '*And* unfair!'

Will shrugged. 'Unreasonable…unfair… You can shout all you like, but, when you're up against the kind of hot-shot lawyers Nikki hired, saying that it's unfair doesn't get you very far. For two years she refused to communicate with me except through the intimidating letters her lawyers would send me.'

'But why would she be like that? You'd have thought she'd have wanted her child to grow up knowing its father!'

'I don't know.' Will rubbed a weary hand over his face. 'The only thing I can think was that she was afraid I'd somehow take Lily away, but I wouldn't have done that, and she had no grounds for suspecting that I would.'

'I'm sorry,' said Alice, appalled at what Will had been through. 'It must have been very hard for you.'

'I didn't react quickly enough.' Will's face was set in grim lines as he remembered that bleak period. 'I'm a scientist. I understand about ocean currents, and protogyny among coral-reef fish, and sampling by random quadrats, but I wasn't well equipped to deal with divorce lawyers. It took me too long to get my own hot-shot lawyers and take the fight back…and by the time I did Nikki had changed tactics.'

Alice frowned. She didn't like the image of Will, bruised from the wreckage of his marriage, frustrated by lawyers and manipulated by Nikki. No wonder there were harsh lines on his face now. 'In what way?'

'She opted for emotional blackmail next,' he said, and, although he was clearly trying to keep his voice neutral, it was impossible to miss the underlying thread of bitterness. 'And very effective it was, too. Lily was already a toddler by then, and Nikki claimed it would be too unsettling for her to see me regularly. I wouldn't understand her needs the way Nikki did. It would distress Lily to go and stay somewhere strange. She didn't know who I was. I wouldn't know how to look after her properly. She needed to be in a familiar environment. It would be too disruptive for her to spend longer than a couple of hours with me. And so on and so on.'

'With the result that you became even more of a stranger to Lily?'

'Exactly. The few times I did manage to see Lily I was only able to take her out for a few hours, and frankly they weren't successful visits. I think Nikki was so paranoid about the possibility of me taking her away altogether that she'd transferred all her tension and suspicion to Lily. It's not surprising that she was nervous of me. As far as she was concerned, I was a stranger her mother didn't trust.'

He rubbed his face again, pushing his fingers back through his hair with a tired sigh. 'It wasn't just Nikki's fault. I didn't know how to reach Lily either. I wanted to tell Lily how much she meant to me, but I didn't know how, and I still don't. I've got no experience of being a father, and, now that I've got Lily all the time, I just feel inadequate. I either try too hard, or I get it completely wrong.'

He sounded so dispirited that Alice found herself reaching out to lay a comforting hand on his arm.

'You got it right tonight,' she told him.

She was burningly aware of his hard muscles beneath her fingers, and wished that she hadn't touched him. She had reached out instinctively, but now that her hand was on his arm it seemed suddenly a big deal, and she felt jolted, as if she had done something incredibly daring.

Which was ridiculous. It was only a matter of a hand on his forearm, after all. No reason to feel as if she had done the equivalent of clambering onto his lap, unbuttoning his shirt, pressing hot kisses up his throat …

Alice swallowed. She wasn't even touching his skin, for God's sake! Will was wearing a long-sleeved shirt rolled back at the wrist, but there was only a thin barrier of cotton between his skin and hers, and she was sure that she could feel his warmth and strength through the fine material anyway.

Horribly conscious of the way her body was thrumming in response, she made herself pull her hand away. She couldn't have been touching him for more than a few seconds, but her heart was beating so hard she was afraid Will would be able to hear it above the crescendo of the night insects.

In this light it was impossible to tell whether he had even registered her touch, and his voice sounded perfectly normal as he credited her with the small progress he had made with Lily.

'Thanks to you,' he said. 'The books were your idea.'

'But you were the one who read to her.' Sure that her cheeks were still burning with awareness, Alice was very grateful for the darkness that she hoped hid her expression as effectively as it did Will's.

'You're good with children,' he said abruptly. 'Somehow I never imagined that you would be.'

'I'm not really,' she confessed, glad that her voice seemed steadier now. 'I'm not usually that interested in them. But I like Lily.'

'You've never wanted children of your own?'

Alice thought about the years she had spent trying to find a man she could settle down and be happy with, a man she could build a family with, a man who would make her forget Will and all that she had walked away from. She had thought she had found him at last in Tony. They had talked about having children, when they were married, when the time was right. But sometimes the time was never right, and, even if it was, it wasn't always that easy. Look at Roger and Beth.

'You can't always have what you want,' she said in a low voice, and Will turned to her, wondering if she was thinking about Tony who she had loved so much, and thinking about how much he had wanted her for so long.

'No,' he agreed. 'Sometimes you can't.'

'It'll rain soon.' Will handed Alice a glass of fresh lime juice chinking with ice, and sat down next to her with a cold beer.

'I hope so.' Alice took the glass with a murmur of thanks and held it against her cheek, letting the condensation cool her skin. 'Mmm…that feels nice,' she told Will, who had to make himself look away from the sight of her, her eyes closed in pleasure as the condensation on the glass trickled down her throat and into her cleavage. It was dark on the verandah, but sometimes not dark enough.

'It's been so hot today,' she went on, languid with heat. 'I took Lily over to see Beth today so we could sit in the air-conditioning for a while.'

With her free hand, Alice lifted a few damp strands of hair that had fallen from their clip onto the back of her neck. 'The heat doesn't usually bother me, but for the last couple of days it's been suffocating. It's like trying to breathe through a scarf.'

'It's the pressure.' Will was dismayed at how hoarse his voice sounded. 'A good storm will clear the air.'

'I can't wait,' she sighed. 'There's no sign of any rain clouds, though. I've been looking at the horizon all day.'

'They'll be boiling up now,' said Will. 'Didn't you notice them at sunset? That's always a sign. It has to break soon.'

He wished that he was just talking meteorologically. A different kind of pressure had been building inexorably over the ten days since Alice had arrived, and Will was finding it harder and harder to ignore.

He had done his best to try and think of her simply as Lily's nanny, but it wasn't any good. She was resolutely Alice, impossible to ignore. It didn't matter if she was just sitting quietly next to him in the dark, or playing cards with Lily or laying the table. It was there in every turn of her head, every gesture of her hands, every sweep of her lashes.

Will struggled to remember how he had disliked her at Roger and Beth's party, but that tense, brittle, superficial Alice had somehow been whittled away by the heat, the sunlight and the warm breeze that riffled the lagoon and rustled through the coconut palms. He had to remind himself constantly that she hadn't really changed that much. She still wore that absurd collection of shoes. She flicked through magazines and talked about clothes, make-up and God knew what else, encouraging Lily to remember her life in London more than Will wanted. She still talked about the great career she was going to resume.

She was still going home.

He needed to keep that in mind, Will told himself at least once a day. She would only be there for another few weeks, and then she would be gone. He would have to start thinking about life without her all over again.

It alarmed him how easily they had slipped into a routine, and he was afraid that he was getting used to it. He left early for work, but for the first time in years found himself looking forward to going home at the end of the day. Alice and Lily were usually on the verandah, playing games or reading together, and he would often stand behind the screen door and watch them, unobserved for a while, disturbed by the intensity of pleasure the peaceful scene gave him. Sometimes he tried to tell himself he would have felt the same no matter who was with Lily, but he knew that he was fooling himself.

It wasn't just the fact that Lily was gradually settling down. It was Alice.

Every night when Lily was asleep, they would sit on the verandah, like now, and they would talk easily until one of them made an unthinking comment that reminded them of the past and all they had meant to each other. And when that happened, the tension a routine kept successfully at bay most of the time would trickle back into the atmosphere, stretching the silence uncomfortably until one or other of them made an excuse and went to bed.

Will had hoped that the weekend would break that pattern, and things had certainly been different since then. He just wasn't convinced that it was for the better.

On the Saturday he had taken the two of them out to the reef in the project's tin boat. Half-submerged in a life jacket that was really too big for her, Lily had clutched onto the wooden seat. Her face had been shaded by a floppy cotton hat, but, sitting opposite her at the helm, Will could peer under the brim and see that her expression was an odd mixture of excitement and trepidation. She'd looked as if she wanted to be thrilled, but didn't quite dare to let herself go.

'Would you like to drive the boat?' he asked her, and her eyes widened.

'I don't know how.'

'I'll show you.'

Will held out his hand, and after a moment, with some encouragement from Alice, she took it and let herself be handed carefully across to stand between his knees. He showed her how to hold the tiller, and kept her steady, guiding the boat unobtrusively from behind. Lily's small body was tense with concentration, and it was hard to know whether she was terrified or loving it.

Over her head, he could see Alice, straight-backed as ever on the narrow seat, holding her hat onto her head. Her eyes were hidden by sunglasses, but when she met his gaze she smiled and nodded at Lily. 'She's smiling,' she mouthed, as if she knew what he most wanted to hear, and Will felt his heart swell with happiness.

The sun glittered on the water, bouncing off every surface and throwing dazzling patterns over Alice's face as the little boat bounced over the waves. Everything seemed extraordinarily clear, suddenly: the breeze in his hair, the tang of the sea in his lungs, his daughter smiling as she leant into him… And Alice, contrary, prickly, unforgettable Alice. At that moment, Will felt something close to vertigo, a spinning sensation as if he were teetering on the edge of a cliff, and he had to jerk his gaze away before he did something stupid like telling her that he loved her still.

Bad idea.

It had been a happy day, though. They pulled the boat onto a tiny coral island, where they could wade into the warm water and watch the fish dart around their ankles, flashing silver in the sunlight. Will taught Lily how to snorkel while Alice sat under a solitary leaning palm and unpacked the picnic they had brought.

Afterwards, Lily dozed off in the shade, and Will watched Alice wandering along the shore. The set of her head on that straight spine was so familiar it made Will ache. Her loose white-linen trousers were rolled up to her knees, her face shadowed by the brim of her hat, a pair of delicate sandals dangling from her hand.

'You won't need shoes,' Will had said when they'd got into the boat that morning, but Alice had refused to leave them behind in the car.

'I feel more comfortable with shoes on,' she had said. 'You never know when you're going to need them to run away.'

'You won't be able to run very far on the reef,' Will had pointed out, but she'd only lifted her chin at him.

'I'm keeping them on.'

Alice would always want an escape-route planned, he realised as he watched her pause and look out across the translucent green of the lagoon to where the deep blue of the Indian Ocean frothed in bright white against the far reef. She would always want to be able to run away, just as she had run away from him before.

She wouldn't be here now if she didn't have that ticket home, Will remembered. It would be foolish to let himself hope that she might stay. She wasn't going to, and he had to accept that now. Consciously steadying his heart, he made himself think coolly and practically. He mustn't be seduced by the sea and the sunlight and Alice's smile. Sure, he could enjoy today, but he wouldn't expect it to last. There were no for evers where Alice was concerned.

When Lily woke up, she ran instantly down to join Alice at the water's edge. Will watched them both, and tried not to mind that his daughter so obviously preferred Alice's company to his. Tried not to worry, too, how she would manage when Alice was gone.

He could see them bending down to examine things they found on the beach. Alice was crouching down, turning something in her hand and showing it to Lily, who took it and studied it carefully.

And then it happened.

'Daddy!' she cried, running up the beach towards him. 'Daddy, look!'

It was a cowrie shell, small but perfect, with an unusual leopard pattern on its back, but Will hardly noticed it. He was overwhelmed by the fact that Lily had run to him, had called him Daddy, had wanted him to share in her pleasure, and his throat closed so tightly with emotion that it was hard to speak.

'This is a great shell,' he managed. 'It's an unusual one, too. You were very clever to find it.'

'Alice found it,' Lily admitted with reluctant honesty, and Will looked up to see Alice, who had followed more slowly up the beach. Their eyes met over Lily's dark head, and she smiled at him, knowing exactly what Lily's excited dash up the beach had meant to him.

Will smiled back, pushing the future firmly out of his mind. He knew the day wouldn't last for ever, but right then, with Lily's intent face, the feel of the shell in his palm, and Alice smiling at him, it was enough.

CHAPTER EIGHT

WILL was thinking about that day out on the reef as he sat on the verandah with Alice and the hot air creaked with the pressure of the oncoming storm. He had done his best to keep his distance from her since then.

Again and again, he had reminded himself that she would be leaving soon and that there was no point in noticing the curve of her mouth, or the line of her throat, or the sheen of her skin in the crushing heat. No point in remembering how she felt, how she tasted. No point in thinking about how sweet and exciting and *right* it had felt to make love to her.

Not doing any of that was definitely the sensible thing to do. But it was hard.

'Listen!' Alice held up a hand suddenly, startling Will out of his thoughts.

'What is it? Is it Lily?' he asked, instantly anxious in case he had missed a cry.

'It's the insects.'

Will looked at her puzzled. 'What insects?'

'Exactly. They've stopped.'

And, sure enough, the deafening rasp, scratch and shrill of the insects, that was such a familiar backdrop to the evenings here that Will barely heard it any more, had paused and in its place was an uncanny silence.

The next instant there was a rip of lightning in the distance, an almighty crack of thunder overhead, and a deluge of rain came crashing down onto the roof. One second there had been the hot, heavy, *waiting* silence, the next there was nothing but sound and fury and the pounding, thundering, hammering rain. It fell not in drops but as a solid mass, bouncing back in the air as it hit solid ground, and overwhelming the gutters so that it simply cascaded in a sheet over the edge of the verandah.

Alice laughed with sheer delight. 'I *love* it when it rains like this!' she shouted to Will, but it was doubtful that he could hear her over the deafening roar of the rain.

Caught up in the elemental excitement of the downpour, she jumped to her feet. The sheer power of it was awe-inspiring, almost frightening, but exhilarating at the same time. Alice could feel the raw energy of it surging around the verandah, pushing and pulling at her, making her blood pound.

Normally she hated feeling so out of control, but a tropical downpour was different. She knew it wouldn't last very long, but while it did she could feel wild and reckless, the way she would never allow herself to be the rest of the time.

She looked at Will, who had got to his feet too, moved by the same restless excitement generated by the breaking of the pressure that had been pressing down on them for the last few days. He was watching the rain, his intelligent face alive with interest, the stern mouth curling upwards into an almost-smile, and, as her eyes rested on him, Alice was gripped by a hunger to touch him once more, to feel his hard hands against her skin, to abandon herself to the electricity in the air.

Instinctively, she took a step towards him, just at the moment when the force of the rain finally succeeded in dislodging part of the roof and poured through a hole directly onto her head. If Alice had stayed where she was, the water would have splashed harmlessly onto the verandah, but as it was she was drenched instantly.

It felt as if someone had tipped a bucket over her, and she gasped with the shock of it before she started to laugh again. It was like standing under a waterfall, the water cool and indescribably refreshing after the suffocating heat, and as it was too late to get dry Alice closed her eyes and tipped her face up to the cascading water.

In seconds her dress was clinging to her, and her shoes— her favourite jewelled kitten-heels—were probably ruined, but right then Alice didn't care. Pulling the clip from her hair, she shook it free and let the rain plaster it to her head as it ran in rivulets over her face and down her throat.

Will had been unable not to laugh at the sight of her ambushed by the leak in the roof, but as he watched her close her eyes and turn her face up to the water, as he watched the fine fabric of her dress stick to her breasts and hips, as he watched the rain sliding over skin, his smile faded at the extraordinary sensuality of the scene, and his body tightened.

As if sensing his reaction, Alice opened her eyes. Her lashes were wet and spiky, and she had to blink against the water running over her face, but her gaze was dark and steady.

There was no need for either of them to say anything. They both knew that the careful defences they had built over the last couple of weeks were no match for the downpour. For tonight, the rules, their hopes and their fears, meant nothing. There was only the two of them, the crackle of electricity, and the drumming rain. When Will reached for her, Alice reached out at the same time and tugged him under the rain still pouring through the hole in the roof.

They kissed with the water spilling around them, trickling

from his skin onto hers, and from hers to his, their bodies pressing so close that it couldn't find a way between them. They kissed and kissed and kissed again, hard, hungry kisses that fed on the power of the downpour and on the spiralling excitement that spun and surged as they touched each other with increasing urgency. Their hands moved instinctively over each other, clutching, clasping, sliding, shifting, finding long-remembered secret places, rediscovering the feel and the taste and the touch of each other.

'Will...' Alice pressed her lips to his throat in fevered kisses, revelling in the feel of his body, in the wonderful, familiar smell of his skin, arching and shuddering with pleasure at the touch of his hands, the taste of his mouth, How could she have told herself that she had forgotten how it felt? 'Will...' she gasped, inarticulate with need.

'What?' he murmured raggedly against her throat. They might as well have been naked already. Their clothes were plastered to their wet bodies, and should have felt cold and clammy, but the heat of their beating blood was keeping them warm. Will wouldn't have been surprised to see steam rising.

Alice didn't know what she wanted to say, didn't know how to tell him how she felt. Her mind was reeling with pleasure, and all she could think about was the clamour of her body, the desire that was running rampant, unstoppable, out of control...

'Tell me what you want, Alice,' Will whispered, and then lifted his head so that he could look down into her face, his own streaked with water now too.

'I don't know,' said Alice helplessly.

But she did know. She wanted him. She wanted more of him, all of him. She wanted him closer, harder, inside her. She wanted him completely—but the very strength of her need was beginning to alarm her, while a small voice of reason inside her was insinuating itself into the wild recklessness that had gripped her, telling her to be careful, reminding her about the past and the future, about the risk of abandoning herself utterly to the moment.

Oh, how she wanted to, though!

'I want ...' she began unsteadily, and then swallowed. 'I want to pretend that this is all there is,' she told him at last.

'This *is* all there is,' said Will. 'This is all that matters.' And, taking her hand, he led her inside and out of the rain.

Alice lay next to Will and let her pounding blood slow, her breathing steady. Her entire body was still thrumming with satisfaction, and she felt heady and boneless. It was impossible to regret what had happened, even now the wildness and the excitement of the night had dissipated. Their bodies had remembered each other with a heart-stopping clarity, their senses snarling and tangling and tantalizing, surrendering together to the soaring rhythm of love until they'd shattered with release.

It had been wonderful. She could hardly pretend otherwise when the glory was still beating through her veins and shimmering out to the very tips of her toes. And it hadn't been wrong. They were both single, both free, both responsible adults. No one was going to be hurt by what they had done.

But...

Why did it feel as if that huge 'but' was hovering, just waiting to be acknowledged?

Alice turned her head on the pillow to look at Will. He was lying on his back, and she could see his chest rising and falling unevenly as his breathing returned to normal. Outside it was still raining, although not with the ferocity of earlier, and the sound was comforting rather than exhilarating. If it had rained like this earlier, would they have still ended up in bed?

Perhaps. Probably, even. If Alice was going to be honest, she would have to admit that she had been finding it harder and harder to resist the tug of attraction as the days had passed. She'd only had to look at him reading a story to Lily, or at the helm of the boat, his hair lifting in the breeze and his eyes full of sunlight, or lifting a glass to his lips, and her mouth would dry and her stomach would clench. She could say what she liked about being friends, but the old chemistry was still there, and they both knew it.

So, yes, perhaps tonight had been inevitable, but what now? They couldn't just go back to the careful way they had been before, but what other choice did they have? A tiny sigh escaped Alice as she stared up at the ceiling. She should have made it clear to Will that it had just been the storm, and that she wasn't expecting anything to change just because they had made love tonight.

'You know, you don't need to fret.' Will's voice came unexpectedly out of the darkness, making Alice jump.

'I'm not fretting!'

'Yes, you are.' Will rolled so that he could prop himself up on one elbow and look down at where she lay, her bare skin luminous in the faint light and her hair still wet and tangled on the pillow. 'I know you, Alice. You're planning your escape route right now.'

'What do you mean?' she asked uneasily.

'You always look for a way out before there's any chance that you might end up committing yourself.'

'That's rubbish!' she scoffed, but not quite as convincingly as she would have liked. Will certainly wasn't fooled.

'Is it? Don't try and tell me you weren't lying there trying to work out how soon you could tell me that you only wanted this for tonight, that it didn't mean anything to you and that it wasn't meant to be for ever.'

'What did you think it was?' retorted Alice, glad that he had found the words for her.

'I wasn't thinking at all.' Will's wry smile gleamed in the darkness. 'I can't say I regret it, though. It wasn't something either of us planned, but I think it was something we both wanted—or are you going to deny that?'

'No, I'm not going to deny it,' she said in a low voice. 'There's always been a special chemistry between us.'

'I know that. You don't need to worry, Alice.' Will reached out and lifted a lock of her wet hair, rubbing it gently between his fingers. 'You don't need to explain or make excuses. I know you're leaving, so you don't have to think of a way out. Let's just leave tonight as an itch that we both scratched.'

It ought to have made Alice feel better, but somehow it didn't. She knew that Will was right, and that he was giving her exactly what she needed, but she didn't want to be an *itch*.

Sitting up, she pushed her damp hair away from her face and reached down for the sheet that had slipped unheeded to the floor much earlier. 'Is that it?' she asked almost sharply as she wrapped it around her.

'What more can it be?'

'Well…there's still three weeks or so until I go,' she found herself saying.

There was a pause. 'What are you suggesting, Alice?' he asked, and it was impossible to tell from his voice what he was thinking. 'That we keep scratching that itch?'

'If that's how you want to think of it.' Alice bit her lip and pulled more of the sheet onto the bed. 'You were right about the way out. There's no point in pretending that I'm not leaving in three weeks' time, so I'm not making any promises. I wouldn't want you to think that I'm talking about for ever.'

'Don't worry,' said Will, at his most dry. 'I learnt a long time ago never to think of you and for ever in the same sentence.'

'Then, if we both know that, why not make the most of it?'

Part of Alice was rearing up in alarm at her insistence, and warning her that nothing good could come of getting involved with Will again. It was all very well to talk about scratching an itch, but, once you had given in to the need, it was almost impossible to stop. It was madness to think that she could sleep with him for three weeks and then calmly walk away. Better to leave things as they were, as Will himself had suggested, and treat tonight as a one-off. She had a nice house and a life to go back to in London. That was enough, wasn't it?

But another, more reckless, part had her in its grip tonight. Why not? it was asking. How long was it since she had felt that gorgeously, fabulously good, that relaxed, that *sexy*? What was the point of not doing it again, when they had another three weeks or more to get through? They both knew where they were. They had no expectations of each other. And it had been great. Did she *really* want that to be the last time?

No, she didn't.

'It would be fun,' she coaxed, realising at that moment that it was a very long time since she had let herself simply have fun. Ten years, in fact.

Will was silent for a moment. 'I don't want to fall in love with you again, Alice,' he said.

'We won't fall in love,' she said. 'We've been there, and we know it doesn't work. That doesn't mean we can't have a good time together.'

'So you just want me for my body?' said Will, but Alice was sure she could hear a smile in his voice.

'We-el…' She let the sheet fall and slid back down beside him, letting her hand drift tantalisingly over his flat stomach, and scratching him very, very lightly with her nails. 'If the itch is there, we might as well scratch it, don't you think?'

The downward drift of her fingers was making it hard for

Will to think clearly. 'So we'll have the next few weeks and then say goodbye?' he managed.

Alice's hand paused for just a second. 'Then we'll say goodbye,' she agreed.

Will knew that he was probably making a mistake but right then, with her fingers teasing him and her lips against his throat, and her body warm and soft and close, he didn't care. Moving swiftly, he pinned her beneath him and put his hands on either side of her face. 'All right,' he said as he bent to kiss her. 'Three weeks. Let's make them good ones.'

It didn't work, of course. They had about a week when they both resolutely closed their minds to the future, and thought only about the days with Lily and the long, hot nights together. It was easy to fall into their old ways, talking, laughing, arguing, making love… And inevitable, Will thought, that he should start wishing that it could go on for ever.

Knowing that, it made him increasingly tense and irritable. He was angry with Alice for her dogged refusal to consider taking a risk on the unknown, angrier with himself for agreeing to the one situation that he had most wanted to avoid.

Because of *course* he had fallen in love with Alice again. The truth was that he had probably never fallen out of love with her, and it wasn't helping matters to have her there whenever he went home, as combative, challenging and stimulating as ever, as warm and responsive every night. Every time Will looked at her, his heart seemed to stop, and the knowledge that he would have to let her go gnawed relentlessly at him.

Three weeks, that was all they had. After the heady delight of that first week, Will did his best to distance himself from her. But how could he when she was there in his bed, when she lay warm against him all night, and her very nearness made his head reel?

Alice sensed his withdrawal, even understood it. It had been a wonderful week, but slowly the sensible side of her was regaining its natural ascendancy. Ah-ha! it cried. Told you you'd regret it! Look what a mess you've got yourself into *now*!

The three-week deadline changed her whole sense of time. Sometimes it seemed to rush forward with dizzying speed, making her panic, and at others it slowed to a lethargic trickle that made it impossible to imagine the future. Alice tried to focus on going home, but her life in England seemed increasingly unreal.

She had expected to start feeling bored by now, to start yearning for shops, cinemas, bars and the gossip and pressure of a proper job, but it hadn't happened yet. She tried to make herself miss them, but how could she think about London when Lily chattered as she swung on her hand, and the lagoon glittered behind the coconut palms, and Will closed the bedroom door every night with a smile?

The arrival of Lily's trunk only underlined how far she was from home. Having made such a fuss about Will not bringing his daughter's things with him, Alice had to admit that none of the clothes were suitable for a tropical island. There were surprisingly few books, and a lot of very expensive and hardly-used toys, none of which seemed to interest Lily very much.

She had to find *some* way of detaching herself from life here, Alice thought with increasing desperation. It was too comfortable, too intimate, with just the three of them. She needed to get out and meet more people, make her life bigger again so that when she left there wouldn't be an aching gap where Will and Lily had been. Deep down, Alice was afraid that she might have left it too late for that, but at least it was a plan.

When Will told her that he and his team were preparing for an open day at the project headquarters that Friday, Alice leapt at the opportunity.

'Can we come?'

'To the open day?' Will looked taken aback at the idea.

'Why not? It would be a chance for Lily to see what you do all day.'

'I'm not sure it'll be of any interest to a child. We've got a government minister coming, but it's really about trying to involve the local community in the project, especially the fishermen, and getting them to understand what we're trying to do.'

'Why don't you lay something on for all the children?' said Alice. 'They're part of the community too, and if you get them on board now it'll make things much easier in the future. You could lay on little trips for them,' she went on, warming to her theme. 'Or have a competition with little prizes…you know, they have to find out information as they go round and answer questions, or find something, like a treasure hunt.'

'I suppose we *could* do something for the children,' said Will slowly.

'It'll be good for Lily to start meeting other children before she goes to school, too,' Alice pointed out.

Impressed by her enthusiasm, Will considered. 'Could you run some activities for the children?'

'Me?'

'It was your idea.'

'But I don't know anything about marine ecology!'

'We can give you the information you need. It's putting it into an appealing format we'd find more difficult, even if we had the time to think about it, which we don't. We've got enough to do setting up displays for the open day as it is, and we're running short of time.'

So Alice and Lily found themselves at the project headquarters. The building was simply, even spartanly, furnished, but everything was very well organised. It was clear that all the money was spent on expertise and research equipment—

no surprise with Will in charge. The whole project had his stamp on it; high quality, integrity, and absolutely no frills.

Will showed them round and introduced them to various members of the team, all of whom welcomed Lily kindly and eyed Alice with unmistakable curiosity. He had introduced her simply as 'a friend', and it was obvious that they were all wondering just how close a friend she was. Alice found herself unaccountably miffed that he wouldn't acknowledge a closer relationship, because clearly they *were* more than friends. They were lovers.

Desire shivered through her at the thought of the nights they spent together. She would never guess it to look at Will now. He was dressed casually but with characteristic neatness in shorts and a short-sleeved shirt, and his face was absorbed as he discussed some obscure issue to do with phytoplankton, whatever that was, with a bearded marine biologist. Looking at the back of those long, straight legs, Alice felt quite weak with the knowledge of how they felt against hers, of what it was like to kiss the nape of his neck and slide her arms around that lean, hard body.

'Shall we go and look at the lab?' Will turned to find Alice staring at him, and she gulped and jerked her gaze away.

'Fine,' she said brightly. 'Lead on!'

In spite of herself, Alice was impressed by what she saw. She hadn't realised quite what a major project it was, and she remembered how glibly she had suggested to Will that he give up his career and find another job in London. It seemed an absurd idea now. For it was clear that he was key to the project's success. The staff made no secret of how much they admired him, and Alice could see why. He didn't raise his voice, or show off or patronise anyone, but somehow he was at the centre of everything. She saw a young diver glow at Will's quiet word of congratulation, and a secretary nod with enthusiasm at one of his suggestions. This was Will in his element, intelligent, focused, completely assured about who he was, what he was doing and why he was doing it.

It was very different from her own world of work where status symbols were so important, and how you looked and talked sometimes mattered more than what you actually did. Alice couldn't help comparing Will with Tony, who was always so careful of his appearance and so competitive. Tony would talk himself up in meetings, never missing an opportunity to tell everyone how dynamic and successful he was, and even at home he hadn't been able to wait to tell Alice how well he had performed in a meeting or how much better his results had been than any of his colleagues.

Alice's own drive was less for success in itself than for the security it brought, but she sensed that the team had some reservations about her, and she supposed she did look a bit out of place in her narrow skirt, sleeveless top and high peep-toe shoes with their pretty candy stripes. Alice told herself that she didn't care what they thought of her, and threw herself into the challenge of taking what she had learnt and making it fun and accessible for children.

Will found her a desk, and she and Lily spent the rest of the day happily playing around with ideas and thinking up simple questions that a child like Lily could answer by looking at the various display boards that were being prepared. Will disappeared out to the reef, and Alice found it easier to settle once he had gone. She chatted to the two locally employed secretaries, who adored Will, and were obviously longing to know more about his relationship with Alice but were too polite to ask outright.

'I'm just helping out with Lily until the new nanny arrives,' she told them, since there didn't seem any reason to keep it a big secret. 'I'm going home soon.'

Perhaps, if she said it enough, it would start to seem real.

She liked the atmosphere in the office. It made her realise how much she missed having to think and be part of a team, a train of thought Alice was keen to encourage in herself. Because missing that meant that she was missing work, which meant, obviously, that she was looking forward to going back to London and applying for what she was determined would be the job of her dreams.

Together with Lily, she came up with a competition and a treasure hunt, and begged the use of a computer to draft fun forms for the children to fill in. Then she rang Roger and cajoled him into sponsoring prizes for everyone who took part, as she was pretty sure Will wouldn't approve of using his precious budget to finance frivolities.

'It'll be good PR for your company,' she told him.

'A bunch of children in fishing villages aren't exactly our target market,' said Roger, but he was happy to humour her, and the cost was negligible for a company like his in any case.

It wasn't long before Alice was coming up with other ideas. She told Will about Roger's offer as they drove home at the end of the day. 'Why don't you make this an opportunity to get more sponsorship?'

'I haven't got time for schmoozing,' said Will, changing gear irritably. He was tense after a day spent trying to ignore Alice's warm, vibrant presence in the office. It had been bad enough trying to concentrate on work before, when his senses had still been reeling with memories of the night before, but today had been virtually impossible. Wherever he looked, there she was, sitting on the edge of the desk, swinging those ridiculous shoes, chatting to the secretaries, bending over pieces of paper with Lily, their faces intent, studying the display boards …

Her questions had been intelligent, and she had made some

acute observations, which shouldn't have surprised him. Nobody could ever have accused Alice of being stupid, and he could see that, although the team had been wary of her initially, they had all been impressed by her ideas in the end. She had flair, Will had to admit. It was hard to put his finger on it, but there was a certain stylishness about everything she did, and there was no doubt that she had already made a huge contribution to the plans for the open day.

So he ought to be feeling pleased with her, not edgy and cross. Grateful as he was for her ideas, he wished that she had stayed at home. Now, when she had gone, he wouldn't even be able to go to the office without memories of her waiting to ambush him.

'You wouldn't need to spend any extra time,' said Alice, taking out her clip and wedging it between her teeth as she shook out her hair. 'You're having the open day anyway,' she pointed out, rather muffled through the clip. 'Why not invite businesses along at the same time and show them what you're doing?'

Twisting her hair back up with one hand, she took the clip from her teeth and deftly secured it into place. 'You're the one who said how important the protection of the reef is to the economy. That makes it of interest to companies who operate here, local and international, and I'm sure lots of them would be interested in sponsoring you. Jumping on the environmental awareness bandwagon makes good PR for them.'

'The point of the open day is to keep government support and to involve the local communities,' Will grumbled. 'You're wanting to turn it into a jamboree.'

'Nonsense,' said Alice briskly. 'All you need to do is lay on a few more drinks, and it'll be worth it if you get some extra money for the project, won't it? Besides,' she said, turning to wink at Lily in the back seat, 'if we make it a party, it'll be a chance for Lily and I to dress up.'

Lily brightened. 'Can I wear my pink shoes?'

'You can,' said Alice. 'And I'll wear my shoes with the bows. What do you think?' she asked, ignoring Will's snort.

'I like them.'

'I'm so glad we've got the footwear sorted out,' said Will sarcastically as they turned into their road. 'Now there's nothing else to worry about!'

Although, as it turned out, there was.

An email from the agency in London was waiting for him when he went into the office the next day. Will sat at his desk and stared at the screen. They had found an excellent candidate, the email informed him. An experienced nanny, mature and sensible, Helen would be able to fly out to St Bonaventure as soon as required. Would he please read the attached CV and their comments on Helen's interview and let them know as soon as possible if he wished to offer her the post.

Will lifted his eyes from the screen. Through the glass wall of his office he could see Alice on the phone. She had taken responsibility for the refreshments, and her face was animated as she talked, one hand holding the phone to her ear, the other gesticulating as if the person on the other end could see her.

When she had gone, he wouldn't be able to look at that phone without imagining her as she was now. He wouldn't be able to sit on the verandah in the evening without feeling her beside him, talking, stretching, waving her arms around, laughing, arguing, her face vivid in the darkness. He wouldn't be able to lie in bed without remembering her kisses, her softness and her warmth, the silken fire of her.

When she had gone, there would be an aching, empty void wherever she had been.

'I need to talk to you,' he said to her that night after they had put Lily to bed.

'That sounds serious,' said Alice lightly. 'Had we better sit down?'

So they sat in their accustomed places on the verandah, and Will tried to marshal the churning thoughts that had been occupying him all day. He hadn't been able to talk to her at the office, and he didn't want to say anything in front of Lily. He'd thought he'd decided what he was going to say, but now that he was here his careful arguments seemed to have vanished.

'What is it?' asked Alice after a while.

'I had an email today from the agency in London. They've found a nanny who sounds very suitable and she can come out next week if I want.'

Alice sat very still. Funny, she had known this was going to happen—it was what she had insisted should happen—but, now that the moment was here, she was completely unprepared. Everything had worked out perfectly. A nanny was available. Lily was going to school soon, and there would be someone to look after her when Will wasn't there. She could go home.

It was just what she wanted.

So why did her heart feel as if it had turned to a stone in her chest?

'I see,' she said, and from somewhere produced a smile. 'Well, that's good news. What's her name?'

'Helen.'

Helen would soon be sitting here with him. Helen would meet Lily from school and kiss her knees when she fell down. Helen would be waiting for him when he got home in the evening.

Is she pretty? Alice wanted to ask. Is she young? Will you fall in love with her?

'When's she coming?' she asked instead.

'I haven't replied yet,' said Will. 'I wanted to talk to you first.' He hesitated. 'I wanted to ask if you would stay.'

CHAPTER NINE

'STAY?' Alice echoed blankly.

'Yes, stay. Lily loves you, she'll miss you. And I'll miss you too,' Will admitted honestly. 'I'm not asking you to stay for ever, Alice. I know how you feel about commitment, but the last couple of weeks have been good, haven't they?'

'Yes,' she said, unable to deny it.

'Then why not carry on as we are?' he said, uncomfortably aware of the undercurrent of urgency, even desperation, in his voice. He cleared his throat and tried to sound more normal. 'You told me yourself that your engagement had fallen through and that you didn't have a job at the moment. What have you got to go home to?'

'My home,' said Alice a little defensively. 'My life.'

'You could have a home and a life here.'

'For how long?' she asked. 'I can't pretend I haven't enjoyed the last few weeks, Will. It's been a special time, but special times don't last.'

'They don't if you don't give them a chance,' said Will.

She bit her lip. The thought of saying goodbye to him and Lily tore at her, but he was asking her to give up her whole life, and for what?

'How can they last?' she said. 'Lily will be going to school soon, and what would I do then? You've got an absorbing job, Sara looks after the house. There's no place for me here, Will. How long would it be before I get bored, and everything that's made this such a wonderful time disappears?'

'You could find something to do,' said Will. 'Look at how you've taken over with the open day. Someone with your organisational skills will always find a job.'

'I might find some temporary or voluntary work, but that's not what I want. I've got a career, and the longer I stay away from it the more difficult it will be to go back to it. I've worked hard to get to this stage,' she told him. 'I can't just chuck it all in now on the basis of a few happy weeks.'

'At least you admit you have been happy,' said Will with an unmistakable thread of bitterness. 'Are you going to be happy in London? No, don't answer that,' he said as Alice hesitated. 'You've always put your career before your happiness, haven't you?'

'At least I can rely on my career to give me satisfaction and security,' she retorted. 'You can't rely on being happy.'

'But if you don't take the risk you'll never know how happy you could be.'

Alice sighed and pushed a stray strand of hair behind her ear. 'We've been through all this before, Will,' she reminded him. 'You've got your career, I've got mine, and they don't fit together. We still want different things from life.'

'So you won't stay?' he asked heavily. 'Not even for a while?'

She swallowed. 'No.' And then, when he said nothing, 'Surely you can see that the longer I stay, the harder it's going to be to say goodbye? It's going to come to goodbye sometime, and I think it would be easier for both of us to do it sooner rather than later.'

'All right,' said Will after a moment, his voice empty of expression now. 'I'll email the agency tomorrow and get them to send Helen out as soon as possible.'

Alice didn't reply. She sat unmoving in her chair, paralysed by the weight of the decision she had made. It was the right one, she knew, but that didn't stop her feeling leaden inside, and her throat was so tight she couldn't have spoken if she'd tried.

Beside her, Will looked out at the darkness, his jaw clenched with disappointment and a kind of rage for allowing himself to even hope that she would say yes when he must have known that she would say no.

The insects shrilled into the silence, and for a while there was nothing else but the sound of the ocean beyond the reef and the sadness of knowing that the love and the joy they had shared wasn't going to be enough.

At last, Will drew a long breath and got to his feet. 'Come on,' he said, holding a hand down to her. 'Let's go to bed.'

He stopped as he saw her expression rinsed with surprise, and the hand which he had reached out so instinctively fell to his side. 'Would you rather not?'

'No, it's not that,' said Alice, faltering. 'It's just…I didn't think *you* would want to.'

'We've still got a week left,' he said. 'You were the one who said that we should make the most of the time we had.'

'Yes.' Alice got up almost stiffly, overwhelmed by the relief that had rushed through her when she'd realised that Will wasn't going to reject her. She wouldn't have blamed him if he had, but the thought that she would never again lie in his arms had been a bitter one. Reaching out, she took his hand deliberately. 'Yes, I did.'

They didn't say a word to each other, but there was a desperation and a poignancy to their love-making that wrenched Alice's heart. There was no need to speak when every kiss, every touch, said more than words ever could how much they were going to miss each other.

By tacit agreement, they both threw themselves into the preparations for the open day. Anything was better than thinking about how they were going to say goodbye.

On Friday morning, Will sat impatiently in the car, waiting for Alice and Lily to appear. He had done his best to talk himself into believing that Alice's departure was for the best. She had worked really hard on the open day, but she didn't really fit in here, he reminded himself constantly. She had been right. There would be nothing for her to do on St Bonaventure, and she would soon get bored and restless. Look how little time it had taken for her to get fed up with staying with Beth. Far better for her to go now than to hang around until her frustration soured everything.

He should never have asked her to stay, Will told himself, drumming his fingers on the steering wheel and glancing at his watch for the umpteenth time. Alice had a pattern of running away at the first suggestion of commitment. She had always done it, and she always would. For someone with such forceful opinions, she was pathetic when it came to taking risks.

Will was conscious of the growing resentment inside him, which he fed deliberately because it was easier to be angry with Alice than to contemplate life when she was gone. Why had she had to come and upset everything? She could have stayed with Roger and Beth. They could have met a couple of times for some polite conversation and everything would have been fine. But no! She'd had to come and live with them. She had turned his world upside down all over again. She had made him fall in love with her all over again, and, now that she had made sure that she was right at the centre of his life and Lily's, she was going to leave them both feeling desolate.

Now the tension between them was worse than ever. They

hardly talked about anything except the open day. The only way they could communicate was in bed, where they made love with a fierceness and an intensity that left them both shattered. Will didn't know whether it making things better or worse. He just knew that his stomach felt as if a heavy stone were lodged inside it.

If nothing else, the delay allowed an outlet for his feelings. He leant on the horn. 'If you're not ready in two minutes, you can get a taxi,' he shouted. 'I've got to go.'

'We're coming!'

Alice and Lily came hurrying down the steps from the front door. Alice was holding Lily's hand and had a straw hat in the other. Will didn't know whether it was deliberate or not, but she was wearing the green dress she had worn at the party when he had first seen her again. She even had the same silly shoes on. It was almost as if she was making an effort to revert to the brittle, superficial person she had seemed then.

His daughter looked charming in a floppy hat, pink shoes, and a straight pink shift that Will didn't recall seeing before.

'New dress?' he asked, cocking an eye over his shoulder as she clambered into the back seat and Alice helped her fix her seat belt.

'Alice bought it for me.'

'A goodbye present,' Alice explained, getting in beside Will and settling herself with much smoothing and twitching of her skirt. 'I thought it was time to get her used to the idea of me going,' she added in an undertone as Will let out the clutch.

Big of her, thought Will sourly, resenting the way she seemed to treat the matter so practically.

'I don't want her to go,' said Lily, whose hearing was better than Alice had imagined.

Now look at the mess Alice had left him in. It was all very well for Alice, swanning back to her oh-so-important career in London, but he was going to be left trying to find a way to comfort a desolate daughter, and he had know idea how he was going to do it.

'Alice has to go home,' he said. 'I'm sure you'll like Helen. She sounds nice.'

Lily's bottom lip stuck out. 'I don't want Helen. I want Alice.'

'I'm not going yet,' Alice interrupted, determinedly bright. 'So let's all enjoy today.'

She might be able to enjoy it, Will thought darkly, but he couldn't. The only advantage was that he was too busy to think much. The open day proved to be a surprisingly popular event and, once the government minister's tour was out of the way, a steady stream of curious visitors came in to look around and find out what the project was all about and how it would affect them. Fishermen mixed with the expatriate crowd Alice had persuaded to come with a view to drumming up some financial support, and between them all ran what seemed like hordes of children who had got a whiff of the prizes. Alice's competition was a huge success, and even some of the adults tried it for fun.

It was a hot day, but Alice was cool and elegant at the centre of it all. It was hard to believe that this was the same woman who had rolled laughing with him in bed, her hair tickling his chest and her mouth curving against his skin, and his heart twisted as he watched her.

She seemed to be everywhere, organizing children, making sure people had drinks, smiling and talking, working unobtrusively to make the day a success. He couldn't help thinking that it would be easier for him if she were being selfish and false. As it was, her every move seemed designed to underline how much he would miss her when she was gone.

And how little she herself cared.

Alice was not, in fact, enjoying the day as much as Will

thought. It was a huge effort to keep the smile fixed to her face, especially when she kept catching glimpses of Will between the crowds. He was dressed rather more smartly today in honour of the minister, but she noticed that he talked to the fishermen in exactly the same way as he talked to the politician.

He'd told her that he only had the rudiments of the local language which he had picked up on previous trips, but he seemed to Alice to be able to communicate perfectly well, laughing and joking with the locals or explaining the project's objectives. She only had to look at how people reacted to him to know that he was able to do that clearly and without being condescending or patronising.

Studying him through the milling crowds, Alice was struck anew by the cool self-containment that set him apart from the others, and she was engulfed suddenly in a giddying thrill of pride and possession that she was the only one there who knew how the muscles flexed when she ran her palms over his back, who knew the taste of his skin, how warm and sure his hands felt.

Her breath shortened as she watched him, and her mouth was dry, and for the umpteenth time since that awful night on the verandah she dithered. Stay, he had asked her, and she had said no. Was she making a terrible mistake? Sometimes, like now, it felt as if saying goodbye would be the hardest thing she had ever done. And why do it if she didn't need to?

But, if today proved anything, it was that Will's career was as important to him as hers was to her. His marine research was an integral part of him, and she clung to her work as the one thing she had ever been able to feel sure of. She loved Will, Alice realised sadly. She just couldn't be sure whether she loved him enough to give up everything else that mattered to her, and, unless she *was* sure, it would be better for her to go home.

'Alice!'

Startled out of her gloomy thoughts, Alice turned to see Roger and Beth advancing on her, both smiling broadly, and quickly she fixed her own smile back into place.

'It's lovely to see you,' she said, hugging first one then the other. 'Thank you for coming—and for all those prizes, Roger! They've been a huge success with the children.'

'Where's Will?'

Alice didn't even have to look. She was always aware of where he was and what he was doing. 'Over there,' she said, indicating to where Will stood talking to a group of fishermen.

Rather overwhelmed by all the strangers, Lily was leaning against his leg, nibbling her thumb, and he had a reassuring hand on her head. Every time she saw them close together, a choked feeling clogged Alice's throat and she had to bite her lip.

Roger whistled soundlessly. 'What a change in them both! Is that thanks to you, Alice?'

'They just needed time to get used to each other,' said Alice, but deep down she hoped that she *had* made a difference. At least Will and Lily would have each other from now on.

She would have nobody.

Roger wandered off to have a word with someone he recognized, and Beth turned to Alice with mock reproach. 'We've hardly seen you recently!'

'I know, I'm sorry,' said Alice, guiltily aware that she had been so involved with Will and Lily that she hadn't given her old friends the attention they deserved. 'It's been…busy.'

'Well, as long as you've been having a good time.'

Alice thought about the day out on the reef. About reading with Lily on the verandah. About lying under the ceiling fan with Will breathing quietly beside her, and the thrill of anticipation when he rolled towards her with a smile. To her horror, she felt tears sting her eyes, and she was very glad of her sunglasses.

'Oh, yes,' she said with a careless shrug. 'It's been fun.'

'We wondered if you'd think about staying,' said Beth, ultra-casual. 'You and Will must have got quite close.'

'Yes, it's been nice seeing him again.' Alice was shocked by how unconcerned she could sound when she tried. 'But, you know, when it's time to go…A new nanny is coming out next week, so there's not much point in me staying any longer. Besides, I've still got my ticket home.'

'Oh, you're going?' Beth looked disappointed. 'You will come and see us before you— Oh!' She broke off abruptly and put a hand to her stomach.

'Beth?' said Alice in quick concern. 'Are you all right?'

'Just a bit sick,' muttered Beth, and when Alice looked closely she saw that, beneath her hat, Beth was looking grey and drawn.

'Come inside,' she said, taking Beth's arm. 'It's cooler in there, and you can sit down.'

She made Beth sit in a cool quiet room while she went to find some cold water. 'Shall I get Roger?' she asked worriedly when she came back. It wasn't like Beth to be ill. 'You don't look at all well.'

'I'll be fine in a minute,' said Beth, sipping the water. She smiled at Alice. 'Don't look so worried. It's good news. Oh, Alice, I'm pregnant at last!'

Alice gasped. '*Beth!* That's *fantastic* news!'

'It's early days yet,' Beth warned, 'so we're not telling anyone yet, but I wanted you to know.'

'Oh, Beth …' Tears shone in Alice's eyes as she hugged her friend. 'I won't tell anyone, I promise, but I'm so, so happy for you! And Roger…he must be thrilled!'

'He is. Neither of us can quite believe it yet,' Beth confessed. 'We've wanted this for so long, and we were just beginning to think it wasn't going to happen. Of course, I didn't count on quite how sick I'd feel!'

Alice was so elated by Beth's news that she forgot her own misery about saying goodbye to Will for a while. Leaving Beth to recover in the cool, she sailed out with a wide smile to find Roger.

Roger being Roger, she found him in the middle of a laughing group. Mindful of the need for secrecy, it took all her ingenuity to extricate him but she finally managed to drag him to a quiet place behind the laboratory where she threw her arms around him and promptly burst into tears.

'Hey, what's the matter?' asked Roger in alarm, enveloping her in a comforting hug.

'I'm just so happy for you,' Alice snuffled against his broad chest.

'Ah.' Roger began to smile. 'You've been talking to Beth?'

'Yes, and I'm sworn to secrecy, but it's such fantastic news,' she said, lifting her head to smile at him through her tears. 'I know how much it means to you both.'

'Well, we're expecting you to be godmother, so you'd better come back when the baby is born.'

For a fleeting moment Alice wondered how on earth she would cope with coming back when she would be bound to meet Will again, but she pushed that thought resolutely out of her mind. It was Roger and Beth who mattered now.

'Of course I will,' she told him. 'Try keeping me away from my first godchild!'

She was still smiling when she and Roger rejoined the party. Beth had recovered by then, but Alice was glad to see that Roger took her away soon afterwards. She couldn't help noticing the tender way he put his arm around his wife, and she watched wistfully as he ushered Beth out to the car.

Their devotion to each other brought a lump to Alice's throat. Roger and Beth were lucky. They loved each other completely and they faced everything together. They had had

their sadnesses, but their life seemed so much less complicated than her own. Everything was simple for Roger and
Beth. Why had she had to fall in love with someone whose
life was incompatible with hers?

Sighing, she turned to find Will watching her. His jaw was
set and his mouth was pressed together in a decidedly grim
line, but Alice's heart still skipped a beat at the sight of him.

'Oh… Hi,' she said.

'You look very sad, Alice,' he said, an edge to his voice that
Alice was too full of emotion to analyse.

'I'm not sad,' she said. 'Envious, perhaps.'

'Of Beth?'

'Yes.' She was a little surprised that he had guessed so
quickly. 'I think she knows how lucky she is.'

'Does she?'

This time there was no mistaking the hardness in his voice,
and Alice looked at him, puzzled. But, before she could ask
what he meant, Will's attention was claimed by someone who
came up to say goodbye.

The event seemed to be winding down, anyway, and,
feeling deflated after the earlier high, she began to help with
the clearing up. In spite of her hat, she was beginning to feel
the effects of standing in the sun too long, and her head was
thumping, so when Will told her that one of the divers had
offered her and Lily a lift home she was glad to accept.

'I'll need to wait and lock up when everyone else has
gone,' he said brusquely.

Alice had put an exhausted Lily to bed by the time he
came back, and she was sitting on the verandah and trying not
to think that this time next week she would be home. She tried
to imagine herself in her flat. She would pick up the accumu-
lated post from the doormat. She would unpack her case, and
put some washing on.

And then what? Desolation washed over her at the realisation that there would be no one to sit down with, no one to have missed her, no one to pour her a drink or put an arm around her and tell her that they were glad she was home. She would be alone again.

'There you are.' Will let the screen door crash behind him. He was carrying a bottle of beer, and although he sat down in his usual chair nothing else was normal. His expression was stony, and he was taut with suppressed feeling, wound up so tight that Alice looked at him in concern. *Something* had obviously happened, but she had the nerve-racking feeling that if she put a foot wrong he would explode.

'Long day,' she ventured cautiously.

'Yes.'

'Still, I think it was a success.'

'Yes.'

There was a pause while Alice eyed him warily. 'Do you want anything to eat?'

'No,' he said, adding grudgingly as Alice raised her brows, 'Thank you.'

'I wasn't hungry either,' she said, and gave up. If Will wanted to tell her what the problem was, he could, but she was in no mood to sit here and coax it out of him if he didn't feel like cooperating. Let him keep it all bottled up inside him, if that was what he wanted.

The silence lengthened uncomfortably. Will drank his beer grimly, until at last he put the bottle down on the table between them with a sharp click.

'I think you should be more careful of Beth's feelings,' he said abruptly.

Alice wasn't sure what she was expecting, but it certainly wasn't that!

'What on earth do you mean?' she asked in astonishment.

'I saw you with Roger this afternoon.'

She stared at him. Surely he wasn't jealous of *Roger*? 'Yes, we're friends. Of course I talked to Roger!'

'What were you talking to him about?'

Opening her mouth to tell him, Alice remembered her promise to Beth just in time and closed it again. 'That's none of your business,' she said after a moment.

'Because *friends* don't usually sneak away behind the lab to have a conversation, or kiss and cuddle each other when they're doing it!'

Will had been gripped by a white-hot fury ever since he had watched Alice drag Roger out of sight. He didn't know what had prompted him to follow them—all right, he did know, he was jealous—but he was completely unprepared for the fist that had closed around his heart as he had seen Alice bury her face in Roger's broad chest and cling to him.

Unable to watch any more, he had turned on his heel and left them to it, and he might have left it at that if he hadn't caught sight of Beth emerging from the office a few minutes later, looking pale and wan. She'd asked him if he had seen Roger, so of course he had said no. He couldn't have her interrupting that scene behind the lab, but, from her drawn look, he couldn't help thinking that she already suspected that something was wrong.

And now Alice wasn't even bothering to deny it.

'Roger and I have always hugged and kissed each other,' she said, her eyes blazing at his tone. 'He's a *friend* and that's what we do. We're not all repressed scientists,' she was unable to resist adding snidely.

'Is Beth a friend too?'

'You know she is.'

'You don't treat her like one,' said Will harshly. 'I saw her today too. She looked wretched, and I'm not surprised, if she has any idea of what you and her husband are up to!'

For a moment, Alice was so outraged that she couldn't speak, could only gulp in disbelief and fury. 'Are you implying that Roger and I are having an affair?' she asked dangerously when she could get the words out.

'I'm saying that you don't behave to him the way you should if you were a good friend to Beth.'

'How dare you!' Alice surged to her feet, shaking with fury. 'I've known Roger for years and there's *never* been anything between us. You should know that better than anyone! I love Roger dearly, but we've never felt like that about each other.'

'Are you sure about that?' Will asked unpleasantly, remembering that disastrous evening when Roger had confessed how he really felt about Alice.

'Yes, I'm sure! And, even if I wasn't, do you really think that I'm the kind of person who would break up a friend's marriage?' She shook her head, unable to believe that Will could be saying such things. 'What do you think I *am*? We've been sleeping together, for God's sake! What did you think, that I was just making do with you because I couldn't have Roger?'

Turning away with an exclamation of disbelief and disgust, she wrapped her arms around her in an attempt to stop herself shaking. 'I suppose you think that after Tony left, I came out here deliberately to ensnare Roger because I didn't have a man of my own!'

'I'm a scientist,' said Will, who didn't believe anything of the kind but who was too angry to think about what he was saying. Seeing Alice with Roger had provided an outlet for all the pent-up anger, confusion and bitterness he had been feeling ever since she had refused to stay, and he wasn't capable of thinking clearly right now. 'I believe the evidence, and I've seen you cuddling up to Roger at every opportunity. You can't tell me that you've never thought what that does to him!'

Alice turned slowly to stare at him. 'I don't believe this,' she said. 'How can you possibly think that about me? You know me!'

'I used to,' he said bleakly. 'I'm not sure I do know you any more.'

There was an appalled silence.

'I think I'd better go,' said Alice in a shaking voice at last, and she turned blindly for the door.

The expression on her face brought Will to his senses too late, and he scrambled to his feet. 'Alice, wait!'

But she only shook her head without looking at him. 'I'll leave tomorrow,' she said, and let the screen door click back into place behind her.

Alice sat carefully down on the back steps next to Lily. She had broken the news at breakfast that she was leaving that day and it had gone even worse than she had feared. Not that Lily had cried or had a tantrum. She had simply stared disbelievingly at Alice out of dark eyes, then had got up without a word and run out into the garden. Heavy hearted, Alice had finished her packing. Now Roger was waiting with a bleak-faced Will by the car, and she had come to try and say goodbye to Lily.

Lily wouldn't acknowledge her presence at first. Her body was rigid, her face averted, and Alice was dismayed to see the closed, blank expression that she remembered from their first meeting.

'Lily,' she began helplessly. 'I'm sorry I have to go like this. I was going anyway in a few days, but I didn't want it to be this way.'

'I don't care,' said Lily, but a spasm crossed her face, and Alice's heart cracked. It wasn't long since this child had lost her mother, and now the next person she had allowed close seemed to be abandoning her too. She tried to put a comforting arm around her, but Lily shook it off.

'Oh, Lily, it's not that I want to leave you,' she sighed.

'Then why are you going? Is it because I've been naughty?'

'Of course not,' said Alice, appalled. 'Of *course* not, Lily. It's nothing to do with you. I wish I could explain but it's…complicated…adult stuff,' she said lamely. She wasn't going to leave Lily thinking that it had anything to do with Will. Her father was the only constant in her life now, and, hurt as Alice was, she wouldn't do anything to jeopardise his relationship with his daughter.

'Helen will be coming soon,' she went on. 'And it'll be difficult for her if I'm still here. I'm going to miss you more than I can say, but you'll like Helen, I promise you.'

'I won't!' Lily jumped furiously to her feet. 'I'll hate her like I hate you!' she shouted, and ran off before Alice could reach out to her.

Unable to keep back the tears any longer, Alice buried her face in her hands and wept.

The screen door creaked, and she could hear steps on the wooden verandah before someone sat down beside her. 'She doesn't hate you,' Will's voice said gently. 'She loves you. She's only angry because you're leaving her, and she doesn't understand why.'

There was a pause, punctuated by Alice's hiccuping sobs.

'I don't have Lily's excuse,' Will went on after a moment. 'I *do* understand why you're going, but I was still angry because I love you, too, and I don't want you to go, even though I know that you must.'

Alice's hands were still covering her face, but her sobs had subsided slightly, and he could tell that she was listening.

'I'm so sorry about last night, Alice,' he said quietly. 'I said some unforgivable things, and I said them because I'm a jealous fool, but really because I was looking for an excuse to hate you, like Lily, because making myself hate you seemed like the only way I could bear the thought of you leaving me.'

Drawing a shuddering breath, Alice lifted her head at last and wiped her eyes with a wobbly thumb. She didn't say anything, but Will was encouraged enough to go on. 'It was a childish reaction, I know, but I haven't been thinking straight recently. I've been flailing round, so wretched and miserable because you were going that I would say anything.

'I lied when I said I didn't know you, Alice,' he said. 'I *do* know you. You're the truest person I know. You would never do anything to hurt Roger or Beth, and I knew it when I was saying it. I just wanted to hurt you so that you felt what I was feeling.'

Alice opened her mouth, but he put a gentle finger on her lips. 'Let me finish. I've made such a bloody mess of everything, Alice. I've hurt you, and because I've hurt you I've hurt Lily, and I don't know how I'm going to forgive myself for either.'

He looked into Alice's golden eyes, puffy now and swimming with tears, but still beautiful. 'I won't ask you again if you'll stay. I know you've got your life to go back to, and goodbyes like these are too hard to go through again. Go with Roger now, and fly home as you planned. I'll look after Lily. She'll be all right.

'I hope you find what you're looking for, Alice,' he went on, although his throat was so tight he had to force the words out. 'I hope you'll be happy, as happy as we were here, and all those years ago. I've always loved you, and I know now that I always will. It's only ever going to be you, Alice,' he said with an unsteady smile. 'I want you to know that if you ever change your mind, and think you can take a chance on being loved utterly and completely, Lily and I will be here for you, and we'll take as much or as little as you can give.'

'Will…I…I don't know what to say,' said Alice hopelessly.

'You don't need to say anything.' Will put a hand under her

elbow and helped her to her feet. 'You need to go home and decide for yourself what you really want, without me shouting at you and Lily piling on the emotional blackmail!'

'Tell Lily ...' Alice's voice cracked and she couldn't go on, but Will seemed to understand what she needed to say.

'I'll explain why you're going,' he said. 'I'll tell her that you know that she doesn't really hate you, and that you love her too.'

'Thank you,' she whispered. She didn't seem to be able to stop crying as she walked through the screen door for the last time and out to the front where Roger was waiting by the car.

'Come on then, waterworks,' he said gruffly. 'I've got your cases.'

'Alice,' said Will as she was about to get into the passenger seat, and she paused, a hand on the door and one foot in the well. 'Thank you,' he said simply. 'Thank you for everything you've done for Lily, and for me.'

Unable to speak, she nodded.

'And remember what I said about being here if you ever change your mind,' he added, his voice strained, and Alice bit her lip to stop the tears spilling over once more.

'I will,' she said. Then she ducked her head as she got into the car and closed the door, and Will could only watch in desolation as Roger drove her away.

CHAPTER TEN

THERE was so much post piled up behind the front door that Alice had to push her way into her cramped hallway. The flat smelt musty and unused, and even when she had switched on the lights the rooms seemed cheerless. Perhaps it was something to do with the dreary drizzle and the muted grey light of a wet Spring afternoon, she thought, and tried not to think of the aching blue ocean, the mint-green lagoon and the vivid colours of hibiscus and bougainvillaea.

Her feet had swollen on the long flight, and she kicked off her shoes with a weary sigh as she sat down on the cream sofa. This was the home she had worked hard for, the home she had been insistent she wanted to come back to. It represented everything she had ever wanted: security, stability, being settled at last. She had decorated it with care in the cool, minimalist style that appealed to her, and it had been her refuge whenever things had gone wrong.

Until now, she had always thought of her home as calm and restful. There was no reason suddenly to find the ivory walls cold, or to notice the roar of the traffic along the busy road outside, the dismaying wail of a siren in the distance, and the intrusive blare of a television next door.

No reason to find herself overwhelmed with homesickness

for a verandah thousands of miles away, where the insects whirred and rasped and shrilled, and the scent of frangipani drifted on the hot air. Alice looked at her watch and calculated the time in St Bonaventure. Will would be sitting there now, still and self-contained, listening to the sound of the sea he loved so much.

The memory of him was so sharp that Alice closed her eyes as if at a pain. Was he thinking of her? Was he missing her?

She had thought about him constantly since Roger had driven her away. The worst thing was realising that she hadn't said goodbye, to him or to Lily.

His words went round and round in her head. It's only ever going to be you, Alice. Lily and I will be here for you if you ever change your mind and think you can take a chance on being loved...

'I don't understand what the problem is,' Beth had said. 'Why are you putting yourself through all this misery? Will loves you, Lily loves you, and you wouldn't be this upset about leaving if you didn't love them back.'

'Love's not the problem,' Alice had tried to explain.

'Then what is?'

'It's everything else. It's not being sure if love would be enough.' She'd twisted her fingers in an agony of indecision. 'Yes, I could go back to Will now, but it would mean giving up my whole life for something that might not work out. It didn't work out last time, so why should it now?'

'You know yourselves better now,' Beth had pointed out, but Alice hadn't been convinced.

'I'm not sure that I do. I feel differently here,' she'd said, waving her arms at the tropical garden. 'But who's to say that what I feel is real? It might just be about being on holiday in a beautiful place. Maybe I'm just getting carried away by the romance of it all.'

Beth had looked thoughtful. 'Then perhaps Will is right. You need to go home and see how you feel when you're there. He's told you that he loves you, and he's not going anywhere, so it's up to you to decide what you want.'

It was deciding that was the problem, Alice thought in despair. She who had always been so clear about what she wanted before was now being tossed about in a maelstrom of indecision that was making her feel quite sick. One minute the thought of never seeing or touching Will again seemed so awful that she was ready to jump into a taxi and rush back to the house by the lagoon, the next she would think about selling her flat and committing herself to an expatriate life where they would move from house to house and none of them would be a home. And she would be swamped by memories of her childhood and all the times she had sworn that as soon as she was old enough she would settle down and make a home for herself.

She wasn't ready to give that up, Alice told herself. At least, she didn't think she was …

She was having to readjust so many of her ideas at the moment, that it was difficult to know *what* she thought. She had been astounded when Beth had told her just why Will had been so convinced that her relationship with Roger was inappropriate.

'It's not so far-fetched an idea,' Beth had said. 'Roger was in love with you for years.'

'What?' Alice had goggled at her, and Beth had nodded calmly.

'He confessed to Will once when he'd had too much to drink, and he was always grateful that Will never told you. He thought it would have embarrassed you if you'd known.'

'But I… But I …' Alice had floundered in disbelief. 'I had no *idea*!'

'Roger knew that. He'd probably have been better to have

told you and got you out of his system, but you know what fools men can be about these things,' said Roger's fond wife.

Alice regarded her curiously. 'Didn't you mind when he told you?' she asked a little awkwardly, not at all sure it wasn't a bit tacky to ask a man's wife how she felt when she'd found out he was in love with you.

'No,' said Beth, smiling. 'He told me that when he met me he realised that what he'd felt for you wasn't the real thing, and I believe him. I know Roger loves me, Alice. He loves you too, but in a very different way. I've always been sure of that.'

'It must be nice to be so sure,' said Alice wistfully, and then her face darkened as she remembered Will's bitter accusations. 'I can see why Will might be suspicious, I suppose, but it doesn't change the fact that he actually thought me capable of coming out here and making a play for Roger.'

Beth sighed. 'He apologised for that, didn't he? The man's desperate, Alice! If you won't go and see him, will you at least ring him?'

But Alice shook her head. 'It wouldn't be fair to do that until I was sure, the way you're sure about Roger, and I'm not. Helen's arriving today. It would just upset everyone if I went back now. My flight's tomorrow, and we'd just end up having to say goodbye all over again. No, I'm going to go home, and when I can think clearly again maybe I'll know how I feel.'

It was all very well deciding to think about her situation clearly, but it wasn't that easy in practice. Alice was convinced that all she needed was a good night's sleep and to wake up in her flat and suddenly she would know what to do, but it didn't work like that.

She did her best to get back into a routine as quickly as possible. She unpacked, shook the sand out of her shoes, washed and put away her holiday clothes and set about finding a new job. She filled in application forms, bought herself a smart new suit for interviews, and contacted friends she hadn't seen before the break-up with Tony.

Grimly determined to enjoy herself if it killed her, she went out as much as she could. Once she bumped into Tony and Sandi, and was appalled to discover how indifferent she felt as the three of them made polite chit-chat. She had been sure that Tony was the man she wanted to spend the rest of her life with, but how could she have wanted him when he didn't have Will's mouth or Will's smile or Will's ironic grey eyes? But, if her feelings towards him could change so completely in a matter of months, who was to say that her feelings for Will wouldn't change too?

So Alice continued, miserably unsure, torn between her determination to get back into her old life and her inability to put her time in St Bonaventure out of her mind. She would be sitting having coffee with a friend, and her eyes would slip out of focus momentarily at the memory of Will's hands around a mug. She let herself into the flat, and found herself listening for the click of the screen door, and if she caught a glimpse of a dark-haired little girl her heart would lurch with the bizarre hope that it was Lily.

She ached for Will, for his cool, quiet presence, his wry smile and his hard body. She missed the constant sigh of the sea and the soughing of the warm wind in the palm trees. She missed the hot nights. She missed Lily desperately, but most of all she missed Will.

Alice longed to hear from him. Every time she went home, she would check for an email, a message on the answering machine, a postcard, anything to show that he was still thinking about her. There was never anything. *You need to go home and decide for yourself.* She could still hear Will saying it, and she wanted to shout at him that she *couldn't* decide.

If only he would make some move, it would take nothing to convince her. Why didn't he just contact her?

She began to set herself little tests. If she could get through the morning without thinking about him, that must mean that she was getting over him, and then she'd know she'd made the right decision. If she hadn't heard from him by next week, she'd know he didn't really care and that it wasn't meant to be. If she could walk to the end of the street without stepping on the cracks in the pavement, she'd be able to make up her mind.

None of them worked.

When her dream job was advertised in the trade journal, Alice could hardly believe it. This, surely, was the sign that she had been waiting for. The job was everything she'd ever wanted. A prestigious company, a promotion, a challenging position that would launch her into a new stage of her career. If she got this job, she was meant to stay in London and get on with her life. What could be clearer?

Carefully, Alice filled in the application form, and when she passed the first hurdle and was asked for interview she had her suit cleaned, and bought a spectacular pair of new shoes to go with it. She prepared for the interview as thoroughly as she could, but she was very nervous as she waited to go in. It felt as if her whole future would be decided by that hour's interview.

Her shoes pinched horribly, but otherwise it seemed to go quite well, and then all Alice had to do was wait.

When her phone rang a few hours later, she practically jumped out of her skin. She had spent the afternoon prowling restlessly about the flat, unable to settle to anything. Too jittery to take off her suit, she was barefoot on the carpet, her poor toes enjoying a respite from being pushed into the shoes that might look fabulous but were in fact extremely uncomfortable.

This was it. Alice stared at the ringing phone for a moment and then picked it up. 'Hello?'

'Ms Gunning?' said a voice she recognized from the interview that morning. 'Thank you so much for coming to see us this morning. We're absolutely delighted to offer you the post.'

The rest of the conversation was a blur of congratulations, but it finished with a suggestion that she go in and see them the next day to sort out the practicalities of salary and starting date. In the meantime, they would courier over her contract so that she could read it at her leisure.

'Thank you so much.' Alice put the phone down slowly.

So the job was hers. Finally her decision had been made for her. She was to stay here, with a great job, a nice flat, and friends. She had a good life, and she was safe and settled again, just as she had always wanted.

She was ecstatically happy and relieved, naturally.

She burst into tears.

Aghast at herself, Alice sank on to the sofa, brushing the tears angrily from her face. What on earth was the matter with her? She had wanted a sign, and this was it. She should be delighted, not sick to her stomach with disappointment.

But, the more she tried to convince herself that she had got what she wanted, the more she cried, until her face was blotched and piggy, and her throat was clogged with sobs.

As if that wasn't enough, the doorbell pealed imperatively. 'Oh, God, now what?' mumbled Alice. She didn't want to explain her wretched state to a neighbour, and she was in no mood for a survey, but it might be the contract. She would have to check.

Cautiously, she put her eye to the peephole and peered through the door. If it was a courier, she would open the door, take the contract and close it again. If it was a friend or a neighbour, she would just have to pretend that she wasn't there.

But it wasn't a friend or a neighbour, or a market researcher, or even a courier. Standing on the other side of the door were the very last people she had expected to see.

Her parents.

Alice was humming as she jumped off the bus and walked back to the flat past the little parade of shops. She waved at the owner of the Turkish greengrocer, and the young boy who helped at the Indian corner shop that sold everything she could ever want in the middle of the night. Stopping at the street market, she bought a bunch of hyacinths, and sniffed appreciatively as she passed an Italian restaurant where something very garlicky was cooking. Two elderly ladies swathed in black were coming towards her, deep in conversation, and Alice smiled as she stood aside for them.

She loved this multi-cultural side to London. The city was looking at its best in the spring sunshine. In the centre of town, the great parks were green and bright with flowers nodding gaily in the breeze, and the very air seemed sharper and clearer, as if the world was conspiring to reassure her that she had made the right decision. Even the bus had come just when she wanted it, and she had enjoyed the ride on the top deck back to her suburb. It might not be as attractive as the centre of town, but it had its own vibrancy and charm. Yes, this was a great city to live in.

Alice couldn't believe how much better she felt for making up her mind. Filled with a sense of well-being, she was smiling as she turned into her street, and it wasn't until she was halfway along that she saw that someone was standing on her doorstep. Someone whose shape and stance was achingly familiar.

Her steps slowed in disbelief, until she stopped altogether with her hand on the gate, her smile fading. He turned at her approach, and as they looked at each other the beat of the great metropolis, the jabber of languages, the constant throb of traffic, the rattle of trains, the blare of music, and the car alarm that everyone was ignoring, faded into a blur. And then silence, until there was just the two of them, looking at each other.

Will.

Alice drank in the sight of him. He looked tired, she thought, but it was unmistakably him. It was as if a high-definition lens had been slotted over her eyes so that she could see him in extraordinary detail: every line around his eyes, every crease in his cheek, the way his hair grew, the set of his mouth...

Oh, that mouth... Her knees went suddenly weak, and she had to hang on to the gate.

'Hello,' she said.

'Hello, Alice.'

He didn't smile, he didn't rush to sweep her into his arms, he just stood there and looked directly back at her. But that was the moment nonetheless when the last piece clicked into place for Alice, and she realised that she wasn't even surprised to see him. All that misery, all that indecision, all that dithering...all had led inevitably to this time and this place, to this certainty that everything would be all right.

Discovering that she was able to move after all, Alice pushed open the gate and pulled out her keys as she walked towards him.

'Have you been waiting long?'

'About forty minutes.'

About ten years, Will amended to himself.

Alice looked wonderful. The mere sight of her was enough to lift his heart, but he was conscious of a sinking sense of consternation too. Part of him, *admit it,* had hoped that she would have been wretched and miserable without him, and that it would have showed, but there was no evidence of that. Instead, she looked glowing and confident in a short jacket with a long flowing skirt and boots, and flowers in her arms. Her hair fell to her shoulders, and when she stood at the gate it shone gold and copper and bronze in the spring light, and her eyes were full of sunshine.

She looked happy, Will realised dully, and he was terribly afraid that he had left it too late.

Alice went into the kitchen and put the hyacinths into some water, bending to breathe in their heady perfume. 'Coffee?' she asked.

'Thanks.' Will wasn't sure how to begin. He stood to one side and watched her moving around the kitchen. She hadn't asked what he was doing there, but presumably she could guess, and surely they had known each other long enough for him not to need to dance around with polite conversation before coming to the point?

'I've been wondering if you'd thought at all about what I said before you left,' he said abruptly. 'Have you decided what you want yet?'

Alice had sat on a chair and was pulling off her boots, but she stopped in the middle of unzipping the second one and smiled at him. 'Yes,' she said. 'Yes, I have.'

'I see,' said Will bleakly. She had decided to stay in London, that was obvious. You didn't buy flowers for a home you were about to leave.

'Shall we go into the sitting room?' Alice suggested before he could say any more, and she carried the tray into a bright room. It was cool and uncluttered, and Will sat gingerly on the edge of a cream sofa. She looked perfectly at home here. If this was her life, he wasn't surprised that she hadn't wanted to give it up for a rickety verandah and creaking ceiling fans.

Alice pushed the plunger into the cafetière and poured out the coffee, wriggling her toes on the carpet. Will was so used to seeing her in shoes that the sight of her bare feet was strangely arousing, and he looked away.

'What are you doing here, Will?' she asked as she handed him a mug of coffee. 'I thought you were going to wait for me to decide what I wanted to do?'

'I was going to—I *meant* to wait—but there came a point when I couldn't wait any longer.' Will put down his coffee without drinking it. 'It's terrible since you left, Alice,' he told her honestly. 'Lily has closed in on herself again.'

Alice bit her lip. 'Doesn't she get on with Helen?'

'Helen's all right. She's done her best. It's not her fault that she's not you,' said Will. 'The truth is that Lily and I are in a bad way. I can't sleep, I can't eat, I can't work properly... We don't seem to be able to do anything but miss you.'

A wry smile touched his mouth. 'I know this sounds like emotional blackmail, Alice, but it's not meant to be that. It's just that it suddenly seemed stupid to just sit out there and hope for the best. I couldn't just watch my daughter getting quieter and quieter. I realised that if we wanted you back in our lives—and we do—I would have to do something to make it happen.

'So I've applied for a job here in the UK,' he told Alice. 'It's as a consultant with an engineering company, doing environmental impact assessments for their marine projects. I'd be based in the North, not London, but it's a permanent job, and a good one. I'd still have to do research overseas, but it would be in short stints, so we could buy a house and settle down somewhere. Lily could go to school, and you could carry on with your career ...'

Will stopped, realising that he was in danger of babbling. He looked at Alice, who was clasping her mug with a very strange expression on her face, as if she couldn't quite believe what she was hearing.

'I suppose what I really came to ask you, Alice, was

whether it would make any difference to your decision if I did get that job.'

Very slowly, Alice shook her head. 'No,' she said. 'No, it wouldn't make any difference.'

'I see.' The belief that deep down Alice still loved him had been keeping Will going through the last ghastly weeks. He knew that she was scarred by her restless childhood and he knew how important the idea of home was to her. Once he had made the decision to change his own career, he had thought that would solve the problem, but he could see now that it had been arrogant of him. Alice had never promised anything beyond the short term.

Somehow he managed a smile. 'I understand,' he said. 'Now that I've seen you here, I can appreciate what this place means to you.' He looked around the room, approving its simple, tasteful décor. 'It's nice here. You've obviously got a good life, and I know how important your career is to you. I hope you'll find just the job you want,' he added heroically.

'It's funny you should say that,' said Alice, a smile hovering around her mouth. 'I was offered the job of my dreams just a couple of days ago.'

'Well…great,' said Will heartily. Abandoning his coffee, he got to his feet. He wasn't sure how he was going to tell Lily, but he would have to find a way. She had been happy to see her grandparents again. Perhaps he should think about moving to the UK anyway, just as Alice had once suggested. 'Good luck then, Alice.'

'Where are you going?'

'I should go and pick Lily up. It was good to see you again,' he said, looking into Alice's golden eyes for the last time. 'And… Well, there doesn't seem much more to say.'

He was turning for the door when her soft voice stopped him in his tracks. 'Even if I tell you that I didn't take the job?'

Very, very slowly, Will turned back. 'You didn't take it?'

Alice shook her head, her smile a little wavery. 'You haven't asked me what decision I made yet,' she reminded him.

'I thought…I assumed …' he stammered as a tiny spark of hope lit in his heart. 'You look so happy, so at home here.'

She tutted. 'That's not very scientific of you, Will. I'd have expected you to look at the evidence, not make assumptions on how you think I look.'

'Evidence?'

Getting to her feet, Alice went over to the table and rummaged among some papers, pulling out a rectangular card. 'Evidence like this,' she said, putting it into a flabbergasted Will's hand. 'It's a plane ticket,' she told him unnecessarily. 'Open it.'

'It's to St Bonaventure.' Will lifted his head from the ticket to stare at her, a smile starting at the back of his eyes.

'And it's in my name.' She took the ticket from him and tossed it back onto the table before turning back to him and taking his hand, smiling as his fingers closed convulsively around hers. 'What does that evidence tell you, Will?'

'Alice …' Unable to find the words for how he felt, Will pulled her into his arms. He didn't kiss her, he just held her very tightly, his eyes squeezed shut, his face pressed into her hair as he breathed in the scent of her, and felt the iron bands that had been gripped around his heart ever since she had driven off with Roger start to loosen.

'I made my decision, Will.' Alice turned her face into his throat and clung to him. 'I chose happiness. I chose you.'

Will's arms tightened around her even further, but she didn't mind. 'You were right about me looking happy,' she went on, rather muffled. 'I was happy because I'd just finished making all the arrangements to let this flat and could go back to you and Lily.'

'But Alice, this is your home,' Will protested.

'It was, but when I came back from St Bonaventure it wasn't home any more,' she said. 'It was just a flat. For a while it seemed as if I didn't have a home at all, and then I realised that I do. It's just not bricks and mortar. Home is wherever you are.'

'Alice… Oh, Alice …' Will pulled back slightly so that she could turn her face up to his, and their lips met at last in a long, sweet kiss. He felt almost drunk with relief and happiness. He wasn't sure quite how it happened, but his dream had just come true, and the proof of it was Alice's lips beneath his, her arms around him, the softness and scent of her hair. 'Tell me that again,' he said raggedly when they broke for air.

'I love you, Will. I think I've always loved you, but I was too stupid and afraid to realise how lucky I was to have found you.' Lovingly, she traced the line of his cheek with her fingers. 'I've walked away from your love three times now, and I don't deserve to be given another chance, but, if you will, I promise I'll never walk away again. I just want to be with you, and I don't care where we are, or what we do, as long as we're together.'

'And you're sure?' asked Will as he bent to kiss her again, and she smiled against his lips.

'Yes, this time I'm sure.'

'What made you change your mind?' Will asked much later when they were lying, lazily entangled, in Alice's bed. He smoothed the hair tenderly from her face. 'You were so insistent that you had everything you needed here.'

'Everything except you and Lily,' said Alice, rolling onto her side to face him. 'It didn't take me long to realise that I might have the security of material things, but none of them were worth anything without you. I knew I loved you, and that you loved me, but I still couldn't bring myself to trust that feeling.

'I was afraid to let go of what I had,' she confessed. 'It was just what you said. I was afraid to give it all up for the chance of happiness.' She linked her fingers with his. 'Once you know what you want, it all seems obvious, and I can't believe now that I hesitated for so long. But then I was going round and round in circles, not knowing what I wanted or what I really thought.

'Strangely, it was being offered that job that convinced me,' she remembered. 'I'd told myself that I would take it as a sign that I should stay here if I got it, but of course, when it happened, I realised it wasn't the sign I wanted. I felt a fool,' she told him with a twisted smile. 'I'd just been offered the job of my dreams, and all I could think was that I didn't want it if it meant I couldn't be with you and Lily. Then my parents turned up.'

'Your parents?' Will sat up in surprise. 'I thought they were in India?'

'They were. Now they're on their way to keep bees in Normandy.' Out of habit, Alice rolled her eyes, but her smile held a kind of wry affection as well. 'They thought they would call in and see me on their way through London, and, being them, they didn't think to give me any warning. They simply turned up on my doorstep, at the very moment I'd just realised that I wanted to be with you, and I was in a terrible muddle about everything.'

Will twisted a strand of her hair around his finger. 'Did they help?'

'Well, that's the funny thing. They did.' Alice pulled herself up to sit next to him, and adjusted a pillow behind her back. 'They've never been what you'd call conventional parents. They're two old hippies,' she said with an affectionate smile, thinking of her mother with her anklets and long braid, her father with his tie-dyed T-shirt and his grey hair pulled back into a pony-tail. 'But when they saw what a state I was in, they swung into their traditional roles straight away! They sat me down and made me tea, and got the whole story out of me.'

She ran her hand over Will's shoulder, loving the sleekness of his skin. 'I told them about you and Lily, and how much I loved you, and that I'd let you down three times now. I told them I was afraid of doing it again, that I was scared that it wouldn't work unless I was sure that I could get it right this time and that it would be perfect.'

Her mother had simply shaken her head. 'Alice, you can never be sure,' she had said. 'All you can do is trust each other and be true to each other and believe in each other. Love isn't something that comes and goes. It's something you have to make together, and if you both work at it, if you're kind and patient and prepared to compromise, if you can stay friends through thick and thin, then you can make it last, but you can't *ever* be sure of it.'

Alice would never forget the way her mother had smiled at her father then, and suddenly they hadn't seemed like faintly ridiculous hangovers from another era, but two people who had found their own way and loved each other a long time.

'Loving someone completely isn't easy,' her father had added. 'It's hard work, and you can decide it's easier never to try, but, if you never do, you'll never be completely happy either.' He'd reached out and took her mother's hand. 'Yes, it's a risk committing yourself to loving someone for the rest of your life. It's a leap in the dark, but it's a leap out of the dark too, and if you don't take it you'll never know the joy and the wonder and the real security which is loving and being loved.'

Alice felt quite teary with emotion as she told Will what her parents had said. 'As I listened to them talk, I realised that I'd spent my whole life running away from the unsettling effects of my childhood—the moving from place to place, never having any real friends, never feeling at home—when I could have been thinking about all the wonderful things my parents did for me.'

She shook her head at herself. 'They gave me the best example I could have of a loving relationship. My father didn't wear a suit, and my mother didn't put on an apron and stay in the kitchen, but they were always friends and always lovers. They laughed and they talked and were true to each other. They took me to places most children never get to see, and showed me how wonderful the world is.

'I had the most incredible experiences growing up,' Alice remembered. 'But, instead of realising how lucky I was, I turned it all into something negative. I became afraid of change, and I confused the security of place with the security of love.' She curved her hand around his cheek and leaned over to kiss Will's mouth softly. 'I won't do that again.'

'Your parents sound like great people,' said Will when he had kissed her back. Alice had never talked much about her parents when they'd been students. He had the feeling they had been in South America then, so he had never been introduced. 'I'd like to meet them.'

'That's good, because they're coming out to St Bonaventure.'

'They are? When?'

'For our wedding,' said Alice calmly, and a smile twitched the corner of Will's mouth.

'Oh, we're getting married, are we?'

'Yes, we are.' She leant over to Will until he slid beneath her, and her face was suddenly serious. 'You've asked me to marry you four times now, and each time I've been the fool that said no, so this time it's up to me. Will you marry me, Will?'

'Alice.' He cupped her face with infinite tenderness. 'My heart, I've wanted to marry you since I first laid eyes on you fourteen years ago, but we don't have to get married if you don't want to.'

'I do want to,' she said, dropping soft kisses over his face. 'You know what a thing I've got about security, and, now I've decided that you're my security, I want to tie you up as close as I can!'

'The tying up bit sounds fun,' mumbled Will between kisses. 'You can tie me up as tight as you like!'

'Good, I hoped you'd agree,' said Alice with satisfaction, and then her blizzard of kisses had reached his mouth and neither of them said anything more for a long time.

'We don't have to get married in St Bonaventure,' Will pointed out some time later, when they had both discovered that they were starving and were in the kitchen making cheese on toast, which was the best Alice could do. 'If I get this job, we'll be moving back to the UK and we could have the wedding here if you like.'

Alice picked a piece of cheese from the grater and studied him. 'When's the interview?'

'The day after tomorrow.'

'I think you should ring up and cancel,' she said. 'Let's go back to St Bonaventure and finish the project. If I'm married to you, I'll be able to find a job doing something, and as long as I've got something to do I'll be fine. I could sort out your fund-raising for a start! Then, when the project's finished, we can think again. Maybe that'll be the time to come back to the UK, and Lily can settle in a school here.'

Will slid his arms about her from behind and kissed the side of her neck, making her arch with pleasure. 'You're a dream come true,' he said, and she smiled.

'That's the plan.'

The sun was just starting to sink towards the horizon as Alice took Lily's hand and walked down the garden and across the track. Ducking under the trunk of a coconut palm that leant down at an extraordinary angle, they kicked off their shoes and walked barefoot across the beach to where Will was waiting for them.

Lily was in a pale pink dress, which she had been allowed to choose herself, and her dark curls were held in place by a satin headband decorated with rosebuds. Her tongue was sticking out slightly as she concentrated on remembering her bridesmaid's duties. Next to her, Alice was wearing a very simple cream-coloured dress with fine straps that left her arms and shoulders bare, and the chiffon stirred against her legs as cat's paw of wind ruffled across the lagoon. There were frangipani flowers in her hair, and she carried a spray of vivid bougainvillaea.

The sky was flushed with a pink that was deepening rapidly to a brief blaze of red and orange as Will turned to watch them walk across the sand towards him, and he smiled. Their plans for a small ceremony had been overtaken by the insistence of the entire project staff on being invited, together with Roger and Beth, Alice's parents, his mother, Sara and a whole lot of other people who'd seemed so genuinely happy for them that it had seemed churlish not to include them in the wedding party too. They all gathered round as Will stood with Alice and Lily before the celebrant.

Alice bent and handed her flowers to Lily, who took them as if they were made of glass and stepped carefully back to join her grandmother. Will took Alice's hand and, as they turned to face each other, his grey gaze travelled lovingly over her, from the tawny hair to those golden eyes and the warm, generous mouth, and then down over the enticing curves of her body to stop at her bare feet.

'What, no shoes?' he murmured as the celebrant cleared his throat. 'How are you going to run away?'

She smiled back at him. 'I'm not running anywhere,' she said. 'From now on I'm staying right by your side.'

* * * * *

BEHIND CLOSED DOORS

Anne Oliver

With thanks to my critique partners Kathy, Trish, Linda and Sharon who encouraged me to just go for it! Thank you also to my husband Henry and life-long friend Sue, both of whom believed in me, and to Kimberley Young for giving me this opportunity.

In memory of my dad.

When not teaching or writing, **Anne Oliver** loves nothing more than escaping into a book. She keeps a box of tissues handy—her favourite stories are intense, passionate, against-all-odds romances. Eight years ago she began creating her own characters in paranormal and time travel adventures, before turning to contemporary romance. Other interests include quilting, astronomy, all things Scottish, and eating anything she doesn't have to cook. Sharing her characters' journeys with readers all over the world is a privilege...and a dream come true. Anne lives in Adelaide, South Australia, and has two adult children. Visit her website at www.anne-oliver.com. She loves to hear from readers. E-mail her at anne@anne-oliver.com

Praise for Anne Oliver

"A tantalizingly wicked read..."
—*www.cataromance.com* on
Hot Boss, Wicked Nights

CHAPTER ONE

IT WASN'T the homecoming he'd pictured. Jack Devlin
pushed his sunglasses higher on his nose and stared at
the two-storey house he'd lived in for the first twenty-
one years of his life. For the past six years he'd been
pretty successful in making a point of *not* picturing it.

Perhaps that was the reason he was tripping through
this emotional minefield now. Being dead didn't exon-
erate his father, but Jack had to concede he himself
should have attempted some sort of reconciliation years
ago.

But he wasn't the same naïve young man who'd left
without a backward glance. The Jack Devlin who'd
scaled that trellis to his room at three a.m. till he knew
the steps blindfolded and backwards seemed like
someone else.

And the woman he was about to come face to face
with was no longer the sixteen-year-old kid he'd left
behind.

He cursed the familiar gut-punch that always accompanied that particular image and hooked a finger

inside the too-stiff collar of the shirt and black tie he'd picked up at Melbourne International Airport. In this suffocating summer heat he could almost feel those memories reaching out to strangle him.

She'd be here. No matter what she'd been up to since Jack had last seen her, Cleo Honeywell would not miss his father's funeral.

His jaw tensed as he reached for his bag. He frowned down at the shirt's packaging creases as he hefted the pack and winced as pain shot through his injured shoulder. So much for returning in style.

The heavy aroma of greasy food wafting through the open windows overlaid the outdoor's fragrance of lemon-scented gums. The resulting nausea churned in his stomach and the headache that had been building behind his right eye now throbbed in time with The Easybeats' 'She's so Fine' pumping from the stereo. No prizes for guessing who'd selected Dad's favourite musical entertainment—Cleo was obviously this afternoon's hostess.

The ground heaved and he slumped against one of the verandah pillars, gritted his teeth. Damn painkillers were wearing off. What he needed was sleep, twelve hours of blessed uninterrupted oblivion. But that wasn't likely to happen any time soon. With a deep breath, he slipped his glasses in his shirt pocket, pushed away and stepped inside.

He'd missed the funeral by a good two hours, but apparently the party wasn't over yet. A motley bunch of senior citizens in psychedelic seventies gear were still in full swing, Ben Hargreaves included. His father's solicitor was wearing a lime and purple tie and flares. A fancy dress funeral. And why the hell not? One corner of Jack's mouth lifted at an irony only he could appreciate. A fitting finale for the quintessential wolf in sheep's clothing.

Then his gaze snagged on the woman in the red and white daisy-splashed halter dress with a spectacular rear end as she slung her arms round Ben's neck for a slow dance. Her skirt—if you could call the scrap of fabric a skirt—hiked several inches to reveal equally spectacular thighs.

A different kind of heat stirred his lower body. There wasn't a whole lot of her, perhaps five-two if you discounted the platform shoes, but the curves were all there and in all the right places. His photographer's eye admired the form, but it was a purely masculine hum that slid through his veins.

Then she turned slightly and he got his first look at her profile.

Cleo.

For the second time in as many minutes the old punch slammed into his solar plexus. He set his pack down before he dropped the thing as what little strength he had left drained from his limbs.

He could try telling himself it was jetlag, or the fact that he'd discharged himself from hospital against the doctor's advice and grabbed the first flight out of Rome. *Face it, Devlin, you've never gotten Cleo out of your system.* Still those slumberous blue eyes, that wild-in-the-moonlight hair. For years he'd imagined how that hair would feel in his hands, how it would look on his pillow.

At sixteen she'd been off limits, a beauty with a chip on her shoulder you could carve a monument from. He didn't know about the attitude, but her looks had only improved.

She'd twisted her hair up into one of those clasp things that showed off her nape and made her look elegant and casual at the same time. Her full mouth, more often than not set in a pout, had been one of his forbidden fantasies.

She wasn't pouting now and her smile was as stunning as he remembered. But then, he thought with a wry grimace, she hadn't seen *him* yet.

His throat was suddenly parched. Right now he'd kill for a cold Aussie beer. Or something stronger to mask the feelings that had sprung to life again as if the past few years hadn't existed.

Watching her, he steeled himself against anger, resentment, regret, and, churning through it all, the burning sense of loss for this girl who'd grown into a woman.

All ancient history. He let out a slow, tired breath. The sooner he finalised his father's affairs, sold the house and got out of here, the better.

He was here.

Cleo knew by the way her scalp tingled the minute Jack Devlin arrived. Her breath backed up in her lungs and the tingling spread from her scalp, down her spine to the backs of her exposed bare legs.

She could feel those hot-chocolate eyes on her, no doubt dark with disapproval at her choice of attire for the occasion. Tough. Gerry had wanted a celebration of his life and that was what she'd arranged.

She might not have been Gerry Devlin's daughter by blood, but he had been her father in every other sense of the word, which gave her the right to do as she saw fit. His only offspring hadn't even had the courtesy to contact her about funeral arrangements.

Typical Jack Devlin. Too self-absorbed to think beyond his next conquest. Her lip curled. More than likely he'd been bonking some bimbo while his father lay dying.

But she didn't feel tough. She felt uncommonly fragile. Through sheer will, or plain old desperation, she restored her smile while she tugged ineffectually at the hem of her dress, then reached up to kiss Ben's cheek. 'Thank you for everything. Gerry would've enjoyed the send-off.'

'A pleasure, Cleo. Anything you need, just name it.' Ben's warm hands clasped her suddenly clammy ones and squeezed. She wanted to hang on, just a moment more—*please*—but his eyes flicked to the door, and her heart jolted. 'I'll be…it's Jack!'

Sucking in a breath, she braced herself. And turned.

But the dishevelled man a few feet away wasn't the fashion-savvy, smooth-cheeked Jack Cleo remembered. Oh, his broad shoulders still blocked the doorway and he still oozed that lazy, raw sexuality. Nor had his dark eyes—make that dark, bloodshot eyes—lost that uncanny knack of appearing hot and cold at the same time.

'Jack, my boy, it's good to see you.'

Ben's booming voice broke the spell she seemed to find herself under. Jack's gaze lingered on her a second longer, then switched to the man beside her.

'I'm only sorry it's under these circumstances,' Ben continued. 'My condolences.'

Jack nodded. 'Thank you.'

Rooted to the spot, Cleo watched them come together and shake hands.

Jack hadn't bothered to shave and he looked as if he'd just left a lover's bed. Unkempt dark hair curled over his collar. His trousers looked as if they'd been slept in, although she didn't imagine Jack slept in anything but a tan.

And did he think that stubble on his jaw was sexy? But her palm itched to touch; she could almost feel the roughness beneath her fingers... Heat rose up her neck and into her cheeks. Lucky for her both men were too busy talking to notice.

If the Jack she knew left stubble on his jaw, it was a skilful designer shadow. One that highlighted that dimple in his chin. The dimple she'd loved to touch just to annoy him. Of course that was before she'd become aware of him as a man rather than a brother—which he wasn't. But there was no mistaking the fact that Jack Devlin was all man.

Once again Jack's attention focused on her.

'I'll let you two get reacquainted,' she heard Ben say as he moved away.

She wasn't sure if the sound of music and conversation behind her dimmed. They simply ceased to exist. All she could hear was her pulse drumming in her ears, all she was aware of was the thick pounding of her heart against her chest. And Jack.

Drawing a deep breath, she forced her legs to move but stopped a safe arm's length away. *Safe?* His unfathomable eyes all but devoured her. She watched them roam her face, felt them as surely as a touch—brow, eyes, cheeks. Lips… If she hadn't known better she could have sworn—

But no. He hadn't come back for her. He'd come back for his father.

She willed away the humiliating sting of tears. *Hasn't he hurt you enough already? He doesn't think of you that way, never has, never will.*

He smelled of the aircraft, new shirt and unfamiliar soap, but underneath she smelled the scent unique to him. The scent that had invaded her dreams for too many years.

Clenching her fists at her sides so he wouldn't see the tremor, she lifted her chin. Even though she wore platform shoes he towered over her. 'So, the prodigal son returns.'

'Hello, Cleo.' Perhaps because it was expected of family, he touched his lips to her cheek. Her breath caught, then trembled out at that first physical contact. Unlike that final fevered and furious night in his room, his kiss was cool and detached.

But no less devastating.

To compensate, she waved a careless hand behind her. 'You're too late.'

'How ironic.' He was still leaning intimately towards her. His lips were smiling, and a casual observer might have thought he was pleased to see her, but his eyes were like granite. 'You said those exact same words the last time I saw you.'

At his twenty-first birthday party.

The night was indelibly printed into her brain. Sam Denton's bloodied nose when Jack had punched him through the car window, his fury as he'd dragged her from Sam's car. The shame when his father had caught Jack hustling her upstairs to his room with his jacket covering her open blouse and bare breasts.

And that final humiliation... She'd gotten the reaction she'd wanted all right, and paid the price. Her attempts to make Jack notice her, just once, had driven him out of her life.

'Or perhaps you were lying that night,' he murmured.

His voice catapulted her back to the present and the reality that he was going to throw all those old hurts in her face when what he *should* be asking about was his father.

He leaned closer. 'Was I?'

'Were you...what?'

'Too late.'

'What are you talking about?'

His voice was even enough but his expression held no hint of amusement. 'Convenient amnesia, Cleo?'

A fist slammed into her stomach. Amnesia would be a blessing. 'You're one to talk about "too late".' His sheer nerve, bringing up *that* night at his father's funeral, made her voice clipped and hard. 'You denied a dying man—a man I loved even if you didn't—his last wish.'

'Which was?'

'To say goodbye to you.'

Something dark and disturbing flickered in his eyes. But not guilt, not even regret. 'I came as soon as I heard.' His voice was rock-hard, like the set of his jaw.

Probably true, but it didn't let him off the hook. No way. She gave him her best impression of 'do I look stupid to you?'—pouted lips, lifted brow, a look she'd perfected years ago that never failed to provoke the heck out of him.

'If you don't mind, *Goldilocks*…' he retaliated in kind as he moved to collect his bag '…I'll dump my gear and wash up. Is my old room still my old room?'

How long had it been since she'd heard that pet name? And hated it?

Since Jack.

Determined not to make it easy for him to simply slip back into her life, she shrugged. 'If you can still find your way.'

As he bent to pick up his bag he staggered again, what little colour he had beneath his stubble leaching from his face. Cleo looked closer. His lips suddenly looked like chalk, the skin around them white and drawn. Alarmed, she fought her immediate response to lay a hand against his sweat-sheened brow and kept her voice impersonal. 'What's wrong with you? Are you sick?'

'Never better,' he said, gripping his bag in one white-knuckled fist. 'Give me fifteen minutes.' The corner of his mouth tipped up in a semblance of that cocky grin that had always set her teenage heart racing.

She'd vowed never again to let that mouth get to her, but her body wasn't paying attention. There was an industrial-strength blender in her stomach whipping up a deadly cocktail of unwanted emotions, forcing her to press a surreptitious fist against her middle.

She drew in a slow, deep breath. To her relief he turned on his heel and walked—make that sauntered—towards the hall as if the last six years hadn't happened.

Some things never changed. And there was still enough of the old Jack to have her traitorous system humming. Against her will, her eyes followed his firmly muscled backside as he disappeared through the doorway.

She curbed the swift desire to scream something obscene at him and screwed her eyes shut. She didn't need him in her life. Not now, not ever. She was going to focus on herself for a change, *her* wants, *her* needs. Forget Jack.

But her eyes flew open at the sound of a heavy thump followed by a short, sharp word, and her breath caught in her throat. Easy to say when the man was stumbling up the stairs like a drunk.

Mumbling an 'excuse me a moment' to anyone within earshot, she hurried into the hall and up the stairs. She stopped at the top and huffed out a breath. Back a few minutes and already he had her running after him. Again.

When she reached his door he was standing at the window, hands braced on the sill, taking deep breaths. She was three steps into the room before she could think that this was a very bad move. It hit her immediately. His scent, his proximity. The intimacy.

Back up. Now. But her feet remained stapled to the floor, eyes glued to his long, tanned fingers as he picked up her Champlevé enamel and bronze sculpture from the little bureau beneath the window.

'Did you make this?'

She bit her lip. He had his back to her, but he'd known she was there. He always knew. 'Yes,' she said finally. 'I've got my own workshop in the garage.'

'Impressive.' He set it down, turned around to check out the room.

His colour had improved, but he still had that greenish tinge. She felt a little faint herself. He was sucking up all the oxygen, taking up all the space. Even with the breeze and the fragrance of frangipani and wattle outside, she wondered if she was going to be the one passing out.

'New quilt,' he said.

Her eyes flicked to the burgundy and green patchwork, then away. She did not want to look at that bed. 'I sewed it at Gerry's bedside,' she said, focusing on the cool blank wall dead ahead and reminding herself Jack hadn't been around to see his dad die. 'It helped pass the time.'

The sudden image of Jack's naked body sliding over those patches she'd sewn burst like a fireball behind her eyes. All that hot, tanned skin rubbing against where her fingers had been… *Oh, Good God.*

Twisting those fingers together, she spun a half-circle, only to come face to face with the object of her steamy imaginings.

While she stared in helpless fascination, Jack

dragged off his tie, tossed it on the bed and unbuttoned a cuff. More hot, tanned skin. 'The old house has seen a few changes,' he remarked.

No thanks to him, she reminded herself again. 'You've been gone six years, Jack. You ran off without a word.'

The brief, mildly civilised interlude disintegrated into a deafening silence. Jack's fingers, already working the second cuff, paused. 'First off, I did not run.' A muscle clenched in his jaw. 'Second, it was time to leave.'

His eyes fused with hers and she knew they were both remembering… She knew what he meant even if she didn't understand why he'd left. 'But without saying goodbye?' They'd shared the shock and grief of losing a parent who'd never looked back—he *knew* how deeply that had hurt. He owed her. 'We deserved that much, your father at the very least.'

'Dad?' Something like anger or regret or both flashed in his eyes as he yanked open the top button of his shirt. 'He said what he had to say.'

She gulped, her eyes riveted to the glint of gold chain at his neck. The crudely shaped medallion nestling in that tempting V of chest had been one of her first attempts in metal-working class in high school.

He still wore it. Something fluttered at her heart, but she fought it down. 'He was your father, Jack. You treated him less than a stranger.'

'You more than made up for it.'

The sharp edge to his voice stung. Did he resent her for that?

'Speaking of parents,' he continued in a more reasonable tone, 'I didn't see your mum downstairs.'

Relieved at the switch in topics, Cleo nodded. 'She met someone through work and got married again.'

'Good for her.' He undid his belt, dropped it on the bed with his tie. 'She deserves some happiness.'

'I agree. They went to New Zealand to meet his family and stayed. She sent her condolences. By the way, I moved out of the flat to be nearer to Gerry since Mum's no longer around.' *And neither were you.*

His brows shot up. 'You cared for him yourself? Here?'

'Of course. When he wasn't having chemo.'

'Did you have help?' One hand shot up and rubbed at the back of his neck, the way she remembered he did when he was unsure of something. 'For God's sake tell me you didn't have to go through his…'

The 'death' word hung unspoken between them. 'I did have a carer help out at the end.' She wanted to reach out, but he deserved to suffer as she had. 'I did what I had to do. Death's part of being human.'

He nodded, still rubbing his neck. 'Big responsibility to take on.'

As if he would know about responsibility. 'Not at all. He was my father in all the ways that count.'

'The Dastardly Duo didn't know what they were throwing away when they left you behind.'

'That was fifteen years ago. I'm over it.' In a familiar but now almost unconscious reaction, she folded defensive arms across her breasts. Despite her plea to the contrary, she'd never been able to come to grips with her own father and Jack's mother running off together.

'Their loss, Goldilocks.' His voice mellowed, a warm, aged-whisky kind of sound that seemed to flow over her. She could almost feel her bones melting under his temperature-elevating gaze. She didn't even care that he'd used her old nickname.

Then he laid a hand on her shoulder, a move obviously neither of them had expected because she felt his fingers tense and heard her own soft inhalation. His hand moved to her neck, the rough edge of his fingertip catching on the silky fabric of her dress. Heat from his hard palm warmed the flesh of her exposed shoulder.

What was she thinking, letting him touch her as if he *cared*, as if he were absorbing the feel of her skin against his, searching her eyes for her deepest, darkest secrets? Simple. She wasn't thinking. Oh, my, but she was feeling. Her senses were so acutely tuned she swore she heard the air sigh. Or perhaps it was her. Or him.

It would be too easy to imagine that touch was more than what she knew it must mean: brotherly support. But his hand slid down, closed around her upper arm. Then both hands, both arms. Not brotherly at all.

A *thunk* downstairs followed by loud male laughter broke the sensual spell that had settled around them. Jack dropped his hands as if he'd touched molten metal. 'You've still got guests.'

The sudden loss of contact was a cold dash of reality. 'Correction—*we've* still got guests.' Rubbing her arms where the imprint of his hands still tingled, she said, 'This is your home, Jack, whether you like it or not, and those people downstairs came to say goodbye to your father.'

'With the exception of Ben, I didn't recognise a soul down there. Where's Jeanne? And Scotty said he'd be here.'

'Jeanne left early and Scott's performing a duty *you* should be doing. He's taking Moira home. Your second cousin once removed,' she reminded him, when he looked at her blankly.

'Ah, the bird lady. The one who talks like her galahs. Thank you, Scotty,' he murmured with a visible shudder.

She shook her head. 'I know more about your relatives than you do.' And that, she thought, said a lot about Jack's attitude towards family.

'You always did. Okay, I'll be down in ten minutes. Right now I've got a date with a hot shower.'

He yanked his shirt-tails out of his trousers and began undoing the rest of his buttons. The sight of that tempting strip of masculine skin had her stomach jigging in anticipation. What would happen if she touched him now, there? With her hands, her lips. With her tongue.

Reality check. Jack was off limits, for her own protection, and that included the scenery. She jerked her eyes back to his.

'So…if you'll excuse me?' Jack had paused, hands on the open sides of his shirt.

'Right.' Turning her back on him, she steeled her

mind to blank out all thoughts involving skin and hands and heat and said, 'I'll see you downstairs.'

The moment the last guest departed, Cleo kicked off her shoes before clearing up while she waited for Scott. He was coming back to check on her before heading home. Ben Hargreaves' son, Scott, and Jack might be best mates from high school, but Scott had been there for her from day one. Which made him the number-one hero in her books.

Forty-five minutes later she swung around as Scott's hands settled on her shoulders. She smiled. 'Hi.' This was more like it. No awkward silences, no shivering nerves getting in the way.

'Sorry I took so long. Moira wanted to show me the aviary. I'm not sure it's legal—all those cockatoos.'

'Galahs. She's lonely. Thanks for taking her home.' Cleo patted his cheek. 'Jack's back.' She heard the breathless sound of her own voice. To compensate, she moved briskly to the bench and busied herself covering leftovers with foil.

'Jack?' His voice brightened. 'Where is he?'

'Upstairs, said he was going to take a shower.' She glanced at the ceiling. 'That was more than an hour ago.' The thread of anxiety that had wound its way through her system tightened. She'd managed to ignore it until now, but, 'Perhaps I should go see if—'

'He'll show when he's ready—or not. You know Jack.'

She hesitated. 'You're right. It's just that…'

Scott leaned forward, cupped her chin in his hands.

Concern darkened his pale grey eyes, turning them pewter. 'You okay?'

'Fine. Why wouldn't I be?' But she pulled away, irritated to find her chest tight.

'Because you've always been hung up on him. Seeing him again is bound to be a bit of a jolt after all this time.'

Was it so obvious to everyone but Jack? With a harsh metallic *swoosh* she ripped more foil from the roll. '*Hung up* on him? Is that what you think? You're wrong.'

'Am I?'

'Yes.' On a crazy impulse, she tossed the foil roll on the bench and grabbed his shirt front. 'Kiss me, Scott. Really kiss me and I'll prove it to you.'

'Whoa, there.' He smiled and ran a thumb over her lips, presumably to take the sting out of his rejection. 'That's pure emotion talking.'

Of course it was. Jack and emotion went hand in hand. Her cheeks hot, she stepped back, picked up a platter of mini quiches and took them to the fridge. 'I'm sorry. That was stupid.'

'Forget it.' His smile widened fractionally. 'Another reason is self-preservation. I bet Jack's still protective of his little sister.'

'I'm *not* his sister.' She slammed the fridge door as irritation niggled through her. 'And I'm not so little any more.'

'Hey. Fine, sorry.' He raised his palms. 'You're *not* his sister. And you've got a thing for him.'

Thing. As in an itch? She shook her head. 'If only it were that simple.'

'The last time you saw him you were a kid. That would have made a relationship between you impossible—from Jack's point of view, at least. Now it's different and you don't know how to deal with it.'

'Is that why you never put the moves on me? Because you knew?' *Way to go, Cleo—put Scott in a no-win situation.* 'Sorry, personal question. Forget I said that.'

He nodded. 'Forgotten.' He picked up his keys, jingled them. 'You still on for tomorrow night?'

'On?'

'As in basketball.'

'Oh.' She pasted on a smile. 'Right.'

'We're playing the bottom team; it should be a walkover. I'll let myself out.' But he didn't give her his customary kiss goodbye. 'See you tomorrow.'

'Bye.' She leaned one burning cheek against the smooth fridge until the sound of Scott's car faded. Cricket song filtered through the open window. She heard a dog bark against the background of traffic, felt the cool dampness of evening on her heated skin.

Only an idiot would yearn half a lifetime for a playboy like Jack over a steady, dependable guy like Scott. A sigh slid from her lips. Scott had been there for her when Gerry's time had come. Jack was his son; where had *he* been?

If the clipping at the bottom of her underwear drawer was any indication, he'd been living the high life in Italy. She knew the words by heart. 'And in Milan, Mr Jack Devlin, up-and-coming fashion photographer, escorting Ms Liana Kumova, a stunning, new...'

Cleo snorted, unsure who she was more disgusted with—Jack or herself for allowing it to still hurt.

What else had Mr Jack Model-a-Minute done in the past six years?

And how long would he stay this time?

CHAPTER TWO

TIME. Cleo glanced at the digital numbers on the microwave. Jack hadn't made that promised appearance downstairs. The one person who might have understood her grief, who might have shared it, simply didn't care.

Pushing away from the fridge, she headed for the stairs. Forget that the earth still moved when she looked at him, that the brush of a fingertip over her skin had sent shock waves rippling through every pulse-point in her body. A normal physical response to an attractive male.

But this attractive male wasn't the man she wanted him to be. Not inside, where it counted. She didn't want him on those terms. *You keep telling yourself that, Cleo. Maybe one day you'll even believe it.*

And while she waited for that little miracle to happen, she intended letting him in on a few home truths. Hers.

Jack's door was ajar, the room dark. The last vestige of dusk slid through the open drapes, outlining a motionless form sprawled over the lower half of the bed.

She slapped a palm on the door, swinging it wide. 'Jack, wake up. I want to talk to you.'

No answer.

From the doorway she could hear his steady breathing. Her own breath caught as the sound of that gentle rumble skated down her spine and the backs of her legs. God help her, she should leave. Now. Before he woke and found her watching him like some star-struck teenager. 'Jack…'

When he still didn't stir, she slipped into the room. She had to make a conscious effort to put one foot in front of the other as she crossed the carpet to switch on the bedside lamp. She adjusted it to its dimmest setting.

It looked as if he'd fallen backwards onto the quilt and hadn't budged since. His open shirt revealed a patina of sun-bronzed skin sprinkled with cinnamon hair that gleamed gold in the low light. A metal-smith's divine inspiration—she could almost feel the flow of molten metal beneath her fingers. It took all her will-power to keep her hands at her sides.

His chain had slipped to the side, the medallion nestled between neck and shoulder. But she frowned at the ugly bruise blooming on the left side of his chest. Then she noticed the bulky surgical dressing over his shoulder just visible beneath his shirt.

'What have you done to yourself this time, Jack?'

He wore bruises like badges, she remembered, always getting into fights, more than likely over some girl or other. This was probably no exception.

She brushed his unruly hair from his forehead. His

brow was cool and smooth—no fever—and she had no business touching him, except that she'd always been a sucker when Jack was hurt.

More fool her.

But worry worked its way through the euphoric haze that seemed to have enveloped her and she gently shook his uninjured shoulder. 'Jack?'

He jerked, eyes suddenly wide and glassy and unfocused. 'Huh?'

'It's Cleo, Jack.' His eyelids slipped to half-mast at the sound of her voice, those dark bedroom eyes barely visible through spiky lashes. She had the weirdest sensation of falling. 'Are you okay?' Leaning closer, she could smell the warm, sleepy scent of his skin. 'Do you need anything?' *Like me.*

For a heart-stopping instant she thought she must have spoken those two reckless words aloud when he murmured, 'Cleo…' then his eyes closed on the word '…Home…'

She sighed. Not a chance—the words 'Cleo' and 'home' did not equate in Jack's vocabulary. Leastways, not in this lifetime.

Deliberately ignoring the unsnapped waistband of his trousers, she detoured to the foot of the bed, tugged off his shoes, then peeled off his socks, sucking in a breath as her fingers came into contact with warm, bony skin.

His bare feet stuck out over the edge of the mattress. Long, narrow feet… God, even his toes were sexy; in a knobbly kind of way. She shook her head in exasperation. Only Jack Devlin could have sexy toes.

She grabbed a light blanket from a chest of drawers and draped it over his inert body. Obviously he wasn't going to surface any time soon.

'Oh, Jack,' she whispered, sinking into the armchair beside the bed. 'We had so many good times when we were kids. You were my best friend. You didn't even get mad when I soldered your meccano set to make a windmill.'

She smiled at the memory, but the smile faded as quickly as it came. 'Why did everything change?'

It had been in this room, she thought, staring at the window. The evening started off okay. The Plan had been to give Jack her virginity and he'd see they were meant for each other. Only the Plan had gone horribly wrong.

Not only had Jack backed away from her when the CD had started a slow dance number, he'd started drinking. A lot. Hurt, she'd flirted with Sam and somehow they'd ended up in the back seat of his car with a bottle of vodka.

Until Jack's fist had appeared through the car window.

The memory struck hard. Unable to sit, Cleo stood and paced the carpet. That night she'd been standing here hugging her arms the same way, but for an entirely different reason. Her new blouse with its tiny front-closing loop buttons had been hanging open, her bra missing.

The party lights outside cast Jack's rock-hard face in an orange glow. Over the ringing in her ears she could hear raucous laughter and loud music.

Jack's fingers dug into the flesh of her upper arms, dark eyes flashing with something so much more dangerous than temper. 'What the hell have you done?'

'What do you care?' Cleo tried to dash the wetness from her eyes but Jack kept her arms pinned to her sides, easily holding her in place.

'You're sixteen, Cleo. Do you know what that means?'

Right now all she knew was she wanted to scream, to pummel him, to throw herself at that broad chest and beg him to make love to her. But that wasn't going to happen. She knew that now. 'I hate you, Jack Devlin. I'm going to find someone who'll show me a good time.' Her lips stretched into a sneer. 'A very good time.'

His fingers tightened, and the look on his face made her shudder with something close to fear. 'You want a good time?' he said between clenched teeth, the words barely audible over the blood pulsing through her cotton-wool head.

His mouth crushed down on hers, hot, hard and unforgiving. She couldn't pull away because his hand had hold of her scalp. Barely able to stand, she stood frozen as his lips mashed against hers, his teeth cutting into the soft flesh inside her lower lip. His tongue plunged through her lips, open with shock.

Then he jerked away, breath ragged and rasping, eyes tormented, his beautiful lips glistening in the dim light. Then he swiped a hand across his mouth as if her taste were poison and strode towards the door. 'You've got two minutes to make yourself presentable and be out of my sight or I won't be responsible for my actions.'

'You're too late, Big Brother,' she shouted at his retreating back.

'I'll kill him,' she heard him say as he slammed the door behind him.

Closing her eyes briefly, Cleo drew the curtain on those memories. She blew a long breath and rubbed her cheeks. Then turned to look at Jack. Still sleeping, thank God.

Jack had made it clear how he'd felt about her six years ago. He'd kissed her and it had disgusted him. He'd been so disgusted he'd threatened her with dire consequences. She hadn't seen or heard from him since.

Leaving the night lamp on, she slipped towards the door. The image of Jack on her patchwork quilt had burned into her brain and warmed up a few erogenous zones besides.

In spite of everything, she still wanted him. 'Sweet dreams, Jack,' she whispered into the semi-darkness. *On second thought make that not-so-sweet dreams*.

Jack knew he was dreaming but that didn't make it less real. His head twisted from side to side, his breathing picked up pace. The sky was bone-white, the land baked and brown. And cold. He shivered as the wind whistled through his sweat-damp shirt, and hefted another boulder from what had once been a simple home.

He could hear a woman wailing, but the ragged

children were silent ghosts watching him out of dark, hollowed eyes in dirt-stained faces. Their village was a pile of rubble. The dead stank.

Then out of nowhere, gunfire and screams. The white-hot sting of metal piercing flesh, the thud as his body hit hard-packed dirt. He writhed on the ground, biting dust while his blood trickled hot over his skin. *Get down! Get down!*

Darkness engulfed him. And somewhere in that dark place filled with pain a familiar voice spoke his name. That hadn't happened in the dream before. He tried to open his eyes to see her but they were glued shut.

Cool hands touched his face, stroked his arms. He smelled jasmine as she stretched out alongside him.

Then stillness, and a tranquillity that went soul deep...

He must have died and gone to heaven. A hazy memory of an angel teased the edges of his mind. A less-than-holy angel with a siren's voice and one hell of a bedside manner. And he could still smell the jasmine... He frowned. Angels wore perfume?

He opened his eyes and found her. A tousled and sleeping angel named Cleo curled up on the armchair beside him. He noticed an indent on the adjacent pillow confirming that at some stage Cleo had lain beside him.

Like a gunshot, something inside him pinged as images of her flooded back. The Cleo he remembered was always moving, a blur of colour and energy. So it was a rare and beautiful sight to see her still and innocent in sleep with the subtle bloom of sunrise on her cheeks, the disorderly halo of golden hair around her face.

But her mouth, relaxed and full—he thought of a plump red cherry. Why did the word *ripe* seem so apt? Perhaps it had something to do with the fact that he'd spent so many years remembering the absolute innocence of her taste and wondering if it had matured.

She sighed as if responding to his thoughts, but her eyes remained shut. She'd covered herself from neck to toes in a cotton sheet. Just as well because he knew the body beneath was way too distracting for a man barely out of hospital, let alone a man who didn't fit in with her life.

Unfortunately his imagination wasn't impaired. Neither was his testosterone. His blood grew thick and sluggish, pooling in his groin. With a harsh sigh he shoved the cover down to his waist, closed his eyes and concentrated on the cool air moving over his chest and face.

Come on, Jack. Think of her as just another photo shoot. Except she'd never be model material. Not enough self-discipline, too small in stature, too many curves. The thought of those delicate curves had his mind wandering in a direction he didn't want to go.

Instead, he set his mind to imagining her *covered* in silk; peach, the colour of her skin. Or reclining in a wheelbarrow, covered in leaves—only leaves, the colour of autumn to match the gold glints in her hair.

But he couldn't get past the image of a crisp autumn wind playing havoc, undoing his artistic handiwork, her rosy nipples pebbly with the chill…

Jack swore silently. He needed a distraction. A run was out; the alternative was a cold shower. He ordered his sluggish body to move, but his legs refused to obey. An instant of pure panic sliced through him.

His eyes shot to the foot of the bed. The small mountain of white fur on his calves seemed to augment as the animal, he assumed it was, uncurled itself. A pair of eyes—one gold, one green—opened, blinked once in disdain, then slid shut. '*What* is that?' he muttered, exhaling on a breath of relief.

'*Who*,' Cleo corrected.

He glanced her way. Coupled with the amusement sparkling in her eyes, her sleep-husky voice conspired to crumble his already-damaged resolve. He looked back at the bottom of the bed and scowled. '*Who*, then?'

'His name's Constantine and he's a very spoilt, very arrogant Persian-cross, but he thinks he's human.'

'What the dickens do you feed him? He's massive.'

'Seven kilos at the last weigh-in. Come on, Con.' An ominous rumble vibrated against Jack's feet as Cleo shoved her sheet off and rose. 'Uh-oh, temper alert. Watch.'

But all Jack could focus on was the tantalising way Cleo's breasts swayed beneath her tiny vest-top with its star-and-moon print as she leaned over him and reached for the cat.

There was an indignant growl and a flurry of loose cat fur as she heaved the white mass onto the floor. Shaking back her hair, Cleo watched him stalk off, tail bristling like a feather duster. 'Trouble is he usually sleeps with me.'

Lucky Con. 'Must get a little crowded.'

Her skin flushed from peach to rose. Grabbing the sheet, she pulled it tight around her like some sort of cotton armour and something more than anger fired those eyes to a hot blue flame. 'You know nothing about me or my life. You never bothered to keep in contact. That makes my social life none of your business.'

Did she think he was suggesting *crowded* as in *bed*? 'I only meant…' He didn't want to know her sleeping habits, wanted to think about it even less. 'Forget it.'

She'd been manipulating boys since reaching puberty at thirteen. It had been a recurring headache, keeping one eye on the rebellious teen and one on her male admirers, and never the twain shall meet. At age twenty-two presumably she had it down pat now.

He rolled to his side, stuck his uninjured hand behind his head and asked, 'Have you been here all night?'

'You were obviously having a nightmare. I was just going to bed and I wanted to check you were all right…' She lifted her chin. 'I fell asleep. If you think it was for any other reason, you're sicker than I thought.'

But she'd thought about it enough to have gotten herself a sheet. In some ways she hadn't changed. The same caring nature inside the same prickly shell. A smile touched his lips. 'A few days' rest and I'll be fine, but thank you.'

That chin jutted up a notch. 'No big deal; I'm used to sleeping upright. I often slept at Gerry's bedside.'

Her matter-of-fact retort came armed with a barb aimed squarely at him. And she'd be right on target. She'd borne a responsibility that had belonged to Jack Devlin.

He wanted to think that if he'd known about his father's illness earlier he'd have come home, that he'd have made some sort of peace with him, but the scars in their relationship ran bone-deep. If he had come, it would have been for Cleo's sake, not Dad's.

'He used to like me to read to him till he fell asleep,' she said softly. 'In the early hours when the pain got bad...' Eyes brimming, she sniffed and grabbed a tissue from the nightstand, but her glare warned him she'd more likely take a chunk out of him than not if he offered any kind of comfort.

So he stayed as he was and asked, 'How long was Dad ill?'

'That a son would have to ask that question.' She shook her head. 'He knew it was terminal two years ago. It didn't get too bad until the last three months—they were hard on both of us, but he wanted to die at home.' Her moisture-laden eyes pinned him to the mattress. 'He wanted *you* here when he died.'

Jack felt the sting of her words as surely as if she'd run him through with one of those metal-smithing tools he'd seen her wield. But the belligerent man Cleo had never seen because Dad had ensured his temper had remained behind closed doors hadn't been the type to apologise. Which left him wondering what they'd have had to say to each other.

'I'm sorry, Goldilocks.'

Cleo stared at him and in the silence he swore the

temperature plummeted. She blew her nose sharply, then walked to the adjoining bathroom to dispose of the tissue, trailing the sheet behind her. 'It wasn't me asking for you,' she said when she reappeared.

If Cleo had contacted him, he'd have made the effort. He'd have moved heaven and earth. For her. But Jack himself had made that connection impossible. 'I didn't know he was dying.'

'And whose fault's that?'

His. Scotty, the only person he'd kept contact with, hadn't let him know. Jack didn't hold him responsible; the blame lay with Jack for not asking. 'Why didn't you hire a nurse sooner?'

'A nurse?' Her eyes flashed again as she hugged the sheet tighter. 'A nurse isn't a substitute for family. *Family*, Jack. But you wouldn't know about that, would you?

'One day, Jack Devlin, you're going to be sorry you turned your back on the people closest to you, the people who care about you, even when they didn't know where the hell you were because you never bothered to write or call or let us know.'

There wasn't much of her, but the raw edge to her anger packed a punch that reverberated all the way to his toes. He'd known she was strong—stubborn was the word he'd used. But now, with her maturity, he could see so much more. Loyalty, for starters.

He deserved every word she hurled at him. Not on Dad's account—Jack would never regret his decision to leave. For not being here for Cleo, for not making contact with her, for causing her pain.

But she'd never seen the whole picture. She'd been

looking through the lens while the action had taken place behind the camera.

He wanted to keep it that way. 'Sometimes things aren't as black and white as you think.'

'You're no better than the parents who walked out on us. In fact, you're worse because you know first-hand how it feels to be abandoned.'

His temple was beginning to throb again and he had no idea when he'd last eaten. 'Cleo, I don't want to fight about this now. If you'll excuse me, I'm going to take that overdue shower.'

'And I need coffee.' She paused at the door. 'Do you require any help with that dressing on your shoulder? And that bruise...' Her eyes slid over his body and away. 'Did you see a doctor?'

'I can manage, and yes.'

'Was she worth it?' Her gaze snapped back to his, as frosty as her voice.

She? 'What makes you think I was with a woman?'

Cleo laughed, a brittle sound that skittered along his bones like chipped ice. 'Try: your reputation. I assume you took it with you when you left?'

'Wouldn't leave home without it.' And it suited him fine to let her think so.

But the deceptive laziness he projected was a stark contrast to the tension stiffening his shoulders and neck as he watched her. Not to mention other body parts stiffening in response to the sight of a tanned bare thigh peeking out from behind her sheet shield. Her wide legged jersey shorts didn't quite cover the curve of one very cute, well-rounded buttock.

'Just because I left home doesn't mean I didn't think about you.' He immediately cursed himself. Why had he said that?

'Yeah, right.' She glared at him, her mouth compressed to a grim line, at odds with the soft play of sunlight over her face. She crossed the room again, coffee obviously forgotten. 'I stopped thinking about *you* a long time ago.'

But just for a second her eyes had that same little-girl-lost look he'd seen when her father had announced he'd fallen in love with Jack's mother, both archaeologists, and they were leaving on a dig in two days. Cleo had been seven years old.

His parents had rented out the flat adjacent to the house to his mum's colleague from uni. They'd become more than colleagues.

From that day on Cleo hadn't spoken a word about her biological father. It was as if she'd buried him. Jack understood her pain. After all, it had been his own mother the bastard had run off with.

Had she buried Jack Devlin in the same dark hole? Not that he blamed her, particularly after the fiasco of that last night... Moving carefully, he sat up, swung his legs over the bed and planted his feet on the carpet. 'Cleo—'

'Don't.' She held up a hand. 'Don't say a word.' Her sheet drifted further apart, giving him a close-up of taut, smooth skin between the hem of her mini top and those sinfully short shorts. Not to mention the shadowed top of one inner thigh. He took a fortifying breath and reluctantly shifted his eyes to hers.

'You're history, Jack. You may think you're God's gift to women, but not to *this* woman. This woman wants more than a quick roll between the sheets and a kiss goodbye.'

The thought of a naked Cleo in bed with some faceless man was a black hole he always took pains to steer clear of. 'I damn well hope so.'

She nodded, aimed a thumb at her chest. 'Good. Because this woman wants a man who's not afraid to stick around for the family and commitment bit.'

Two of the words he feared most. 'I'm not big on family and commitment. I learned from the best.'

Cleo snorted. 'I was there too, remember, and I haven't inherited your aversion. Don't blame others for your inadequacies, or your fears.' A disgruntled meow and the sound of claws sharpening on upholstery somewhere in the hall interrupted her. 'I'd better let Con out. Like most males I know, he thinks the world revolves around him.'

Jack waited till she left before easing off the bed. 'Whoa.' Dizziness surged through him and he sat down again, clamped his hands to the mattress and took slow deep breaths. A few minutes to get his bearings and he'd be right. Nothing some good Aussie tucker and a couple of painkillers wouldn't cure. He was home, safe and *almost* sound.

Home. The word slipped subtly into his mind before he realised. He'd taken great care not to use the term, because it invariably engulfed him in memories he'd wanted to forget. Now here he was. Swamped.

Thank God for his camera. Freelancing the world

had kept his focus off what he couldn't have and directed it down more productive paths. Four years ago he'd traded glitz and glamour for war zones, lived for the present and refused to think beyond his current assignment. It was better than beating himself up over what he couldn't change.

His current assignment was sorting out Dad's finances and selling the house.

Not as straightforward as he'd imagined. Pushing up slowly, he winced as stiff muscles protested. So Cleo was no longer in the flat. No, sir, she'd made herself quite at home in the house.

Shaking off the niggling discomfort at living in such close quarters with the girl he'd wanted almost for ever, he moved to the window and looked out at the rainbow-coloured rose garden below. She had every right to be here. She'd nursed his father and presumably seen to the upkeep of the house and the well-tended grounds while Dad's health had declined. Alone. He couldn't very well ask her to leave straight away.

He rubbed at the back of his neck. Perhaps she'd consider taking the flat again—rent-free of course. He could arrange for her to continue using the garage as a workshop until an alternative venue could be found.

Guilt speared up and lodged like a sharp splinter in his chest. Hell, he didn't even know whether she'd had to give up a job, if she sold any of the stuff she made, whether Dad had given her an allowance.

Nor did he want his father's wealth. Leastways not for himself. He'd put it towards the rebuilding efforts he'd been supporting overseas. As far as he could see, money came with a heap of its own problems, and he'd been doing fine on his own minus the complications.

But he owed Cleo. One hell of a complication. Until he figured out the best way to repay that debt, he was stuck here in the danger zone, and this time there was no airlift out in sight.

CHAPTER THREE

JACK took his time washing the sweat of travel from his skin. The steam felt like a balm to his body, the warmth easing stiff muscles. He felt almost human again. Until he wiped the moisture from the mirror with his palm.

He shook his head. 'You've looked better,' he muttered. Couldn't do much for the eyes, but he reached for his razor and began scraping away a few days' worth of beard.

That task completed, he gingerly peeled off the dressing on his shoulder. He could've used some help but the thought of Cleo's neat little hands anywhere near his flesh convinced him to deal with it himself. Not a pretty sight and the wound burned like a devil, but he cleaned and dressed it with one of the sterile packs from the hospital.

Finally he pulled on jeans and an old black T-shirt that was soft against his bruised body, and ran a comb through his overlong hair. He grimaced at his reflection. He'd *definitely* looked better.

He left his room and walked down the hall, his bare

feet almost noiseless on the smooth parquetry floor. He noted the walls were a warm cream rather than the austere white they'd always been. The stairs and banister gleamed and a fresh lingering fragrance of lemon polish mingled with the smell of coffee—and was that pizza?—and the homey sounds of clunking dishes and breakfast radio.

Two steps down, he stopped and stared at the statue at the base of the stairs. Spikes of metal speared and curled into sinuous curves, giving an impression of intertwined limbs, an unmistakable breast... How had he missed this piece of metallic erotica last night? One of Cleo's pieces, obviously.

'Now there's a face I haven't seen in a while.'

Jack turned at the sound of Scott's voice. 'Scotty!' His childhood buddy stood in the entry foyer, looking much smarter than the uni student he remembered, in a lightweight Armani suit and royal-blue tie. His liberal dousing of Calvin Klein wafted up the stairwell. Jack grinned as he descended. 'Still as ugly as ever.'

Scott grinned back. 'Not as ugly as you.' He crossed tiles in three strides and grasped both Jack's hands.

'Got to agree with you there.' Relief sighed through Jack at the open and uncomplicated welcome. 'So... what's with the clothes?'

'I'm on my way to a client.'

'Ah, of course. Scott the lawyer now. Father and son team.'

At the mention of family ties Scott paused, looking uncomfortable as he rocked back on the heels of his shiny black shoes. 'Sorry about your father.'

'Yeah.' Jack couldn't think of anything else to say.

'How's it feel to be back?'

'I'll let you know when my body catches up.'

Scott gave Jack a thorough once-over. 'You haven't changed much. Perhaps a bit leaner and meaner.' His eyes slid over Jack's hair. 'No scissors where you come from?'

Jack shoved a hand through damp strands. 'No time.'

'Jeanne can trim it. Sis has her own salon now.'

'Good for Jeanne.' But Jack was super aware of Cleo moving about in the kitchen and didn't want to be overheard. 'What's a hot-shot lawyer drive these days?'

'Jeep Cherokee Sports.'

'Let's take a look.' They wandered out the front door and down the path to the driveway where Scott's car gleamed silver in the sun.

Scott opened the car door, released the bonnet. Both men ostensibly studied the engine but Jack knew they had stuff to talk about. 'Had it long?' he asked.

'Four months.'

'I'll have to road test it some time.' Jack ran a hand over the bodywork. 'You didn't let on he was sick.'

'I took over some of Dad's clients when he had his heart attack; your father was one of them. He gave specific instructions about not trying to find you till it was over.'

Jack almost smiled. Dad hadn't filled Cleo in on that information. Jack could only presume his reason was to make him look like the heartless son. 'So he never knew we kept contact?'

'No. Nobody knew. Had to do some fast talking to our girl here. Told her I hired an investigator.' Scott shook his head. 'The Middle East, Jack. Every time I heard of a foreigner being kidnapped I thought of you.'

Jack shuddered inwardly at the blurred memories of the field hospital, the airlift to Rome when he'd stabilised enough to be moved, then forced a casual grin. 'Life on the edge.' No way did he want to relive the past couple of weeks, not even with Scotty.

'You make a habit of landing in hospital, then?'

'Not since I was here.' Again Jack's mind spun back to his twenty-first birthday, but this time it was the dark recollection of his father's fists.

'You should've pressed charges, Jack. Two broken ribs and multiple bruises. It wasn't the first time.'

'But it was the last.' He shrugged to cover the emotional pain that still stabbed through him at the memories. 'Forget it, it's in the past. Fill me in on Cleo.' At Jack's own request they'd never discussed her while he'd been away. He'd mistakenly thought it would distance her from his mind, from his heart. Wrong.

'She's fine,' Scott said. 'We've gotten close over the years.'

Jack's gut cramped at the unwelcome image that popped into his head. 'How close?'

Scott grinned. 'Told her you'd do the brotherly protection bit. We're friends, that's all.'

Jack shoved his hands behind his head and linked his fingers to ease the tension between his shoulder blades. 'You think she and Sam…?'

Scott laughed. 'After That Night? Hell, no.'

Jack imagined punching a triumphant fist in the air but remained outwardly calm. 'I think she hung around those types just to rile me.'

'She succeeded. You got into more than one fight on her account.'

'For all the good it did. She was a messed-up kid.'

Scott lowered the bonnet with a mechanical click and pierced Jack with a look that had Jack's outward calm ruffling at the edges. 'She's not a kid any more.'

Too right she wasn't, and it scared the living daylights out of Jack. 'I've already noticed she's more than capable of looking out for herself.'

'Are you guys coming in for breakfast or what?' Cleo called from the open doorway.

'Coming,' Scott called back and clapped Jack on the shoulder. 'Let's go eat.'

When Jack entered the familiar sunny yellow kitchen Cleo was unloading the dishwasher. She wore hip-hugging jeans with rainbow pockets and a shrunken violet vest-top that left a tantalising strip of midriff bare. The top stretched over her breasts surely tighter than would be comfortable. Her puckered nipples looked as if they needed rescuing.

He imagined putting his tongue in the curve of her waist, then working his way up, sliding his fingers under that snug fabric to ease her distress—and give him access to all that smooth skin and those two perky little buds.

She stopped in mid-stoop when she saw him looking. He caught her eyes, and for a brief second he thought he saw a flash of something intimate, then... nothing.

'Help yourself,' she said, closing the dishwasher.

He drew in a deep breath. Was it the smell of food or the sight of woman that had his juices flowing, his mouth watering? A lack of both had sharpened his senses and he aimed for the nearest chair and collapsed onto it.

He was right about the smell—it *was* pizza, along with mini quiches, toasted sandwiches and half a soggy pavlova loaded with strawberries and cream.

Scott seemed to know his way around their breakfast table and was already pouring coffee into mugs. 'You going to give Jeanne a try?'

'Why not?' Jack said, wondering if his taste buds could cope with pepperoni pizza this early in the morning on an empty stomach.

Scott pulled out his mobile phone.

'Good idea,' said Cleo, and sat down. Her arm, sprinkled with tiny gold hairs and smelling like jasmine, passed in front of Jack and hovered under his nose as she selected a toasted Vegemite sandwich. She cast a glance over his hair. 'Though it does give you a certain untamed appeal. Some women might find that attractive.'

She'd admired that untamed look six years ago, he remembered, though *feral* might be a more apt word for the guys she'd mixed with. It soured his mood and did nothing for his appetite. 'So you go for what—slick and sophisticated nowadays?' he said.

She snatched her hand back. 'Isn't that *your* preference?'

He felt the sharp edge to her voice like a knife between his ribs and paused, pizza poised halfway to his lips. Her expression wasn't any softer than her tone. Ignoring both, he bit off a mouthful and chewed, but the flavour had lost its spice.

What kind of man *did* she go for now? He'd resigned himself to the fact that she'd have had men in her life. But seeing the stunning woman she'd matured into, sharing the same air and breathing her scent… The thought of any man touching her peachy skin was an exercise in torture. And something he'd have to get used to fast.

'We weren't discussing me,' he said at last. 'Hopefully you've gotten some wisdom along with your maturity.' Now he was really starting to sound like a big brother.

'Your appointment's for ten,' Scott said, setting the phone down. 'Jeanne's looking forward to seeing you again.'

'Thanks, Scotty.'

'So, Jack.' Cleo sliced herself a generous serving of pavlova. 'Tell us about yourself. Rome, wasn't it? I think I read something about it in some magazine.' She lifted one shoulder, took a gulp of coffee. 'Photographing all those Italian beauties. Must be a hard life.'

'I—'

Scott's mobile buzzed. Scott spoke briefly, disconnected. 'Those Italian beauties will have to wait. I've got to run.' Rising, he drained his coffee. 'Cleo, can you take Jack to the mall later?'

She answered with a hesitant, 'Okay.'

Jack understood her reluctance and was tempted to cancel the whole business and go back to bed. Or perhaps she had someone else she wanted to be with today. 'I can find my own way,' he said, eyeing her over his mug. 'If you're expected elsewhere...'

He was dismissed with a curt, 'Don't be ridiculous, you're in no shape to drive. I'm taking you and that's that.' She shrugged as she licked cream from her fingers. 'I've nothing better to do.'

But as Jack watched Cleo clear and stack plates her quick and edgy movements let him know she'd agreed only as a favour to Scott. She still had that chip on her shoulder, though she'd smoothed the edges some. And he couldn't help thinking what a nice shoulder it was.

To distract himself from the sight of that trim body, he directed his gaze through the glassed doors that opened onto the patio, and beyond, to the bottom of the garden. 'The old wattle tree's still there.' Dense with foliage, it was still a perfect spot for a cubby or a cuddle...

'Where you got a little too friendly with a certain Sally Edwards,' Cleo reminded him.

'Thanks to you, one of my less memorable moments.' Unbeknown to him, Cleo had watched the proceedings from above, and just when things had been getting interesting she'd decked him with her shoe. Unfortunately Sally hadn't seen the humour in the situation.

Cleo turned to look at him. 'Remember that time I climbed higher than you?'

'An unfair contest—the branches didn't support my weight.'

'Ah, but you were taller. Bet you couldn't do it now.' Her voice held a definite sneer.

Jack recognised the old challenge, and met her eyes. 'That sounds suspiciously like a dare.'

She tossed out a laugh as she filled the sink. 'Hardly, for someone in your condition.'

But the triumph in her eyes was enough. 'You're on, but I've got something better.' And something a man recovering from concussion and assorted wounds probably shouldn't attempt, but pride was at stake here.

'Like what?' He saw the flicker of alarm in her eyes as he strode to the glass doors, slid them open. 'Coming?'

'Jack, wait.' His strides took him to the front of the house while Cleo sputtered behind him. 'Whatever you're planning, don't.'

Jack allowed himself a rare moment of light-headed amusement as he put one bare foot on the first rung and gauged his ascent up the trellis to his window while Cleo tugged at his arm, her nails pressing into his flesh. He liked the way she clung to him a little too much.

Definitely light-headed. Temporary insanity even. That was what he told himself as he planted a quick hard kiss on her parted mouth and swung up. 'If I fall, I want my ashes scattered on—'

'Shut up and get down or I'm going to kill you myself.'

His own lips tingling from the unexpectedly lush heat of Cleo's mouth, he gritted his teeth, wincing as pain sang through his body. 'Like riding a bike,' he muttered, picking his way through a forest of ivy. Virtually one-handed was only a minor handicap. He was fitter at this point in his life than he'd ever been.

But his head was spinning and he was sweating with a sudden dose of something he refused to consider as the shakes when he hauled himself through the window. Still, he managed a wave at a white-lipped Cleo below.

Then he flopped onto his back on the floor and closed his eyes. The room tilted. His shoulder screamed. The throbbing in his temple grew to epic proportions. *Don't pass out, for God's sake.*

But he didn't have time to enjoy his pain in solitude because in the next moment Cleo burst through his bedroom door and was bending over him, wild-eyed and spitting mad.

'You idiot!'

He would have smiled if he'd had the energy—it had been a long time since anyone had shown emotion of any kind towards him. He closed his eyes. 'Hi, Goldilocks. You made good time.'

'Shut up, Jack.'

Her voice was breathy, impatient. Like an aroused woman. Cool fingers slid his T-shirt up his chest, working gently over and along every tender rib. One, two, three…

His breath stalled in his lungs. It was too easy to imagine those fingers sliding lower, dipping beneath the waistband of his jeans. His suddenly very tight jeans. He might hurt more than he'd admit, but he wasn't dead. Yet.

'Piece of cake,' he told her, pushing up, mostly to

cover the incriminating evidence in his lap. The eyes that met his were stormy pools of blue. The light fragrance wafting from her skin made his head spin again for a different reason entirely. 'I used to do it regularly. Don't worry.'

'I wouldn't waste my time.' She pushed away the hand he'd automatically lifted to her cheek and stood, fisting her hands against her sides. 'We leave for the mall at nine forty-five. Don't be late.'

'I'll be ready.'

Not one of your more intelligent ideas, Jack, he thought, when he was alone again. Trouble was he'd quickly rediscovered that, where Cleo was concerned, emotion rode roughshod over sense.

Which didn't bode well for however long it took to settle Cleo in a place of her own, wrap things up and be gone.

Under an array of brilliant down-light, Hair's Jeanne was bustling with the sounds of scissors and dryers, the smells of shampoos and lotions.

An attractive brunette like her brother, Jeanne smiled from a distance while she put the finishing touches to a client's hair. But Cleo noted Jeanne's eyes were all for Jack this morning. And why not? The woman was alive, wasn't she?

Knowing it would be rude to take the single, safer chair on the opposite wall when there was a space beside him— even if it was a very small space—Cleo sat on his right.

Her arm was hard up against Jack's. Their jeans-clad thighs brushed. Obviously Jack didn't experience the same jolt that sent heat spiralling through her system. With a casual ease she envied, he picked up a periodical and began flicking through it.

It was impossible not to see his reflection in the salon mirrors. His eyes were on his magazine and all she could see were the long, dark lashes. And the dimple. And that mouth. He could have been in front of the camera instead of behind. She scowled. That might make him poster-boy material, but it didn't make him a better person.

So why did she feel so weak, so…hot? And what was she going to do about it?

Remember what he did.

Forcing her eyes away, she reached for distraction with a copy of *Cosmopolitan* and opened it at random. As Jack turned a page one hair-dusted forearm grazed hers, sending sparks of awareness shooting to her shoulder. *Hurry up, Jeanne*.

She needed a job, something part-time to get her by until she could earn enough with her jewellery and metalwork creations. She had a few shop owners taking orders on commission, and a few art pieces in a couple of galleries, but not enough to live on.

She flipped the page, looked closer. The woman in the picture wore a silver ensemble—G-string and feathers. She was gripping a pole with her thighs, one arm behind her head, fingers artfully rippling through her hair.

'Executive by day, stripper by night.' She hadn't realised she'd read aloud until Jack shifted a shoulder and glanced at her magazine.

'Can't they come up with something better than that?' he said.

But she saw it had his attention. His eyes barely flickered as he studied the two images. One was of a woman in a conservative navy suit carrying a briefcase, the other was a long-legged, sultry blonde.

He flipped a page of his own magazine. 'And the camera angle's all wrong.'

Cleo rolled her eyes. *Yeah, right.* 'One way to earn extra money…' She watched him perk up at that, then he narrowed his eyes just enough to provoke her into saying, 'And you'd know all about photographing naked women, wouldn't you?'

'I do not photograph naked women,' he said, stiffly.

'I've seen the evidence, Jack.'

At fourteen it had been too painful and too personal to talk about. Years later it still hurt. She'd barely glimpsed the careless spread of nude photos on the table before his father had swiped them away with apologies on his son's behalf. But not before she'd seen the one including the same woman draped over a formally tuxedoed Jack with a Chesire-cat grin on his face.

'I don't know what you're talking about,' he muttered with a dismissive shrug as he turned the page.

No, he probably didn't even remember—all in a day's work. She directed her attention to the magazine again. 'Cherie here calls it exotic dancing. She says it pays the rent and keeps her flexible.'

He made a guttural sound in his throat. 'If you want flexible, try yoga.'

'I do. I also play basketball and take a weekly jazz ballet class, and it's great, but it doesn't pay the bills. Besides, Jack, I'm sure you've seen your share of "flexible", and I don't think they were performing yoga.'

His jaw kind of clenched but he didn't reply.

Guilty as charged. 'At least she's got a figure, unlike those broomsticks you associate with.' She shrugged at his frown. 'I've seen a picture or two... Somewhere.' The woman draped over his arm in the magazine clipping had been tall, blonde and beautiful. And skinny.

Cleo read on. 'Says here she made enough money to put her through business school. That's how she got where she is today.'

'And where, exactly, is that? With her face splashed all over this magazine, who's going to take her seriously in the workplace?'

'When she's dancing I doubt anyone's looking at her face, Jack.'

Jack made his living out of women who used their bodies in a similar fashion. Even if modelling wasn't stripping, it wasn't far off with today's designs.

'Money's not a problem for you,' Jack said. 'We'll get you settled somewhere and you can—'

'Get...me...settled...somewhere?' She said each word slowly and distinctly between clenched teeth. It took all her self-control to stay seated. 'And if you think money's not a problem for me, you haven't eaten from the plastic spoon I was born with.'

His jaw tightened. 'No, but I've tasted tin a time or two.'

'I make my own decisions. I'm not a kid any more.'

'No. You're not.'

His eyes were focused on her mouth. She could almost feel them sliding over it. Hungrily. She licked her lips. Saw the instant response of his own mouth.

'Which is why I know you'll look at this situation calmly and rationally.' His clipped, dispassionate tone was like a slap in the face. No more hungry eyes. In fact, they looked as dark and remote as a midwinter's night. 'We're going to straighten out a few things while I'm here.'

We? Mr Cool Detached Take Charge Devlin was back with a vengeance. Setting the magazine aside with admirable control under the circumstances, she rose. It gave her a slight advantage in height and some illusion of being in control.

The anger and disappointment simmering in her veins told another story. 'And we have plenty to straighten out. Like I said, I make my own decisions. I'll be looking for a job as soon as possible.' She lifted her chin to stare down her nose at him. 'Perhaps I'll try some of the clubs around town, see if there are any openings for exotic dancers.'

Apart from a tick at the corner of his eye, he didn't react in any way except to say, 'Sit down, you're making a scene.'

Oh. She realised her voice had risen on the last few words and this was Jeanne's place of business, for heaven's sake. For that reason alone, she did as he asked.

But she wasn't finished. His high-and-mighty

attitude needed taking down a peg or two. Leaning over, so she was sure he could see her cleavage, she continued in a lower voice. 'Do you think I'll make a good exotic dancer, Jack?' She toed off her sandal and ran her bare foot under the leg of his jeans, over his shin. And felt him shudder. The hair tickled the sole of her foot, sending ripples up her leg to settle between her thighs.

'Your immaturity's showing,' he muttered, shifting to the left.

'Or pole-dancing,' she continued, undeterred. 'I imagine it's quite...*stimulating*—all that twisting and writhing...' She watched his jaw clench and knew she'd achieved one thing: if she set her mind to it, she could turn him on. Astonishing. However, the operative word here was *if*. 'It's probably quite lucrative. I might look into it.' Satisfied that he was properly *stimulated*, she picked up her magazine and pretended to read.

Thanks to Jack and the mixed signals he was sending her, she was riding an emotional roller coaster. Okay, rule number one: *Keep it light, no one gets hurt.* No way was she going to set herself up for that kind of heartache again.

'Hi, Cleo. And Jack!'

Cleo looked up as Jeanne all but leaped at him. Already standing, he enveloped her in his arms, then kissed her full and firmly on the mouth. A wave of heat plunged through Cleo. He hadn't hugged her like that, hadn't kissed her as if he wanted to eat her alive. So much for light.

That smile, all that devastating Devlin charm, apparently didn't extend to surrogate sisters. He hadn't been on such easy terms with Cleo since she'd been thirteen. She forgot all about keeping it light as a sense of betrayal knifed through her.

'Jeannie,' he said when he came up for air. He stepped back. 'Let's have a look at you.' Jeanne did a quick pirouette, arms outstretched. 'All grown up.' He laughed, low and deep. 'I can hardly believe I'm about to trust little Jeanne with my hair.'

She laughed right back. 'I promise to be gentle with you.'

Cleo knew Jeanne meant nothing by her flirtation, but, feeling as out of place as a chocolate éclair on a platter of prawns, she tapped Jeanne's arm. 'I'll leave you to it, then.'

'Cleo, isn't it great to have him home?' She slung an arm around Cleo's shoulders. 'Are you going to bring him to the game tonight? It'll give me a chance to flirt some more.' She batted her eyelashes at him and grinned.

So much for tonight's idea of escaping his presence for a couple of hours. 'I don't think—'

'I'll be there,' he said.

'Great. Hey, I could maybe rustle up a uniform…'

Cleo's pulse skipped a beat. *Thanks, Jeanne.* She definitely did *not* want to see Jack's tanned, sweat-sheened and muscled body in those ultra-short shorts and loose top. Besides, he was injured.

To her relief he said, 'Not tonight. I think I'll stick to the spectators' stand. My skills on the court are a little rusty.'

Cleo doubted his skills were rusty in any area of his

life, but, after the high-rise stunt he'd pulled earlier, it was a relief to hear him decline.

'Okay, we've sorted out the evening's entertainment.' Jeanne crooked her finger. 'Follow me, Jack.'

'I'll call back in half an hour,' Cleo said, and headed out into the less-unsettling mall.

The strong yeasty smell of hot doughnuts accosted her from the little stand under its pink and white umbrella. For once, her stomach, already tied up in knots, revolted, and she hurried out of the shopping centre into the balmy morning sun.

She walked to the café a few minutes away where the air was fresh and smelled of summer grass and ordered a juice at an outside table. Sparrows darted between patrons, pecking at crumbs. Striped awnings flapped lazily in the drift of warm air.

She leaned back while the waitress set a long, tall glass in front of her.

Why was it so easy between Jeanne and Jack? And why hadn't Jeanne given him the cold-shoulder treatment? Jeanne knew the hurt he'd caused her, even if she didn't know the full story—Cleo wasn't about to let anyone in on that. Was Jeanne taken in by his looks and charm? *Traitor.* It had to be a be-nice-to-the-customer thing.

Even if there was still that rugged, almost primal attraction she doubted any woman under the age of eighty could ignore. The memory of that fast, hard meeting of lips back at the house brought back the giddy rush. Now *there* was a kiss, even if he hadn't meant anything by it. Keeping it light. Except...

She stirred her juice vigorously with the straw and let herself brood. She was going to move out as soon as she could. It wouldn't work at home with Jack there night and day, his scent in the air, that face at the breakfast table, that long, lean body sprawled on the sofa. Not again.

She drummed restless fingers on the table. It wasn't fair that he could simply walk back into her life and turn it upside down. Drag all that old stuff to the surface. Stuff she'd thought she'd buried for good.

His rough-grained voice, the up-for-a-dare attitude they'd shared since childhood. And how, when it had really counted, he'd always, always looked out for her, even if it hadn't been in the way she'd have liked. Even if she'd never admitted it.

Until he'd left.

Her fingers tightened on the glass. *Remember that cold, hard fact.*

She didn't need him looking out for her now. And she certainly didn't want to hear that 'morning after' voice or see those too-clear images it conjured: hot suggestions, hotter bodies…

She rolled the glass against her brow to cool those rampaging thoughts. 'Get over it,' she said aloud. She'd done it before, she could do it again. It was just a matter of will-power.

CHAPTER FOUR

CLEO swiped at her brow, then braced her hands on her thighs as Scott slam-dunked the ball for another two points. The smell of stale sweat and rubber filled the four-court gym. Umpires' whistles, shouts of players and spectators ricocheted off the walls.

So what if she'd heard Jack talking on the phone in the study just before they'd left? In smooth, sexy Italian. She understood the words, *'Ciao, bella.'* And if she'd gotten to the phone first, she'd have known more.

She jogged down the court as Scott dribbled the ball towards the scoring end. Every time she glanced Jack's way he was watching. She ordered herself to concentrate on the game, to ignore the way those dark eyes focused wholly on her. *Will-power, remember.*

But with his hair cut close to his head he looked more like the Jack she remembered and it did strange things to her tummy despite her good intentions.

'Cleo!' Jeanne's shout came too late.

Cleo fumbled for the ball as a blur of brown whizzed past her shoulder. Bugger.

The umpire's whistle sounded. 'Sub. Forty-two out, thirteen on,' their coach, Mike, called, jerking his thumb at Cleo.

Disgusted and worse, humiliated—thanks to Jack— she headed for the bench.

'Your game's off tonight,' Mike said as she grabbed her water and sat down beside him.

'Mmm.' She scowled as her eyes connected with Jack's and felt that stab of heat before she returned her resolute gaze courtside. 'Blame it on hormones.' She yanked the lid off her water bottle.

'Ah.' Mike nodded in understanding.

He didn't understand at all but it let her off the hook.

They won, thanks to Scott's three-pointer on the bell. As the players dispersed Jack joined Jeanne and Cleo as they collected their gear.

'Hey, Jack, still got what it takes?' Scott called, jogging towards them.

Too late Cleo saw the ball leave Scott's grasp. She shot forward to intercept the throw, but it hit Jack high in the chest. She winced as she watched Jack stagger backwards. 'Scott, he's—'

'Fine,' Jack wheezed. But colour leached from his face. He shot a quelling look at Cleo. 'Out of practice.'

He retrieved the ball, tossed it back to Scott, but he didn't fool Cleo. Beneath the grin, she saw the pain the others didn't—Scott was too busy exchanging a male bonding slap with another player and Jeanne was guzzling water.

Turning her back on Jeanne, she glared at him. 'Go ahead, be a superhero,' she muttered.

Jack merely grinned again. 'Give it a couple of weeks.'

'We'll be waiting,' Scott said, turning to stuff gear into his gym bag. 'Okay, one family-size pizza coming up, I'm starved.'

The steamy air carried the odour of hot asphalt and exhaust fumes as they walked across the car park. With what appeared to be some fancy manoeuvring on Jeanne's part, she took the front seat with Scott, leaving Cleo to sit with Jack.

'How do you like Jack's hair?' Jeanne said, buckling her seat belt.

'Good job,' Cleo replied, looking straight ahead. She'd already seen more than she needed to have her fingers tingling at the thought of running them through those gleaming dark strands, touching that bare neck.

'Better than good.' Jeanne turned to grin at them—correction: Jack. 'He looks movie-star gorgeous.'

Scott reversed out of the parking bay, glancing in the rear-vision mirror. 'Our old Jack's back.'

Almost against her will, Cleo slid Jack a sideways glance. He might look more like her old Jack, but for the second time in as many days she reminded herself that looks were deceiving. Behind that movie-star bone structure, under that dark wash-faded T-shirt...

She narrowed her eyes at the darker stain that had spread near his shoulder. Forgot all about keeping her distance and leaned closer. Musky male sweat met her nostrils...and the faint metallic scent of fresh blood.

In the car's semi-darkness she could see the perspiration glistening on his upper lip, the tight muscles in his jaw, the hands clenched into fists on his thighs, but when she opened her mouth his eyes flashed a warning.

'Scott, I think I'll pass on the meal,' she said. Her eyes flicked to the rear mirror and Scott's frown, then back. 'I'm all pizzaed out, and after the stress of yesterday… I'm feeling a little nauseous. Nothing an early night won't cure.'

'Okay,' said Scott. 'You want Jeanne to—'

'Jack'll keep me company…' she lowered her brows at him '…won't you, Jack?'

Scott glanced at Cleo in the mirror again. 'I thought Jack and I might—'

Jeanne's quick not-so-discreet jab cut him off. 'Jack's not the best either, Scott. Can't you see that?' Jeanne shot Cleo a knowing look, a smile hovering around her mouth. 'Men. They never notice.'

Jack made an almost inaudible rumbling sound in his throat.

Cleo sighed. Now wasn't the time to set Jeanne straight. She wasn't sure whom she was madder at, so she settled for as far away from Jack as space allowed, let her head fall back and closed her eyes.

Five minutes later she made a show of dragging herself up the steps to the front door. Bad move, because suddenly Jack was at her side, his palm warm and firm on her basketball singlet, searing her skin and making her jump.

The instant Scott's car disappeared down the drive she jerked away. 'Stop it.'

Undaunted, Jack closed the space again. 'You did this for me.' His breath caressed the side of her face.

The scent of blood and sweat was closer now. 'You're not sick. You go till you drop.'

'And so will you in a minute. Too stubborn to admit when you need help. Well tonight, like it or not, you're going to get it.'

'I can tend my own flesh.'

'Jack. You don't come with me and let me see, I'm going to drag out the old truth-or-dare, and, trust me, you wouldn't like the questions. Take your pick.'

Her heart was pumping in anticipation, but she marched to the kitchen flicking on lights as she went. The first-aid box was in the cupboard above the sink. 'Sit down,' she ordered without turning. Easier to keep her mind off that hot body if she concentrated on what she needed.

She heard the scrape of wood over tile as she set the box on the sink and her heart skipped a beat as she fumbled for a gauze pad and tape.

'When did you develop this bossy, take-charge attitude?' he grumbled.

'Since I took charge when your dad got sick. Take off your T-shirt.'

'I don't need a nursemaid, just give me the box.'

'Save the heroics for someone who cares.' She squirted antiseptic into a bowl of tepid water. 'I know you too, Jack Devlin. Never did want a nurse even when I wanted to play.' She set the bowl on the table. 'Well, I'm going to get my turn now. And it's probably going to hurt...'

Oh, boy. Her breath backed up in her lungs. He'd gotten rid of the T-shirt. Naked skin. Man skin.

Gleaming rich bronze, like polished wood. Heat rolled off him in waves that seemed to soak into her own skin, making her feel hot and shivery at the same time.

'I get the impression you're going to enjoy this.'

His voice held a hint of a smile, and she dragged her eyes to his. There was humour there, and warmth, and for a few seconds she basked in the glory before the ugly sight of his wounds took precedence.

Bruising marred the gorgeous skin, and beneath the shoulder bandage she saw the bright seep of fresh blood. Patches had dried and stuck nastily to his flesh and she winced. 'Ouch.'

'Cleo?' The sharp edge to his voice broke her concentration. 'You sure you're up to this?'

No, she wasn't sure at all, but not for the reasons he thought. The sight of blood didn't distress her; the fact that this was Jack's blood, on Jack's chest, did.

She shrugged to hide her distress. 'What's the big deal?' Biting her lip, she eased away the blood-stiff dressing, and felt him tense when her fingers skimmed over his skin. 'Sorry.'

He hissed out a breath between his teeth, then grinned. Sort of. 'There's a fine line between pleasure and pain.'

'Is that so?' she murmured, chewing her bottom lip some more as she tugged the last corner of the pad from his flesh.

Her breath stalled; she couldn't seem to drag her eyes away from the small, neatly stitched wound and surrounding bruise. 'Is…that…what…I…think…it…is?'

He looked down at the wound then up at her. 'Depends. What do you think it is?'

'You were *shot*?' Her whole body went weak. A ball of ice formed in her chest. A little lower, further to the right, he'd never have come home. She glared at him. 'And what the hell were you doing to get yourself shot?' she snapped, her voice rising a notch. 'A jealous husband?' She raised her hand. 'Don't tell me, I don't want to know.'

She busied herself by cleaning off the dried blood with a cloth dipped in antiseptic. 'It seems to have stopped bleeding.' Her clipped voice betrayed none of the emotions running through her at the thought of losing him for ever.

Yet hadn't she accepted that until yesterday? She shook her head. Not this way. Not dead.

She unsealed a sterile patch, cut two lengths of adhesive tape. 'This'll have to do.' His breath was warm on her hand as she worked. 'It should do the job. For now.'

'Cleo, look at me.' He tilted her chin up until her eyes met his. There were tiny flecks of gold in his irises. She'd never noticed that before. Then again, she'd never been this close, this intimate, for this long, before. 'No jealous husband.'

'Caught between two lovers?' Why was she taunting him? She'd already told him she didn't want to hear.

'You've always had a poor opinion of me,' he said tersely. 'I have not, nor do I intend, to juggle two women at once.' He pinched her chin before dropping his hand, and his eyes hardened. 'One's more than enough.'

She stepped back, heart pounding, mouth dry as jealousy stabbed at her. Who was she—The One that was enough for Jack Devlin? 'Whatever you say.' She busied her hands and eyes repacking the first aid box. 'Go put a clean shirt on; I'll soak this one.'

'Forget the shirt, and the box.' His hand shot out and grabbed her wrist. Hard. She could feel the tension in his fingers, could hear it in his voice, and knew she'd see it in his eyes, but she didn't look.

Instead she stared at her hands, small and fragile-looking against his work-rough ones. Surprising for a photographer, she thought, in some faraway part of her mind.

'You know what really ticks me off?' He said it quietly but Cleo heard the ice-tipped steel lance through it. 'When people closest to me don't accept what I say, don't accept *me*. Dad never did and that's the...' Abruptly he snapped his jaw shut, released her wrist. She saw the shattered look in his eyes before he turned away.

Perhaps he had cared about his father, but something had happened between them that had hurt Jack deeply. Whatever it was he didn't want to show it. Nor did he want to discuss it.

Bright, shiny grief twisted inside her. *I want to accept you. You don't know how much.* Instinctively she stepped back, away from his height and the proximity of that naked chest with its badges of pain.

Through a haze that verged on tears she watched him ball the cloth and walk to the door, the movement as tight and controlled as his face as he turned to look at her for one long, tense moment. And then he was gone.

* * *

The following morning Cleo faced Scott and a stony-faced Jack across a pile of legal documents on the rosewood dining table. She wondered if Jack felt an ounce of the grief that consumed her. It certainly didn't look like it, but she didn't know with Jack any more. Scott didn't look much better; she could have sworn he was nervous.

Scott's jaw tightened, his fingers tense as he shuffled the documents. 'In your absence, Jack, Gerry named you and me co-executors of his will.'

Jack leaned back in his chair as if distancing himself and waved a hand. 'Leave the fine print for now and give us the layman's version, Scotty.'

'He wanted me to read this before the will.' Scott looked at Jack as he unfolded a single handwritten page. '"I have to believe that you, Jack, have taken pity on a dying man, forgiven him and come home."'

Cleo saw Jack's mouth tighten infinitesimally. Enough to know he wasn't as immune to the grief as he'd have her believe. It triggered an echo in her body, a mix of pain and sympathy. She bit her lip and willed herself not to cry. But tears lurked nonetheless.

'Cleo?' Scott leaned across the table and touched her elbow. 'You all right?'

She nodded, thankful it wasn't Jack's hand or she was sure she'd fall apart—from hate, love, anger or grief, she hadn't a clue at this moment.

'Okay.' Scott straightened, eyeing them both in turn. 'Gerry left a substantial estate. Very substantial.' He tabled the documents, then drew a breath. 'Cleo, you are the sole beneficiary of Gerry's will. His bank accounts, stocks and shares, the house and surrounding property.'

Cleo swallowed as her throat closed over. It took a moment to comprehend Scott's words, another to absorb the implications. 'Everything?' Her voice cracked on the word. 'The house and all his money…to me?' She rubbed the heel of her hand over her chest. It felt too tight, too full. *Gerry, how could you do this?* To her. To Jack.

Almost afraid of what she'd see, she lifted her gaze to Gerry's rightful heir. If Jack was disappointed or angry, he didn't show it. In fact, she saw nothing in his dark eyes. And that was the most worrying of all. 'This isn't right, Jack.' She had to work at keeping the tremor out of her voice. 'I know it; you know it.' She pushed the tabled documents firmly towards him. 'It's your family, your inheritance.'

He shook his head. His eyes still gave nothing away. 'Family's not only about blood, as you've demonstrated so well over the past couple of years.' Another man might have sounded bitter. Not Jack. 'It's about caring and compassion and giving. You deserve it.'

Then he flicked the documents as if they were last week's junk mail and the torment she saw beneath that one careless action wrenched at her heart. 'This saves me the hassle of putting the house up for sale. As soon as we've dispensed with the legalities, I'll be gone.'

The cold simplicity of his words slid like ice through her veins. Cleo twisted her hands together beneath the table. If he left mad, hurt, humiliated, it would never be right between them. She had to do something, but what? Nothing could alter the fact that his father had left his inheritance to her.

Scott's eyes softened with sympathy for his friend as his fingers slid back and forth over the papers. No wonder the poor guy looked as if he'd rather be somewhere else. 'Jack,' he said. 'Probate could take up to four weeks.'

When Jack exploded out of his chair, Cleo jolted and looked up sharply. His back was rod-stiff as he strode to the window and she had to stop herself from going to him.

She'd wanted him to help her sort out the legal issues his father's death had left, and God knew he owed her for all those years away. When it was finished, she'd told herself she wanted him gone. No reminders, no pain.

But not this way. Never this way.

She pushed up on wobbly legs. 'I can take care of myself, Jack, but I don't want you leaving with this between us.'

When he didn't reply, she dug down for strength and walked up behind him. His scent, familiar, clean and woodsy, surrounded her. She tapped him on an unyielding shoulder. 'I dare you to stay, Jack Devlin.'

Jack winced. He could feel Cleo's eyes like twin lasers on the back of his head. That compact, curvy body lined up behind him. Too close, too hot, too...Cleo. Stay a month? Out of the question. Hell, staying a day was a day too long. 'You win this one, Goldilocks.'

'Win? This isn't about winning, Jack. It's about having the courage to work with me and make it right. Not a dare, then—I'm *asking* you to stay. To help.'

The quiet sincerity in her voice tugged at his heart. A man could be tempted by that voice, by that woman's scent wafting over his shoulder.

But was that all an act? The splinter of thought struck out of nowhere and festered instantly in his mind. Had Cleo known about the will all along? The more Jack thought about it, the more credible it seemed that she and his father had cooked it up between them. Their relationship had changed to more than father-daughter over the past six years, and Jack was the one on the outside.

Fury erupted like molten poison through his veins. He closed his hands into fists and forced himself to turn and look at her. Had his father's cruel hands—the ones that had broken his ribs—stroked that smooth female flesh?

Was Jack the only one here who didn't know?

Jaw tightening at the sight of her innocent-looking face, he fought back the anger, the bitterness. 'Just think, in a matter of weeks you can play lady of the manor.'

Her face paled, those beautiful blue eyes widened. Then they narrowed and her whole body tensed. She drew a breath and said, 'Now wait just a minute. I'm confused.'

He shook his head to clear it, couldn't stop the sneer that curled his lip. 'That makes two of us.'

'You've made it plain all along you didn't want anything to do with Gerry, and now you act as if I tricked him into leaving me the house.'

'Did you?' The words were out before he could censor them.

She reared back as if he'd slapped her. 'You'd even *ask* that?' Her eyes sprang with moisture, but she swiped at her cheeks with the backs of her hands. 'How could you? How dare you? I'll sell the house. You can have the money or I'll give it to charity; either way it doesn't matter. Money's never mattered to me.'

Her anger only fuelled his own. Questions and doubts hammered in his head. His vision greyed and that throb in his skull was back. 'Unfortunately that's not an option at the moment.' And she'd know it. 'If you need to contact me I'll be down the road at the Sunset Motel.'

Swinging away, he made it through the door and managed to point himself in the direction of the stairs.

'Time out, Jack.'

He slowed in the hallway at the sound of Scott's voice but didn't stop. 'Not now.'

He heard Scott slide the dining-room doors shut. 'I'm sorry, Jack,' he said in a low voice. 'It's a tough break, but you have responsibilities. There's documentation to deal with. You need to be here.'

Jack swung to Scott and met his direct gaze head-on. 'You're co-executor, and the lawyer. You'll manage.'

'What about personal effects?' Scott waved a hand, his frown deepening. 'And the study's full of papers that need going through. Are you going to leave all that to Cleo?'

Too full of anger—and, dammit, pride—to stand

still, Jack paced the hall. Not only had his father denied Jack his inheritance, he'd had the gall to rub his nose in it.

He thought of the school he'd been helping to rebuild before he was shot, the new wells they'd begun to sink. Fresh water and education where it was so desperately needed. That money would have helped.

The old man was counting on Jack's own feelings for Cleo to see it through. If someone had squeezed a round of bullets into his heart it wouldn't have hurt more. His father knew how Jack felt about her. And despised him for it, as if it had been some sort of contest.

Why? Dad had done his damnedest to make Jack look bad in her eyes. Jack always suspected the man couldn't face the prospect of not having a female in his life, as if it was a bruise to his male ego. His cancer would have been the perfect trigger to win over Cleo's sympathy. Or more.

As he passed the dining room he saw Cleo through the glass doors. She was still standing by the window, hugging her arms and looking out across the lawn. Her hair caught the light around the edges, creating a halo effect.

His gut cramped. That damn angel again. Even if she'd been his father's lover, he couldn't cut off his feelings for her any more than he could cut off his own arm. That didn't mean he had to stay and torture himself.

'Jack?' Scott asked quietly.

Not ready to commit to anything yet, Jack rammed a fist into his open palm. 'I'll let you know.'

The back door slapped shut behind him as he crossed the neatly manicured lawn to the place he'd always taken his troubles. The old wattle tree. Beneath its branches the air smelled of summer and dry leaves and solitude. He sank to the ground, leaned against the trunk. Drawing up his knees, he let his forearms rest on them and closed his eyes.

Doc Romano had told him it was important to avoid stress during recovery. *Slow deep breaths, muscles loose. Relax.* But his muscles remained clenched despite his best efforts.

The old *dottore* hadn't met Jack's family.

If you could call it a family. One word summed it up. Dysfunctional. And now the man who called himself a father was leaving someone else everything he owned.

He didn't hear Cleo, rather he felt her presence; a stirring of the senses, like an approaching change in the weather. That light mix of jasmine and woman drifted over him. He wanted to capture that fragrance and carry it next to his heart for the rest of his miserable life. His *solitary* miserable life.

'Jack?' She spoke softly, tentatively, as if unsure of his response. He felt her kneel in front of his raised knees. 'This is new,' she began. 'You were always so revved. I could almost believe you're sleeping.'

He let his eyes remain shut and absorbed the velvet sound of her voice.

'So…if you're asleep you won't hear me apologise for what happened back there.'

An apology? From Cleo? Another reminder that she

was no longer a kid but a mature woman. Question was, what was she apologising *for*? He opened his eyes, then wished like hell he hadn't.

Sunshine and sex.

How was a man supposed to avoid stress, let alone think rationally, when the girl of his fantasies was at his knees, her face inches away from his crotch? He would have risen but for the sudden bulge that surged uncomfortably against the tight seam of his jeans and the fact that he didn't think his legs would hold him.

'Honest to God, Jack, I had no idea about the house.'

'Forget the bloody house. It's just a house.'

She leaned nearer. Her strawberry top gaped, giving him a bird's-eye view of soft shadows and curves. Then, by God, she placed those long, slender hands on his knees.

'Not just a house,' she said. 'And I'm *not* going to forget it. We have to talk.'

The pressure of her fingers burned through his jeans, sending hot darts of pleasure—or was it pain?—shooting up his thighs. The thought of those fingers sliding over his bare flesh, inching up… He cleared his throat, patted the ground beside him. 'For God's sake, sit down.'

To his relief she did as he asked for once. Sunlight dappled her skin as she tilted her head and studied him. 'I don't know the man you've become, Jack. But I want to. We're both different people now. Perhaps we could work on something together, get to know each other again.'

'I'll think about it.' If he could get his brain in gear. Right now the only thing his scrambled brain could conjure up involved nothing more than the two of them and a bed. Maybe not even the bed.

She clasped her arms around her own upraised knees. 'I've been a pain in the bum over the years, I admit it. But you weren't exactly Mr Congeniality yourself.'

He almost weakened. The urge to reach out, to open up and tell her all the reasons why, welled inside him. But the past half-hour had changed everything.

Watching him with those wide, slumberous eyes, she waited for him to respond. To deny his lack of congeniality, perhaps? But she was right on; at this point he felt anything but.

Her jaw firmed, her delectable mouth pursed. 'I assume by that surly expression the answer's no?'

'I said I'll think about it. What do you want, a promissory note?' She blinked at him and he felt a stab of guilt. 'Give me a break, Cleo.'

'Give *you* a break?' She straightened and pulled away. There was a steely edge to her voice that warned him she was stronger than he'd ever given her credit for.

'Do you realise what you said inside?' she continued in that razor-edged tone. 'I don't want your father's money and I'll tell you now, Jack, I won't stand for the verbal slurs you cast on him and me. If you want to follow that path, you can just follow it right back to Italy.

'I want you to stay,' she continued, but he heard a thread of silk through the steel. 'At least until probate's finalised.' She hesitated as if weighing her words. 'I need you.'

The images those three words conjured. His erection quivered and strained against his fly, forcing him to shift position. The sultry glide of her flesh against his as she panted those words into his mouth. His lips sliding lower, driving her desperation higher as her panting turned to whimpers...

Scowling into shrubbery, he avoided the hopeful, vulnerable look that had crept into her eyes, which reminded him his imagination was leading him down the path to self-destruction. He let out a long, slow breath. He could be here for four weeks. Twenty-eight long days. Twenty-eight endless, frustrating nights.

'Think about it, Jack,' she said at last, rising abruptly. 'We'll talk later.'

He remained as he was—hard, frowning—watching the sway of her jeans-clad hips as she walked away. Her gold hair showered over creamy bare shoulders. For a moment he was tempted to follow, just to breathe in its scent again.

He twined his fingers around a slim branch and inhaled the fragrance of the grey leaves instead. Then he rammed a fist against the tree trunk. *Don't be an idiot.* How many men had fallen victim to those blue eyes and pouty mouth in his absence? His own father had left her his entire inheritance—didn't that tell him anything?

But his heart wasn't paying attention to his head. The one girl he'd made off limits was the only girl who'd ever slipped beneath that barrier he'd erected around it.

Damned if he wasn't going to get some answers.

CHAPTER FIVE

JACK followed Cleo at a discreet distance. She headed to the shed at the back of the garage—her workshop, he remembered. He watched her take a key from her pocket, unlock the door and disappear inside. Was she going to fire up her soldering iron or celebrate her inheritance in private?

The images invading his brain tore him to shreds. His father and Cleo. He was so preoccupied with the fist clenched round his gut he didn't knock, but walked right in.

The smell of metal and dust met his nostrils. He gazed at the mess. It was like being back in a war zone. Scrap iron and old pipes were stacked against a wall. Bicycle wheels littered the floor at one end, along with half a dozen metal sculptures—works-in-progress, he assumed, because they didn't look like anything he'd ever seen before. A trio of bronze-forged lilies speared out from a metal cylinder.

A goggled Cleo perched on a stool, head bent over a piece of wire, a snipper of some sort in her hand.

She'd pulled on a pair of grey overalls over her clothes. They swamped her small stature and made her look vulnerable. *We'll just see.* He dragged an overturned crate over the concrete floor, positioning it so he could get a good clear look at her expression, and sat down.

'I'm behind in my orders,' she said, without looking up. She reached for a small mallet and began pounding the metal.

He studied her face. 'Some people might wonder why Gerry Devlin left his house and entire life savings to you over his son.'

The rhythmic thuds continued, but her expression barely changed. 'Perhaps they'll think it's because Jack Devlin didn't care enough to come home when it mattered. But no one's going to wonder, because no one's going to know. We're going to sort it out before they do.'

He watched her clever fingers manipulating the wire as the end took on a flattened oval shape. How clever would they be manipulating his flesh? Or his father's? he thought, clenching his teeth. 'You're not blood kin,' he continued. 'You're a young and available woman. People talk.'

He saw her fingers tighten on the mallet, watched her jaw drop, her throat bob as she swallowed. And waited for her next response. One second, two. Three.

With slow, deliberate movements she set the tool down, slid the goggles to the top of her head, and raised her eyes to his. Their blue fire arced across the space between them. No guilt, no guile. Just simple, honest-to-goodness fury.

Right response.

'What *exactly* do you mean by that?' She spoke each word as if she'd snipped it off with her tin shears. Twin spots of colour bloomed on her cheeks, a stark contrast to the pallor of the rest of her stricken face.

Now he saw the pain warring with the anger in her gaze. He had his answer. Relief pumped through him, but he kept his cool, on the outside at least. And made his decision. 'Exactly what it sounds like,' he replied smoothly. 'Another reason for me to stick around. Quell any speculation.'

'That's obscene.' She glared at him for a full five seconds until he had to glance away. 'The people who knew Gerry and who know me would *know* that's obscene, and they're the only people who matter. Everyone else can go jump.' Her fingers clenched the hammer again. 'That includes you. Money's one thing, but what you're sugges...' Her free hand paused halfway to her goggles. '*Another* reason to stick around?'

'I'm staying till everything's finalised.'

A heavy beat of silence. The only acknowledgement was a curt nod. Snapping her goggles in place, she picked up the wire and attacked it with a vengeance.

Jack couldn't move. He'd hurt her, insulted her, compounded her grief. He slid damp palms over his jeans, curled his guilty conscience into fists against his thighs and swallowed the apology he owed her. If he moved so much as an inch closer, if he let slip one iota of his emotions right now, he'd be lost. He'd have that stiff-as-a-post, overall-covered body against his so quick she'd never know what happened.

'I don't need an assistant,' she said, tossing the mallet down and snatching another. 'And if you don't leave in a matter of seconds, I won't be responsible for what I do with this hammer.'

Without looking at her again, he pushed up and made his way into the fresher air outside. His throat was parched, his chest too tight, his skin damp and prickly. He leaned against the shed wall and took a steadying breath before starting slowly back to the house.

Cleo needed her hammer and hot sticky workshop to sweat out her emotions. In his current medical condition how was he going to sweat out his own?

In the family room he stretched out on the familiar brown leather couch, now covered with a buff throw-over and buttercup cushions. When they were younger, he and Cleo had spent time together in this room, watching videos, playing computer games, listening to music.

He punched a cushion, stuck it behind his head. Responsibility wasn't something he'd had to think about for a long time. He wasn't sure how it fitted on his shoulders. But when it came right down to it, the solution was a perfectly simple three-point plan.

Stay for the next few weeks.

Help Scott tie up his father's affairs.

And walk away.

Oh, yeah, simple. As a distraction, he reached for the TV remote on the coffee-table in front of him and channel-surfed till he found the cricket. Australia versus the West Indies.

The next thing Jack was aware of was the phone ringing. By the time he'd got his brain working and his backside off the couch, Cleo had answered it. He glanced at his watch. Two hours had passed.

He almost groaned. Great. She'd have seen him zonked out in front of the TV, a flaw she'd never failed to point out. He crossed the carpet square and rifled through the neatly shelved books for something to read, but found nothing he could put his mind to. Not that he could put his mind to any damn thing.

A sliver of sun slanting through the window reflected on a gilded hand-decorated box tucked against the wall beside a stash of old vinyl LPs.

Curious, he pulled it out and set it on the coffee-table. Couldn't be personal or it wouldn't be here, he decided, and lifted the varnished découpage lid. In side he found a photo album. Gold lettering spelled 'Twenty-First' across the front. His heart missed a beat and the old yearning kicked in.

He'd hated missing Cleo's entry into adulthood, even though she'd looked entirely adult enough on her sixteenth. On a spur-of-the-moment thing, he'd sent her an anonymous bouquet of roses for her special day; the only contact he'd ever made. Some comfort that now he could see how she'd celebrated it through another photographer's lens.

'You're awake. Oh…'

He looked up to see Cleo's startled eyes glued to the box. At least she seemed to have worked off her mad. 'If it's personal…'

She shook her head. 'I brought it down the night

after Gerry died. It's been in my room since I put it to-gether.' She lifted a shoulder. 'No one's ever seen it.'

'Not even Dad? Why not?'

She folded her hands together at her waist, and he could see the white-knuckled grasp as she twisted them together. Her face was pale, devoid of make-up as she raised her eyes to his. 'I wanted you to be the first.'

Her choice of words sent heat spiralling through his lower body. He clenched his jaw at the disturbing image of her spread beneath him, slender limbs gleaming in the moonlight, silver hair tangled in his fist, her breath warm against his neck.

Of course his mind was playing tricks. Reading something into her words that wasn't there.

Or was it?

Was there something deeper in that clear gaze? They'd always been close, until she'd grown overnight into the leggy teenager he'd barely recognised. Suddenly he hadn't understood her, hadn't understood himself. The brotherly affection had morphed into something much more dangerous. He'd spent more time with his mates and girls his own age and made a heroic effort to treat her like a kid sister, or, worse, as if he were some sort of father-figure.

She seemed to pull herself together and straight-ened. 'It's not my twenty-first album, Jack. It's yours.'

His. The breath stalled in his lungs. She'd kept a part of him close all these years. In the sudden stillness that enveloped them he swore he heard his heart beating in time with hers.

He shifted, shaking off the too intimate feeling.

'Why would you do that?' he demanded. 'I'd've thought you'd've burned it by now.'

'Don't think I haven't considered it. I naïvely thought you'd come home.'

All this time he'd imagined her relief that he was finally out of her life. He'd made her existence hell: an older brother's duty. And she'd returned the favour in spades. In fact she'd dug the hole and buried him.

Had he misunderstood her hostility towards him? But he remembered the devastation on her face when he'd kissed her that night. Her mouth swollen and trembling, her eyes filled with shocked horror.

'I'm not so naïve now,' she said. She crossed the room to sit beside him. The heat of her thigh burned through his jeans as she leaned closer to lift out the album.

The first page was a full-sized photo of the three of them. Dad, and a starry-eyed young Cleo gazing up at a younger Jack Devlin. A tumult of emotions washed through him. How many times had he wished he could go back to that point in his life and start over?

'He was like you,' Cleo said, looking at his father's face. 'Quick to butt heads.'

'Yeah.' But Jack wasn't thinking about his father. As she turned the pages he found her time after time, looking too much like a woman for her sixteen years, her heavily made-up eyes sparkling, smile radiant.

Smiling at *him*.

How had he missed that? Because he'd been too busy keeping his own libido in check to pay attention. Something else had been going on beneath that don't-

give-a-damn attitude. She'd seen something worthwhile in Jack Devlin.

He'd kissed that goodbye when he'd walked away.
For her own good. She might be all grown up now, but
a relationship was still impossible—for different
reasons. *Family and commitment.* Her words echoed in
his head.

He wasn't ready for either. For those reasons alone,
no way would he start something with Cleo he didn't
intend to finish. Nor was he sure he didn't carry his
father's violent genes. How many fights had he got into
protecting Cleo? He'd prefer burning in hell to hurting
her.

He squeezed the hand lying on the album. 'It's a fine
record, Goldilocks. Thank you.'

'I didn't do it for you,' she replied, her voice cool.
She pulled her hand away. 'I did it for me.'

Beneath the album at the bottom of the box he saw
a newspaper clipping, birthday cards, and the single
yellow rose he'd given her on the night, carefully
pressed.

'Photos were all I had left of you,' she said. The
anger he might have expected, and would have preferred, dissipated beneath a kind of resigned accep-
tance as she replaced the album in its box and set it on
the table.

'Cleo, there were reasons…' None of which he wanted
to share, he realised as soon as the words were out.

Folding her legs beneath her, she slid one elbow
along the back of the couch and faced him. 'I'm listening.'

He hesitated. How to answer? She wasn't ready for the truth so soon after the old man's death. He wanted to stand up, shift away, put some space between them because at that moment he didn't trust himself not to take what his father had accused him of taking that night.

Also preferable to the alternative of looking into those expectant eyes while he concocted a half-truth that might or might not satisfy her. He made a vow then and there that she'd never hear the whole truth from his lips.

'After the party, Dad "requested my presence" in the study to discuss…you.' It had been close on dawn, he remembered.

'Oh…' He saw the flush rise up her neck to stain her cheeks. 'He was pretty mad, I know, but he's never once mentioned that…moment on the stairs…'

Jack knew it had looked bad for him. 'I told him it wasn't what it looked like.' Close enough, though. He'd wanted her so bad he'd ached. *…be out of my sight or I won't be responsible for my actions…* The memory of that defiance, that girl-woman who'd rocked his existence, still haunted him.

'Dad was sloshed and angry with it. We argued. He told me if he saw me again it'd be too soon.'

Right before his iron fist had landed Jack on the floor. *Come on, Jack, boy, fight back like a man.* Closed windows and drapes, low voice. No one ever heard Gerry Devlin raise his voice in anger. Jack had been too busy trying to breathe. By the time he'd managed to half crawl, half stagger to the phone and call Scotty for help, his father had been sleeping it off in his room.

Cleo hesitated as if trying to reconcile what Jack

said with the Gerry she knew. Then a brittle laugh shot from her mouth, shattering the sudden stillness. 'Don't give me that. You and I both know it was the booze talking. You could've waited or come back when he'd slept it off—when you'd both slept it off and cooled down. Why didn't you?'

'Trust and respect, Cleo. Dad gave me neither.' Then he lied when he said, 'I packed and caught the first available flight to Sydney.'

'You know something, Jack?' She leaned towards him, her subtle fragrance filling his nose. Her eyes flashed, an electric-blue charge that seemed to sizzle through the air and along his bones. 'There's more to this than you're telling me.'

He'd been right about not wanting to look at her. She was far too perceptive. He had to look away. 'So now you're a psychologist.'

'No, I'm a woman.'

No argument there. He had a sudden insane urge to give in to his temptation. To absorb all that female energy shimmering from her, to taste it on his mouth, to feel it beneath his palms. Instead he smiled with intended cynicism. 'A man doesn't stand a chance against such powerful logic.'

The air cracked as she slapped an open palm on the couch between them. 'There you go, making fun of me, still treating me like I'm only sixteen.'

'You were never *only* sixteen.' And that had been the crux of the problem.

'How would you know? You barely gave me the time of day except to snap and snarl.'

'Doesn't mean I didn't notice you.'

'You *notice* a toothache. What's more, you do something about it.'

'I did do something about it—I removed myself from the source.' And suffered the pain of loss as keenly as a death. 'It wasn't about you,' he said. 'It was about me.' But he saw the same suffering in her eyes.

Without thought he reached out. He could handle her anger, but not her pain. 'I never meant to hurt you.'

Cleo stared at him, her eyes stinging. The gentle pressure of his fingers, warm, rough-textured as they touched hers, did nothing to ease the ache that gnawed at her heart. Nor did the dark, impenetrable eyes, the musky scent of masculine skin. How could an intelligent, female-savvy man be so dense? 'You really don't get it, do you?'

Or was he playing dumb, refusing to acknowledge what a blind man would recognise when she looked at him? Ignoring her because, let's face it, she was no glamour puss. It was too mortifying to contemplate. And if she didn't do something—anything—she'd dissolve in a puddle of frustration or self-pity. She'd sworn she wouldn't let him make a difference this time—with her head. Her heart wouldn't cooperate.

She forced herself to straighten, pushed up off the couch and away from that male warmth and moved to the door.

'What do you want from me?' she heard him growl behind her.

Gathering what little emotional strength she had left, she turned back. Afternoon sun spilled through the window over his shoulders, a burning aura against the dimness of his face. In his black T-shirt he was the dark fantasy of her dreams.

But unlike in her dreams, he didn't smile and hold out his hand. He looked hard and remote, his lips pencil-thin, the groove cutting between his knitted brows deep and shadowed.

'Nothing. Not a thing.' *Nothing you're not prepared to give willingly.* And, desperate not to give any outward sign of her turmoil, she turned away again before he could answer and fled upstairs to his father's old room.

Closing the door to the room she'd become so familiar with over the past couple of years, she leaned back against it. She could still feel the heat of Jack's hand on hers, could still feel that potent gaze on the back of her neck.

A hint of Gerry's Old Spice cologne, which he'd used till the day he died, clung to the fixtures. For a moment time ran backwards and he was there again, on the silk-covered sofa, his gaunt face turned to the window, eyes fixed on the world beyond. Just as she'd watched through her own window as seasons and birthdays had come and gone.

Waiting for Jack.

Pain sliced through her. Tears clogged her throat. Two people whose stubbornness had cost them one of life's most precious moments—that last chance to say goodbye. Jack had to be wrong. Gerry hadn't meant what he'd said about not wanting his only son to come home.

Though the air was balmy, she rubbed suddenly cold arms. She needed work. Hard, physical work would ease some of the frustration that had built up inside her till she felt ready to explode.

Gerry's bathroom. Not that it needed cleaning—she'd scoured the whole house in the last few days—but working with water always smoothed the rough edges of her mood.

An hour and half a bottle of shower scrub later, she peeled off her latex gloves. She smelled of rubber, probably sweat too, as she pushed a damp tendril of hair from her face. The rest was shoved haphazardly into an old scrunchie she'd found in the vanity. Her eyes caught her reflection in the mirrored wall. And didn't she look like something the cat had dragged in? Thank God she was alone.

As she re-entered the bedroom, the absolute stillness, the emptiness, struck her like a physical blow. To compensate, she switched the CD player on low and let the Beatles sing about 'Yesterday'. Then she walked to the window and pushed it up.

A snappy breeze fanned her overheated face and neck. As she lowered herself to the sofa her fingers closed over the lambswool throw-over and she drew its softness to her cheek. 'You're free now. Free from the pain.'

She hadn't cried at his bedside when Gerry Devlin had breathed his last breath though the grief had cut to the bone. Nor at the funeral; he'd wanted a celebration. But now those tears sprang to her eyes and she let them come. They spilled down her face, cooled by the breeze.

Her hiccoughing breath caught at the sound of the door knob turning. She swiped at her damp cheeks. She could picture Jack standing just inside the doorway, one arm propping up the door-frame, those knobbly toes curling into the carpet, dark eyes watching her.

Watching her lose it.

She tightened her grip on the wool and closed her eyes. Ashamed, embarrassed. Frustrated. 'Go away, Jack.' When he didn't answer, she waved a hand behind her. 'Can't you see I'm having a private moment here?'

He switched off the CD, once again filling the room with silence. 'I've been looking all over for you.'

The air stirred, but he wasn't leaving. Now, when she wished him a thousand miles away… Wasn't it like Jack to be contrary? Her attempt to draw breath came out like a snuffle.

She jumped like a rabbit at the touch of his hands on her shoulders. Awareness sharpened as those hands tightened in a brief squeeze. His heat, his scent, the sound of his breathing washed over her. She felt the sofa dip as he sat down behind her.

'I should've been here for you, Goldilocks.'

'Well, you weren't, so get over it. I have.' *And you're such a lousy liar, 'Goldilocks'.*

'You think things will go on for ever the way they are,' he said. 'That people in your life will always be there, then bam! You wake up one day and everything's changed and it's too late to say all those things you wanted to say, share those thoughts, relive the good times.'

She buried the naïve but romantic thought that he'd

wake up one day and realise all those things could belong to them. And where would she be then? In a nursing home, most likely.

His hands slid from her shoulders, down her arms, and locked in front of her so that she was enveloped in the hard warmth of his body. She gazed down at the sinewy forearms with their sprinkle of cinnamon hair over her own and wondered if she was dreaming.

Her head fell back against the soothing pad of his shoulder as if it had been made for that express purpose. For now she needed his simple offer of comfort. 'I never had a father I want to remember,' she said. His fingers tightened again, and she snuggled deeper into the circle of his arms. 'Not the kind who makes time for you, who loves you for nothing more than for who you are. Your father gave me that.'

'I know.'

She felt the subtle change in his posture. So the reason Jack had dubbed her Goldilocks and said it in that derogatory way of his was a kind of payback.

'We both know he drank too much. The woman he loved was gone, his son...' What could she say? Gerry had seemed indifferent to Jack in the early days, which had developed into open dislike over the years. 'You were rude, always out with your mates. Or some girl or other.'

'You weren't much better.'

She knew he was referring to the rough crowd she'd hung around with—to get his attention. Any attention had been better than none. 'I was pretty obnoxious, I admit it.'

'We were a pair, you and I. Your own father didn't give a second thought as to how his actions affected his daughter. And I lost the mother I loved to him.'

Bitterness flavoured his words and she twisted around in his arms to look up at him. And saw an echo of her own bitterness in those eyes for what their parents had done.

'Jack.' In an automatic response she reached out to his face, wanting to give a little back, to show she understood, that she shared the memories, and the pain.

At the first touch her heart leaped. She absorbed the wonder of the warmth of his skin, the soft stubble beneath her fingers. But his eyes reflected the same shadowed mystery that told her he might have allowed this moment of togetherness but he hadn't lowered his guard.

'I lost a parent too.' Wanting to soothe, she traced her fingertips lightly down his cheek to the line of his jaw. She felt it tighten as he sucked in a harsh breath. Something dangerous flashed in his eyes.

The sweet fledgling elation that had swept her up took a dive. He didn't want her. The stinging heat of rejection rushed to her cheeks. The old, familiar brush-off. Jack didn't like being touched. Leastways not by her. Not home-grown Cleo Honeywell, almost-sister. Six years hadn't changed that.

Blinking back tears still lurking behind her eyes, she curled her hand and fisted it against her breasts. 'I swear, Jack, you wouldn't know if your arse was on fire.'

'Cleo—'

'Don't say it.' She punched the space between them. 'I don't want to hear it.' She could have socked him one for the humiliation alone, but right now that jaw looked as ungiving as granite.

'The back door was open…'

The familiar voice had them both turning towards the door. Cleo wasn't sure who sprang up and apart first. 'Scott.' She forced stiff lips into something resembling a smile. 'Hi.'

Scott stood in the doorway, his business shirt unbuttoned at the neck, tie loose. 'Hi.' Jingling his keys, he glanced from Jack to Cleo, back to Jack. 'If this isn't a good time…'

'It's the perfect time,' Cleo said. Hugging her arms. Achy and embarrassed. How much had Scott heard? She was careful not to look at Jack, but she could feel the tidal waves of tension emanating from him.

'Hey, Scotty.' Jack's voice, all husky and deep and not quite steady.

'So…you two got plans for the evening?'

'No,' Cleo shot back. Not with that sensual scene fresh in her mind. She could still feel Jack's skin against her fingers, his scent filled her nose. His rejection was a raw, throbbing wound that needed attention. Alone. 'I'm going to have a bath and pamper myself. No males allowed.'

'Actually, it was Jack I was after,' Scott said. 'You won't mind if I steal him for a few hours?'

Cleo stifled an almost-laugh. She wasn't invited in any case. 'Go ahead, steal away.'

From the corner of her eye she saw Jack hunch his

shoulders, stick his hands in the back pockets of his jeans and heard him say, 'What did you have in mind?'

'Thought it was time you lost the struggling-photographer look and bought yourself some new clothes. It's late-night shopping in the city. We can take a taxi, grab a meal and a few beers after. Like old times.'

Jack nodded. 'Sounds like a plan. I'll get my wallet.'

As soon as Jack left the room Scott said, 'I interrupted something.'

'You interrupted *nothing*. Have a good time.' *Not.* Avoiding his penetrating eyes, she moved to the door.

He touched her shoulder as she slipped past. 'Don't wait up,' he said softly.

'I don't intend to.' She hadn't fooled him—not best buddy Scott, now Jack's best buddy Scott. She'd been passed over for a guy—how much more depressing did it get?

In her book, depressed equated with a long hot bath, a glass of wine, and a mountain of chocolates. And she had plenty of time to wallow in both the mood and the water.

In Cleo's own bathroom, ferns spilled from hanging pots, towels of peach complemented a wall papered with forest green leaves. It was too early to light candles with the sky still bright with twilight. Said who? In defiance of her own rules, she lit five then steeped the water with a blend of rosemary, lavender and geranium essence. She stripped and sank into the fragrant warmth with her fluted glass and bowl of chocolate truffles.

She'd told Jack she'd forgotten him when he'd left. But she'd kept Pandora's little box of hope tucked away deep in her heart. Believed he'd come home one day and tell her he'd missed her and how she'd grown up and what a big mistake he'd made.

Well, he'd come back, hadn't he? But the rest... She'd almost succeeded in telling herself she didn't care, but seeing him again had undone all that hard work.

It was she who'd made the mistake.

She tossed the glass of bubbly down her throat. And now she was tied to this house by love for his father and a duty to abide by his last wishes.

When the water cooled and the chocolates were gone, she dried off and reached for her pink shortie pyjamas. The soft airy cotton was comforting as she slipped it over her skin.

She padded to her bedroom window and pushed it higher. Outside, the humid, cloud-heavy evening had darkened to indigo. She watched the city lights blinking in the distance, breathed in the scent of damp foliage and frangipani, then switched off the light and climbed into bed.

It was only nine-thirty and she knew she'd not sleep. Not with her traitorous imagination straying to that long, hard body that would be warming the sheets a few feet away when he came home. What would it be like, warming her instead? Her body tingled with the imagined heat, a low throbbing began to pulse in her lower abdomen. She shoved the cover down with an angry sigh. A *frustrated*, angry sigh.

If he came home. With two unattached, attractive men out on the town, she had to face the possibility he might not come home till morning.

CHAPTER SIX

'I WALKED in on something back there.' Scott settled back in the cab, a genuine concern etching his brow and an obvious readiness to listen.

Jack turned to the view beyond the window. He didn't want to discuss it. 'Family politics—a difference in perceptions,' he muttered. Storm clouds were smudging the crimson glow over the city skyline. Inside, the cab's air-conditioning cooled his face if not his body. Somehow Cleo had slipped under his guard.

He'd intended leaving her alone, *should* have left her alone. But he'd had to go find her, hadn't he? After all, he'd laid some heavy-duty information on her this afternoon. But those few moments on Dad's sofa hadn't been about his father so much as comfort. It had nearly cost him his hard-earned self-control. Jeez, if Scott hadn't turned up…

He shifted, suddenly uncomfortable as a surge of re-membered heat swamped him.

'I take it you mean your father?' Scott asked quietly.

Jack nodded. 'He meant a lot to her. I can't just hit

her with the truth. I don't think she could deal with it. Nor should she have to,' he finished harshly.

Scott squinted into the sun setting below the band of clouds and the silhouettes of Melbourne's approaching skyscrapers then turned to him. 'What are your plans for...after?'

'You mean after probate's granted? I've unfinished business overseas.' Nothing had changed. His job as a photographer was still open; he could resume it if he chose. Or he could return to the town he'd been helping rebuild before he'd been shot.

'Unfinished business,' Scott repeated, breaking into his thoughts. 'Anyone special we should know about?'

Anyone special. Cleo's scent still clouded his mind, the imprint of her hands were still fresh on his face. Needing a distraction, Jack inched the window down a fraction. Air laden with exhaust fumes and hot bitumen rushed past his ears. He laughed without humour. 'You know me—too many to count.'

'I do know you, Jack, perhaps better than you know yourself. If you get close and personal with Cleo then skip out on her, she's going to hurt.'

'I haven't laid a finger on her.' Yet. 'That's why I want this over. She doesn't need me screwing up her life.' He shrugged at Scott's intense scrutiny. 'I'm surprised she's not already attached. She must have men in her life. You, for instance.' And as much as it pained him, if Cleo and Scott had something going, at least Jack could rest almost easy knowing she'd be okay.

'Me?' Scott shook his head. 'She doesn't look at me

that way.' He cocked a brow. 'But she looks at you. She's always looked at you.'

A strange but powerful sensation steam-rolled through Jack, leaving him feeling bruised and breathless. He'd seen it today, in the photos, on the sofa—a woman's eyes, a woman's desire. But no matter how much he yearned to fill the empty space inside that he'd always held for her—only her—he must discourage any feelings she had for him. He covered his regret with a dismissive gesture. 'I'm never in one place long enough, Scotty, you know that. Cleo wants a home and family. She deserves it. But after what I went through as a kid, family life's not for me.'

'Give it time, Jack.'

He smothered the sigh that came from his heart. 'I won't be here long enough.'

Jack was still brooding about that two hours later as he drew wet circles on the buffed wood-grained table with his moisture-slick glass of beer. His fourth, or was it his fifth? He shrugged, took another gulp. Its yeasty taste slid down his throat. Who the hell cared? If he wanted to get plastered, that was his business.

Laser lights swirled, bass thumped. The music was hot, the entertainment hotter. His eyes might be directed at the dance floor but his mind was fixed on the distressed woman he'd left in the hallway.

He shouldn't be staying in that big old house alone with Cleo. Yet he had no choice with his father's mess to tidy up.

She'd *looked* at him. And he'd felt the intensity all the way to his soul. Even half-crazed with jealousy and liquor, it hadn't been disgust he thought he'd seen in her eyes that night six years ago—she'd wanted him. And he'd hurt her. Even then she'd not given up on him.

She should have.

It would only lead to heartbreak. He wasn't ready to settle down, and if he ever was it wouldn't be in that house, with those memories.

'Scotty, go get us a couple of shots of Jack Daniels each, would you?'

While Scott fought his way to the overcrowded bar, Jack scowled some more while the action played on around him.

'Admiring the talent?' Scott said, setting the drinks in front of Jack.

He poured a shot of the potent liquid down his throat.

Scott laid a hand on Jack's shoulder. 'You're going to hate yourself in the morning.'

'Might as well make it worthwhile.'

'Time to go, pal.'

He pushed out of his chair, slung an arm round his mate's neck. 'Let's go home.'

Scott steered him towards the exit. 'We'll swing by my office on the way and pick up your shopping. Perhaps you'll have sobered up some by the time we get there.'

Jack wasn't sure how many drinks he'd consumed but it annoyed the heck out of him that Scott was still ostensibly sober when they arrived home. He'd always been able to drink Scotty under the table. A side-effect of surgery? He patted his dressing; at least the booze had dulled the ache in his shoulder, if nowhere else.

The house loomed ahead in the sweep of headlights. What the hell time was it? Apart from the security light that winked on as the taxi approached, the house was in darkness.

He hauled himself out, and, swaying a little, stared up at the second storey windows. One in particular. The warm evening breeze stirred the leaves and caressed his face. The way Cleo had caressed his cheek this afternoon.

She must be in bed. He imagined that compact little body warming the sheets, hair spread like a golden fan, and fantasised a moment about what she'd be wearing. Silk, lace, cotton? Or nothing at all.

His whole body went tight as a bow string. Did she sprawl, those slender, creamy arms and legs tangling with the linen, or did she like to curl up? He wished he didn't want to know.

He dug in his pocket for his keys as he made his winding way up the path. No stars tonight. Thunder rumbled in the distance. The air was thick and still.

'Jack, wait up.'

He turned, noticed his legs wobble, and squinted at Scott striding towards him with an armload of shopping bags. 'Thanks.' He took the bags, and, full of good cheer, gave him a hug. 'You're an okay guy.' Then he gazed up at her window again. 'Beam me up, Scotty.'

Scott's eyes followed. 'Not a good idea, my intoxicated friend.'

'I guess you're right.'

'I know I'm right. Can you make it upstairs yourself? The traditional way?'

'Sure. Just like old times, eh?'

'You got it.'

'Later.' Jack raised a hand in farewell as he leaned against the verandah's stone pillar and watched Scott climb into the cab and disappear down the drive and into the night. Yep, just like old times.

Except… This afternoon everything had changed. Jack sucked in a lungful of the heat-drenched evening to clear the alcohol-induced haze. The one thing that hadn't changed was how he felt about Cleo. Always that gut-churning, heart-grabbing reaction, an ache so familiar it had become a part of him. He fumbled the key in the lock.

And seeing her again…the instinctive urge to reach out and touch that petal-soft skin, to drag her against him and bury his nose in all that fragrant hair, hadn't faded.

It had just grown stronger.

He heard a rustle in the bushes as he opened the door. 'Evening, Cont…Constantine,' he managed around a rubber tongue. 'An evening out with the ladies?'

Con prowled over and wound his way once around Jack's legs before shooting inside. Jack thumbed on the hall light to see his way upstairs and followed the huge furry shape. Con stopped at Cleo's room, flicked his tail, obviously irritated to find the door shut.

'You and me both,' Jack muttered. She must have

taken a shower—he could smell the fresh scent on the air mixed with the familiar smells of polish and wood.

The light in the stairwell threw long shadows down the hall. He was inebriated enough to consider opening her door and finding out if his fantasy about her preferred sleeping position was true, but—sadly—not inebriated enough to carry through. So he stood a moment breathing in her fragrance while Con sat watching the door, his mismatched eyes expectant.

'If I can't, you can't,' he told Con. No way was he going to open that door, even for a cat. Especially not for a cat. Royally ticked off, Con rose and stalked on down the hall, tail bristling.

'Okay, time for bed.' The floorboard creaked beneath him. Leaning against the wall, he toed off his shoes. 'Sh. Mustn't wake Cle…'

The almost inaudible click of the door froze him in place. The door opened and a cloud of tousled hair glinted in the light, then an elegant bare shoulder.

Holding his breath, he watched from behind while thousands of forbidden thoughts played through his mind, all of which involved that bare flesh. Starting with sliding his hand under that skinny strap and easing it down…

'Bastard,' he heard her mutter quietly. Then she turned his way.

She wore a tiny pair of pale panties that flared at the hem, exposing the tops of her smooth, creamy legs, and a matching top that stretched over her breasts like opaque cling-wrap. In the soft yellow light the colour blended with her skin, making her appear naked. God help him.

Her hand flew to her throat. 'Jack! What are you doing here?' She didn't look pleased to see him.

He thought he felt a grin spread over his face. Or a grimace. 'Loitering?' When she simply gaped at him, he straightened—or tried to. 'Chain me to your bed. Make me confess, I—'

'Shut up, Jack,' she said, between clenched teeth. 'If you have to bring your playmates here, at least have the decency to keep it discreet.'

He frowned. 'Say what?'

'The woman you brought home with you.' She glanced up and down the hallway. 'The one you were talking to.'

'The one I...uh...Con. I was talking to Con.' Perhaps that was why his tongue felt thick and furry.

On cue, the fluffy feline padded out of Jack's room towards them.

'Oh.' She flushed and lowered her head. 'There you are, you naughty boy,' she said as Con disappeared into her room. She raised her eyes to Jack's. 'I apologise... I shouldn't have jumped all over you like that...'

All over you. 'Like honey over hot fudge.'

'What?'

Had he lost control of that thick, furry tongue too? 'Nothing. No need to apologise, s'okay.' He took a step, tripped on his own damn shoes that he'd forgotten he'd removed. Uh-oh. Fighting inevitability, he stumbled forward, trapping her against the wall.

Her breasts collided with his chest. Her eyes flew to his, wide and almost green in the light. He could see the pretty pulse beating fast against her throat, matching his.

His hands had connected with her shoulders. He wanted to slide them down her arms, to feel that warm, silky skin and the firm muscles beneath, to watch her eyes widen with awareness while he did, but opted for the wall on either side of her head.

He should step away now, go to his room, but it was as if he were encased in stone. He sucked in air, immersing himself in the fragrance. 'You smell like a garden.'

'Can't say the same for you; you smell like a brewery.' Her breath whispered over his skin. His gaze dropped to her full, sensuous lips, slightly parted. She remained as she was as if waiting.

Thunder rolled across the sky. Through the open window in her room a layer of humidity swamped them, making her skin dewy and slick.

She moved oh-so-subtly, so that he felt her nipples rise like two little beads against his shirt. And felt the hot, liquid slide towards total meltdown. Sweat broke out on his brow; his arms were beginning to tremble. Her mouth was a whisper away. He was hard and hot and only human.

That first contact was like laying his lips on a live wire. The sensation sizzled along nerve endings and spun through his head. He tangled his hands in her hair as he'd always imagined doing, let the silky strands caress his fingers, and shifted nearer.

In response, she moved her hips lightly against him, a soft noise coming from her throat, like a purr. He felt her mouth soften and give and took instant advantage, plunging deep, dancing his tongue over hers.

He'd known how she'd taste without the bitterness of anger. Exquisite. Sweet, dark and rich, like the imported cherry liqueur his father kept for special occasions.

Coming home.

This was what he'd wanted all these years. What he'd never found with any other woman. This connection, this rightness.

Then he couldn't think, didn't want to analyse. His thumbs moved to her face, exploring the satin softness of the skin beneath her jaw, her neck, the little hollow above her collar-bone where her pulse jittered.

He felt her arms slide around his waist, the heat of her hands burning a trail up his spine as she stroked him. She shifted, arching towards him.

Wanting more, he slid his own hands lower, over soft cotton and feminine curves. His thumbs whisked over taut nipples beneath the cling of fabric. With something close to reverence he filled his palms with the firm but luscious weight of her breasts.

Her quick intake of breath, the moan from her throat, brought him up and out of the grip of his sensual haze. What in hell was he doing? Clutching for some shred of sanity, he jerked himself away. His lungs burned, his lips were on fire. And his rock-hard erection throbbed like a wound.

She blinked at the sudden movement, those thick gold lashes sweeping her cheeks, then stared up at him, eyes glazed. Something dark and passionate simmered in their depths, and something more: shock.

And no wonder. The scene was like an old movie

rerun. Except that this time he'd not stopped at a kiss; he'd groped her like a randy teenager. His drink-hazed mind rejected the knowledge that she'd done her own groping.

Cleo. The kid who'd smeared jam on his bike when she'd been too young to ride with him, the one whose knee he'd tended when she'd sneaked out to road test that same bike.

The girl who'd always been there, in his life, in his thoughts. The girl he'd never been able to touch.

And he still couldn't touch her because he'd made a promise to himself.

Because they were shaking, he lowered his hands, forced them into fists at his sides. Took a step away. Futile to hope she hadn't felt his arousal.

She wouldn't know it went so much deeper than sex—after all, he'd done it before with much the same result. Pain clawed viciously around his heart. 'I'm sorry.'

Pathetic. He wasn't sorry. Already he wanted to do it again.

Her eyes widened and the limpid pools hardened to glacial ice. The mouth that he'd all but devoured thinned. Then one hand shot up and he felt the sharp sting of her palm against his cheek.

The slap echoed like a gunshot in the muggy still-ness. Then she hugged her shoulders as she backed towards her bedroom doorway. Her eyes glittered with unshed tears; her lips still glistening from their kiss, trembled.

'Cleo…'

She flapped a hand and he had to stop himself from reaching for her. 'Just so you know,' she said, her voice husky, breaking. 'That's for the apology.'

Before he could get his head around her words the door slammed shut, rattling the trio of watercolours on the wall.

He stood watching it a moment, rubbing the hot, stinging spot on his cheek. The *apology*?

He'd changed their relationship yet again. One thing hadn't changed: his feelings towards her. But now, whenever he looked at those lips, he'd remember how they'd felt in the bloom of passion.

And want it again.

Scott was right. Jack Devlin was going to hate himself in the morning.

Cleo sagged against her door. She barely registered the flash of lightning through the window. Barely noticed the first big drops of rain plopping on the leaves outside.

Her whole body felt as if it were on a knife's edge. Weak, helpless, burning… She lifted trembling fingers to her mouth and a whimper escaped. Oh, she burned all right, from the tingling in her still kiss-sensitive lips to the wave of liquid heat low in her belly, to the soles of her bare feet.

He'd wanted her. He'd wanted her as a man wanted a woman. She'd seen it in his eyes, smouldering and ready to ignite. She'd felt it in his unsteady breathing, the way he'd tensed his muscles as he'd leaned into her.

And most telling of all: he'd been big and hard and

all male. She might not be too familiar with male arousal, but she'd known exactly what she'd felt nudging her belly. She shivered at the thought of that impatient masculine part of him sliding inside her.

And the memory of his hot, restless hands cupping her—her breasts felt full and heavy beneath her pyjama top. Her nipples, still tight and erect, prickled.

Her jaw tightened. The impact of what he'd done seeped through the heat haze and her anger resurfaced. He'd *apologised*. He'd denied what they had, denied both of them.

He'd lifted that lid on her Pandora's box, shown her the delights inside, then slammed it shut. And apologised.

How dare he? The jerk. Was he sorry because he was drunk or because he'd kissed her?

She hadn't waited to find out. She'd had control over that small action at least. But the rest… Her breath whooshed out. Unable to think beyond the moment, she'd been all but molten metal in his hands, letting him mould her to his will with his clever fingers, his mouth, his body…

She needed to lie down.

Her legs felt weak as she crossed to the bed. The inside of her thighs felt chafed, sensitised from the rough weave of Jack's trousers.

Con swatted an impatient paw when she pushed at him, and stalked to the foot of the bed—typical male, wanting it all his way.

Punching the pillow, she flopped backwards and lay in the murky evening-scented stillness, gazed at the ceiling. 'I've got news for you, Jack. Tomorrow you pay.'

CHAPTER SEVEN

CLEO was awake with the dawn's first streaks of crimson and gold. The night's storm had blown away, leaving the clear blue sky of another hot day. Thanks to Jack she'd tossed all night, but she rolled out of bed with a plan.

She hadn't discussed the mutual project idea she'd come up with yesterday but the sundial and memorial garden she'd intended creating was something they could work on together.

Dragging on her gardening shorts and jersey top, she rooted in her closet for her old sneakers. Something to focus on might ease the awkwardness she knew she'd feel when she saw him again.

All Jack's fault. And what did she have to feel awkward about? She paused in her task of tying her laces. But, ooh, could the man kiss when he put his mind—and lips—to the task. No wonder he had females lined up. He could make a woman feel as if she were the only one in the world. A dangerous skill, she decided, glaring up the hallway at his closed door before descending the stairs to the kitchen.

She fed Con, then grabbed a peach. As she bit into the fruit she tried not to imagine the same body that had plastered her against the wall last night sprawled on the bed upstairs. Reckless thoughts like that could sway her from her intention to make him pay this morning. She hoped he felt like hell when he woke. Apology *not* accepted.

She grabbed a mug and herbal tea bag, slammed both on the counter and poured boiling water over, nearly splashing herself in the process. Would he agree to her idea?

She shrugged it away. What was not to agree? He had nothing but time on his hands. Might as well put those hands to good use. Her nipples sprang to attention when she remembered the use he'd put those hands to last night.

Clenching her teeth against the traitorous tingle, she twisted her hair into a knot, shoved it under an old baseball cap and let herself out into the fresh morning air.

She was *not* going to think about it. He probably wouldn't turn a hair when he saw her again.

She needed to maintain an it-happens-all-the-time façade. So she would not let him see how embarrassingly inexperienced she was. She'd managed to carry it off at sixteen; she could do it now. He didn't need to know that, apart from one not-so-memorable night months after Jack had gone, she'd not let any guy past first base.

She headed for the gardening shed, anxious to get a head start before the day grew hot. The door opened with a scrape of wood on stone, and a musty, earthy smell met her nose. Selecting tools, she dumped them in the wheelbarrow.

The spot she'd chosen for the garden was in the centre of the front lawn. Using stakes and twine, she marked out a circle, then dug a groove with the tip of the spade.

She leaned on her spade and swiped at her brow. She'd made the sundial and gnomon using scrap metal and an old piece of iron lace she'd salvaged at a demolition site. She would ask Jack to help select the flowers, and, if his shoulder was up to it, he could plant them. That way, they both had a hand in creating a lasting memory.

But his injury had her thinking again. What had he been involved in to get himself shot? She'd have to pry it from him the way she tackled her metalwork— slowly and sensitively.

But slow and sensitive wasn't the way she intended waking him this morning. She checked her watch as she headed for the house, mentally rubbing her hands at the prospect of rousting him out of bed and seeing him suffer the effects of his overindulgence. Or his underperformance?

Squeezing her eyes shut, she mentally counted to ten. In Chinese. She was thinking about it again. The thing she wasn't going to think about. The lip-smacking, hip-grinding thing. If they were going to complete this project, she was going to have to stay cool—a problem if Jack was going to look at her the way he'd looked at her last night. That hot, hungry way.

Last night had not been the act of a man in control. A man recovering from God knew what—he hadn't let her in on his past. A past he was going back to. Didn't that tell her anything? He didn't want to be a part of her life.

So it suited the mood she'd talked herself into to rap once then push the door open. She stood a moment, letting her eyes adjust to the semi-darkness, trying not to inhale the not-so-subtle smell of stale booze and male sweat.

Jack was flopped on his stomach, one sinewy arm hanging over the bed. The sheet was scrunched at the bottom of the bed. A surge of heated excitement raced through her body, and pooled between her legs. She was right—Jack Devlin slept in nothing but a tan.

The acre of bare bronzed back and the long dimpled spine had her palms itching to touch. But she was powerless to resist following the tight curve of his slightly spread muscular buttocks with its shadowed cleft, to the darker hint of male anatomy between two firm thighs... The moist heat between her legs intensified and her pulse rate soared. The fact that she was viewing something forbidden only added to the mix. Her common decency seemed to have deserted her.

She licked her lips. The urge to trail her tongue over all that taut, hot skin overwhelmed her. And how was she going to keep that emotional distance? She'd never be able to look at him again and not remember.

Finally, reluctantly, she dragged her gaze to his pillow. His mouth was full and gorgeous and relaxed in sleep. She remembered only too well how it had felt against hers, how persuasive that mouth could be.

Scowling, she huffed out a breath, stuck her itchy hands in the back pockets of her shorts and said, 'I knocked.' The dark lashes didn't so much as flicker. 'Wake up, sleeping beauty, time's wasting.'

She moved to the curtains. They slid apart with a swift whoosh. Air that had been trapped behind the drapes wafted fresh and cool through the window and over her skin. Sunlight flooded the room.

'God,' a voice rasped from the bed.

She took some satisfaction at seeing him wince. 'No, just Cleo, I'm afraid, with your not-so-early wake-up call.'

'I didn't order any wake-up call,' he mumbled.

'Rise and shine, we've got work to do.'

He started to roll over, then stopped. 'Hey, I'm naked here.'

'Well, you're conscious, at least. Downstairs, ten minutes, if you want breakfast.'

She flicked the switch on the radio and racked up the volume on a heavy-metal station on her way out. If he swore, she didn't hear.

When he made his appearance twenty minutes later, it didn't look as if he'd be big on conversation this morning. His face was drawn and slightly green, accentuating his stubble, but he'd taken a shower, leaving his hair damp and smelling fresh and spicy. He was wearing long shorts and a ratty T-shirt he must have unearthed from his six-year-old supplies. He walked carefully, as if measuring his steps.

'No breakfast,' he said in a downright pitiful voice as he filled a mug with water at the sink.

'Oh?' When he scowled at her, she pointed to the fridge. 'Tomato juice is good for hangovers.'

'Don't need it,' he growled, zapping the mug in the microwave, then dunking a teabag in.

'Glad to hear it, because we've got work to do.' She pushed up. 'Bring your tea and come with me.'

Moments later they stood on the lawn where Cleo had marked out the circle.

Jack was silent a moment, his expression blank. 'A garden? Or are you planning a pond?' *And what do you need my approval for?* his expression said.

She could almost feel his head pounding as he shaded his eyes from the morning glare. 'A memorial garden with a sundial,' she explained. 'Our mutual project.'

His dark brows lowered, his mouth turned down. Yesterday she might have laid a hand on his shoulder, but this morning was an entirely different matter. Instead, she stuck her hands on her hips. 'You have a better idea?'

'You have to know how to make a sundial,' he said with an arrogant wave of his mug. 'You need to find north, know the latitude, you can't just—'

'Done already.' Annoyed that he assumed she hadn't done her research, she crossed her arms over her breasts. 'All you have to do is help with the garden.'

'Hmmph.' He squinted as he surveyed the circle.

'I know your shoulder's still healing. I can dig—'

'I'm not an invalid.' He rotated his shoulder. The muscles bulged like coiled rope in his forearm as he flexed his hand.

'Good.' He was standing too close. Scowling. Looking dangerously dishevelled, smelling of soap and man. 'I'll get the hose and soften the ground.'

She swung away, intent on putting some distance between them, but he grabbed her arm with one firm hand, tossing his mug on the grass with the other.

'Not so fast.' Strong fingers closed around her wrist. Useless to try to pull away. 'We need to clear the air first.'

She looked up into dark, whiskey-coloured eyes. 'Clear the air?' The air she could feel pulsing thick and charged between them?

'I shouldn't have kissed you like that.'

'Like what?' *Like a man kisses a woman?*

'In that condition. I wasn't at my best when I got home last night.'

'That's too bad.' She couldn't help the inward sigh. How would his best feel? Not that she was going to find out. *Remember the Rule.* Playing it light, she patted his T-shirt, concentrated on its wash-worn softness and tried not to think about the hard chest beneath. Then she grinned and said, 'I wasn't at my best either.'

Something dangerous speared into his eyes. She could almost feel the heat. Her stomach muscles curled. She tried to step away, but his hold was like a steel band. 'Play grown-up games the way you did six years ago and live with the consequences.'

A flush crept up her neck at the memory. 'I'm old enough to play grown-ups now, Jack. And have been for some time.' She meant *old enough*, but by Jack's glowering expression he was stuck on the *playing grown-ups* bit.

His jaw clenched, and his grip on her wrist tightened. 'You want to be real careful about airing your conquests to me, Cleo.' Beneath the holier-than-thou attitude she remembered so well, his eyes smouldered with that same hot spark she'd witnessed last night.

In daylight with the sun catching the red-gold strands in his dark hair, with the sound of birds and breeze, it was no less potent. But she saw something darker flicker in their depths now.

Lord in heaven…could he be jealous? She almost laughed aloud. Jealous of her non-existent love life. But her pulse picked up as the flicker in his eyes intensified to an all out blaze, and a fine tremor shivered through her limbs. 'Women don't make *conquests*,' she retorted, maintaining her calm. 'We're far too evolved.'

'The way you went about it at my twenty-first you could've fooled me.'

Because his rejection had forced her to do something she'd never done before: come on to a guy. 'I've seen you in action too, remember.' Memories she wanted to forget. Snapshots of nudes and Jack, a hidden photo in her drawer she wished she'd never seen.

'That was a long time ago. It's a new day and I'm sober.' He was rubbing a callused thumb lightly over the pulse in her wrist now and watching her with such tenderness, she wanted to sigh.

Suddenly his lips were a whisper away from hers, his breath warm and smelling of tea. Her mouth dried up; her knees went weak. He pulled her closer, dropped her now-limp hand to slide his thumb across her lower

lip, leaving tingles of sensation. A hot shiver rippled
down her spine. Nearby, a lawnmower droned and the
smell of fresh-cut grass lay on the morning air.

'Jack...' She let out a shaky breath as his mouth
skimmed a lazy path along her jaw. Coherent thought
spiralled away on the breeze. Her eyes drifted closed
at the stunning sensation of his lips on her skin. The
warmth dancing on her eyelids faded as Jack's head
blocked the sun. Anticipation quivered through her.

His lips moved to her neck, he released her arm,
leaving both his hands free to caress up and down her
spine. The world tilted on its axis and then... No more
Jack. She heard a sharp sigh as he stepped back. She
let her own sigh out slowly. Raggedly.

'Hell,' he swore softly and turned away.

Her fingers fumbled as she straightened the cap on
her head. 'You kissed me last night, Jack. You might
have been under the influence, but you wanted me.'

He paced away, dragged a hand over his head, then
swung to her. 'Cleo...' There was something horribly,
ominously final in that one word. He started back,
stopping when he was an arm's length away. She saw
his Adam's apple move as he swallowed.

Yes, he wanted her. But he didn't love her. Not the
way she wanted him to love her. Could she settle for that?

She'd waited a long time for him to open his eyes
and look her way. Tears gathered at the back of her
throat. She tugged the bill of her cap down further so
that it shaded her eyes. She didn't want to see him,
didn't want him seeing her humiliation.

He moved closer, placed impersonal hands on her

shoulders. 'I don't want to start something I can't finish. You mean too much to me, Goldilocks. I'm not a permanent kind of guy; I only came back to finalise Dad's affairs.'

She knew that, she'd always known it.

You mean too much to me.

Desperate not to let him see how much it hurt, she shrugged beneath his hands but they stayed firm and uncompromising, the way his six-foot height towered over her. 'That's right, Jack. Don't let a little lust over a home-town girl get in the way of life's priorities.'

His eyes darkened. 'Don't cheapen what we have, or who you are.'

'What *do* we have?'

Hesitation. A muscle tightened in his jaw. 'I don't know.'

She shoved at his hands and this time he let them fall to his sides. Anger exploded out of her. 'You haven't been paying attention, Jack.'

'Oh, I've been paying attention. You've made it plain that you disapprove of my choices and the way I live my life. I have to think about this…for both of us. That kiss last night—'

'What kiss?' she hurled back. 'And I do my own thinking.' This time it was she who stepped away. 'When I decide what's right—for *me*—I'll let you know.'

'Another day with no one but Jocular Jack for company and I'd've gone crazy.' Cleo faced Jeanne across the café's red-and-white-checked table cloth and stirred her coffee. 'Thank God for you, Jeanne. Our Sunday-morning brunches are a life-saver.'

Jeanne smiled. 'Is Jack giving you a hard time?'

'Try *any* time.'

Jeanne's smile faded. 'Oh.'

'He's been back over a week and I still don't know the real Jack Devlin.'

'Does anyone ever know the real anyone?' Jeanne bit into her apple Danish. 'It's bound to take some adjusting. He's been gone a while.'

'I guess.' Frowning, Cleo lifted her cup to her lips. They'd stuck to their agreement and worked on the sundial thing. They'd dug dirt together, positioned the dial, planted petunias. Talked in monosyllabic sentences.

So much for getting reacquainted.

'I take it your feelings haven't changed,' Jeanne said.

When Cleo could only shake her head, Jeanne reached over and patted her hand. 'Go ahead, let it all out. You're talking to Auntie Jeannie here.'

'It's embarrassing. Humiliating, even.'

'Why, for God's sake?'

'Well…' She swallowed, unsure how or even whether to go on. 'I look at the two of you. You're great together.'

'Of course. He's a friend, but—'

'He hugged you. Kissed you.' *And practically stuck his tongue down your throat.*

Jeanne nodded. 'A natural enough way to greet a friend you haven't seen in six years.'

'He didn't hug *me* like that.' She couldn't help it; her lip curled. 'All spontaneous and smiley.'

'Oh, Cleo, don't be mad at him. Jack and I have always been close.'

'That's just it—you two are so natural and easy with each other.'

'Yes. We're comfortable together. But there are no sparks,' Jeanne said gently. 'We're like brother and sister. Whereas you two... You strike so many sparks off each other, it gives me the hots. You were a kid when he saw you last. Even then I saw the way he looked at you, but he was way too nice a guy to take advantage of your youth and innocence.'

'So what, now I'm old and experienced?' Cleo shook her head. 'And he still hasn't taken advantage of me.' She was older of course, but experienced...hardly. Not when her love life had been on hold since Jack had left.

'He's still getting to know the grown-up version,' Jeanne said, skimming a spoonful of froth off her cappuccino.

Cleo propped her chin on her hands. The memory of just how well he'd been 'getting to know' her passed in front of her eyes. 'He kissed me the other night. Drunk as a skunk, but he kissed me.' And she could still feel the press of that hard male body against hers.

Jeanne leaned forward, spoon poised halfway to her mouth, her expression bright and interested. 'Well...?'

'Then he apologised.'

Jeanne made a sound that was part sympathy, part amusement. 'Poor Jack.'

'Poor *Jack*?'

Jeanne-the-traitor smiled. 'What happened then?'

'Nothing. Oh, I slapped him.' At Jeanne's incredulous expression, Cleo waved her hand. 'For the apology. We talked around it a bit the next day. We argued. No more kissing, no more talking. Said he wants to think about it for both of us. Like I've got no say in the matter.' Anger prickled her skin just remembering it. 'Can you beat that?'

'I can't, but you can.'

'Me?'

'Yes, you.' Jeanne fixed Cleo with a straight look. 'Nothing's stopping you taking the initiative, is it?'

Cleo frowned, considering the notion. 'I guess not.'

But could Cleo Honeywell the homebody really measure up to Jack's ideal of a desirable woman? Did she want to know? Could she live with the answer? Only one way to find out.

Jeanne's nail tapping on the table cut into her thoughts. 'If you want him, do something about it. Leave him in no doubt about what *you* want. Then leave the rest to him.'

Cleo had never turned down a dare. She stood at the base of the trellis attached to the wall outside Jack's bedroom, chewing on her lower lip and toying with the zip on her black figure-hugging jumpsuit. Her new black lace bra and panties from Bedroom Secrets itched something fierce.

Lucky for her no one had ever asked for the impossible or even slightly dangerous.

Until now.

Now she was asking for it for herself. For Jack. For what they could have together if only he'd let it happen.

She knew she was risking a broken heart... A quick glance up had her amending that to maybe a broken neck? She figured it was worth it.

The moon was on her side for once, spilling light through the frangipani branches, clearly outlining her own personal stairway to heaven. She plucked a frangipani blossom and tucked it in her hair. Checked her watch by moonlight. Jack's room had been in darkness for fifteen minutes.

She wanted to give him time to be relaxed and receptive to her. Over the past few days she'd watched that self-contained, remote Jack take over. It was up to her to bring out the Jack she'd only glimpsed in the past two weeks.

The fun-and-games Jack who'd scaled this very trellis on that first morning, that sensitive guy who'd comforted and talked with her in Gerry's room after the fiasco with the will.

The drunk, dishevelled and definitely dangerous man who'd pushed her up against a wall and put his mouth on hers. The memory sent an instant shard of heat searing a path to her lower abdomen.

Since Jack obviously wasn't going to, she would take that next step towards intimacy herself. An intimacy that went so much deeper than the sexual act. A bond, she knew, that could never be broken, no matter where in the world he went, no matter how hard he tried to deny it.

Nerves pinched her skin and fluttered in her tummy as she contemplated the climb. 'Okay, Jack,' she murmured, placing a bare foot on the first rung and gripping it with her toes. 'Ready or not, here I come.'

CHAPTER EIGHT

CLEO SWUNG UP onto the first rung. Her pulse raced, a nervous excitement jittered up and down her spine. She climbed steadily upward, concentrating on not looking down. She'd seen Jack do it with an injured shoulder, how hard could it be?

But her palms were damp, her heart seemed to have lodged in her throat. Branches tapped lightly at the ground-floor window. Somewhere she could hear party music, the thump of bass on the air in time with blood pounding in her head. Just a few more feet…

Uh-oh. Wrong window. Of the two windows in his room, contrary Jack had left the wrong one open… *Don't look down.*

She looked down.

Her head spun nastily. No way could she go back the way she'd come. The white-knuckled fingers of one hand clung to the trellis while she pried one hand off to tap at the pane. 'Jack.' Her voice came out barely above a whisper. She was afraid if she raised it, somehow she'd be flung from the wall and land in a heap below. A *broken* heap. She gritted her teeth and tried again. 'Jack.' Louder. Her whole body was taut as wire, aching with the tension of holding on.

A face appeared. Thank God. She almost wept with relief. 'What the hell?' it shouted.

So much for a dramatic entrance. 'It's me, Jack. Open up.'

The window shot up with a sharp riff and Jack leaned out, peering at her over the window ledge. 'God, are you crazy?'

Not just a face. A body. A very *naked* body from what she could see. 'Just help me in, Jack.' Calm voice. Calm, in control voice. Not-so-calm pulse.

Two strong arms reached out, lifting her bodily through the opening as if she weighed no more than the shadows surrounding her.

'Thanks.' Her valiant attempt to appear nonchalant failed miserably as her legs turned to jelly. She clutched those, strong safe arms while her chest ached and her lungs burned from holding her breath.

'What in hell do you think you're doing?' he demanded in a dangerously low voice.

The bright slash of moonlight carved an equally dangerous expression on his face; his arms, shoulders, chest could have been painted with it. His eyes glittered, smoke and silver in the dimness.

'I wanted to see you…' *Wrong choice of words. Wrong, wrong, wrong.*

Her gaze kind of slid downwards. And stuck. An instinctive feminine awe speared through her body. Her blood turned to quicksilver in her veins. It looked…*he* was…magnificent. And growing more magnificent even as she watched.

'Congratulations,' he said tautly, his voice thick. 'I think we could say you've achieved that.'

He tilted her chin with a thumb and finger till she had no choice but to look into those dangerous eyes and not at the action taking place below.

'Listen, and listen good, Cleo. Don't you *ever* try anything like that again.' He tightened his grip on her chin. 'Understood?'

'No, not understood.' She batted his hand away. 'You give yourself permission to take risks and I'm not supposed to? And don't give me any of that chauvinistic crap because I'll refuse to discuss it.'

His lips firmed into a blade-thin line. 'Okay. Have it your way. For now.'

'I…' Her voice hitched, then trailed off as her breath rushed in and out. The traumatic ascent and the sight of all that masculinity had made her light-headed, and her whole body trembled.

'Come on, sit down before you fall down.' Sweeping her off her feet, he deposited her on the side of the bed, managing to drag the sheet around his hips at the same time.

His hand wasn't steady as he switched on the bedside lamp at its lowest setting, surrounding them in halo of soft amber light. He drew a deep heartfelt breath and let it out slowly, watching her in a way that had her stomach twisting into knots again.

'If you wanted to see me you could've tried the traditional method and used the door,' he said at last.

'It was a dare; I didn't have a choice.'

'Who the—'

'I challenged myself. I figured you'd take more notice this way.'

He shook his head and she saw the tension in his features relax a little as a corner of his mouth quirked. 'So is it Cat Woman, or Tropical Island Barbie?' he asked, touching the flower she'd forgotten.

'*Barbie?*'

'Your hair's just like that Barbie doll you had as a kid—of course that's only the visuals,' he hurried to explain. 'Comes from working behind the camera.' He leaned forward and sniffed, rubbing the tips between his fingers. 'But the feel and scent's your own.'

'Gee, thanks.'

He cocked his head. 'You're like a young Goldie Hawn; all sleepy eyes and hair.'

'I'm not sleepy now.'

She should have done something different with her hair. Barbie or Goldie was *not* the look she'd tried for, and both were decades older than her. She'd hoped to look like one of his models—sleek and sophisticated. Like Liana what's-her-name. Impossible given Cleo's generous breasts and lack of height.

But a week ago he *had* looked at her; he had kissed her.

He had wanted her.

And she'd wanted him. It had been sheer torture to step back before he did. A win for her.

Now all she had to do was keep that upper hand.

Keep it light. She touched the zip tab lying between her breasts. Imagined Jack's hand closing over hers…

He'd lower the zip an inch at a time and find the black lace bra. His long fingers would slide over the top of her breasts, then lazily back and forth before dipping beneath the lace. Taking it slow, driving her wild with wanting.

But she'd wait, because she wanted it to last. He'd find her nipple and she'd sigh as he rolled it gently between his fingers, pushing the lace aside to lower those hot, full lips and… Yes!

No. She bit back a moan of frustration. As if he'd read her thoughts, he leaned away, putting his weight on one hand on the bed behind him. Backing off.

'So…' he began. 'You wanted to see me about…?'

'Us, Jack.' Ignoring the inner voice whispering that he wasn't exactly falling into her plan, she forged on. 'I've been thinking, *for myself*, and I've decided what's right for me.'

She was going to seduce Jack. Oh, God, had she really been thinking that? Her stomach turned a double somersault. The Jack who'd be all too familiar with seduction, who'd had a string of beautiful women, who lived his life on his terms, as he chose.

The Jack who looked a little nonplussed right now as her presence in his room, her little speech—and the implication—penetrated.

His free hand crept up to rub at his neck. 'I think—'

'Don't.' She reached for the medallion, felt a rush of heat as her fingers brushed soft, masculine hair.

Metal winked in the light and was warm from his skin. 'Don't think, don't say anything. Listen. Why do you still wear this misshapen, unevenly forged scrap of metal?'

He opened his mouth to speak, but she tugged at the chain, bringing him closer. His breath whispered over her face. 'I said listen.'

Eyes darker than midnight locked on hers as she placed the medallion over his heart. 'Wherever you've been, I've been with you. Every woman you've slept with, I've been there, between you. Yet you still wear it, next to your heart. What does that tell you, Jack?' She could feel its fast thud beating beneath her hand.

'Cleo…'

'I'm not done yet. I want you to think back to that last night.' Those whirligigs in her stomach were spinning like windmills now, but it was a powerful feeling, having Jack at a disadvantage.

She leaned nearer. He leaned away. She could smell his soap, his skin, could see the muscles in his rock-hard abdomen straining as he struggled to remain upright. One gentle nudge and she'd have him right where she wanted him; on his back.

She laid her palm on that corrugated-iron belly and felt his muscles tighten as he sucked in air through his teeth. His eyes flashed a warning. She paid no heed as her hand crept higher, lightly over the ridge of newly healing scar tissue, then moving on to explore chest hair and one flat male nipple.

A sigh barely escaped his lips as she circled the soft areola with her fingernail. 'Are you still thinking about that night?' she reminded him. 'I was waiting for you. Did you ever wonder who stowed the rug and champagne in your car, Jack? Who organised the "Slow Dance Favourites" CD when it was my turn to dance with you?'

'I guess I know now,' he said, fingers closing around hers so she could no longer touch him. His thumb chafed her palm, the sensation exquisite torture. 'You decided Sam was a better option.' There was more than anger and accusation in his tone.

'I used Sam. Shamelessly. Stupidly. I realise that now. I wanted you to notice me.'

'Oh, I noticed all right.'

She threaded the fingers of one hand through his soft hair and pressed a kiss to the corner of his mouth. 'I was trying to make you jealous. Did you even figure that out?'

'I had no right to be jealous.' The hand holding hers tightened on the last word.

'*Were* you jealous, Jack?'

'You were sixteen, Cleo, for God's sake!'

'You haven't answered my question.'

He released her hand to swipe at his neck. 'You were sixteen; that *is* the answer.'

'Dear Jack.' She splayed a hand against his chest. 'Stubborn as ever.'

And with that promised nudge he slid bonelessly back onto the mattress. In one quick smooth motion, Cleo flicked the sheet aside. And went weak all over. Her hand fell away. Her mouth dried, her pulse picked up as excitement stabbed through her.

He was all fully aroused, heart-stopping male. From the powerful jut of his thick sex, the broad chest, to the tight, stubbled jaw.

He projected an image of laziness, but she felt the lethal undertones, like a lion ready to spring into action. And…in this position, he was also vulnerable.

With fingers that shook annoyingly, she kept her eyes on his while she lowered her zip to her navel. Her lace-covered breasts spilled out. For all the good it did; his eyes didn't leave hers—unreadable—but the muscles in his jaw were clenched, the tendons in his neck stood out and his breath was forced and harsh.

Slowly she lowered her upper torso to his, and, letting instinct guide her, moved against him. She rubbed her belly against his hip and watched the way his mouth moved. Silently, as if he was swearing. Or praying.

She caught his face between her hands, saw his eyes widen, darken. With a dizzying rush she felt an awesome female power she'd never experienced swell within her.

'I'm not sixteen now,' she breathed. And pressed her lips to his. They were warm and full and luscious and she was going to have him on toast for breakfast. The only barrier was her faux-leather suit, but as she moved against that hard wedge of masculine flesh she felt it buck. His hands fisted in the sheet.

He made no attempt to reciprocate, but neither did he push her away. Encouraged, she slid her tongue along the seam of his tight mouth and sampled his taste.

Jack didn't budge. Didn't dare. He'd left his retreat too late. Any movement would cause friction between their bodies and set off a chain reaction he didn't want to think about. His rock-hard erection strained and chafed as that slippery catsuit tormented and teased. Every muscle in his body, every square centimetre of skin, every cell, burned.

She changed the angle of the kiss and rubbed up against him like an eel, her warm, slippery length sliding over his thigh, the soft pillow of her breasts a sinuous, torturous caress against his chest.

His angel in temptation's clothing.

Her mouth was sweet sin, the kind that made a mere mortal man want to sin some more. A lot more. He clung to the hope that he had at least a shred of integrity left in his heat-ravaged body.

But the taste of her tongue as it explored the shape of his mouth was dark and rich and seductive. He felt the slow slide towards surrender as he drew it into his mouth to tangle with his in a slow, deep dance that had him straining for another kind of slow and deep.

Her hand left his face to trace a scorching path down the front of his body; over nipples, ribs, abdomen… His sex jerked at the first touch of her hand, then she slid her thumb over the moist tip and he teetered on the edge of madness.

With the strangled sound of a drowning man, he tore his lips from hers. 'Cleo,' he whispered.

Her hair fell in a silky curtain of moonshine as she lifted her head and leaned over him. 'Yes,' she whispered. 'It's me.'

With the practised art of a seductress, she brought those wet fingers to her mouth while she watched him. She licked them slowly with the tip of her tongue, one at a time, leaving them glistening. 'You taste good, Jack.'

His mouth fell open; rational thought deserted him. Then, God help him, she enclosed him again in that sleek wetness. 'Stop!' A second longer and he'd embarrass himself into her hand. He lurched up.

She stopped. 'Did I hurt you?'

'No. Yes, no. *Hell!*'

'I'm not doing it right. I don't…I'm not…' Her glazed, passion-filled eyes stared into his.

Innocent eyes. He grabbed her wrist, held it as far away as his trembling arm allowed. Had she lied that last night in his room?

They remained in that gridlock for several long, tension-filled seconds, their eyes fused. His body was ready to explode, his breath ragged and he knew his hand grasping hers was shaking.

'All that self-control's not healthy, Jack.'

'But necessary.' He cleared the sandpaper rasp from his throat. 'A dare's one thing; this…*this* is…'

'What I want; what you want,' she finished for him.

Fighting a battle he was rapidly losing, he shook his head. As soon as probate was granted and he was satisfied all was well, he was gone. He could give her that, if nothing else.

'Goldilocks…' He loosened his death grip on her wrist to soothe the satin-smooth flesh. Her face was flushed with anticipation, her lips rosy from the kiss.

The kiss that shouldn't have happened. Wouldn't have happened if he'd acted sooner. 'What I want has nothing to do with what's right and fair,' he said.

The passion in her eyes turned dark, her arm tensed beneath his hand. 'To hell with that.' She looked pointedly at his throbbing erection, which only made him ache more, then back to his face. 'You don't want me to go.'

'We are *not* doing this.' The denial came out harsh and forced. The air simmered between them, a brooding stew of hot emotions and unfinished business.

Then she dropped her gaze to her own lap, her shoulders drooped and he felt her pain right down to his toes. 'So...' she said. 'I came on to you—totally not your fault—but when it comes right down to it, I'm not good enough.'

She was so wrong. And that was the killer, testing his resolve down to the wire.

'Cleo, Goldilocks...that's not true, you were...' *Back off now.*

Her Cat Woman suit made a shooshing noise as she slid to the edge of the bed. Unshed tears shimmered in her eyes, tiny diamonds on her lashes, but blue fire burned in their depths. 'No need to explain. I know home-town girls aren't to your taste.'

His fingers itched to wipe the damp away. Face it, his fingers itched for entirely more basic reasons. His self-disgust was complete. Here he was imagining how it would feel to touch her, really touch her, when she was hurting and humiliated. She was better off not knowing how he felt, how he ached.

She patted his hand, making him feel like a total bastard. 'I'll leave. I've always been real good at making a fool of myself in front of you. I should be used to it by now.' She rose, hands fisted at her sides. 'Think of me when you're lying here alone tonight. For that matter, you can spend the rest of your life being right and fair. And *alone*.'

She shook her head when she reached the door. 'But I guess you won't be alone for long, will you, Jack?'

And while his brain tried to catch up with the rest of his body, she slipped away.

Jack dragged the last box from his father's wardrobe and sat on the floor to sort through it. It had been a huge job over the past two weeks, sorting clothes for the Goodwill box, hours on the phone and in Scott's office going over paperwork so all would be in order for Cleo.

He'd taken long jogs around the neighbourhood and spent hours at the local gym where he'd punished his body till there had been no room for thought.

His shoulder had healed well enough to join the basketball match last week, but Cleo had begged off, pleading a migraine.

When they had shared a meal—the only thing they seemed to share these days—they had talked like strangers. Polite, distant. The subject of their relationship remained off limits for both of them, something he'd have to deal with before he left. He couldn't, *wouldn't* leave without addressing Cleo's loss of self-esteem.

He missed her sunny, outgoing personality, her

forthright nature. Who else could put him in his place the way Cleo did? He missed her smile at the breakfast table. She was in her workshop before six o'clock most mornings and often managed to be elsewhere when he was around.

Could he blame her? Blowing a harsh breath, he lifted the lid. Sixties *Rolling Stone* magazines and paraphernalia. He put them aside for the recycling bin and looked deeper.

Photos. Black and whites. His father had preferred to work with the drama of shade and light, whereas Jack liked the vividness and immediacy of colour. Jack had learned photography by osmosis—one of the few positives he'd inherited from his father.

He sifted through some nudes, all of the same woman—a well-endowed brunette. Dad's? Then he frowned. The last one was of Jack in a tux taken at his eighteenth with the brunette snuggled up against him. Naked. What the…? Disbelief plunged through him. Dad's handiwork, he realised. His father had enjoyed experimenting in the dark room. He'd merged two shots. Why?

Then he recalled the conversation. What had Cleo said? *You'd know all about photographing naked women… I've seen the evidence.* He clenched his fist around the photo and threw the crumpled paper at the wall. Bastard. Another one of his father's attempts to make Jack look bad in Cleo's eyes.

Disgust filled him. Was there no end to this man's hidden talents? This man who was his father.

Not for the first time another equally abhorrent

thought slid through his mind. He carried his father's genes. Jack never used his camera to lie, but the violence…

Agitated, he got up and prowled to the window. Hadn't Jack pounded anyone who had tried to put the moves on a young Cleo? Like the bastard who'd told Scott what he wanted to do with her. The satisfaction of bone crunching bone. The hot smell of blood. Did that make him a violent man?

Too right. He clenched his fist against the window pane till his nails bit flesh. Didn't matter that the other guy had thrown the first punch. An unenlightened Cleo had been appalled at Jack's behaviour when word had got out, whereas Dad hadn't batted an eyelid. Like father, like son.

Yet another reason to stay the hell away from Cleo.

No one had been good enough for her because *he'd wanted her for himself*.

The reason he'd left.

The reason he'd leave again.

Because he wasn't good enough either: *family and commitment*.

He hadn't needed to try very hard to keep his distance today. She'd breezed out this morning and he hadn't seen her since. He checked his watch—four p.m.

And wondered where she was now.

'We need a girls' night,' Jeanne said as she and Cleo strolled the mall licking ice-cream cones. Jeanne closed up shop at one p.m. on a Saturday, and they usually spent the afternoon together.

Cleo had reported her failed mission with Jack, and Jeanne obviously felt she should try to lift Cleo's spirits. 'Good idea,' Cleo said, feeling duty-bound to agree, even though she'd prefer to hole up in bed with a book or a mind-numbing bottle of red.

'Girls' night, as in *in* or *out*?' Jeanne asked before wrapping her tongue around her chocolate pecan ice-cream.

'Out. Definitely out.' Cleo took a chunk out of her raspberry-flavoured one. 'It's been three weeks since... Since Jack and Scott did the town. It has to be our turn.'

'You want cool and classy or hot and sweaty? As in nightclub hot and sweaty,' Jeanne added with a grin.

Images of Jack in the garden minus the shirt, his skin slick and gold in the sun while they turned soil for the sundial, snuck up to mess with Cleo's hormones. And as for the Cat Woman scene— *Don't go there. Don't go remotely near there.* Hormones were off limits. Jack was off limits. She'd humiliated herself enough.

'Cool and classy,' she said. 'I don't think I can cope with hot and sweaty of any kind right now.'

She stopped in front of one of the mall's fashion boutiques, attracted by a low-cut watermelon-pink top and matching handkerchief skirt. That didn't mean she couldn't dress hot.

She caught her reflection in the boutique window and frowned. Boring, boring, boring. The top she wore must be four seasons old. And she lived in jeans or overalls. How long since she'd splashed out on something feminine? Something that would knock Jack's eyeballs to the back of his head.

She lifted a shoulder. Not that she cared what he thought. *Liar.* More like she wanted Jack to see what he was missing out on. 'I wonder if they have that outfit in my size,' she said, and, handing her ice-cream to Jeanne, she went inside to ask.

Back at Jeanne's apartment, Jeanne twitched at Cleo's gauzy layers of skirt, then stepped back with a smile. 'Stunning with a capital S. You sure you don't want to go somewhere more crowded to show it off? Seems a waste to spend the evening eating seafood at Ritzy's with plain old Jeanne when you could have a nightclub full of men at your feet.'

Cleo did a slow turn in front of Jeanne's mirror, checking out the back view. 'I don't want men at my feet.'

'Okay, it doesn't have to be your feet.'

'Ha ha.'

But Cleo did feel a little like Cinderella going to the ball. The top fit like a glove, showing a flattering cleavage, hinting at more. Sparkles spilled down the single spaghetti strap and swirled over the bodice. Matching strappy pink stilettos completed the look, and underneath she'd purchased a strapless bra, and, in a daring move, a hot-pink thong. The chiffon skirt, with its six points of sheer fabric reaching just below the knee, gave the outfit a whimsical feel.

A warm glow of pleasure spread through her body. Not bad. Not bad at all.

Until she looked at her face.

Some of that pleasure dulled. She wasn't Cinderella,

she was still Cleo Honeywell. Worse, she was still
Goldilocks. 'I need a fairy godmother with her magic
scissors.' She turned to Jeanne. 'Will you cut my hair?'

'Sure, a quick trim would—'

'I mean *really* cut it—short as in…s-h-o-r-t.' She held
up her thumb and forefinger an inch apart. She didn't tell
Jeanne about the picture of Liana what's-her-name
draped over Jack's arm with short, spiked, *sophisticated*
hair.

The Goldilocks/Barbie image had to go.

'God.' Jeanne straightened, her expression one of
astonishment. 'I'd kill for your hair and you want to cut
it off? Have you thought about this? What'll Jack say?
He's crazy about your hair.'

Barbie doll hair. Cleo turned away quickly and
caught her own mutinous reflection. 'I'm not doing it
for Jack.'

'Right,' Jeanne said. 'Bugger Jack, the man's an
idiot. A woman should do what pleases her. Still, it's
rather drastic.'

'I'm feeling drastic.' A new and exciting anticipation slid through her. She stripped off her new clothes.

Jeanne tossed her an old shirt. 'Okay, let's do it.'

A couple of hours later Cleo stood in front of her own
mirror studying the transformation with a mix of horror
and exhilaration.

She'd covered her hair in a sun hat and sneaked in,
but she needn't have bothered. Jack was napping in
front of the TV tennis while Sweden and the U.S.
battled it out for the Australian Open.

Oh. My. God. She raised a hand to her hair. What there was of it. Jeanne had put highlights and something called styling mud through it and it stood up in soft little tufts all over her head.

She looked at the whole picture. The lack of hair seemed to augment her eyes; they looked brighter and lighter, and her diamanté studs actually showed.

She laughed out loud. It was totally *out there* along with body piercings and tattoos. And which of those would come first? Probably neither, since both involved pain, but it was satisfying to know she could. If she chose.

Today she'd made a decision solely for herself. It felt good, and liberating. She was definitely going to do it more often. She held the pink outfit aloft on its hanger and laughed again. Starting tonight.

Two hours later, fresh from a long scented bath and a careful make-up session, she watched Jack from the edge of the family room. He'd stretched out on the floor in baggy shorts and a T-shirt with the sleeves ripped out. One hand curled around a can of beer. His head was propped on a cushion and he was watching the TV news between the V of his long, sexy feet. His hair was mussed.

As she watched his free hand pushed the T-shirt higher, over hair-sprinkled, taut gold skin and scratched lazily back and forth.

Heat flashed through her blood. The thought of those long fingers cruising slick and slow over her own belly seared through her brain. She took a deep breath to calm herself. Another before she said, 'Jack, I won't be home this evening. There are a couple of frozen dinners you can microwave if you want.'

'Hmm...okay.' He didn't tear his eyes from the sports news.

'Don't wait up.'

He glanced her way, then seemed to turn to stone. His beer-can hand paused halfway to his lips.

Give him time to look, but not to ask questions.

She felt the slow slide of his gaze from the burnished, highlighted tips of her hair to her freshly lacquered toenails. Back to her head. Shock furrowed his brow, darkened his eyes. And something more—her skin prickled—something...hot.

'Your hair...'

'Jeanne did a good job, didn't she?'

'Ah...'

Slack-jawed and speechless. A first for Jack Devlin.

Keeping to her plan, she glanced pointedly at her watch. 'Gosh, is that the time? I've got to go.'

'Wait up...'

But she was already halfway across the room, her stilettos clicking over the tiled foyer. Timing was critical.

'Where are you...? I'll drive you.'

She beamed at him—over her *exposed* shoulder—as she reached for the door knob. 'No, thanks, I'm fine. Bye.' And pulled the door shut behind her.

She didn't know if Jack would come after her, but she did know by the heat on the back of her neck that he was watching from the window. Good. Great. Satisfaction had never felt so good.

Her mood lighter than it had been in a long time, she walked to her car without looking back. 'Enjoy your evening, Jack. I intend enjoying mine.'

CHAPTER NINE

JACK checked his watch for the umpteenth time, then punched the wall. Two a.m. Where the hell was she? Who was she with? Of more concern, what was she doing?

Forcing the unsettling images away, he went back to standing at his window in the dark, willing her car to turn into the drive. A gentle night breeze flirted with the curtain, cooling his naked, sweaty chest. He saw Con crouched on the porch like a great fur log with whiskers. The stillness of the night was interrupted briefly by a dog barking, the call of a night bird.

But no Cleo.

Her mobile was switched off. Why was it off? Letting out an impatient snarl, he slid to the floor and leaned back against the wall.

The image of her as she left was seared into his brain as clear as any photograph. How many times had he studied it tonight?

She'd cut her hair. What was all that about? And that outfit— Whew. His hormones kicked in again at the memory. He'd never seen her in anything so feminine, so…startling. So un-Cleo.

But he'd detected a glint of mischief in those big blue eyes. As if she knew something he didn't. He cracked his knuckles. He hadn't liked not being in control of that situation one bit.

Two-ten a.m. Blowing a harsh breath, he watched the streetlight and shadows play on the wall. Apart from a couple of evenings out with Jeanne, since he'd been back, Cleo hadn't been on a date.

Was this a damn date? Did she date regularly? He hadn't been around Cleo, the adult.

The woman.

The woman he'd held in his arms not so many nights ago. The woman who'd slapped his face, then scaled a wall to be with him. How could he not be moved by that unique spontaneity?

And, yes, he was going to stand by and watch someone else have her. Because it was best for Cleo. *Take a bow, Jack Devlin.*

So why was he sitting on the floor—while his bum went numb—counting the minutes?

The sound of a car's tyres had him scrambling up, his heart pounding with relief. But his relief was short-lived. When he looked down, an old Toyota Corolla with a dent in the front passenger side pulled up as the security light winked on.

He craned his neck—the car was directly below and the angle was wrong—but he could just see the pale but indistinct shape of two faces in the dimness.

His fingers curled on the window sill as a minute

ticked by. Two. Three. What was she waiting for? It became obvious when the two faces merged into one for a second or two.

Two seconds too long. The hot quick flash took him by surprise. *Not* jealousy. But it snaked through his body like venom. And still he stood, unable to turn away, while the passenger door opened with a groan of tired metal and Cleo stepped out, laughing at something lover-boy said.

She looked young and vulnerable with that short hair, her slender body reflected in the porch light. For a nerve-racking moment he thought she was going to bring him in too, but she pushed the car door shut and waved, disappearing from view as she stepped onto the verandah.

He pried his fingers from the sill, unclenched his jaw and ordered himself to get a grip. Take a cold shower. Go to bed.

But he wanted to see her again. Simple as that.

And just as simply, he turned and walked to his door to wait for her to come up to her room.

When she didn't come, he paced the floor, then— to hell with it—he stalked downstairs. He found her in the kitchen, pouring milk into Con's bowl while Con wound his way around her perfectly shaped legs. He had an insane urge to slide right on over and do likewise. All that exposed creamy skin made him think of warm milk and honey and how smooth and sweet it would taste against his lips.

Which made him scowl as he propped himself on the door jamb and crossed his arms over his chest.

'What's the point of having a mobile if you switch it off?'

She whirled, spilling drips of milk on the floor and over her hand. 'Jack!' She did a quick scan of his body—naked but for midnight-blue boxers—then concentrated too hard on the milk carton as she replaced it in the fridge. 'You're still up.'

'Yes.' More than she knew. Shifting to hide the augmenting evidence, he crossed his right ankle over his left. He stared hard at her until she met his eyes. 'The phone?'

'Oh. I only switch it on in an emergency,' she said. Her tongue darted out to lick the milk off her hand. Still holding his gaze. As if she knew what was going on a few hands lower and wasn't game enough to look.

He cleared his throat. 'How do you know if there's an emergency if you don't keep it on?'

'I mean, if my car breaks down, or something.' She ripped off a piece of paper towel and crouched to mop up the spill. Con lapped up the stingy milk offering and walked off in disgust towards the stairs.

'So…did your car break down tonight?' he asked in a reasonable voice.

She rose slowly, walked to the bin and tossed the paper. Then she leaned one hip against the counter. 'No, but I don't like the way you said that. It had a definite edge.'

'An edge.' She was trying to put the blame on him? His temper spiked. He reined it in, barely. 'Wasn't your car I heard pull up.'

'I had a couple of drinks. I left my car at Jeanne's.'

'Jeanne's?'

Her own temper fired up in those blue eyes. 'Why are my words coming back at me, and what's with the eyebrow lift?'

He shrugged. Let her dig herself into a hole. 'Wasn't Jeanne who drove you home.'

'No. It wasn't.' She watched him for a long moment. He thought he saw regret or hurt flicker across her features before she blanked all expression. 'Jack, you made it quite clear you didn't want me in your bed—'

'Bed?' Cleo naked beneath him, her pale body writhing on his black silk sheets... Before the erotic image could take hold he cut her off with a quick slash of his hand. 'Did I say anything about bed? I only mentioned a lift home.' He pushed away from the door. It wasn't only temper now, it was anger and pain and a load of other stuff he couldn't seem to sort out.

She toed off one pink shoe, then the other, shrank a couple of inches. 'I didn't think—'

'Obviously not.'

Without her shoes, she looked like a little girl lost with her raggedy hair and skirt. He wanted to take her in his arms and make everything all right. He wanted to shake her till she told him the truth.

Mostly he wanted to knock lover-boy's balls into his throat.

'Is that why you're late?' *Because you've been in some man's bed?*

She walked to the sink, took a glass from the drainer, filled it with water and drank it with her back to him.

'Before you rudely interrupted, I was going to say I didn't think it would matter to you. What I did. After all, you don't want me.'

He watched her slender bare neck as she rinsed the glass. *Not want her?* He should be relieved, even pleased. He'd achieved what he'd set out to accomplish.

So why did he want to hurl the nearest available object?

She reached for the tea towel and made a major production out of wiping her glass. 'That makes it none of your business, Jack.'

'The hell it doesn't.' His anger had claws. Anger at himself and anger at her because she made him forget. 'You're family, remember? That makes it my business.'

'No. I'm Cleo Honeywell, all by myself.' She turned her back on him. 'I'm nobody's business.'

'Wrong.' He slapped a palm on the table. Her words struck like a knife all the way to his soul. And he was responsible. She'd built a wall around herself to shut out the hurt. To shut out Jack Devlin.

He turned his anger on himself, raised a conciliatory hand towards her, let it fall, useless, to his side. 'You'll always be my business, Goldilocks.'

'Fat lot of good that'll do me on another continent,' she shot back in a voice that belied her small stature. 'Assuming I wanted your assistance, which I don't.'

In a lightning-quick move he was behind her. He could feel her heat, could see each tiny gold hair on the back of her bare neck. The subtle bouquet of feminine scents—perfume, shampoo, makeup—filled his head, leaving no room for reason.

All he knew was need.

She turned. Sucked in a breath as their bodies bumped. Wide, shocked eyes flew to his. Her breasts grazed his chest, the little beads on her top abrading flesh that was suddenly way too sensitive. If glass beads could do that, what havoc would warm bare skin and tight nipples wreak?

His hands streaked over firm shoulders, smooth arms. Grasping her hands, he brought them to his lips, slid his tongue over her palms, then the delicate inside of her wrists where her pulse beat like a fury. Her taste was all he'd imagined and more, sweeter than honey, smoother than milk.

And his eyes didn't leave hers. *I want to do this to you until there's not a patch of skin I haven't tasted.* He watched those eyes sharpen, deepen, saw the moment she registered his unspoken message.

'We have now,' he murmured. Then speech was beyond him. Waiting was beyond him.

Releasing her hands, he held her face between his palms. Saw his own arousal mirrored there in the flushed cheeks, lips parted in anticipation. He lifted her onto the counter top so they were eye to eye.

Then he set his lips on hers. Now had no beginning, it had no end. Now was all he needed, this moment, this woman, the hot, slippery slide of her tongue against his. At her soft moan he plunged deeper. She grasped his medallion, fisted a hand around it and tugged him closer.

She was in his head, his heart, his soul. Even in the

harsh glare of the kitchen light, by the night-darkened window and fully dressed, she surrounded him.

A strangled groan rumbled in his throat at the first whisker-light touch of her fingers over his chest, then again, God help him, when they scraped and rubbed over his nipples.

Sanity flew out the window, long-denied passion rushed in to fill the void.

Closer. More. More skin to skin. His hands trembled as they left her face and slid the single tiny strap off her shoulder, down her arm.

His senses absorbed the blur of hot-pink lace, soft flesh, the rasp of his own breathing as he unsnapped her bra, tossed it aside and filled his hands with the womanly weight of her breasts.

With his hands on her bottom, he slid her to the edge of the counter. He put his hands on the silky firmness of her thighs, pushed them apart and stepped between them. His erection came up hard against hot, damp panties.

'Jack.'

His name on her lips, breathy and demanding, drove need towards desperation as her hands clawed at his nape and her head fell back.

Then his mouth was on her neck. On that smooth, vulnerable place where the blood pounded like a drum and her moans hummed like music against his lips.

He was blind, deaf and dumb to everything but her. The warning voice thrumming at the back of his mind grew muffled, distant, until he could no longer hear it. Could no longer drum up the energy or the inclination to heed it.

He heard Cleo's voice against his ear, felt the brush of her breath as she said, 'So live the now, Jack. For once in your life let yourself go.'

Cleo's mind spun. Was she dreaming? Was this the Jack who'd tossed her out of his room not so many nights ago? Breathless, she put her hands on his shoulders, nudging him back so she could see him. She watched his eyes glaze over.

Right where she wanted him, and she hadn't even tried. The only way she'd known she'd ever get Jack in bed was if he wasn't thinking of consequences and all those other issues he had with her. Like now.

The urgent need to have that naked body—all of it—against her, in her, was like a fever in her blood. And the hot, hungry, almost unbearable anticipation had her squirming to get closer, her sweaty thighs sticking to the counter top.

As they watched each other he slipped an impatient hand under the strap of her thong. She felt a finger sliding along the moist folds, then inside her. She gasped and saw his eyes flash with heat and wanting. Her inner muscles contracted, liquid desire pooled as he manipulated her flesh with fast, flicking passes, but she grabbed at his hand. 'Not here,' she managed.

'Where?'

Every pulse point hammered out a primitive beat at his feral growl. *Somewhere close.* 'Family room.' She wrapped her trembling legs around his waist, her arms around his neck, and he dragged her off the counter into his arms.

Half walking, half stumbling, Jack made it as far as

the doorway. Her breasts were flattened against his chest. She wiggled, wanting more friction between their bodies. More Jack.

He pinned her against the door jamb to devour her mouth once more, then released her slowly. She slid down between cool, smooth wood and the hard, hot length of him. He wrapped a hand around the back of her neck, his fingers pressed against her flesh. 'You make me weak.'

Upper body gleaming in the slant of light from the kitchen, he looked anything but weak as he hooked a finger in the thong. And tugged. She felt callused palm and silk slide down her inner thighs. The scrap of fabric pooled at her feet and she toed it aside.

He shoved his boxers down and oh…my…God. A fully-primed-and-ready-for-action weapon. And she had no doubt it had destroyed more than its fair share of the female population.

He'd slept with so many beautiful, experienced women. She wasn't beautiful or experienced, and she felt a quick lick of fear that he'd find her lacking.

But that didn't seem to be a problem for him right now. In the slant of light from the kitchen he looked like a bronze sculpture. A wickedly gorgeous, delicious male sculpture who was obviously more than capable of doing wickedly gorgeous, delicious things to her.

Her legs turned liquid. She was pinned there by his hands on her waist and one power-packed, hairy thigh between her legs.

Hard and hot as molten steel, his thigh pressed

upwards against already sensitised flesh, the hair-roughened skin rubbing, abrading as he rocked against her, his breath coming in short, sharp bursts. Her back and head slapped against the wood. All she could do was hang on.

Fast hands rushed up her body, over her breasts, stroking, squeezing, kneading. Her fingers dug into his upper arms, and beneath her palms she could feel the bunched ropes of sinew and muscle.

He swore—a rough-edged, almost violent sound—and for one panic-filled moment she thought he was going to back out again and she'd have to kill him. But he crushed his mouth to hers again, and, with their lips locked, he lifted her, whirling her across the room as if they were performing some mad, erotic waltz.

They hit carpet, collapsed onto the floor in a tangle of limbs and pink chiffon. It broke the connection, but only for a second. There was a cool draught down on the carpet and the scent of summer roses from the vase on the coffee-table. She'd never smell roses again and not think of this moment and Jack.

The kitchen light was behind him, leaving his face in shadow. Only his eyes glittered in the dimness as they fused with hers. The glint of his watch caught the light as his hands shoved her skirt up to her waist, then raced over breasts, belly, thighs.

Lower.

Quick, clever fingers plunged hard and deep into her heat. Her breath caught at the shockingly intimate intrusion and she made a sound somewhere between a whimper and a purr. But she wanted this, wanted more. Wanted all.

Her thighs fell open under his skilled assault. He knew his way around a woman's body. Knew where to stroke, how to rub, and—oh, God—he slid his knuckles back and forth along her quivering flesh until her bottom lifted off the floor. 'Jack!'

She was flying apart, hurtling towards the edge of the world and didn't know if she'd ever find her way back. Reaching down, she rode his hand to anchor herself.

Then his mouth was on hers again, hard and unforgiving. There was an edge of desperation in the way his tongue invaded her, as if he were battling a war he'd wanted no part in. Arching her back, she willed him to love her as she was and let it be enough.

Abruptly he reared up, shoulders broad and dark as he rolled on top of her, his heavy thighs pushing her legs even wider. She felt the smooth, wet and hot tip of his erection against her exquisitely aroused inner flesh.

He looked into her eyes for a freeze-frame of time. And they were children again, poised on the edge of innocence.

In one long, liquid thrust he drove into her. The breath left her lungs in a whoosh; her inner muscles contracted around him as she struggled with the shock and speed of that first penetration.

He went absolutely still. She could feel his heat throbbing inside her. His hands gripped her hips, holding her prisoner while his eyes turned molten. 'Why didn't you tell me?'

'It's okay; I'm okay. *Please.*' She arched against him once more, drawing him further inside her. Already she wanted that urgent thrust of carnal power and heat again. And again and again.

Slowly he withdrew, creating a delicious friction and anticipation, then plunged deep a second time. *Yes.* A third.

She moved with him, learning his rhythm as if her body had been tuned to his, only his. His head dropped to her breast, his mouth suckling and feasting as their hips slapped together in perfect unison.

She ploughed her hands through his short silky hair, clenched them as pleasure built and swirled like ribbons through her body.

She wanted to stay here for ever, with Jack a prisoner inside her body, the cool blanket of night to protect them and the rest of the world asleep.

She was hot, so hot, her skin slick with perspiration, yet she shivered with every thrust, every glide of his tongue, every stroke of his hand. Each new sensation brought new delight and took her higher.

Harder, quicker, deeper, in perfect synchronicity, dancing to music only they could hear. The tempo grew wild, a primal beat that echoed in her blood, in her mind, until there was nothing but Jack, sweat-slick skin and hot, shallow breaths.

He tensed suddenly, his muscles quivering as he supported his weight on his arms, watching her, the tendons in his neck and shoulders standing out like ropes.

The ribbons of pleasure swirled low in her belly,

then coiled. She was back on the edge of the world, but this time she wasn't alone. And when she took that final leap, he poured himself into her still-pulsing body and was with her all the way.

Jack watched Cleo sleeping in the pre-dawn dimness, pale and luminous as a pearl on black velvet, her head against his shoulder, one hand curled on his chest. Some time ago he'd carried her to his room, a rag doll in his arms.

His jaw tightened and an ache spread through his body. Her crumpled dress on the floor was a stark and appalling reminder of what they'd done. What *he'd* done.

Cool, dew-scented air wafted through the windows and the silence in the house was absolute. As real and absolute as his self-contempt. Not only had he let his body do the talking instead of his brain, he hadn't used protection.

He hadn't used protection.

Of course, he hadn't come downstairs with the intention of having sex, but when he'd seen her bending over the cat the rational part of his brain had simply shut down.

Her legs beneath the hot-pink hide-and-hint skirt had made him want to pant. But he'd held it together. Hadn't he restrained himself from salivating at the sight of her newly bared neck, a particular weakness of his?

Until she'd laid that all-by-myself none-of-your-business crap on him.

All his self-talk, all his noble intentions had flown out the window. He'd lost it, plain and simple.

She'd been his business since the first day he'd laid eyes on the scrawny seven year-old with pigtails in her hair, a man-sized toolbox of scrap metal under her arm and the biggest blue eyes he'd ever seen.

For the past six years not a day had gone by when he hadn't thought about her. Until he'd left home he'd made it his duty to look out for her.

That made her his business.

No reason it should change now. Except that last night Scotty had told him that probate was final. The only thing missing was Cleo's signature on the documents and the estate was hers. She was an independently wealthy woman.

That didn't mean he *had* to exile himself. It only meant… He blew out a slow breath. What *did* it mean?

One thing for sure; everything *had* changed.

CHAPTER TEN

CLEO smiled as she surfaced into semi-wakefulness. Her body felt like molten gold. As if Jack were the metal-smith and had forged the ordinary into something shiny and beautiful.

When he shifted, she protested with an indistinct, 'No.' She wanted his weight on her, his body joined to hers a little longer. A lot longer. Her limp hands slid bonelessly up and over the hard curve of his shoulders.

'So this is what all the fuss is about,' she murmured, nuzzling her face against his chest, hearing the ponderous beat of his heart.

Making love.

Making real love.

If only tonight, the Now, could last for ever. She breathed in the musky warm air between their bodies that smelled of their lovemaking, and opened her eyes. The half-dream fled. Bright early morning light tinged with pink already flooded the room.

Jack's room.

Jack's bed.

Jack's body beside hers, *not* joined.

'You let me fall asleep,' she accused him, still hung over with sleep. Oxygen starvation probably had something to do with it since her nose was buried in his chest hair. 'Did I miss anything?'

She wriggled upwards till they were nose to nose, bellies brushing, and not only bellies... Feeling adventurous for so early in the morning, she traced a finger down the line of their bodies, and moulded her hand around him.

It bucked against her as if it were a living thing with a mind of its own—probably why they said men thought with their—

A sound rumbled in his chest and he closed a hand over hers. 'Cleo...' He drew both to his lips, entwining their fingers. 'We have to talk.' He said it as if they were discussing the economy rather than sharing body heat.

Ignoring the tone, she kissed the sexy stubble on his chin. 'No talk.'

'Yes talk.'

A huge ball of uncertainty lodged in her chest. 'Don't you *dare* apologise.'

'I could have made you pregnant.'

'Oh.' Relief washed through her, easing tensed muscles. 'Is that all?'

'Is that all? You don't think that might deserve an apology?'

'There's no chance of pregnancy; I'm on the pill.'

His expression didn't soften or relax. It remained grim, perhaps even grimmer.

Her muscles tensed again. 'Ah…after the Sam thing and my ladder trick, I suppose you'd be forgiven for jumping to conclusions, but it's a female problem. The doctor said the pill should correct it. And it did; I—'

'Are you…were you…' he seemed to struggle with the words '…last night, was I the first?'

Last night had been…hot and fast and furious, against the wall, on the floor…

Heaven.

But she supposed he could feel bad if he thought she'd been a virgin, which she *almost* had been—if such a thing were possible. She pressed her lips together, then asked, 'Does in and out count?'

She almost smiled at his hard-edged confusion when he frowned and said, 'Want to explain that?'

'Just what I said. One in, one out.' She shuddered at the memory of that bungled encounter. 'Once was enough.'

His eyes darkened. 'Sam?' She shook her head. He didn't look appeased. 'Did he hurt you?'

'No.' Not so much body as heart. 'I thought I wanted it, thought if I closed my eyes and imagined…'

'Imagined what?'

That it was you, you idiot. But she only shrugged her shoulder and said, 'Can't remember now.'

After that terrible, mortifying night she'd known it could only be with someone she loved. And she loved Jack Devlin. Only Jack. With an ache so big, so wide, so high, she wondered that her heart didn't burst out of her chest.

So tell him, whispered a little voice.

But how would he react to that profound piece of news? How would he rate his feelings for her on the love scale? She really didn't want to know. Because, no matter what he said, she knew he didn't want anything permanent, and long-distance love wasn't her idea of happy-ever-after.

'Who was your first, Jack?' She stroked his collarbone, turning attention on him and away from her inner pain.

His lips twitched as he remembered. 'Kitty Cartwright.'

'Oh, my God.' Cleo couldn't hide the grin. 'The photographer's apprentice. So, who apprenticed who?'

'I'll leave that for you to consider. Are you going to fill me in on yours?'

'Not on your life. My first time was last night.' She met his eyes. Last night's heat and speed still vibrated along her nerve endings and shimmered in the air between them.

Jack cupped her face in one hand. 'I shouldn't have been so rough on you.'

'I wanted rough; I asked for rough.' She closed a hand over his. 'In fact, I think I begged.'

'Ah, Cleo,' he murmured. 'I thought that was me.' As if in apology he lowered his lips for one long, soul-destroying kiss that stole the breath from her lungs.

His hard, masculine body slid over hers while his soft, full lips nipped at her chin, her neck, then closed hungrily over her mouth.

She melted under his hands as they warmed and teased. Not rough this time, but slow and deliberate, seeking out all the places that begged to be touched: her breasts, nipples, the hollow at the top of her thighs, just a scant fingertip away from her—

'Jack?' Scott's voice. Scott's face peering at them from the open doorway. 'You through with those…' The sound of a throat clearing. 'Morning.'

Cleo stiffened, appalled. She'd invited Scott to breakfast and here she was laid out like the main course. The warm, melty feeling disappeared. Now it was a warm, flushed, embarrassed feeling from head to toe and every place in between.

When she tried to push up to cover herself, Jack's body prevented her. Without looking at the morning intruder, he stopped his busy hands, and he raised his head enough to swear against Cleo's mouth. 'Ever hear of knocking, Scotty?'

'Sorry. I'll make coffee. Hi, Cleo.'

'Make it a long black,' Jack called back as Scott retreated down the corridor. 'Very long. How did he get in?' Obviously not embarrassed about being caught in the act, he took up nibbling where he'd left off. 'And what's he doing here on a Sunday morning at nine a.m.?'

'He and Jeanne both…have keys, and I invited him—*them*, actually. But Jeanne couldn't make it.' Jack was kissing his way over a breast, making it hard to concentrate. 'The three of us often have…' her breath hitched '…Sunday brunch.'

'I'd've thought brunch leaned more towards eleven a.m. onwards.'

'Ummm.' Frustrated with the interruption, she puffed out a sigh. 'Jack…'

'You don't want to continue this right now, do you.' A statement, not a question. He rubbed her arm before rolling off her.

'I can't—not with Scott prowling around downstairs.' Probably tripping over her discarded underwear. Her very new, very sexy underwear.

Her morning-after glow had been tarnished. Suddenly she felt more than naked. She felt exposed, and wished they were in the familiarity of her own bedroom.

'I'm going to take a shower,' she said, getting up and grabbing his sheet from the bottom of the bed. No way was she making that trek down the passage bare-bottomed.

'You know, we could share a shower,' he said with a sexy lift of his brows.

She paused as she adjusted the sheet over her shoulder. The idea had appeal. They could lock the door and...

His eyes took a leisurely stroll over her sheet-clad body. 'I could wash your back for you.'

'Mmm.' Not nearly as exciting as having her front washed, but she'd take what she could get.

She made her own journey over Jack's still relatively unfamiliar terrain. Taut, tanned skin stretched over muscle and bone, the little dip in his navel and the not-so-little jut of masculinity that beckoned every female cell in her newly awakened body.

Her eyes flicked to his face and the more familiar but no less arousing sight of that brown-eyed gaze, looking at her in an entirely new way, deep and penetrating.

Like last night.

And if she stood here any longer she was going to do much more than look. With an effort, she moved to the door, tossed a sexy glance over her shoulder. 'I'll bring my own soap.'

A few minutes later, clutching her toiletries and some hastily hunted-up clothes, she made her way back to Jack's room. The sound of his voice had her hesitating at his door. He was on his mobile phone and using that voice he reserved for women.

'Just some of those complicated family issues to resolve,' she heard him say. He nodded at something the caller said, throwing in a sexy laugh for good measure. 'Yes, I'm still interested. Very interested…' Pause. 'Tomorrow?' Another pause. 'Eleven-fifteen, Café Medici. I'll look forward to it. Ah. Can we keep this just between us for now?'

Cleo swallowed over the sudden grip on her heart. *Just between us.* But she stepped away, turned, and, hugging her bundle, fast-tracked back to her room. Closed the door. The fragrance of the Yves Saint Laurent soap she hoarded for special occasions filled her nostrils. It was a painful but necessary reminder that this might not be a special occasion for playboy Jack.

Did tigers change their stripes? She walked into her bathroom and turned the shower on full blast. She was probably being paranoid, but she'd wait to see if he was going to let her in on his secret rendezvous. *Okay, Jack. Let's see how you play this. Then I'll know.*

* * *

'Is that what I think it is?' Scott said as Cleo entered the kitchen.

She snatched up her thong at the doorway and her bra from the counter, averting her eyes from the man who knew too much, and sighed. 'You tell me.'

'It looks like Black Forest cake.'

She looked up. He was standing in front of the open refrigerator.

He licked a finger. 'Tastes like Black Forest cake.'

'Go ahead, it's all yours,' she said, looking for a spot to hide her undies. She gave it up—what was the point?—and put them on a chair.

He cut off a wedge. 'Want some?'

'I'll stick to fruit and coffee.'

'That doesn't sound like the Cleo I know.'

'Maybe I'm not the Cleo you know.' She took a knife and plate to the breakfast bar, sat down on a stool and reached for an orange.

'I've been trying to figure out who you look like without the hair. Tinkerbell,' he decided.

'Great.' So much for sophisticated.

'What does Jack think?'

'I'm not sure.' She wasn't sure about anything where Jack was concerned any more.

'So...' Scott set his cake down and sat on the stool beside her. 'You and Jack, huh?'

The fresh tang of citrus scented the air as she sliced her orange. They couldn't pretend nothing had happened, but she so didn't want to discuss it with Scott right now. 'Can we talk about something—'

'Where did you get to, Goldilocks?' Jack breezed in as if nothing had changed. He nuzzled her neck briefly, his soapy smell reminding her of the shower she *hadn't* shared, and whispered, 'Get rid of Scott. I want to talk to you—among other things,' then nicked a slice of her orange.

She watched him suck at it while he poured coffee. The long, hard length of him was now casually covered in shorts and T-shirt, but she could still see him last night, against that door less than a meter away. Naked, primal and fully aroused. The tiger and his stripes.

He'd been sucking her with the same enthusiasm. A tide of hot flushes washed through her as her body remembered and responded.

She was still watching and remembering when he stopped in mid-pour and frowned, his attention drawn to something beyond the window.

'Scotty?' He jutted his chin in the direction of his glare. 'Whose car's that?'

'The Corolla? It's a friend's. I lent him my car for the weekend. Had to drive his mother to her sister's in Ballarat.'

'So you drove Cleo home last night. Thanks.'

'No worries.'

Jack continued to top up his coffee, but Cleo saw the tension in his shoulders ease. In fact he looked extraordinarily pleased, she thought with a snarl as she picked at her orange. Smug, even.

Did the man always get what he wanted? 'I'll be out back,' Cleo said, grabbing her coffee as she rose.

Jack looked up sharply. 'Hey, I thought…'

She met his eyes and acknowledged the heated look that told her exactly what he thought. 'I'm behind in my commissions. I need to clock up some work hours.' *And you have something to tell me.* Or did he?

His lips curved in a sexy grin. 'Perhaps I can help.'

She nodded. 'Perhaps you can.'

'Wait up,' Scott said, reaching for the file beside him on the table. 'Before you both disappear I need you to sign these papers. Then the estate's done and I can leave you alone for the rest of the day.'

Knowing how hurt and humiliated Jack must feel, Cleo gritted her teeth and replaced her mug carefully on the table. This morning had taken another turn for the worse.

Jack sat in his father's big leather chair and scowled at the papers in his hand. He'd always avoided this room. This had been his father's domain, where he'd doled out verbal and physical abuse behind closed doors.

So why was he sitting in this monstrosity of an office when the woman in his life was a thirty-second walk away?

Because she'd told him she needed to work on her jewellery. He could understand her wanting some space. A simple signature and she had just become an unwillingly wealthy woman. He understood that.

But was that all that was bothering her? They'd both known the score on that point and he'd accepted it. Still, she'd seemed on edge when he'd joined her in the kitchen.

Was it the fact that they'd made love? He shook his

head. It wasn't her first time. He had to smile at her confession, and at the same time he had to hate the guy who'd taken what Jack had tried so hard to keep intact.

No. He'd noticed…something in those big blue eyes as she'd left for her workshop. Was it the Corolla moment? She'd managed to keep him guessing there. Perhaps she was disappointed he'd discovered her little secret.

The other reason he was here instead of trying to entice Cleo back inside and into his bed was because he'd also promised Scott some info a week ago and he'd promised to have it by the end of today.

Unfortunately it involved sorting through his father's filing system and desk drawers. He made a half-hearted attempt to start, then gave up, rolled the chair back and deliberately jammed his feet on the polished mahogany desk with its dark leather inlay.

His head was too crowded with thoughts and images of Cleo. The way those creative jeweller's hands had worked their magic on him, and her body so snug and so right against his. The scent and taste of her soft, milky skin, her sexy moans when she came—that had to be the most incredible moment of his life.

And the whole thing might not have happened if he hadn't seen her rock up in another man's car and pan-icked—Scott, as it turned out; the only man he trusted, the man he owed big time.

But Cleo was a family-and-commitment girl with her roots firmly in her home town whereas he needed to return to Rome, at least for a few weeks. He had ob-ligations—Domenic and Carmela for starters. Carmela had informed him the old man was out of danger. He wanted to see for himself without a bullet in his chest.

But where was home? Not Rome. But for him, thanks to his father, home was a dirty word. Family was a dirty word. Jack loved the travel, the freedom of being his own boss, the love-'em-and-leave-'em credo he'd lived by for the first couple of years overseas.

Filming in war-ravaged areas had changed the way he looked at the world, and he'd been bound by a sense of duty he hadn't thought he'd had to stay and help. He'd thrived on the challenge.

Could he give all that up? And if he did, if he stayed...was he being fair to Cleo? With his father's violence and his mother's wanderlust in his veins, he was a bad bet.

Last night the cold, hard reality of seeing Cleo with another man in the shadowy confines of a car had tipped him over the edge. He lowered his feet and pushed away from the desk to pace. He'd lost it, big time. Lost control. Like his father. He struck a fist on the filing cabinet, tugged at a drawer. It opened with a sharp metallic sound. He had to get this done and get the hell out of his old man's office.

He dealt with the paperwork, saving a padded envelope Scott had handed him as he'd left today till last. As he sliced it open a gold key fell out, tagged 'lower desk drawer'. Fingers of tension gripped his neck as he studied the key in his hand. 'Okay, old man, what little surprise have you left me now?' Nothing pleasant, he was sure.

He fitted the key, opened the drawer and found a

letter addressed to him in his father's handwriting. Expelling a four-letter word, he considered tossing it out, but perhaps it had some info that pertained to Cleo or the estate.

The letter was dated six weeks before his death.

Jack,
As you read this, Cleo has inherited my estate. I knew I could count on your feelings for her to see it through.

I understand why you didn't return sooner, even if Cleo doesn't. I made mistakes but I had my reasons.

'Is there a valid reason to beat your son?' Jack grated through his teeth.

I fell for your mother knowing she was on the rebound. We married within a month and seven months later you were born. But I soon discovered domestic life didn't suit Atta. She was always off on some research caper or studying.

Then after thirteen years of marriage she announced that our tenant, John Honeywell, and she were involved in more than research. Their decision to join that expedition to Antarctica meant dumping you kids. They just forgot to collect you on their return.

Another surprise. Years ago a routine examination revealed I was firing blanks. I am not your father, Jack. Perhaps that helps you understand why I could never love you; even before I found out, in my heart I knew.

As for Cleo—who wouldn't love her? And she was the only person who loved me for myself. You threatened that relationship. I did what I had to do to keep it.

Discovering you're only half a man makes one look at things differently. I needed a woman in my life. I needed Cleo.

You're wondering why I didn't pack you off to your mother when I discovered you weren't my son. You were already eighteen. Cleo adored you—she would have followed. I couldn't let that happen. But if I could convince her that you weren't worthy of her love…

Jack shook his head. 'You were one sick son of a bitch, Gerry Devlin.'

Finally, you won't be aware Atta and John first knew each other as uni students twenty-eight years ago. I met Atta after John took off on some overseas research scholarship. Make what you will of that.

Jack's fingers tightened on the paper. He'd been born twenty-seven years ago.

What you tell Cleo and how you deal with it is up to you. Perhaps you'll curse me for telling you, perhaps you'll thank me…

Jack didn't read any further. He couldn't seem to hold the paper steady. His stomach pitched and rolled; his eyes wouldn't seem to focus. Dates and years and calculations rampaged through his mind.

Think! But he didn't want to think. To think was to know. He slammed a fist on the desk. The glass lamp trembled. Papers sailed onto the floor as he swept them aside with a slash of his hand.

To *know*, was to know what his father was capable of. The part about John Honeywell had to be a lie. Deep down in some dark corner of his heart he knew it was a lie, but true to form, his father—*not* his father—Gerry had set him up to doubt. He refused to doubt.

But he had to be sure.

To do that he had to find his mother. Even if Honeywell hadn't been his mother's lover twenty-eight years ago, he couldn't put Cleo through the pain of knowing he was meeting her. Nor could he could tell her why.

Dad's—*Gerry's*—*coup de grâce. Your father could be my father.* The words shredded the very fabric of his life as he knew it, and he didn't know how he'd ever stitch it back together. 'Cleo.' Her name vibrated on his lips. She was the only thread that could save him.

He fumbled with the phone and had to punch in Scott's number twice. 'It's Jack.' He steam-rolled over Scott's cheery good morning. 'Drop whatever you're doing, I need your help.'

Fifteen minutes later, Jack had a bag packed, a seat

on the next flight to North Queensland, and Scotty's word to keep his mouth well and truly sealed. Thank God Scott the lawyer had his mother's address on file.

Depending on what he found he had to prepare for the possibility of severing all ties. Cleo could start a new life, be happy. Without him. That prospect wrenched at his heart till there was no room for anything inside him but pain.

He rang for a taxi, parked his bag by the front door and took a deep breath. All he had left to do now was inform Cleo he was leaving.

Therapeutic. That was what Cleo told herself as she pounded the sheet of metal. The forging hammer felt good and solid and familiar in her hand as she worked. Something she could control. An outlet for her emotions. She imagined it ran a close second to a punching bag.

She should be working on the silver and amethyst drop necklace she'd been fretting over for weeks, but it demanded intricate and exacting work, and she needed something more physical.

Which of course segued straight to Jack. She'd inherited what was his. That earned a chime of metal on metal that jangled through her hand and up her arm. She intended changing that as soon as Scott could do the paperwork.

Half an hour had passed and Jack hadn't come to talk to her about his coffee 'date'. Another clang. How could he make love to her as if she were the only woman in the world and arrange to meet another without telling her about it? Was she being paranoid? Probably.

'Knock knock.'

Cleo looked up, almost dropping her hammer with relief at the sound of Jack's seriously deep voice, and smiled. 'Hi.'

'I hope I'm not interrupting anything too complicated.'

Now he just sounded serious. A shadow seeped into her bones and her smile dropped away. She picked up a probe, began scoring the metal's surface and said, 'Would it make a difference?'

'This time? No. Cleo... I came to tell you I'm—'

'Leaving.' She closed her eyes.

One word to sum up Jack Devlin.

The loneliest word in the world.

He was going to put her out of his life now and move on. Like last time. No, not like last time, because this time he was taking more than her broken heart. He was taking the memories of one glorious night together—because she would *never* think of it again.

He was taking away hope. Her hope for a future with Jack, the home they could have shared, the babies they could have made...

Carefully, so he wouldn't see her hand shake, she swapped the probe for her hammer, ran it through her fingers, tapped it against her palm.

In the silence she heard the tinkle of her metal wind chimes outside the door, the neighbourhood sounds of someone's power tool and traffic and birds. Homey sounds. Sounds Jack didn't take the time to hear.

She forced herself to take one last look at him before she put him out of her mind, and her heart, for ever.

Dark—and was that troubled?—eyes met hers. The amorous, casual guy from breakfast had disappeared behind a stone façade.

His eyes flicked to the hammer she'd forgotten about. She tapped it against her palm again, harder, so that she felt the jolt sing up her arm. 'Someone beautiful offer you something better than love, Jack?'

He flinched at the word. She saw the stone wall crack a little and something infinitely sad clouded his eyes before anger took hold. 'Don't piss me off with crap like that. I'm coming back, Cleo, and we'll talk.'

'You know something, Jack? I don't want to talk to you, ever again. And I *want* to piss you off. I want to piss you off so bad that you never come back. And if you do, by some miracle, come back you won't find me here. Because I won't wait for you again.

'I love you, Jack Devlin. I love you more than I can say, more than you'll ever know. If I got down on my knees and humiliated myself some more and begged you to stay, or to take me with you, would you, Jack?'

His jaw tightened and he closed his eyes briefly. Then he lifted a hand, let it fall. 'Cleo, I—'

'Didn't think so. I'm through waiting for you. Goodbye, Jack.' Biting down hard on her lip to stop it trembling, she turned away and pounded metal to metal.

She didn't hear him leave, but a few minutes later, when her arm burned with the effort and she'd all but flattened her strip to smithereens, she realised she was alone again.

The knowledge left her reeling with grief. She wanted to love him, wanted him to love her, so desperately, so completely, she'd just shouted the word for all the world to hear—three times, for God's sake. *Idiot.* She threw her hammer across the room, then swiped a piece of pipe from her workbench and threw that too.

But Jack had never mentioned love. Jack was incapable of loving—he hadn't even mourned his father. One thing was certain; she couldn't stay here. *Wouldn't* stay here. Wouldn't be waiting for Jack if and when he decided to come back.

CHAPTER ELEVEN

'THANKS for letting me and Con stay here, Scott. You're a real hero.' Cleo was on hands and knees trying unsuccessfully to tempt the hulk from behind Scott's sofa with a bowl of chopped ham.

'No problem.'

She glanced up at the sombre tone to see Scott in the doorway, arms crossed and a frown line between his brows. 'Do you think Jase'll mind?' She had a sneaky feeling Scott's flatmate wasn't particularly fond of cats. Or of Cleo herself, for that matter.

'This apartment's half mine; it's okay.'

Not the answer she was hoping for, but Jeanne's tiny one-bedroom apartment didn't allow pets. And she absolutely, positively couldn't sleep alone in her house tonight. *Her* house. The reality only compounded her misery.

Giving up, she pushed the bowl towards the two eyes glinting in the dimness amongst the dust bunnies. 'I hope he finds the litter tray, he's not used to being inside all the time.'

'He'll find it,' Scott said, stepping away from the door. 'Come and sit down. We have to talk.'

Shifting an assortment of clothes to one end of the sofa, she let out a half sigh, half laugh. 'You mean I'll talk and you'll lend a sympathetic shoulder.'

'No, I have some things to say too and you need to hear them.'

Her attention snapped to the grim-faced stranger standing in the middle of the room. Scott had never sounded so terse. Not the same guy who'd turned up with banana caramel pie a couple of hours after Jack had left and saved her from herself. Suspicion narrowed her gaze. 'Jack put you up to this afternoon's tea party, didn't he?'

'He was worried about you.'

She snorted. 'Not worried enough to stick around or let me in on his plans.' Straightening, she said, 'I'm imposing; I'm sorry. I'll ring a cattery and book into a motel—'

'Your choice, but you'll hear me out first.' He jabbed a finger in her direction, his pewter eyes brooking no argument. So not Scott's manner.

Her surprise morphed into anxiety and some of those knots in her stomach tightened. She sat down. Scott remained standing. Okay, no sympathetic shoulder to lean on. 'All right, what's this about?'

'It's about Jack.'

She threw up a warning hand. 'If he wanted me to know, he would've told me.'

Scott shook his head. 'No. He wouldn't.'

His voice changed, making her super aware of the

vice squeezing her heart. Whatever Scott had to say, she didn't want to know. 'The trouble with Jack is—'

'Shut your mouth, Cleo.'

Reacting out of pure shock, she did.

'For once in your life listen to Jack's side.' He paced away towards the window where twilight was settling over the suburbs. 'It started about thirteen years ago…'

Cleo wrapped her hands around her knees, hugging herself in a dismal effort to contain the heartache. She felt the sofa dip as Scott sat beside her. He'd said plenty and now he didn't seem to have any words left. Nor could she get her own words out over the lump in her throat.

The man she'd loved as a father wasn't the man she thought he was. She felt numb, as if she were having the nightmare where she was running from something, only she couldn't move and it was dragging her down. She'd hit rock-bottom this time and there was no waking up. Today she'd lost not just one man she loved, but two.

She clenched her fingers till her nails bit into her palms. She wanted to lash out at someone. Anyone. Mostly she wanted to lash out at blind Cleo Honeywell. 'I should have seen it.'

'Don't blame yourself, Cleo.' She felt Scott's arm squeeze her shoulders in an attempt to comfort. It didn't. Nothing would.

'I should have known something wasn't right.' That Jack's bruises weren't always from backyard brawls, but something so much more sinister.

His father.

The man had abused his own flesh and blood.

'No one knew—Jack made sure of that. So did Gerry,' Scott finished.

All those years Jack hadn't let on. Cleo felt the burning sting of tears for what Jack had put up with. He'd stayed to look out for her. For the rebellious girl who'd given him grief at every turn. And when he had left—and she understood why now—he'd used Scott as back-up for her. Because he cared about her.

She'd been so wrong about him.

And like his father, she'd told him not to come back.

Cleo pushed off the sofa, rubbing her upper arms. She felt chilled to the bone despite the warm evening. 'You know where he is. Tell me, I must make it right between us.' *Even if it's only to say goodbye.*

'I can't. I gave my word.'

Defeated, she closed her eyes and nodded. Scott would never betray a confidence. She had no choice but to accept it.

'Give him the time he needs, Cleo. He'll be back when he's ready.'

'Will he?' Why hadn't he let her in? Even in his pain he'd held her at arm's length. Heart cramping, she gazed beyond the window, watching a jet's lights wink high in the sky. Perhaps because his heart now lay an ocean away on another continent. She thought of the café date he'd arranged. Or he'd found someone closer. She struck her palm against her thigh. 'I feel so powerless.'

'You love him.'

She continued to gaze out the window. 'I've waited for Jack more than half my life. Waited to grow up, waited for him to look my way, waited for him to come back. It's no secret to anyone but Jack.'

'Tough, isn't it? The waiting. The wanting.'

Cleo turned at the subtle undertone. Scott was hunched forward, forearms on his knees, his eyes unusually intense…and focused on her.

Uh-oh. *Scott?* How had she missed this? But he looked away, down at his hands. He made two fists, rubbed them together. 'You looked, and maybe you missed seeing Jack's response for a few years back then, but he was looking back.'

She felt those words all the way to her soul.

A corner of his mouth kicked up in a semi-grin as he finished, 'Discreetly, mind you.'

'Scott, I…' She mentally closed her eyes remembering Jack's first night back when she'd tried to kiss Scott to prove Jack didn't mean anything to her. *Stupid, stupid.* 'You're the big brother I never had. Something Jack could never be, because of how I felt about him.' How she'd always feel about him.

And not once in those six years had Scott made a pass at her. He'd never tried to be more than her perfect Sir Galahad.

Why not?

Somewhere in her brain a light switched on. Scott wasn't talking about waiting for her, about wanting her… A mix of disturbing emotions knifed through her. A strange heat danced through her belly. 'You… wanted…Jack.'

Their eyes met with new awareness and he nodded. 'Jack never knew, and I wasn't ready to deal with my own sexuality. I spent the past few years in denial. Then five months ago I met Jason.'

'Jason. Oh, Scott.' She knelt before him and grasped his hands still clenched on his thighs. 'Does Jeanne know?'

When he didn't reply, she tightened her hold. 'These days it's no big deal, and I know Jeanne will accept you and…Jason.'

He nodded, blew out a breath. 'Seems like now's a good time to bring it out in the open. You and I have both learned the painful lesson that secrets don't do us any favours.' His hands turned palms up and linked with hers. 'Enough for now, you've had a rough day. Jase'll be back soon and I'd rather not have him walk in on our conversation.'

'I'm sorry, but I don't want to go home, Scott. Those terrible secrets are embedded in that house. I don't think I can face them alone. At least not yet.' She laid her head on their joined hands.

'I invited you here, didn't I?' Dropping a kiss on her hair, he said, 'Take the main bedroom; it's got its own bathroom. You'll be more comfortable and it'll give you privacy. Jase and I'll take the spare room. Just give me a moment to grab our toiletries.'

She was too tired and wrung out to argue. 'Thanks.'

He tightened his grip on her hands briefly before releasing them and rose. 'Sleep in as long as you like. I'll see you tomorrow after work.'

* * *

That night Cleo lay in the dark, breathing the earthy, masculine scents of the room and listening to the muted TV on the other side of the wall.

Her world as she knew it had come apart. Her trust and her beliefs about family, life and love had been shattered. Her eyes had been opened and her innocent view of the world had altered for ever.

But Jack... Her heart squeezed tight, so tight she wondered that it didn't crumble. Jack's own beliefs had been shattered more violently, more personally, years ago.

No wonder he didn't trust family.

No wonder he wanted nothing to do with love.

Between spring-cleaning Scott's apartment to channel that nervous energy, checking job vacancies—because she'd need a job when she signed the house over to Jack—and talking Jeanne's ear off in the evening, Cleo should have been exhausted. But over the next couple of nights fragments of her life intruded on her dreams. Images of Jack's bruised body kept her awake and pacing the floor.

Somehow she had to show Jack that love and trust and family didn't have to be a lie. In her newly awakened view of the world, the one thing she could be sure of was her love for Jack. Everything else would grow from there.

That didn't mean she wasn't angry with him for keeping everything to himself. Before they sorted out their relationship one way or the other, she was going to set him straight—sharing was non-negotiable.

As dawn lightened the sky on the third day she took a shower and spent a long time letting the soothing spray massage her skin. Not bothering with a bra, she pulled on one of Scott's comfortable flannel shirts over her panties.

Creeping into the kitchen to make a hot drink, she noticed the microwave clock flashing five-thirty. She made a cup of chamomile tea and took it back to bed.

Slivers of pink and purple were streaking the sky when she stretched out and willed herself asleep.

As the aircraft dipped below the clouds on its final approach into Melbourne, Jack's gaze shifted from the early-morning glow to the small dog-eared photo in his hand. The man looking at the camera could have been him. Dark hair, olive skin, dimpled chin. Steve Jackson.

His father.

Regret churned through him for what he'd lost. But Steve Jackson had been killed before Jack had been born. His mother had named him for the man who'd given him life. She just hadn't bothered to inform Jack, or Gerry, as it turned out—he almost felt sorry for the man. Almost.

His mother had looked frail and weather-beaten from years out in the field, so he hadn't told her about the abuse that had begun after she'd left. His fingers tightened on the photo. Seeing her again had dredged up an inconvenient surge of emotion from some deep forgotten corner of his heart. Something of the same had reflected in her eyes as, out of some warped sense of duty, he'd kissed her goodbye.

He hadn't looked back.

She'd chosen her life, let her live it. It was time Jack Devlin chose his. A new determination coursed through him as he thought of Cleo. She'd probably still be asleep when he arrived, which would give him an opportunity to sneak in and wake her for once, instead of the other way round.

His blood pounded in anticipation as he thought about how he might accomplish that. His loins grew heavy just thinking of those long lashes fluttering open, her husky morning voice. That erotic feline way she'd arched her back and stretched as if waiting to be petted the last time they'd woken together.

But his heart tumbled over in his chest as he thought of the whole woman. A woman that got to him on every level. With every layer he'd peeled away, he'd discovered something new or long forgotten, from the creative way she stacked the unwashed dishes, to the soft core she guarded beneath all that attitude.

She could freeze him out with just one look and have him melting with another. She had drive and tenacity and, once she made up her mind, she let no one steer her off course. She also had compassion and empathy and put her needs on hold to help others— Gerry and himself for starters.

And he wanted it all, the complete package.

Family, Jack. But you wouldn't know about that. He looked at the photo in his hand again, before slipping it into his pocket. Perhaps he did now. He *did* know he was going to give it his best shot.

She'd been spitting mad when he'd left, understandably so. He'd been hurting too. Cleo had always been feisty and up front—another aspect that he loved about her. Scotty understood her too. His buddy would reassure her.

She knew how he felt about her. Hadn't they made mad, glorious love only hours before? She'd know he was coming back; he'd told her. He'd kept it low-key because of possible complications, but she didn't know any of that. Like any woman, she'd overreacted.

She'd wait. She'd told him she loved him. Rather, she'd spat it at him. A smile touched his lips and he let his head fall back on the headrest and closed his eyes. His whole body brimmed with something close to awe. Everything would be fine when he explained.

Rubber hit the tarmac with a thud and the aircraft roared as it slowed, then taxied, the low sun glinting bronze on the glassed terminal building as they neared.

A frustratingly slow hour later he paid off the cabbie and stared at her bedroom windows. One was open as usual, but the curtains were closed. Yes, still asleep.

He could almost believe he was nervous. He'd detoured to a florist for a peace-offering, and the scent of the long-stemmed carnations mingled with the familiar scent of morning-damp grass. Magpies warbled in the eucalypts. He had to force himself not to sprint to the front door.

This homecoming was so different from the one he'd faced a few weeks earlier. He wasn't coming home to a house. He was coming home to a woman. To family—his family. The warmth of that rightness seeped through his blood like the early-morning sunshine and settled comfortably in his bones.

A freeze-frame of Cleo, round with his baby, stopped him in his tracks. *Their* baby. He let out a breath. *Whoa. Back up. One step at a time.* Apologies and explanations first.

Letting himself in, he dumped his bag in the hall. He noticed it immediately. The stillness, the emptiness. No Con, no inviting breakfast smells.

Quick as spit, his buoyant mood evaporated. This didn't feel good. *I won't wait for you again.*

His heart lurching, he took the stairs two at a time. The unslept-in bed confirmed it. His fist tightened around the flowers. She loved this house—she *owned* it, for God's sake.

So where the hell was she?

He all but leapt down the stairs, snaffled keys from the hook in the kitchen and headed for Gerry's Daimler, praying there was enough fuel. *Think.* Where would she go? He didn't have Jeanne's phone number handy, but he keyed in Scott's mobile number. Voice mail. He swore, left a message and tossed the phone onto the seat.

Tyres screeching, he swung out of the drive and headed for Scott's apartment five minutes away. Jeanne would already be at the salon—Scott's place was closer. He saw Scott's flatmate Jason's car pull out as he turned into the apartment building's parking lot.

He leaned on the doorbell, tried the door. Finding it unlocked, he shoved it open and followed the smells of burnt toast and sounds of activity to the kitchen.

'Jack.' Scott was wiping what looked like the remains of cat food off the floor but he tossed the cloth on the sink when he saw him. 'I expected you to call—'

'I did; you didn't pick up. Where's…'

Scott's bedroom door opened off the L-shaped entertaining area and a sleepy-eyed woman stumbled out. In a too-big flannel shirt, and nothing much else by the looks of it. '…Cleo?'

He took in her quick indrawn breath, the wide, stunned eyes. 'Jack!'

His fleeting relief turned to something hot and sharp that slashed through him like a knife. He kept his eyes pinned to hers. He wanted to read the truth in those eyes. More, he wanted to avoid the bare legs and the ample show of cleavage that told a story he didn't want to hear.

A story that told him she didn't love him enough to wait. That she'd carried out her threat. That she'd turned to Scott, his mate. The stab of the twin-pronged betrayal had him itching to pound…something. Anything. Instead, he tightened his fist around the flowers, and, still watching her, he planted them firmly, squarely, on the coffee-table. 'Surprise.'

For a moment she seemed confused at the venom in his voice, which he hadn't tried to disguise. Then she glanced down at herself, one hand rising to fumble with the single closed button. 'I was…asleep…I…'

That husky morning voice that always turned him on scraped over his already raw emotions. Jack took a step back, still unable to comprehend the scene that was playing out right in front of him, like something from a soap opera. He glared at Scott, then Cleo, back to Scott again. 'What the *hell* is going on here?'

Scott moved to the table, stuffed some papers in his briefcase. 'You're jumping to the wrong conclusions, Jack.'

Jack's glare swung to the sofa. No evidence that anyone had spent the night on it. 'Am I?' The fact that Cleo stood between them prevented Jack from crossing the room and doing something he'd possibly regret later—or would he? 'Only one other bed... You telling me you're gay now, Scotty?'

Jack's ex best buddy exchanged a covert glance with Cleo as he snapped his briefcase shut. 'I'm due in court in an hour,' he said. 'I'll leave you to it.' He paused at the door. 'Tell him the truth, Cleo. All of it.'

And the door closed with a click.

The truth. How far back did that *truth* go? A chill settled over Jack's body like a shroud, almost suffocating him. Double-crossed by the two people he'd trusted above all others, who meant more to him than anyone.

He'd learned the rules young. Putting your heart out there on the landscape that was life was asking for it to be trampled on. Which was why he preferred the role of spectator, viewing life through the lens of his camera. Detached, alone, heart intact.

He hadn't learned a bloody thing.

'The truth then, Cleo,' he said at last, hearing the bleak sound of his own voice. Or perhaps it was the sound of his heart being torn apart. Irrevocably, finally.

She moved to the window. Avoiding eye contact. Avoiding him. The sun carved bars of gold over her through the vertical drapes, making her seem even more inaccessible.

'The *truth* is I couldn't stay at the house alone, Jack. Not after...' She seemed to shrink before his eyes, hugging her arms around herself. '...Scott told me about...your father.'

Great. Just great. He rubbed the back of his neck where a tension headache was beginning to throb. 'Let it go; I have.' She'd loved the man; Jack had wanted to spare her the gory details.

'What he did to you...' At last she turned to face him. A well of emotions darkened the misty blue of her eyes. 'I'm sorry—'

'I don't want your pity—'

'You don't have it,' she shot back. Gripping her upper arms with white-knuckled fingers, she glared at him. 'I was going to say I'm sorry you didn't tell me. What I *am* is *angry*. Why didn't you ever fight back? I never saw *him* bruised and battered.'

He shook his head. 'Fists, violence of any kind never solved anything. It frustrated the hell out of him when I didn't retaliate. The anger and unhappiness in his eyes each time I walked away gave me a twisted sense of satisfaction.'

'And didn't you think I had a right to know? All that time you let me love that man...'

'He loved you too.' The bastard. 'I didn't want to hurt you.'

'You kept the truth from me. You lied to me. You went away without a word and kept it to yourself. *That* hurts.'

'I—'

'Six years of your life are a mystery to me.' She

sliced her hand through the air, rattling the blinds and cutting him off. 'You never trusted me enough to open yourself to me, to let me in on your thoughts and experiences. *That* hurts. You're like the silver bangles I make. Beautiful, strong, solitary and *closed*.'

She shut her eyes, but a single tear tracked down one pale cheek. Jack yearned to pull her into his arms. He wanted her body against his. He wanted to catch that tear with his tongue and taste the saltiness, to share his own pain, a pain that right now was tearing his heart to shreds.

Yes, he'd hidden the truth about Gerry. And he'd do it again. But he'd kept too much from her. Gerry was one thing; shutting her off from the past six years was as bad as cheating. Letting her believe he'd been living a life of indulgence and women had been a ploy to keep her at arm's length, but it was still lying.

He'd been an idiot. If she'd turned to Scott for more than comfort, he had no one to blame but Jack Devlin. He'd deal with Scott later; right now he had to get Cleo back. He had to convince her that they belonged together. But not here. 'Get your stuff; we're going home.'

Her damp eyelashes flicked up and she looked at him, her eyes twin pools of blue misery. 'You can still call it home?'

'It's all we've got at the moment. Sometimes, Goldilocks, you have to face problems where they lie.'

Cleo stared at him. His voice was steel, his eyes like flint. But the message in his words... *We're going home.* The way he'd coupled them together sent hope soaring through her heart. If only. She wanted to believe. She dared not hope. Not yet.

'My car, Con…'

'I'll deal with Con. Get dressed; we'll pick up your car later.'

She cringed at the way his eyes slid over Scott's shirt. 'I didn't…' she began, but he'd already turned away to hunt up the cat.

Five taut, silent minutes later she sat in Gerry's car, staring at the house that had been given to her. Her mouth turned dust-dry, her body tightened a little more with every painful beat of her heart. Once upon a time she'd never imagined not belonging here.

Now she didn't belong anywhere. To anyone.

Jack sat beside her, his familiar scent surrounding her. She understood his wanting to go back to Rome. He'd made a new life there. At least her head understood, even if her heart couldn't accept it. Now she was independent it made sense he'd want to get on with the rest of his life without those bad memories.

She was part of those bad memories.

On legs that barely held her, she climbed out of the car, opened the carry cage and let Con out. He scurried away, then glared at her from beneath his favourite bush. 'Sorry, big guy,' she murmured. At least someone wanted to be here.

Turning, she saw Jack watching her from the driver's side, looking remote behind his sunglasses. 'Let's go,' he said. Curt and unsmiling. So not the way she'd imagined.

The moment Jack unlocked the door she fled

upstairs to her bathroom, closed the door. Grabbing her toothbrush, she cleaned her teeth to chase away the sour taste of dread and to regain some sense of normalcy.

An impatient knock on the door was accompanied by, 'If you're not out in one minute I'm coming in to get you.'

His ultimatum sent a tingle dancing down her spine. She rinsed, patted her mouth dry, and, bracing herself, opened the door.

But what she saw stopped her dead. Jack Devlin, stubble-jawed and totally masculine in tight blue jeans and white T-shirt, lying on her bed and surrounded by pink satin and lace.

But it was his eyes that held her. It was as if they could reach deep down and see into her soul. He held her heart and her will in those dark eyes.

As if tugged by their magnetism, she drifted across the room, stopping in the centre of her pink sheepskin rug. The faintest of breezes carried the delicate fragrance of morning, and Jack.

The muscles in his forearm twisted like rope as he plumped a frilly lace cushion and set it behind his head. 'We're going to talk; we might as well be comfortable.'

Talk. Honestly, she was all talked out. What she wanted was body contact and lots of it.

When she didn't answer, a corner of his mouth kicked up. 'Isn't that what you women want to do? Talk? Lay it all out on the table? Dissect and analyse and rehash?'

The sight of those more-than-capable hands and long, sensuous fingers as they smoothed the quilt beside him sent a thrill of remembrance racing to her feminine centre. 'At this particular moment, not especially. Is that what *you* want to do?'

The flash of heat in his eyes disappeared beneath a darker, sombre patina, lightning behind storm clouds. 'It's a start.' He jerked a thumb at the bed. 'Sit down. I've made up my mind about what I want to say and I'd rather say it with you beside me.'

She walked the rest of the way but perched herself on the edge of the rose-printed quilt and folded her hands. Took a deep breath. Swallowed. 'I'm listening.'

He rubbed at the back of his neck. 'I've been to see my half of the Dastardly Duo.'

She blinked in surprise. At no stage had either of them considered tracing the whereabouts of their respective absent parents. 'Why?'

'Take a look at this and tell me what you think.' He handed her a creased photo, warm from his pocket.

She saw a handsome dark-haired man with a dimple in his chin. 'He's the image of you,' she said slowly, comparing Jack and the photo. 'A relative?'

'He was my biological father. He's been dead for over twenty-seven years.'

Shock, disbelief and the chilling knowledge that they'd both been betrayed shivered through her. 'Gerry…Gerry's not your father.' Each word was wrung out of her.

'No. Gerry left some…info; I had to check it out.'

The cold, flat tone, the hard, obsidian eyes were a

Jack Cleo had never seen before. 'What information? Jack, you're scaring me.'

'Which is precisely why I couldn't tell you. Scared the hell out of me too. He told me mum had known your dad around the time I was born. A lie, but I had to be sure.'

She took a moment to absorb the implications. 'He thought my father was…yours too?' Her chest was too tight, her throat so dry she could barely get the words out.

'He *didn't* think it.' Jack's jaw tightened. 'Gerry just enjoyed messing with my head. Punishing me for learning he was sterile and the kid he'd raised all those years wasn't his own.'

'Oh, Jack.' That sense of betrayal erupted into an icy ball that left no room for the place in her heart where Gerry had been.

'There's more.' He put the photo on Cleo's nightstand before he continued. 'I haven't been fair to you. One of the reasons I haven't talked about those missing years is because some of it's not pretty.'

'It's okay,' Cleo urged, shifting closer. 'I want to know. All of it.'

He scrubbed a hand over his face. 'I landed a job as a fashion photographer in Rome for the first two years. After that I took up a post in the Middle East. I've seen first-hand what war does to families, children, lives. It affected me so much I stayed on to help.'

She frowned. 'Scott told me you were in Rome when he contacted you.'

He nodded. 'I was in hospital when I got the call.'

The gunshot wound.

He'd been in a *war zone*. She could sense it all: the desert haze, the terrible sounds of gunfire and men, the hot smell of metal and sweat, the cold shroud of fear. For a terrifying moment she was with him in that dark place looking into the jaws of hell.

Too agitated to sit still, she jumped up, paced away. She'd all but accused him of being with a woman when she'd seen that wound, and he hadn't said a word in his defence. She wanted to kick that stubborn, sexy backside into next week.

She swung to face him, a brew of anger and pride, admiration—and love—simmering in her heart. 'Silly stubborn...*man*. You put yourself in danger and I—'

Shrugging deprecatingly, he said, 'You'd prefer I walk away and pretend I didn't see?'

She almost laughed at the irony. 'Didn't you do exactly that to me, to us?' She was coming apart, but she pushed the words out over the lump in her throat. 'Is that what you're going to do now, Jack?'

He shook his head, watching her with a sensual heat that seemed to flow out to her like a deep-moving river. 'What I'm going to do now is something I've wanted to do for a very long time.'

CHAPTER TWELVE

CLEO didn't need the words to know what he wanted. What he intended. He was going to make love to her. The slow, bone-melting kind that she'd waited half a life time to share with him.

So why did she want to cry? Because that kind of loving came from the heart. At least it did in her books. It came with love and commitment.

Jack didn't believe in love and commitment.

Cleo believed in love. Despite her childhood, she believed in commitment. She longed to show Jack how love could mend the hurts of the past. She ached to unlock that something he'd closed off from the rest of the world. To give him a reason to stay.

To tell him she loved him without anger to taint the words.

And to hear those same words from his lips. She felt her eyes fill and blinked the moisture away.

His languid expression faded and his brows puckered. 'You have a problem with that?'

Definitely, absolutely. *It will hurt too much when you*

go. She swallowed over the ball of pain lodged tight in her throat and blurted, 'You're so clever, you figure it out.'

He stared at her, a help-me-out-here plea in his eyes. 'I can't think of a damn thing,' he said. 'Unless I was mistaken the other night…'

She remained where she was, too far away to touch him, but close enough to smell warm skin, to see the wear-and-tear marks on his medallion and the tiny gold flecks in his dark irises. 'The night we made love, I thought…' *You loved me.* She shook her head. Naïve and wishful dreams. 'I didn't think, neither of us did.'

'It doesn't always pay to think too hard,' he said softly, reaching for her.

And wasn't that the cold, hard truth? She stepped further out of his reach and said, 'I don't know how to play this. Relationships aren't my forte.'

With a rasp of denim over cotton quilt, he shifted on the bed so that his body angled towards her. 'You could start by coming over here.'

She hesitated, torn between throwing herself into his arms and running from the room. Neither option would give her what she craved.

'Come here, Goldilocks.' His tone dared her. 'Or are you afraid?'

'Oh, you don't play fair, Jack.'

'Cleo.' His eyes held a quiet torment. 'You've healed me, hit me, seduced me, refused me. And now you're damn near killing me.'

It wasn't a challenge or a dare. It was a simple plea that squeezed at her heart. Cautiously, she sat on the edge of the bed again. She didn't want to fool herself into thinking this was any different for him than any other woman he'd had. But, oh, if she could only convince him… 'Our relationship's always been a roller coaster ride.'

'But what a ride.' He sat up. She could feel the heat pumping from his body, his warm breath caressing her cheek as he spoke. 'And you're finally ready to admit we have a relationship. So am I,' he finished quietly.

His fingertip touched her nape. Barely there, but, oh, what a feeling. 'We practically grew up together,' she managed. 'Of course we have a relationship.'

'A very close, very personal, very intimate relationship.'

His finger slowly tracked down her spine, setting each vertebra on fire and making her shiver at the same time. Her eyes closed at the scorching, sensual pleasure. But she shook her head. 'You denied us that, Jack, when you left.'

'I'm not denying it now,' he muttered, his voice rough with emotion. 'Say yes, Goldilocks. Tell me you want me.'

Her body was melting like metal beneath her blow-torch. Her brain wasn't faring any better because she couldn't seem to remember why she'd thought letting the man she loved touch her was such a bad idea. She sagged against the solid wall of muscle behind her. 'Yes. Yes, Jack. I want you.'

With a low growl that vibrated against her back, he pressed his lips to the pulse in the sensitive hollow above her collar-bone. She felt her legs tremble as he tugged her gently to her feet with him so his thighs touched the backs of hers and his hands warmed her belly through her vest-top. So he surrounded her.

'I want to do things to you. I want my name on your lips when you come,' he murmured, and stroked a moist tongue over her ear lobe.

His words slid like mulled wine through her system, intoxicating her with their promise, blinding her to consequences. Jack wanted *her*, so-not-sophisticated Cleo Honeywell in her oldest vest-top and frayed jersey shorts.

The hot press of his palms on the soft cotton shifted lower. She felt the roughness of callused skin as his fingertips slid over her belly, the gentle glide of fabric as he eased shorts and panties down over her hips until they fell softly to her ankles.

Desire coiled low in her belly, dampening the place between her legs and filling her with restless anticipation. 'Jack…' Her arms seemed heavy as she lifted them, pushing her fingers through her short cap of hair, then twining them about his neck behind her so that her breasts lifted, tingling and full.

But he didn't touch them, not yet. He slid his hands over the cloth one more time, tracing the dip in her navel with a fingertip, then shimmied her top over her head. Her breasts spilled free, swollen and heavy.

'No bra,' he murmured.

'Was in a hurry.' Her pulse thundering in her ears, she waited on a razor's edge. She heard the rustle of fabric behind her as he stripped off his own clothes.

At last he turned her in his arms. His gaze locked

with hers. She saw his need in the dark soulful eyes, felt it in the quivering muscles in his arms. Felt that need nudge hot and hard against her belly.

It made her feel female and powerful.

He disabused her of that notion when he swept her up and laid her on the bed as if she weighed no more than a puff of air. He was the one in control here—but he was the one trembling.

A rainbow danced overhead as the sun-catcher in her window twisted in the breeze, catching the glints of chestnut in his hair. For a long hot moment they simply stared at each other. She absorbed the long, lean lines of him, from the broad, muscled shoulders, to the tapered waist, to the brutally masculine jut of his sex.

He drew in a long, unsteady breath. 'You have the most exquisitely beautiful body I've ever seen.'

And for the first time in her life she felt beautiful. Almost as beautiful as the models he worked with. But perhaps he was a mind-reader because he said, 'I want to photograph you, just as you are now.'

'Really?' She shifted on the cool coverlet, restless with the promise in his husky voice, aching with need under his scorching, sensuous gaze.

'Really.' Sinking to the bed, he stretched out over her, his spread knees capturing her hips. He held her face in his hands as if he held something special. 'Later,' he whispered, and lowered his mouth.

Surprisingly soft. Sinfully seductive. He was all she could think of—his unique taste, the scrape of stubble against her chin, the caress of his breath on her cheek.

Hot, masculine flesh rubbed against her belly, one hard-packed muscled thigh between hers. She heard her own low moan as she clutched the hard curve of a shoulder, rubbing her aching nipples against the plush roughness of his chest.

Sensing her need, he eased her back. 'Let me.' He filled a hand with her breast, rubbed a maddeningly slow thumb over the tip. 'So firm, so beautiful.'

'So oversized,' she whispered, hearing the trace of her earlier vulnerability creep into her voice.

'Never.' He cupped both breasts in his palms. 'See? The perfect fit.'

He lowered his head again. The deep, wet pull of his mouth on her nipple, the slow, gentle glide of his hand over her belly, her hip. He suckled the other breast while his fingers parted her woman's flesh, slipped a finger inside her and slid it out slowly. Over and over. His unhurried gentleness, the fine tremor in his hands undid her.

And frustrated her. Somewhere in her befuddled senses, she was aware of the tension behind the quiver, the strain in his breathing. He was holding back. 'Jack—'

He groaned. 'For once in your life don't argue with me.'

'But, Jack… Now,' she begged.

'Demanding woman,' he muttered against her ear. But she heard the smile settle in his voice as he pressed her into the mattress. 'I'm going to have to teach you to be patient. Especially in the bedroom.'

'Might take a lot of practice.' In the bright light of

morning, his two-day beard showed up stark and bristly
against his tan, reminding her of what he'd been
through the past two days.

He was here now, and she revelled in the hot, hard
weight of him. Revelled in the feel of flesh sliding
against slick flesh, the scent of morning and hot skin
filling the musky air between them. Lifting her hips,
gripping his arms, she opened to him, poised at the
edge of her control, desperate for this completion, this
merging of bodies, of selves.

Eyes locked on hers, he eased himself inside—
slowly, drawing out the moment, filling her with his
heat and strength. Her inner muscles quivered, drawing
his hard, throbbing length inside her until she couldn't
tell where she ended and he began.

He muttered something she didn't catch; cursing
God or thanking Him. His eyes still focused on her,
only her, he withdrew slowly before thrusting into her
again, with more insistence.

The harsh groan torn from his throat sounded like
music to her ears, her own rising to accompany him.
Her heart beat against his in a duet of passion. He filled
her, completed her.

His hands found hers, palm to palm, fingers entwining, then he dragged her down into the velvet depths
of passion in those dark eyes only to toss her up to a
place full of light and life. And love.

Sensation pin-wheeled over sensation, creating a
whirling galaxy of jewels, each one glittering and
unique. She caught the edge of the spiral as it hurtled
towards the stars, higher and higher. She wished it

could go on and on, that she could gather all those precious treasures to her heart and hold them for ever.

But Jack wasn't a for ever guy.

So she had now, and the little dip in her happiness smoothed out as he pinned her hands with his above her head. Breath mingled. Sweat slicked their bodies. There wasn't an inch of skin that wasn't melded with his.

Then he thrust hard once, twice, and liquid warmth flooded inside her as he shuddered, rasping out her name and taking her to the stars with him.

Cleo floated back to earth. To reality. To the soul-destroying knowledge that Jack still had a job overseas, a life beyond Melbourne suburbia. Right now he was sprawled half on, half off her, in no apparent rush to change the status quo.

She closed her eyes, reliving their lovemaking, storing it for later. But wait… Had he said, *I'm going to have to teach you to be patient*? A glimmer of hope lit inside her. Did that mean he wanted to stay a little longer? With her?

As if he'd heard her thoughts, she felt Jack push up. When she opened her eyes his head was propped on one elbow and he was watching her. Serious eyes. Serious mouth. No more body contact.

'Cleo—'

Shaking her head, she sat up, wishing she had the sheet to cover her. 'Don't.' *Don't spoil what we shared, don't take that away from me.*

He captured her wrist. 'Listen to me. I need you, Cleo, and not only in bed. My life's a dull black and white without you.'

What? What was he telling her? 'Say that again,' she said slowly.

'You colour my world, Goldilocks.' He sat up too, and cupped her face. 'You have looks, loyalty, courage and optimism. You're the most beautiful person I've ever known, inside and out.'

She wished she didn't hear a *but* coming. For the sake of her pride, for her heart, she forced a smile. 'That's the best recommendation I ever had.'

He frowned and she could see he was offended. 'I'm being serious here, I'd appreciate it if you'd be too.'

'Okay. On a serious note, then...' She dug down deep for some of that courage to say, 'I overheard you making a date at Café Medici the other day. You laughed—the way you always laugh when it's a woman on the phone.' She ignored his raised brows. 'You told *whoever* you were interested. When you didn't tell me about it, I assumed...' She lifted a shoulder. 'So, what are you trying to tell me here, Jack? Because I sure as heck don't follow.'

He looked thoughtful a moment, then he grinned. 'You reneged on our shower. I was discussing a job opening for a photo-journalist. In Australia.'

Australia. That glimmer of hope flared, but she had to know more before she started tap-dancing. 'Why would you do that? What about your other...interests?' She studied his face, searching for subtle cues as she said, '*Ciao, bella* ring any bells?'

Another brief pause. 'Carmela,' he said finally. 'She and her husband Domenic rented me a room when I first landed the job in Italy. Domenic's ill. Carmela's been updating me on his progress.'

'Not Liana.' Had she really said that aloud? Oops. Big mistake bringing up a past lover.

'Liana…? Ah, the Armenian designer. Haven't seen her in years.' He narrowed his eyes. 'And you know her how…?'

'Um, a magazine…?'

'Milan.' His eyes lit with gentle teasing. 'Does that mean you were jealous?'

I've been hung up on a woman he hasn't seen in years. She swiped at his shoulder. 'What do you think? I love you, Jack, that's unconditional. It's not a choice, it simply is. Doesn't mean I didn't hate you for leaving me. Twice.' She prodded his chest. 'And for not telling me about the job opening in Australia.'

'That was an hour before I read Gerry's letter. You were in a snit at breakfast, didn't seem like the time to—'

'Because of the phone call,' she interrupted, prodding him again, harder.

'I didn't know that, now, did I? I wanted to tell you over a celebration dinner. I wanted to tell you…' His tone turned sombre as he trailed off, rubbing the back of his neck. Nervous. Definitely nervous.

'Hey,' she said softly, and tugged his arm, felt the ropey sinews twist beneath her palm. 'Tell me now. We're both naked here, seems like a good time to bare our thoughts as well.'

He nodded, fingering a spike of her hair and kissing her forehead. 'I've learned from you these past weeks.

Your commitment to family and your inner strength gave me the courage to look inside myself. I discovered something greater than my fear. Love.'

A lump rose in her throat. She looked into those eyes that knew her so well. Not vulnerable and guarded now, but clear and filled with hope. She pressed her palm to the side of the face she loved. 'I'm glad I could help.'

He covered her hand with one of his. 'Only you.'

'So, you're ready to come home.'

'I want to spend the rest of my life with you; it doesn't matter where. You *are* my home.'

His lips found hers, letting all the emotion of his words flow into one long, deep kiss. Then he lifted his head just enough to look into her eyes and say, 'I love you, Goldilocks; I always have.'

Her heart wept for joy. Words more precious than diamonds. 'Can I have that in writing?' she murmured against his mouth.

'You bet.'

Wrapping her arms around his neck, she pressed herself against him, mouth to mouth, skin to skin, heart to heart. She felt his hands, hard, possessive, seeking, as they slipped around her waist, over her back, circled over her shoulders and finally, finally found her aching breasts.

He leaned back to look at what he was touching, and a hot tide of lust and love washed through her. No one had ever been able to turn the heat up like Jack. 'You've made me feel good about myself,' she whispered. 'You even make me feel sexy and desirable.'

'Even?' He shook his head. 'Get this through that beautiful, stubborn head, Cleo. You *are* sexy and desirable. And much, much more. It's not your clothes or the way you wear your hair. It's *you*.' He leaned back to look into her eyes. 'Marry me, Cleo. Let me spend the rest of my life showing you.'

The sexy rumble of his voice echoed deep in her heart, filling all those empty places only Jack could fill. Tears sprang to her eyes. 'Oh, Jack, yes. Yes, I'll marry you. But I don't want to wait.' She pulled his long, hot and incredibly sexy body on top of her. 'Start showing me now.'

A long time later, their bodies warm, sated and entwined, Cleo twirled Jack's well-worn medallion in her fingers. 'You never forgot your roots, did you? After all that happened, even when you were injured, you cared enough to come back.'

'To you, Goldilocks.' He pressed an open-mouthed kiss against her neck.

She basked in the stunning sensation, her happiness spilling over when he murmured, 'Is a month enough time to organise a wedding?'

'As long as I can find a dress to knock your socks off. And lingerie, and sleepwear…' If she needed sleepwear. Her mind spun at the images.

'Speaking of sexy outfits,' he said, in sync with her thoughts, 'do you still have that black catsuit around here somewhere? I'd like another chance to take it off you.'

Arching her foot over his leg, she slid it down his shin, enjoying her new-found role of seductress as his body jerked to attention. 'I think that can be arranged.'

EPILOGUE

JACK waited for his wife to finish duty-free shopping with Jeanne at Melbourne International. Cleo had refused to let him accompany her, saying she couldn't shop with him breathing down her neck. He planned to do a lot of that. Tonight.

His wife. He tried unsuccessfully to wipe the silly grin off his face that seemed to have become a habit over the past few weeks. They'd been married in a small civil ceremony less than five hours ago. He still couldn't quite believe it.

They'd put the house up for sale and were going to tour Italy and catch up with Domenic and Carmela before settling in Melbourne's suburbs. The clichéd white picket fence was looming closer.

He didn't mind a bit.

He turned to his best man. 'Scotty, you and Jason have a major responsibility there looking after Constantine.' He was still getting used to seeing Scott and his partner as a couple, but he'd never seen his buddy so relaxed.

'Don't worry about the big guy,' Scotty said. 'He'll be fine until you get back. Your bride's on her way,' he said with a grin, glancing over Jack's shoulder.

Jack turned. And there she was, all lusciously curved five-feet two of her in crisp white slacks and an emerald jacket, confetti still stuck to her spiked hair, eyes sparking with excitement, her face aglow.

He didn't need his camera to know he'd remember the scene for ever—and the one of her in her spectacular dress as they exchanged vows. But he snapped a shot anyway before saying, 'Hi.'

She answered with a breathless 'hi' of her own. That husky sigh got to him every time, on every level. He stepped closer, relieving her of a mountain of shopping bags. Their gazes fused, their hands brushed. The air between them flared with heat.

They were in the middle of a noisy tide of humanity, lights and announcements, but all he could focus on was the subtle scent of her skin and the way her lips curved as she shared the moment with him.

Somewhere to his left, he heard Jeanne cough loudly, then say, 'Come on, you two. Get on board that aircraft before we all start melting here.'

'We're on our way.' With his eyes still on Cleo's, he raised her left hand, pressed a kiss to the gold-set ruby flanked by diamonds and the filigree wedding band Cleo had made herself. His own matching band glinted in the airport lights. 'Ready?' he said.

She nodded, her blue eyes as warm as the summer sky. 'Oh, yes, I'm ready.' Her smile widened. 'I've been ready for a very long time.'

Their eyes lingered a second or two over their joined fingers. He smiled back, filled with love for the woman who was his wife. 'Then let's get started.'